Praise for James Carroll's

THE CLOISTER

"A sweeping, heartbreaking blend of history and fiction. . . . [Its] entwined stories move at an engrossing rhythm, making this a very magnetic, satisfying novel." —*Publishers Weekly*

"Fascinating in its evocation of the twelfth-century Catholic Church in France, this lavishly detailed historical novel serves as an education in historical philosophy, a poignant tale of devoted love, and a portrait of a postwar human crisis influenced heavily by both. . . . A thought-provoking book." —*Booklist*

"Carroll blends his well-aired interests in history, theology, and literary fiction in this deftly told story that partakes richly of all. . . . A rich, literate tale well told." —*Kirkus Reviews*

"A novel that shifts seamlessly between epic love story, the anatomy of a crisis of faith, family tragedy and trauma survival saga. . . . Both moving and enlightening, *The Cloister* will engross readers." —*Shelf Awareness*

"A literary detective game. . . . In pushing his readers—in both his fiction and nonfiction—to ponder tough religious topics . . . Carroll is continuing the important discussions made famous by Peter Abelard." —*New York Journal of Books*

James Carroll

THE CLOISTER

James Carroll is the author of twelve novels and eight works of nonfiction. He lives in Boston with his wife, the writer Alexandra Marshall.

www.jamescarroll.net

THE CLOISTER

THE CLOISTER

A NOVEL

JAMES CARROLL

Anchor Books
A Division of Penguin Random House LLC
New York

FIRST ANCHOR BOOKS EDITION, JANUARY 2019

The Library of Congress has cataloged the Doubleday edition as follows:
Names: Carroll, James, 1943– author.
Title: The cloister : a novel / James Carroll.
Description: First edition. | New York : Nan A. Talese/Doubleday, 2018.
Identifiers: LCCN 2017016952
Classification: LCC PS3553.A764 C58 2018 | DDC 813/.54—dc23
LC record available at https://lccn.loc.gov/2017016952

Anchor Books Trade Paperback ISBN: 978-1-101-97158-1
eBook ISBN: 978-0-385-54128-2

Book design by Maria Carella

www.anchorbooks.com

Printed in the United States of America
10 9 8 7 6 5 4 3 2 1

For Julia

Beloved, let us love one another: for love is of God; and every one that loveth is born of God, and knoweth God.

— 1 JOHN 4:7

Author's Note

Quotations from Abelard's *The History of My Calamities,* and from the letters of Abelard and Héloïse, are from the classic seventeenth-century rendition by the French Enlightenment figure Pierre Bayle, *Letters of Abelard and Héloïse,* which appeared in an English translation by John Hughes in 1782. Other quotations are from *The Lost Love Letters of Abelard and Héloïse,* edited and translated by Constant J. Mews; from Peter Abelard's *Collationes,* edited and translated by John Marenbon and Giovanni Orlandi; and from a letter of Bernard of Clairvaux to Pope Innocent II, translated by Bruno Scott James. In these citations, I have taken some minor editorial liberties for clarity and style. Biblical quotations are from the King James Version or, to reflect mid-twentieth-century Catholic usage, the Douay-Rheims Bible. The anathemas from the twelfth-century Council of Sens are from Heinrich Denzinger, *Enchiridion: Decrees of the Solemn Magisterium.*

THE CLOISTER

PROLOGUE

In the Duchy of Bourgogne in the year 1142, the largest church in Christendom stood on a hill above the tidy village of Cluny. That church, with its towering belfry, Corinthian columns, and massive rectangular pilasters, defined the pulse of the Benedictine Abbey of Cluny, a large walled complex itself the center of a vast monastic empire, counting ten thousand monks and nuns in foundations spread across the continent, from the Mediterranean to the British Isles. The sharply pointed Cluny belfry was visible for miles around, and had served, across the last phase of a long journey, as the locating focal point for the small band of horsemen that approached now, making its way up the final slope toward the monastery gate.

The palfrey on which a heavily cloaked rider sat, as it slowly ascended the hill, was a lighter-weight horse, and its unsteady gait suggested what a distance it had come. Trailing behind were four other ridden horses, and a hitched pair pulling a covered cart. The wind was howling from the valley spread below, and the sun was low at the distant ridge. The stout wooden gate banged open. The porter rushed out, going to the first horse, to take its headstall and stirrup. In a bustle of activity, others of the minor orders followed from within the monastic enclosure—the almoner, oblates, and lay brothers. A knot of black robes, they surrounded the riders and the cart. With the porter's help, the first rider dismounted, throwing aside the covering woolen mantle, and being seen only then for the religious woman she was. The porter bowed, showing his tonsure, muttering, "My lady."

Two others in the party were religious sisters, clothed, like the first, in a long gray belted tunic, scapular, white coif, and veil. Except that the fabric was the gray of rough, undyed wool, the garb was the habit of the Benedictine Order. They were nuns.

The party's six accompanying men were the horse master, the marshal, two armed henchmen, and two stewards. As the first nun, walking erect and at an authoritative clip, led the way through the gate, the receiving monks bowed, even while stealing glances at her sharply concentrated face. With whispers, they had spoken of this arrival, although this woman of slight stature and medium height did not match the measure of the songs sung in her name. She was the Abbess Héloïse, Mother Superior of the Abbey of the Paraclete, a ranking convent several days' journey by river and rough trail to the north. In those whispers, they had spoken of what she would be coming for. There would be further songs.

The porter had been instructed to show her at once into the main Cloister garden, to which women were ordinarily forbidden entrance, but the instruction had come from the Abbot Primate himself. At this time of year, the garden was still bare of fruit and berries, but twigs shone with the fresh scales of buds and shoots. The waters of the central fountain, drawing on the stream that ran below the monastic kitchens and toilet block, had quickened in recent weeks, but would not splash again until the coming spring rains replenished the flow. The normally bright marble of the arches and pillars of the surrounding arcade was dusky gray now, for the shadows of evening had settled on the place, like loneliness. The Vespers bell would be ringing soon.

The porter gestured at a garden bench, but did not wait to see if Mother Héloïse would sit. She watched him hurry away, as relieved to be alone as, after the day's ride, she was to be standing.

It was not long before the Abbot Primate entered, coming from the chapel. Because his cowl was up, his face was shadowed. Across his chest was the leather strap of a pilgrim's satchel, hanging at his side. The unfettered stride with which he crossed to her suggested the depth of feeling she knew was there. His arms were stretched toward her, but as he drew close, she genuflected, a proper obeisance. With her head bowed, she reached for his hand, pulled it to her mouth, and kissed his ring. Grasping her upper arms, he lifted her. He lowered his cowl, unveiling sadness.

"Where is he, Most Holy Father?" she asked.

The Abbot Primate turned slightly, gesture enough to indicate the Chapter House, the darkened room, close at hand, separated from the garden by a large arcaded gate of three stout arches, each one upheld by a clutch of fluted pillars. Mother Héloïse peered into the room. Under the interlacing of groined ceiling vaults, the open space was large enough to accommodate the professed members of the monastic family, with each monk sitting at the wall, on the stone bench that defined three sides of the rectangle. Now the room was vacant, but as her eyes adjusted, she made out the dark form of the catafalque standing in the center. She should have sought the Abbot Primate's leave to move away from him, but did not. Instead, she simply walked out of the garden, crossing through the arcade, to enter the Chapter House, going directly to the one for whom she'd come.

Leaves of lavender and woodruff, and dried rose petals, were scattered on the floor; pots of rose water stood at the four corners of the bier; but still the fetid odor of his decomposition came to her. He was clothed in his black habit, and his hands were hidden under the folds of his scapular. But the sight of his sharp-featured face, with its distinctive brow and aquiline nose, made her stop. *Oh, Peter.*

Lifeless, yes. But also old. He had come into his seventh decade, yet she still thought of him as they had been before. The lids of his eyes were down, but his lips were slightly parted, the lips from which the most precious words had pierced her, the lips with which her own had been so sweetly caressed. His lips. She bent to them, touched them lightly with her cheek, then put her mouth on his. *Oh, my Peter.*

The Abbot Primate took up a place behind her. To her back, he said quietly, "When I sent for you, I assumed he would still be alive at your arrival. I am sorry." He waited.

When, finally, she turned to him, she said, "They condemned him because of me." Her voice was shot through with feeling, a mix of grief and anger. "Because I refused to renounce my love; because he remained mine through all calamity. I will publish his virtues across all the world, to punish the age that has not valued him."

"It is true, Mother. They hated him for what he had in you. But he opposed them in their vain repudiations of God's mercy. By the end, he was the exemplar of mercy. That is what he had from you. Mercy. Against all charges leveled at you, the measure of your love was mercy, not licentiousness."

"He disowned our promiscuity. I did not."

"He did what was necessary to keep his authority—as you yourself wanted. You flogged him with your writing, to re-enter the fray. And he did."

"But look!" Her hand swept across the corpse. "What authority has he now? They betrayed him, all of them."

"Not all."

"You, my lord, were his only friend."

"No, dear Mother. Many, many loved him."

"Where were they, then? When the *Damnamus* was pronounced, and pronounced again, where was a hint of objecting murmur?"

"You were not there, Mother."

"But I was."

The Abbot looked at her aslant, as if to diagnose derangement. "Impossible. A Canonical Council? No women were present."

"Enthroned beside King Louis? Does your monkish vow prevent even the *perceiving* of the female form?"

"The Queen? Yes, the Queen was there. *Pro forma.* But otherwise—"

"And the Queen's party, the Ladies-in-Waiting, in the loggia, nearly out of sight."

"Ladies-in-Waiting?"

With a half-curtsy, the nun mocked herself.

"You? A consecrated woman among the courtiers?" The Abbot checked his first reaction, and smiled. This Héloïse was indomitable.

"Disguised as the widowed cousin of Her Majesty," she said. "A consecrated woman dressed, illicitly, in the mourning clothes of a widow. But a widow is what she is." Héloïse turned back toward the bier, perhaps in part to face away, as she said then, "In the hour of his great test, I would not abandon him—unlike the others. It was as close to him as I could be. If the Abbot Primate is obliged to censure an undisciplined religious woman, so be it."

"Mother, what the Abbot Primate does not know, the Abbot Primate is under no obligation to censure. I know nothing of the Queen's Ladies."

"Queen Eleanor, as you *do* know, is a patroness of the Paraclete."

"Her Majesty is a devotee of the storied niece of Canon Fulbert. Your former notoriety defines her interest."

"Not 'former,'" the nun said, but quietly.

The Abbot Primate continued, "The Queen cares only for romance, nothing for theology. And at the Council of Sens, theology was at issue."

"Romance and theology, Father. Only eunuchs would think they are unrelated." Mother Héloïse raised her hand, a fist. Then she checked herself, biting her knuckles, letting her eyes fall again to the face of the dead man before her. "Despite what they had done to him because of me, and despite his palsy, Peter Abelard was the only one in that large nave with manliness. The only one, I mean, besides you." She raised her eyes. "Your bold statement rang like the Word of Jehovah."

"I could not save him. All I could do, as his canonical superior, was confirm his appeal to the Roman Pontiff, and guarantee it."

"An appeal that was then promptly denied. The Pope excommunicated him, burned his books in front of Saint Peter's Basilica, condemned all those who dare to follow in the way of Peter Abelard. *Anathema sit!* The greatest man in Christendom!"

"Yes. All of which I then *myself* appealed, with Peter's approval. The Pope is reassessing, even now. I succeeded in getting Clairvaux to second my petition."

"Bernard! That false prophet! It was he who betrayed Peter."

"Yes. But he is remorseful. His support will help Pope Innocent overturn himself. The excommunication will be lifted. Now, more than ever, I will see to that."

"But again, I ask: if so many others loved him, where were they when Clairvaux led that chorus of *Damnamus*?"

"Afraid. They were afraid, Mother. The winds from Rome are fierce. And not only Rome." She knew this, of course. Peter Abelard, by the end, was tied by his enemies to the restlessness of the schools, but rowdy boy-geniuses were the least of it. Abelard and the thinking he promoted were blamed for the rebelliousness of burghers; he was faulted, even, for the deceptions of the Jews. In those days, princes challenged bishops; but, then, yeomen challenged princes. Peasants, obviously, would be next. Order was shaken—inside the Church, but outside, too. The King's sworn duty was to restore that order—everywhere. Fierce winds, therefore, blew from his palace, too. The savvy Abbess understood. Alas, she had not understood soon enough. Yes, she had flogged him to re-enter the fray, entirely underestimating how lethal such an action might be.

She said, "Peter Abelard was an apostle of *caritas,* yet he was damned."

"The excommunication will be lifted," the Abbot said forcefully. "I will make it happen. Then the gates of heaven will be opened to him, we will be authorized to inter him in sacred ground, and we will do that here at Cluny."

"No! I will have him at the Paraclete. I will have him with me. It's why I've come. Any ground that receives this man will be sacred."

The Abbot Primate began to object, but she raised her hand again, stopping him. He stared at her. She did not blink. Finally, he lowered his eyes. One of the most powerful men in Christendom—yet he yielded to this woman.

"As for tonight," she said, "I will not have this Chapter House plunged into darkness. I want torches here until Matins. And the paschal candle." The dynamic between Abbot and Abbess had reversed. Each saw it; each assumed it. "I want water brought in," she continued. "Heated water, and cloths. Incense. And scented oil. I will bathe him." The Abbot Primate bowed. She added, more quietly, "And perhaps a mat. Bundled straw will do." She would not be leaving him.

"Yes," the Abbot said.

"I will depart with him tomorrow, at first light. I will need fresh horses. He will be mine, at last."

After a long silence, the Abbot pulled back the flap of his leather satchel and withdrew a sheaf of beribboned vellum sheets. He said, "Peter asked me to return these to you."

Mother Héloïse received the bundle solemnly, knowing at once what it was. Her letters, all that she had written him. Once, Peter had said that it was womanly to save such letters, implying he never would. Yet he had.

And then the Abbot produced another pair of bundles. "These also. His Credo, a last explanation of himself." Solemnly, he handed her the sheaf. "And one other . . ." He held the second, hesitating. "An unfinished treatise, what he called *Dialogue with the Jew*. I alone have read it. Guard these words—"

"Peter was never guarded with words." Héloïse received the pages, but she was bristling.

"Guard these words, Mother! Clairvaux's dark angels are everywhere—spies!—even here at Cluny. He joined with me in the petition to Rome only because he thinks he has heard the last from Peter Abelard. This treatise must not be published! They condemned him once because of the Jews. They will again."

"Jews are being attacked, murdered. If Peter wrote of Jews now, despite the Council's *Damnamus*, it was to defend our Lord's own cousins, for was Jesus Christ not a Jew?"

"Mother! There are reports of Jews slaughtering Christian children, to get their blood."

"That is nonsense."

"Perhaps. But Jews murdered their own children in Mainz. That is certain."

"To prevent their being kidnapped by the crossbearers and forcibly baptized. That was not murder; it was martyrdom."

"Be careful of that! These are fires from which we must protect Peter Abelard's name. Jews be damned. The battle now is for Peter's eternal salvation. We must have the anathema voided. Guard those words if you want the papal rescript granted." Father Abbot took hold of her forearm, fiercely. "For the sake of his eternal soul, Mother. Guard those words."

She clung to the pages. Despite the hot rush of what she felt, she nodded. A promise.

The Abbot held on to her arm for a moment more than was seemly. He said, despite himself, "Your obstinacy is what Peter knew of you. But I see it, too. Beware of your obstinacy, Mother."

To his surprise, she leaned against him. "Inside, Holy Father, I am anything but obstinate. I am egg custard, fallen."

"The jongleurs sing otherwise." The Abbot laughed, gave her one squeeze with his enclosing arm, and released her. "You, the infamous Héloïse," he said, with a sudden rush of affection. "Their lyrics sing happily of your damning of the Church. An Abbess who damns the Church!"

"And you, the Abbot Primate, who receives her with a gentle hand." She straightened her spine, an unconscious gesture of will. She clutched the vellum pages close, deliberately pushing the bundle against her breast, to feel the pressure of the small ring of gold, suspended on a chain, hidden beneath her habit, against her flesh.

The Abbot stepped back.

But now, with a bolt of feeling, she reached for him. "Will you be at the gate in the morning, my lord? I will pray your blessing."

"You will have it, Mother. You will have it always. And now I must order your torches, the oils, and water." His authority was back. "I will send in bread and fruit, a cup, and the holy image of our Lady." With that, the Abbot Primate turned and walked out into the Cloister, the budding garden, over which darkness was soon to fall.

CHAPTER ONE

Father Michael Kavanagh was at the Communion rail, moving smoothly along, placing the wafer on the outstretched, glistening tongue of each of the ladies and the few gents who had come forward to drop to their knees. *"Corpus Domini . . . nostri Jesu Christi . . ."* he intoned, but under his breath. Rubrics required him to recite the entire formula for each communicant, but no one did that. Aware of the swirl of his vestments, nicely in sync with the sidling altar boy, he kept the clip, speaking a phrase above each open mouth. *"Custodiat animam tuam . . . in vitam aeternam."* The trick was to keep from touching the knuckle of one's forefinger to the actual tongue, its saliva. *"Amen."*

This was "the Six," the first Mass each weekday morning. Counting the Monsignor, there were five priests on the staff of Good Shepherd Parish in Inwood, on the far tip of Manhattan—the only Catholic church on Broadway, even if it was a dozen miles north of the Broadway that counts. Kavanagh, at thirty-eight, was senior to one of his fellow curates, and could have drawn a later Mass, but what the hell—his eyes routinely popped open at five. Anyway, he found the jumble of the faith fully convincing only when it was dark outside.

And here was Mrs. Heaney, in her black shawl and firmly shut eyes, an "Irish divorcée"—a woman whose husband had simply taken off, never to come back. She clutched rosary beads. *"Corpus Domini . . ."*

Sergeant Kelly, uniformed and ready for the precinct follies, offered a trembler, the nervous tongue that, outside of church, habitually curled itself around the unlit stub of a cigar. One of Kelly's secrets was his Bell's palsy, a slight facial droop, which that cigar disguised, while plugging the drool. *". . . nostri Jesu . . ."* The priest knew Kelly's other secret—that, hitting the bottle, he hit his wife—because Kavanagh's priesthood was centered more on the Confessional than the Communion rail. He was regarded in the parish as kind, and a long line of penitents stood outside his booth every Saturday, which may have said more about his sternly judgmental brother priests than about him. In truth, sins whispered in the dark made Kavanagh as sorry as the one whispering. He was not so much kind as aware of his own free-floating compunction, which made the priest's side of the Confessional box his personal holy-of-holies. As for Kelly, the priest knew that the cop never took Communion unless he'd kept his fists in check at home. Good man, Sergeant, Kavanagh thought, but said only, *". . . Christi . . ."*

And here was Benjy Foley, the proprietor of the candy store across from the church, whose clientele was divided among schoolchildren, policy players, numbers runners, and whackers. Never one for the Sacrament of Penance, Foley knew that if he ever showed up on the other side of the sliding screen from Father Kavanagh, he'd be forbidden to take Communion, despite the priest's famous kindness, until the rackets went. Too many paychecks left at Foley's, too many legs broken by Foley's collectors, too much hidden juice. Kavanagh knew that the bookie's throwing himself on his knees next to Sergeant Kelly was all part of the game. But it wasn't a priest's part to openly refuse Communion—*". . . custodiat animam tuam . . ."*—even to this bastard.

When Father Kavanagh moved toward the next bent person along the rail, the sharp scent of Old Spice cologne hit him. The man was a lean, hunched-over figure, with linked fingers clamped like a helmet to his head, which bent forward from the upended collar of a gray tweed overcoat. Because he was out of place in that company, Kavanagh quickly took in his appearance. His trousers, emphatically displayed by his kneeling, were dark, sharply creased. He wore expensive-looking brown wingtips. His longish hair, in the interlocking thatch of his fingers, was a silvery blond. There was something supplicant, or defeated, in the posture, which did not square with the well-cut downtown clothing. The priest broke stride, hesitated. The altar boy missed his step, tilting the golden plate he carried, the paten. Then the man lowered his hands, raised his head, and brought his sad black eyes up to Kavanagh. His straight and steady gaze belied its bloodshot rheuminess. His necktie was loosened, and his collar was unbuttoned. There was exhaustion in the man, but also a kind of ferocity. Kavanagh froze, because, despite smart grooming rarely seen at Good Shepherd, and despite how the face had been touched by time, he knew it at once. *Runner!*

The man met Kavanagh's recognition with his own, but only for a moment. Without extending his tongue, he lowered his head again, bending forward, clasping his fingers atop his hair. The posture itself was an utter rejection of Communion. Kavanagh was stock-still, confounded. This had never happened before. The man's refusal to open his mouth and take the Host seemed personal, a refusal not of God, but of the priest. An indictment?

There was nothing to do but move along the rail. The next communicant—another rosary-clutching, shawled grandmother—had left space between herself and the well-dressed man, yet Kavanagh came at her aslant in order to keep the man in sight. By the time she had received and made the sign of the cross, the man was up and moving away. He was tall, and still had the smooth stride of an athlete. *Yes. Runner.*

After Mass, in the sacristy, Kavanagh removed the vestments quickly, assuming the man would be waiting in the shadowy rear of the church. But when the priest went out there, he was gone. Had this just been a dream? No. The air in the far vestibule, when Kavanagh reached it, carried the lingering aroma of Old Spice, the rooting detail. He went out the heavy oaken doors. The damp November chill hit him square. In fact, that weather—vividly dank and gray, an endless threat of true winter—perfectly matched how Kavanagh had come to feel about himself, a perpetual inner bleakness, yet always short of the true misery he'd have had to acknowledge. He could still deny the state he was in.

He stood on the landing atop the wide staircase that ran down to the Broadway sidewalk. In the early-morning fog, he glimpsed the lanky form, heading south at a steady clip. The man made his way past the rarely shuttered Green Acres Bar, the A&P, Connors Funeral Home. There were a couple of liquor stores on that block, but he passed them quickly. "Go, Runner!" the guys had called after John Malloy at track meets. His speed in footraces had given him his nickname. "Runner" could do the hundred-yard dash in eleven seconds, the 220 in twenty-three. Because of him, the much-disdained Saint Joseph's Seminary out of Yonkers, an unofficial entry, had unforgettably beaten Columbia and Fordham both, in the 1935 Eastern States Interscholastics, fifteen years ago.

John Malloy, assuming it was him, crossed 207th Street, moving purposefully. Why would he so pointedly show himself, then disappear? Kavanagh, in his cassock, was not dressed for the street, but he followed anyway. He practically had to run to begin to close the distance. By the time he neared the corner, he had fallen in with the line of early-shift workers making for the subway, and his billowing black robes drew glances as the people made way.

Kavanagh could just see him when Runner veered west at Dyckman Street, heading onto the overgrown pathway of the hilly bushland that separated Inwood from the Hudson River. To the working-class Irish of Good Shepherd, this end of Inwood Hill Park, running into Fort Tryon Park, was a forbidding place—forested and cleft by ravines and gulches, an old-growth nature preserve more than a playground. Younger boys made use of the near margins of the park to drift behind ill-kempt hedges for a smoke, and older ones, with girls, found nooks for making out, but otherwise all but the wildest kids avoided the place. There were caves, it was said, in which Indian bones and arrowheads could be found. More likely, the "caves" were the hollowed-out undersides of untended shrubs, ad hoc housing for the fearsome vagabonds who jungled in the park—but that was not Runner Malloy. Kavanagh had lost sight of him.

He stopped, checked his watch. He was the duty priest until mid-morning, and had to get to the hospital, to administer Viaticum in the intensive-care ward. "May the Lord Jesus Christ protect you"—the words popped into his head—"and lead you to eternal life."

A COUPLE OF hours later, dressed now in a plaid flannel shirt, sweater, and windbreaker, the priest tucked his breviary under his elbow, together with the small volume that was his current spiritual reading, and set out for the park again, not to find Runner Malloy, but simply to dispel the energy the phantom had ignited in him. That Kavanagh had last glimpsed his old friend disappearing into the rough preserve lent the park a kind of mystical aura that morning, and it drew him. By the time Kavanagh had finished the morning rounds at the hospital, he'd begun to wonder if he'd been mistaken at the early Mass. He hadn't seen Runner Malloy since the seminary, not long after that astounding track meet. But who presents himself at the Communion rail and then rejects the sacred Host? What the hell?

Fort Tryon Park was nestled under the pinnacle, and to the north, of Washington Heights, the city's highest point. The only vista from which the park's own sharp elevation could actually be appreciated was across the river, in New Jersey. Once a stroller left Broadway to enter the reserve, the air of an aboriginal landscape quickly imposed itself, and the place felt alien.

Kavanagh did not know what he was looking for. There might have been vagrants lurking in the hollowed-out shrubs, leftovers from the summer, when the park was said to be alive with hoboes, down-and-out drifters whose encampments the police would have ignored as long as they kept their distance from the museum that stood atop the hill. In fact, not so many tramps made their way this far uptown, a hardscrabble district, home to doormen and hacks, where panhandling wouldn't pay and free soup was scarce. As for the museum, it was an obscure outpost of the Met downtown, and the Irish of Inwood gave it a good leaving alone.

At a parking lot inside a pair of tall stone pillars, it occurred to Kavanagh that Runner might have left a car here. But at the far side of the park, at 190th Street, there was an out-of-the-way subway station, so perhaps he'd simply headed there, for the A Train that would take him all the way to Lower Manhattan, where his fancy duds would fit in.

Parking lot? Subway? That Kavanagh did not know what the striding John Malloy had been gunning for underscored his perplexity.

As he wandered the paths, he thought of those first days that had made them friends. They arrived at Saint Joseph's Seminary in Yonkers on the same day in 1932, alike in being twenty years old, and in having a tremulous readiness to throw themselves off the cliff of God's grace, as the retreat master described what they were doing. With God's help, the priest said, they would find a way to fly. And did they ever!

Dunwoodie, as the place was called for the once-pastoral corner of Yonkers it occupied, was the former country estate of a railroad baron. The already opulent mansion had been expanded—a license to crenellate, in old country argot—into Patrick Cardinal Hayes's neo-Gothic fantasy of an Irish great house. Its demesne consisted of a hundred acres of rolling lawn, which the Sulpician Fathers had seen fit to turn into a golf course for the lads. It was easy to believe in miracles if, in the thick of the Depression, you went from being the unpromising second son of an unemployed Hell's Kitchen longshoreman or, in Runner's case, of a long-laid-off Poughkeepsie millworker, to being a connoisseur of golf clubs, knowing the difference between a brassie, a spoon, and a mashie niblick. On long, easy strolls between tee and green, Runner and Kavanagh had become chums. That Runner had later dropped out of the seminary, and of Kavanagh's life, had left Kavanagh in a lurch from which, apparently—given the sense of dislocation just triggered by the man's abrupt reappearance—Kavanagh had yet to extricate himself fully.

He wandered the park for most of an hour, and was in the thickly wooded well of a glen when it began to rain. He wasn't sure which way was out. The path ahead ascended steeply, and he took it, cursing himself for not having worn a hat. At first, the rain was light, but it began to come down sharply, and he picked up the pace, moving steadily uphill. Because the path was serpentine, the foliage overgrown, and the downpour heavy, he could not see ahead, and it surprised him when, as he was taking a last turn, the huge museum building appeared above, looming like a granite butte. He headed for it.

An American Catholic should have loved that place—the museum took the form of a medieval monastery, with elements plucked from the rubble of a long-lost Europe and lovingly restored on a pinnacle overlooking the Hudson River—but at that point, few Catholics did. The Cloisters housed the Metropolitan Art Museum's masterpiece collection of tapestries, altarpieces, frescoes, sculpted figures, fountains, and stained-glass windows—all dating to between the twelfth and fifteenth centuries. But The Cloisters was not a true monastery, or even an authentic imitation. It was a Rockefeller-funded fantasy structure, a mishmash of belfries, architectural fragments, aged pillars, arched doorways, stairways, arcades—all tastefully reassembled to evoke the high romance of Gothic revival that had so quickened the patrician imagination of the Gilded Age. The inspiration here was not Saint Henry, the patron hallow of the childless and the handicapped, but Henry Adams, for whom Chartres's triumph was only aesthetic.

In fact, the museum was a stunning monument to the artistic achievement of Catholic high culture, but Kavanagh's parishioners knew better than to consider it theirs. What were a bunch of moth-eaten old wall hangings or limestone statues with smashed faces, anyway? What counted in monasteries were the monks and nuns and their spiritual works of mercy—men and women on their knees, not gawking at pictures. To the good people of Good Shepherd, The Cloisters seemed a peculiar, haunted emptiness, and, but for the handful of Irish who found employment there as guards or maintenance men, the parish was content to ignore it.

Kavanagh rushed into the place, for its shelter from the rain. Inside the entrance, a prim woman sat at a desk. She looked up, startled. There was a box for a voluntary contribution. "Cats and dogs out there," Kavanagh said. He threw some change into the box, picked up a brochure, and turned to enter, shaking water off his shoulders. His books were tucked under his jacket. He'd be a Prod tourist for an hour. What the hell.

He'd been in there once, years before, but had forgotten that the first sensation was of claustrophobia: the entranceway was a long, low, windowless corridor, sloping upward, evoking the dark tunnel of a mythic initiation. The corridor led to a set of rough stone stairs that spiraled up to the next level, to a great stone octagonal antechamber, higher than it was wide, that served as the museum's true entrance hall. From clerestory windows above, the dull November light washed down on the several artworks that decorated the walls: artworks here, but once they had been consecrated altarpieces. Kavanagh recognized, because of the pictured staff and animal-skin cloak, a primitive portrait of John the Baptist, together with a rendering—the lion—of Saint Mark. Another woman sat at a desk in a corner, focused on pages under a gooseneck lamp. Several doorways led, multidirectionally, out of the hall, and Kavanagh chose one at random, having to stoop slightly as he passed through. He was startled to hear the atonal chanting of monks, just audible, as if coming from a nearby, closed-in chapel. But it was newfangled piped-in music, fake.

A short walk down a stone corridor—hung with a gruesome crucifix, a penitent Magdalene, and a sorrowful Madonna—led into a large rectangular enclosure organized around a glassed-in courtyard, a classic rendition of the ancient monastic hub. The quadrangle was defined by a long four-sided arcade that begged to be walked around. Originally, the space would have been open to the air, a garden for growing herbs and fruit, centered on a fountain. The limestone fountain was there, but dry, and the few potted plants suggested that most others had been taken to some greenhouse for the winter. Above, on the paneled glass canopy, the rain danced, but soundlessly. At the far opposite side of the colonnade, a small group of people were gathered around a painting, too far away to notice or care about the complications of a momentarily thrown middle-aged priest.

To his right, through a semicircular arch whose Romanesque sturdiness jarred with the more delicately pointed Gothic-era arches of the arcade proper, was a vacant, unfurnished, low-ceilinged hall with a stone bench running along all three walls. He went in, as if the room had been his destination all along, and he took up a place on the bench, as if he had a right to be there.

Alone, he unzipped his jacket and put his books on the bench beside him. He resolved to block out the canned Gregorian chant, but then realized the ersatz music was sparing him the problem of a deadly silence: in holy silence, so the prophets say, men like him are supposed to hear the voice of God, but Kavanagh never heard a thing. He picked up his breviary again, and reflexively flipped the ribbon to the appointed page. He began to read the day's Psalms as if he were a monk.

"Cloister," he heard some moments later. "From the Latin, *claustrum.* For 'closed.'" A voice had finally come to Kavanagh, but it was some woman's. He did not look up. "In French," she continued, "we say *cloître.* In this museum, we have five distinct cloisters: hence the plural of the museum's name: 'The Cloisters.' But this one—dating to the twelfth century—is the jewel, the one around which all the others are organized. The reason we are here."

When Kavanagh raised his eyes, it was to find that, instead of along the arcade or at the closed-in quad, the woman was looking directly at him. She was a museum docent, clearly. She was giving instruction to a clutch of ladies whose look was fixed the other way, down the aisle of the colonnade along which the docent had been pointing. She had spoken enough so that Kavanagh took in her French accent. There was an aphonic quality to her voice, low-pitched, rough, suggesting a whisper, even though she could readily be heard. When their eyes met, they held each other's gaze for a long moment.

Then she faced away and resumed, "When this cloister was in its monastery, La Chapelle-sur-Loire, in southern Bourgogne, its dimensions were twice this size." The ladies earnestly looked about the quadrangle, taking in its pink marble arches and supporting columns, capitals elaborated with carved pinecones, acanthus leaves, and animal heads. A gray pallor hung over the scene, because the glass roof above showed the weather. The ladies, in from Scarsdale or someplace, wore tailored suits of coral, mauve, pale green, but even those colors seemed subdued by the downwash of murky air. They wore flat-crowned hats and sensible shoes, with handbags at their elbows.

"Constructed most of a thousand years ago"—the docent took several steps away from the group, letting her long, thin arm carve a graceful arc, encompassing the entire scene, an unfeigned gesture of delight—"this was the enclosure onto which all of the monastic buildings would have opened—the chapel, refectory, dormitories, kitchen, and Chapter House." At this last phrase, she threw a sidelong glance Kavanagh's way, which made him realize that "Chapter House" referred to the room he'd settled in. She resumed: "The Cloister provided the monks or nuns with isolation from the world outside. In this courtyard, the monks or nuns grew vegetables, prayed, read, took meditative walks—and washed themselves. Here. In this very place. Picture them. All in silence. *Magnum silentium.*"

As if in emphasis, she stopped speaking, quieting even her gaze, which lifted to settle on the roofline of the arcade. Through the glass could be seen ocher tiles with lips curving over the limestone entablature resting on the ranks of columns and arches. It seemed wrong, suddenly, that the rain was blocked from falling into the courtyard.

The docent turned, taking a few steps along the arcade. The ladies followed. "This cloister," she continued, carefully pronouncing each word, but with that Gallic intonation, "formed the center of one of the network of Benedictine foundations attached to the great abbey at Cluny. . . ." She described Cluny's place on the plain between the Loire and the Rhône, strategic river openings to the Atlantic and the Mediterranean both. "Cluny," she said, "was a fulcrum of culture, or, as we say in French, *le point d'appui.*" Her spiel was practiced, but did not seem canned. She simply knew what she was talking about. She had fallen into an unselfconscious pose, letting her fingers rest in a stone crevice joining a pillar to its sculpted capital, her hand at a level just above her head.

She was tall. She was dressed unremarkably in black laced Oxford shoes, a long dark skirt, and a white blouse whose pointed collars were slightly askew above a formless, fully buttoned cardigan sweater. She wore no jewelry. The slender hand at her hollow cheek emphasized an overall litheness. Her black hair was cut short, like a man's, close against her skull. Her clothing hung on her loosely. She was not lithe, he saw now, but extremely thin, as if her body had known malnourishment. A wasting disease in her past, perhaps—consumption, tuberculosis. The only skin showing was at her hands and face, but it carried the hint of an ashen hue.

"If you please," the woman said, moving the group along, "this carving of a double-headed monster . . ." They began to drift away, toward a new threshold. ". . . which invites the viewer to contemplate, as the monks and nuns always would have . . ." Her last words carried back to Kavanagh. ". . . the great struggle between vice and virtue." Then they were gone.

His reading of the breviary amounted to going through the motions. He put the woman out of his mind, but then had to fend off memories of Dunwoodie again. In fact, the museum's piped-in syllabic chant fueled the distraction, since Runner had chaired the schola, the small seminary choir that led the way each day through the communal incantations of Matins, Vespers, and Compline. Here the recorded music, with antiphons and responsories, was on a ten-minute loop that circled from the Kyrie to the Spiritus Domini to the Laetatus Sum, and back again, but under it all, Kavanagh kept hearing Runner muscle through the high notes of Panis Angelicus.

"I beg your pardon, sir."

Kavanagh looked up, surprised to find the docent standing before him, at the threshold of the so-called Chapter House. She was hugging herself against the chill, which made her seem even more slender, as delicate as one of the thin pillars in the arcade behind her. Her fingers were long, bony.

The expression on her face was neutral, but Kavanagh felt rebuked nonetheless, as if he'd stayed past closing time. He lifted his book, letting its ribbons drape, and attempted a smile. "No actual prayers allowed?"

She smiled, but thinly, ignoring the little gibe. "I simply wanted you to know there will be another general museum tour in fifteen minutes, if it pleases you." He sensed that her job depended on having people actually show up in this remote outpost, and then bother to follow her around.

Kavanagh was relieved to have his brooding interrupted. When he looked at his watch, though, she took it as refusal, and half turned away. He stood. "I'm Father Kavanagh, from Good Shepherd, the church up Broadway a few blocks." He stepped toward her and offered his hand. He smiled. "Out of uniform."

"Hello, Father." She took his hand. Her grip was firm, but her fingers, yes, were very bony. Still, something soft was showing itself, something vulnerable. "I am Rachel Vedette," she said.

"You're French."

"Yes."

"That's a coincidence." He turned back to the bench, to pick up his other book. "I've been reading a French woman's book." He displayed it.

The docent glanced at the volume. "Simone Weil," she said, but with a sort of wince.

Her expression surprised him. Weil was much written about that year; her book was something of a sensation, even among New York intellectuals.

"Why do you cringe?"

She shook her head.

"No, really," the priest said. Her slight but visceral recoiling could not have been more surprising.

But she deflected him. "Perhaps you could say what you admire about her."

He gestured with the book. "It's called *Waiting for God.*"

"Yes. Letters she exchanged with a priest."

"That's right. But that's not why I'm reading it."

"Why, then?"

"Because 'waiting for God' implies she doesn't have Him. Nothing pious here. She is with the misfits and the outsiders."

"She is with the anti-Semites."

"What?"

"Simone Weil was an anti-Semite."

"An anti-Semite?" he answered. "I thought she was a Jew."

"She was born a Jew, but her embrace of the Church fueled her contempt for her native Judaism. The worst kind of anti-Semite." Her hand went to her mouth, as if to shut it. "But I am sorry," she said. "It is rude of me to speak so bluntly."

"Embrace of the Church? She could never accept baptism. She writes harshly about it." Kavanagh was thrown that the docent had indeed spoken so directly. Her accent lent authority to her surprising statement. Still, lifting the book, he ventured, "She says she would never join an institution that regards itself as identical with Christ."

The woman checked herself. "You are correct, Father. I spoke wrongly. Her embrace was of Jesus, more than the Church. Although, as I recall, she spoke of her love for Him as remaining—how do we say this?—unconsummated." She lowered her eyes, suddenly shy, as if the word's implications embarrassed her.

Kavanagh suddenly saw the docent's gaunt appearance as a version of the French mystic's. Weil had been famously malnourished. Indeed, she died from a self-imposed hunger strike—an ultimate identification with victims of the war. To Kavanagh, Weil had seemed a kind of martyr, and he'd found her book, with its rejection of conventional religiosity, an astonishment. But now he saw that this woman before him, even in deriding Weil, was like her—not only gaunt, but brusquely candid. She said what she thought.

Unlike me, Kavanagh said to himself. He was a maestro of indirection. For example, this unexpected exchange had made apparent that the docent herself was Jewish, yet the priest could not ask the question that prompted: what is a Jew doing here, in this artificial homage to Christendom, giving tours on medieval monasticism? Instead, trying to demonstrate some further appreciation of the French writer, he said, "Perhaps it is for her seriousness in the face of what happened in Europe that Simone Weil is valued."

"Is it serious," Rachel Vedette said with fresh severity, "to analogize the ancient Hebrews with the Nazis?"

"Does she do that?"

"Yes. Despite having been forced out of her teaching post because of Vichy laws against Jews. Ancient Israel, to her, was 'the beast.' Although you may not know this, because I doubt that her *cahiers* . . . notebooks . . . have been published in English."

"It's true. I don't read French. This is the only book I know."

"That one is a good book. I agree. It displays her empathy with suffering, which was limited, but quite real."

"And her longing for transcendence," Kavanagh dared to say.

"Yes, that, too."

"And as for the complications of her being Jewish . . ."

Miss Vedette shrugged. "You are right. 'Complications of being Jewish.'" She smiled. "Why not?"

That she had no interest in judging him, or in puncturing his pretensions, made it possible for him to ask his question, although still obliquely: "So your expertise is Catholicism?"

"French history, in point of fact. *Le Moyen Âge.* The Church, of course, is necessary for that."

"Of course."

"Although, unlike Simone Weil," she said, "I do not know priests."

Kavanagh bowed slightly. And she returned his gesture with a slight bow of her own. She looked at her watch. "So, I said before, fifteen minutes. Now it is five minutes."

"I wish I could join you," the priest said. He placed *Waiting for God* together with his breviary and slipped the pair of books under his arm. "Some other time, perhaps."

"Yes," she said, and put her hand out. They shook. *"Bonne chance, mon père."*

She turned and walked away. Kavanagh knew that, given his response to her, the expected thing would be for him to zip up his coat and leave. He'd made it seem that the press of his schedule precluded his joining the tour, but in fact his next obligation wasn't until midafternoon, religion class for the sixth- and seventh-graders. He had turned down her invitation reflexively. It wasn't a docent's spiel he wanted. What, then?

Instead of resuming his place on the stone bench of the Chapter House, he turned and entered the ambulatory, falling into the slow pace proper to a monk reciting the Office. Would he resume the business of seeming to pray? He could not have explained his impulse to remain in the museum. Had the enchantments of the place trumped his parochial resentments? No. Something else.

He took up his breviary again. Priests like him called the black Psalter with gold leaf pages "the wife." That they called their chosen spiritual reading, his other book, "the mistress" did not seem funny now; indeed, the Simone Weil volume rode with fresh awkwardness beneath his arm. Kavanagh flipped the breviary ribbon and read, *Exaudi, Deus, orationem meam cum deprecor; a timore inimici eripe animam meam.* He muscled his way through the Latin: *Deliver my soul from the fear of the enemy.*

Cradling the breviary, pressing the Weil against his side, he had made two complete circuits of the colonnade when he saw the woman again, this time without a group. She was unaware of him as she entered the Cloister, and when she stepped into the arcade, as it happened, she cut him off. He stopped.

"My goodness," she said, startled. "I am sorry." Now she, too, was holding a book, a thin leather-bound volume.

"My fault," Kavanagh said. "Please, pardon me." He adjusted a ribbon and closed his breviary.

"I thought you had gone," she said.

"Wasn't ready to face my afternoon." He smiled. "Sixth-graders." Because Kavanagh had been walking, and because the arcaded promenade invited it, he started to resume his pace, then stopped. With a gesture, he invited her to walk beside him. She hesitated.

He apologized: "I've cluttered your space, haven't I? You came in here to—what do we say?—perambulate?"

"It's true. When no one arrives for the guided lecture, I come in here alone."

"'Preserve your solitude,' Simone Weil says."

The woman only looked at him.

"I feel bad, then," Kavanagh said. "I should have joined you for the tour."

"Why are you still here?" she asked.

Her direct question threw him. Also, it made him want to answer. He looked up. The rain was drumming the glass canopy. "I was hoping it would stop," he said. But the rain was not what had kept him here, and it suddenly seemed deceptive to imply that it had. He said, "Something bothered me this morning. I came to The Cloisters by accident, but it feels like the place to be."

"I understand." She looked around. "I imagine the men and women who built this place, a thousand years ago. It consoles me."

"Consoles you . . ." Kavanagh said slowly, surprising himself. "From what?"

Instead of answering, she stared at him coldly. Or rather, as he realized then, her stare was her answer. He said, "I'm sorry."

She said calmly, "It would be rude of me to ask, 'What bothered you this morning?' How could you imagine I would explain myself to you?"

He glanced around. "A thousand years, you said. The place surprised me, that's all. You surprised me." What had she said about Weil? "Her empathy with suffering, which was limited but quite real." This woman and Simone Weil, he thought again, were alike. He said, "You seem to say what comes to mind. For a change, that's what I did just now. Not like me. But I take your point. And, yes, it was rude. None of my business. The Cloister is no excuse. After all, it is not real."

"But it is. This very place. Abbots and Abbesses; monks and nuns; we know their names. They were trying for something that cannot be seen. Something that lasts. Such men and women should not be forgotten." With that, she made a slight gesture with her book.

"Cluny, you said."

"La Chapelle-sur-Loire."

"But now a museum."

She shrugged. "Cluny itself is a museum now."

Kavanagh felt entirely displaced, as if he and this woman were meeting in a realm apart, speaking a language that, whatever it was to her, was new to him. "The place no longer serves its purpose," he said.

"But its purpose was always to remember, no? A museum, a sanctuary—all the same."

"But in the museum the past is dead," Kavanagh said carefully. Such a portentous statement was unlike him, yet he pushed it further, saying, "Remembering can be a death grip. The sanctuary is for life."

A dark expression came over her face, unpleasant, almost mean. But she banished the dour look and held up her thin volume again. "You have your books, Father. I have mine. History. *Le Moyen Âge.*"

The priest thought, finally, of Runner again. He wanted, all at once, to tell someone what had happened at Mass that morning. That strange, unsettling apparition. And now this woman, too. Another sort of visitant. He had met her because of Runner. She was a match for Runner. Strange. Unsettling. He said, "You say it would it be rude of you to ask what bothered me, but what if, despite myself, that's why I mentioned it? Hoping you would ask."

Rachel Vedette, again, answered with her stare. Finally, gesturing at his breviary, with no hint of her public face, she said, "You should complete your obligation, Father." With that, she turned and walked out of the Cloister.

CHAPTER TWO

Rachel Vedette carried it with her everywhere, a gnarled scar on memory, the sweltering day when all had changed—July 16, 1942. Life can be transformed in a snap, a cosmic shift determined by one hour that glows red through the chilly gray of mundane experience ever after. Since then, she had sought not to undo what had happened—impossible!—but only to find again, and claim, any one of the many aspirations that had belonged to her before.

She was twenty. As she hurriedly set out for home from the Musée de Cluny that afternoon, even the wide sidewalks of Boulevard Saint-Germain were deserted, which had not been the case the other times. The vacant street amplified her alarm. She was already running, and now ran faster. The skirt of her loose-fitting summer dress flared at her knees. Unruly wisps of her dark hair, having come loose from the plaited coil of her tightly pulled-back bun, flew at her face. Rumors had yet again swept Paris. But this afternoon, in the archive of the Institut Médiéval, housed in the Musée, a clerk, who had often looked her over but never spoken to her, approached her work-table, under the cone-shaped hanging lamps of the high-vaulted reading room, to lean close and whisper, "The Germans are arresting the Jews."

The shock of what the man said was compounded by her instant question: *How does he know I'm Jewish?*

But then he said, "The wandering days of *les youpins* are over," and she realized he was including her not in the insulted group but in the group having the right to slur. He did not know. She turned away and began to gather her papers, but he touched her arm. "You should not go out. Let the Krauts do their business."

"Their business?"

He shrugged. "It's only Jews."

"Only *Jews?*" she replied sharply. And then, at the mercy of a bolt of anger, she added recklessly, "My father is a Jew."

He drew back, quizzically.

"And so am I," she added, although it was only her father of whom she was thinking.

"But you . . ." He glanced at the pages on the table, her own handwriting and the manuscript facsimiles that she was copying—musty texts that he himself had delivered to her. The clerk had seen her at this table for months—an unusual *doctorante*, so young and pretty. He'd used the rumor about the Jews as a pretext to approach her.

"But what? I work on Peter Abelard?" she said. That unforgotten man of *le haut Moyen Âge* had spoken from and to the soul of *la France* for most of a thousand years—but what meaning could the infamous Catholic monk have for Jews? "Is that your question?" she asked. Rachel read the confusion so clearly in the man's eyes that she sternly made his question even more explicit: "What is Peter Abelard to a Jew?"

"Nothing," he answered, but he was backing away now.

"That's what you think," she'd said. She'd left the manuscript stack for him to refile, pushed the last of her own pages into her briefcase, and rushed out of the archive.

Now, at Rue Dante, she dashed across the oddly vacant boulevard into the narrower street that would take her to the river at the Pont au Double, and to the islands beyond, including hers. Now she ran along the very center of the street itself. That the city was deserted frightened her. Over the previous year, the other rumors of Jews being arrested had never proved accurate, and she hoped that this one, too, was false. At each of those other reports, a new clique had disappeared from the Marais, the Jewish quarter on the Right Bank, a

mile or more from the apartment she shared with her father. But
those Jews had not been arrested; they had fled Paris. And each time,
Saul Vedette had pleaded with his daughter to go, too. But her father,
severely diabetic, was tethered to the local chemist who supplied his
insulin, and she'd have had to go without him—unthinkable. Since
his wife had died five years before, Vedette had become wholly depen-
dent on Rachel, even as the disease had progressively weakened him.

Rachel was like her mother in thinking of herself as French first,
which meant being more detached from Jewishness than her father,
who was a professor, after all, of medieval Jewish history, specializing
in Talmud. In the beginning, she'd found it impossible to believe
that the jeopardy of the Jews of France could be real, but the sequen-
tial promulgations of the Statut des Juifs since 1940 had made her,
too, understand that a noose was tightening on the Israélite throat—
especially once her father was dismissed from the university. Still,
they encouraged each other in the belief that they'd be safe because
they did not live in the Marais, among kosher butchers, Judaica shops,
and synagogues. Indeed, few Jews lived on their island in the Seine,
and since her father's banishment, when even the institute was closed
to him, he had rarely shown himself in public. The Germans were
said to be scouring municipal census records for Jewish names, but
"Vedette," a military term meaning foremost sentry, had been adopted
by a forebear serving in Napoleon's Grande Armée, an assimilation-
ist betrayal of God's people for which, at last, Saul Vedette could be
grateful.

Rachel, for her part, had easily continued to blend in as just
another Sorbonne *étudiante,* even as she surreptitiously took up her
father's research in the archive. As far as most of his former colleagues
knew, Saul Vedette was simply one of those Jews who'd already taken
the hint and fled Paris. So once more, the terrible thing she'd done hit
Rachel: as of only the month before, there were some who knew very
well who and where he was—and they knew because of her.

As she drew closer to the river, with her satchel banging at her
side, Rachel pictured him, dozing in his chair by the window. Beside
him would be a last ribbon of smoke rising from the ashtray on the
table. Next to the ashtray would be the worn leather volume *Historia*

Calamitatum: Heloissae et Abaelardi Epistolae, a text that he had come
to know so well he needed not to read but only to fondle it. On that
table, also, would be assembled numerous pages of manuscript in her
own hand, alongside other pages that she had herself put through the
typewriter—his dictation. Behind his chair, on the small bookcase,
would be other stacks of such pages, in both handwriting and typescript, Latin and French. Flanking the bookcase would be the bentwood chairs that had last been used when the review committee had
come to the apartment for that awful hearing—again, because of her.

Now, running along the boulevard, she conjured images of home
as a way to fend off panic—the picture of her father dozing. Her mind
flew ahead. As always, she would rouse him softly with a kiss on the
forehead, then stand aside while he made his way to the water closet.
She would go to the sink in the small kitchen to wash her hands.
When he returned, he would have left his shirt out of his trousers,
ready for the injection. By then, she would already have prepared
the cotton swabs with rubbing alcohol, and retrieved the insulin
syringe and the rubber vial-cap, both of which she'd have sterilized
after the morning shot by boiling them in a small cast-iron pressure
cooker on the stove.

When he sat again, she would take from the shelf above his chair
the mahogany jewelry box in which, once, Rachel's mother had kept
pearls and rings, and the small silver mezuzah she had from her rabbi
grandfather—the mezuzah she could neither hang at the door nor
part with. But the box now held Saul's insulin vials. Rachel would
open it, remove the active vial, and cap it with the rubber stopper.
Raising the syringe to eye level, against the window light, she would
expel its air. She would push the needle through the vial cap and, once
more against the light, carefully draw exactly eight units of serum
into the barrel. Eight units in the late afternoon. Six units in the early
morning. Then, with her father pinching a fold of flesh at his abdomen, she would stab the needle in, expertly push the plunger, pull it
out, and swab the pasty flab, all in one continuous movement. *"Voilà,
Papa,"* she would always say, putting the needle aside. Only then, having winced not at all, would he greet her, reaching up to grasp her
shoulders, pulling her cheek down to his, first one, then the other,

and saying, as he always did, *"Merci! Merci!* I would be lost without you, my dearest, dearest girl." Then he would turn away to hide his eyes—so full of water, not from pain, but from feeling.

She tore across the Pont au Double, onto the Île de la Cité, ever more troubled at how godforsaken Paris felt. There seemed to be no river traffic, no taxis at the stand. Approaching the Cathedral, she was relieved to see a clutch of people in the plaza, but they were heading into the great church—a dozen old women, she saw now, widows of the Great War, famously appointed to pray the daily rosary for the dead heroes of France. Rachel had heard it said that Catholics, when they recited the Ave these days, substituted the name of Marshal Pétain for Mary.

Notre-Dame, of course, was the storied demesne of Abelard and his famous lover, Héloïse, but that day it was a mark on her passage home, that's all. The towering Cathedral was roughly the midway point between the museum and the book-lined apartment she shared with her father on Île Saint-Louis, the villagelike cluster of faded mansions and subdivided townhouses on the Cathedral's sister island. On most days, coming home from the museum, she would see off-duty German soldiers sunbathing on the grass behind the apse, but now they were not there. She imagined the soldiers mustered, fully uniformed, at loose in the streets, rifles at the ready, in their brown trucks, mounted on motorcycles, blowing whistles, slamming through doors, boots loud upon stair treads. And, indeed, just then she heard the faint wailing of far-off sirens, the urgent up-and-down of a screeching beast. The high-pitched squeal was coming, yes, from the Right Bank, around Rue Saint-Paul—the *Marais,* with its closed-in streets, lanes, and squares, to which, for more than a year, her father had forbidden her to go.

Of course, what were sirens in occupied Paris? French police rushing from one bureau to another; ambulances carrying the valorous near-dead from the Front; Wehrmacht brass in train with their escorts. Sirens were nothing, she wanted to tell herself. But these sirens, she was certain, were coming from the Jewish quarter. *Thank God, we don't live there!* She might have dropped her satchel, to run faster—to hell with the thing—but at the archive she had gathered up two weeks' worth of copying and frantically stuffed the pages into the bag. Pages, she believed, despite the dismissive verdict of the Sorbonne reviewers, that were still keeping her father alive. However desolate he'd become, she had helped him continue with his project. Each page she carried home was a token of his hope. Each one a talisman. Magic.

Normally, when crossing the last bridge into her own home enclave, she relaxed, comforted by the special island air of exemption from the stresses of Paris that had defined Île Saint-Louis for two hundred years. But now she became even more frantic. These streets, too, were empty, and that seemed, if anything, still more ominous than the far-off sirens. At the corner café, Deux Garçons, where Rue Jean du Bellay met Rue Saint Louis, she had an impulse to rush in and ask Monsieur Beguin if it was true, the Germans were coming? She glimpsed him, standing in the window in his black vest and bow tie, perhaps raising his hand to wave, but she simply ran past.

Two blocks along Rue Saint Louis, she came, finally, to their apartment house. She turned her key quickly and bolted through the small entrance foyer, but not so swiftly that she failed to notice Madame Boudreau's firmly shut door. Usually, the door was kept slightly ajar at all hours, enabling the concierge to track the comings and goings of the two dozen people who lived in the once-grand old building. Rachel ignored the closet-sized elevator—its electricity had been shut off the year before—and took to the winding staircase. By the time she reached the fourth floor, she could hardly breathe, but then she saw that the door to their apartment was standing wide open. She forgot her exhaustion, and stopped.

She stood at the threshold, looking in. The main room, with its glass-fronted armoire and stuffed sofa, was orderly, as was, beyond the separating arch, the far alcove that served as her father's study. His chair was there, by the window, but with her father gone from it, the piece of furniture seemed defective. The pair of bentwood chairs were in place, at the bookshelf. The only sign of disarray was a fan of papers on the floor. But then she saw that the sheets half covered her father's black yarmulke, which, when he was awake, indoors, was always on his head. On the floor beside the yarmulke were his spectacles. Rachel dropped the satchel and moved slowly into the apartment. "Papa? Papa?"

He was not there. This recognition, oddly, cauterized her panic, and all at once a calm detachment came over her. She stooped to retrieve his yarmulke, held it briefly to her breast, then put it in the side pocket of her dress. His meerschaum pipe was in its ashtray. She picked it up. Cold. She crossed to his bedroom, then to her own small, curtained-off corner. She opened the door to the water closet. She craned into the tiny kitchen. Back in his study, she stooped to retrieve her pages from the floor and carefully aligned them on the table, beside the worn leather volume that always sat there. She flicked a pinch of spilled ashes away.

Slowly turning, she surveyed the bookshelves, the typewriter, the reams of manuscript. The jumble was normal untidiness. On impulse, she went back to her father's bedroom and opened his closet door, to see his heavy winter shoes properly in place on the floor. If she'd been a detective, she'd have been making notes on her pad. But then, in her father's study again, her eye went to the shelf above his chair, and, snap, like that, the rush of feeling returned, a dammed torrent breaking loose in her breast again. The mahogany chest was gone: *Papa's insulin!*

Saul Vedette's diabetes meant that his pancreas failed to produce a sufficient quantity of the hormone that allowed his body to process sugar properly. Without his shots, his body would not absorb sugar, and would effectively starve itself. His blood-sugar levels would quickly become impossibly high, causing severe dehydration, and within days, coma would follow, and radical organ failure, beginning with the kidneys.

Whoever had taken her father had taken the chest, too. She imagined her father having the presence of mind to insist upon it. But that would have meant taking also the syringe and rubber vial-cap, which, after sterilizing, she routinely kept in a freshly laundered linen sleeve on its own shelf in the kitchen. She went there now and, to her dismay, found the needle still in its cloth holder. Saul Vedette, without his shots, was dead.

Rachel left the syringe where it was, and rushed from the apartment and rapidly down the stairs; she was quickly at the door to Madame Boudreau's room, and banging on it. The woman's voice, plaintive and obviously afraid, came back at her: "Please, please . . ." The door opened. The bent old woman looked up at Rachel as if expecting to be hit. Over her black housedress, she wore a dark-blue smock. She was clearly startled to see Rachel, and opened her mouth to speak. But no words came. The blow of her foul body odor hit Rachel.

"What happened? Who came?" Rachel asked. An inane question, of course.

"They did," the old woman answered. "They did. They took the professor."

"Who? Who? Germans?"

"No. Not Krauts. Gendarmes. French police." The woman tried to close the door, but Rachel stopped her.

"French police!?"

"Yes. French."

"Took him where? Where?"

"Who knows? Gone. He is gone. If you were here, they'd have taken you, too. You would not fool them, as you do everyone else." Suddenly, the woman uncurled herself, almost straightening her back, to lunge up at Rachel, contemptuously. "You have brought trouble on this house. You and your father." She pushed on the door again.

This time, Rachel shocked the old lady and herself by forcefully slamming the door all the way open. The woman fell roughly to the floor, and Rachel crossed into her room, a tiny space, holding only a narrow cot, a cluttered deal table, and a doily-backed chair. A small wall-shelf had been converted, by means of an unevenly pleated faux-satin scarf, into a pathetic Marian shrine. Behind a thin vase with its bud, and a curled rosary, stood the Virgin. Made of cheap molded plaster, shoddily painted blue and white, the figure was poised with her face demurely down, as if averting her eyes from what this ferocious, invading Jewess was about to do.

Only then did Rachel see what was on the table, amid the clutter of newspapers and dishes: the mahogany chest. Her father's mahogany chest; her mother's. Its lid was up, showing its store of glass vials, insulin. At once, Rachel understood. After the police took her father away, the concierge stole into their apartment, saw the jewelry box, mistook it for what it once had been, and made off with it.

Rachel wheeled on Madame. "You dare to take this! You thief! You fiend!"

The woman's eyes cast about, as if help would come. She shielded her face. "I saved it for you," she whimpered.

The lie so infuriated Rachel that she slapped the woman. It was the first blow she'd ever struck against another human being, and at once Rachel fell back, her hands at her mouth, mirroring Madame Boudreau. Rachel lurched toward the table, closed the lid of the mahogany box, clutched it inside her left arm, and turned back toward the door. But the old woman was in the way. Furious, she sent a wad of spittle into Rachel's face. "Jew!" the woman screeched. "Stinking Jew!"

Once again, Rachel's reaction was visceral, instant, and unwilled. Instead of hitting the woman, she swung her right arm toward the wall-shelf and swept the statue of the Virgin away. It crashed to the floor, smashed into pieces. Quickly, she was out, rushing up the stairs. The words "Stinking Jew!" were alive in her ear, but her mind roared with the question, *Who am I now?*

By the time she was back in the apartment, the vise of her will had closed down on the terrors. With the back of her hand, she had wiped her face clean of saliva. She moved swiftly and steadily, as if through a routine instead of through a sequence of actions she had never imagined. Yet she knew exactly what to do. First, she gathered the foolscap typescript from the bookshelf, and a stack of her own handwritten pages. She stuffed them into the satchel she had carried from the institute, then went into her father's bedroom. At his closet, she knelt and pushed his brogans aside, along with a hodgepodge of old journals and items of soiled laundry. She pulled out a small battered suitcase. This left exposed the wide pine boards of the narrow floor space. Craning in, she pushed down on the rearmost floorboard, at a knot by the wall, a particular pressure point that brought the other end of the board up just enough for her to grasp it and pull it free, opening a below-deck space between the joists. She pushed the satchel into the well, an ad hoc vault, then closed the plank again, snapping it back into its close fit.

She took the suitcase to the small table by the kitchen and, in short order, carefully filled it with the insulin vials, the syringe kits, the linen sleeves, and the pressure cooker. She took a brick of chocolate from the counter, wrapped it in paper alongside a small folding knife, and put it in the case, together with three precious bananas, a sack of nuts, and a pair of apples. From the highest shelf, she took the hoarded coupons—*cartes de rationnement*—essential to acquiring meat, bread, and eggs, as well as a stash of several thousand paper *francs*. From the edge of the sink, she took the toothbrushes and tooth powder. Then, from their separate drawers across the room, she took underwear for both of them, his fresh shirt, her sweater. At the suitcase again, she cushioned the medical gear with this clothing and with a small pillow from the sofa. Before closing the suitcase, she looked around carefully. Her eye fell on the small stack of books on her father's table—the Bible, a commentary by Nachmanides, and, on top, the worn leather volume of Peter Abelard's *Historia Calamitatum*. She retrieved all three, and placed them on the pillow, as if enthroning texts on the bimah. The Abelard struck her: yes, a story of calamity—precisely.

She took her father's yarmulke out of her pocket and placed it on the book, then closed the suitcase. Pressing down, she forced away the question: how had this happened?

Saul Vedette had been a senior *directeur de recherche* at the Institut Médiéval—a key figure in the modern recovery of medieval manuscripts that had been cast aside in the anti-Catholic frenzy that shook all of France after the Revolution. In addition to the great biblical and theological texts of Christendom, the major monasteries had preserved Jewish and Islamic works, too, and the work of the institute was to reclaim them. Beginning as a young Hebraist, Vedette had done his life's work there, at first a decidedly Jewish project of cataloging fragments of the foundational Talmudic and Kabbalistic documents that had been spirited away by monks. But Saul Vedette had become one of the most revered professors at the institute—revered, so Rachel had thought, by everyone. Her mistake.

One last glance around. What else? His glasses! There, on the floor. She crossed, picked the spectacles up, and put them in the pocket of her dress.

Still looking, she asked herself again: what else? She was certain there was something, but could not think what. Then she knew. She returned to her father's closet, reached in between the hanging items of apparel, and from the breast of his overcoat ripped off the yellow star, stamped *Juif,* that she had sewn there herself the year before. He had never once gone outside wearing it. In the kitchen, she found a pin, and with it attached the badge to her dress, at her breast. That was all.

As she went past Madame Boudreau's door, she again noted that it was firmly shut. Also firmly shut was Rachel's heart against the woman. Only moments later, Rachel presented herself at the Deux Garçons, the corner café. Three out of the seven tables were occupied. At one of those, before a pair of dark-suited men, Monsieur Beguin was placing first one demitasse, then the other. When the café proprietor saw Rachel standing in the doorway, he stood motionless, staring. The yellow star on her breast had registered. At first he seemed only perplexed, but then his face softened. Still, he did not move. Rachel entered the café, crossed to the zinc-topped coffee bar, put the suitcase down, and stood ready to place an order. Monsieur Beguin came to her, but on his side of his counter.

"Whom else did they take?" she asked abruptly. She was thinking, for starters, of the Lévys, a family living two doors down from the café, and of the Brissards, an elderly couple whose flat was above the patisserie in the nearby square.

"They came only for your father, it seems," the man replied. "No one else on our street was arrested. They went right to your place, direct. They took him, and they left. In and out." Monsieur Beguin looked down, ashamed. "There was nothing to be done."

"How did they know?" she asked.

He shrugged. "The 'denaturalization' rolls?"

"My father never registered."

"Still, they knew." He held her eyes with his. "As I say, they went direct. Only for your father. They took him."

"French police. Not Germans."

"I know," he said. And his face reddened with further shame.

Rachel withdrew a cigarette pack from her pocket. By the time she'd placed a cigarette between her lips, the proprietor was ready with a match. She took the flame, exhaled. "You might as well serve me coffee while I wait," Rachel said.

"Wait for what?" Beguin asked.

"The police. I want you to call them. Tell them you've captured a Jew of your own."

He shook his head no—never. When he lowered his eyes, they snagged on her yellow star. Rachel knew it was unfair to unload this spite on her cowardly neighbor, but she did not care. She said, with a calm that sounded eerie even to her, "Call the police, monsieur. Then, if you please, serve me a coffee."

She went to the small table by the window, to wait. Soon enough, Monsieur Beguin placed a demitasse in front of her. By then, though, she was lost in the pool of her own eyes, reflected in the window. But instead of her own face, what she saw was her father's.

It was the year before, when Saul Vedette found himself barred from even entering the archive room at the Musée de Cluny, that Rachel, weighing in, had made her first great mistake. She understood that he'd come to live for his new project, and she saw how this final banishment shook him. She insisted that he continue. It was unthinkable to her that his friends on the faculty would not welcome the work once it was completed—and she said as much. She volunteered to exploit her own minor *étudiante* status at the Sorbonne to become her father's discreet research assistant. Enrolled in the standard history course, she would be free to roam the archive. "Only point me to the texts you need," she said, "and I will reproduce them for you."

Vedette was in his chair, pipe in hand. She was standing before him. He smiled sadly. "And bring the occupiers down on you?"

She shrugged. "I am a Jew—but like Mama was."

Vedette smiled. "Modern."

"If I am Jewish, my teachers and fellow students care nothing for it. No one at the institute knows me. As for the Germans, what are the dusty folders of Cluny to them?"

"The dusty folders hold texts cluttered with insular Latin script—difficult to read."

"Which I can readily master. Why else," she said, grinning, "did you send me to the *lycée classique*? As you know, Latin was my best course." She laughed, because such a claim was so unlike her. And she sensed that he was seeing the way forward—her way. Except on matters of his diet and the disciplines of insulin injection, Rachel had rarely pushed back against her father's will, yet it was all at once apparent that he had raised her for this moment.

She said, "The only question, Papa, is—are you right in what you propose about Peter Abelard, or are you wrong?"

"I am right."

"And your findings could help our people?"

"They could. They could, if somehow my voice was heard in France."

"Your voice," Rachel said with the absolute certitude of a worshipful daughter, "*will* be heard."

His eyes brimmed when he said, "As yours is now."

Abélard et Israël was to have been the book's title, a direct elucidation of the medieval philosopher's radically ecumenical attitude toward Jews—an attitude that had been lost to history. Saul Vedette meant to offer a new interpretation of Peter Abelard's known work, and an argument that heretofore anonymous texts unusual in their Jew-friendliness belonged in the Abelard canon.

Less a pedant's dry treatise than a robust narrative, the work aimed to lift up Abelard as an alternative model of French *esprit* for the widest possible readership. Vedette's igniting hope was that, with the imprimatur of the Institut Médiéval, his book would be published—anonymously, of course—and presented at a Sorbonne symposium, all under the noses of the Nazis, to whom arcane Gallic medievalism would be angels dancing on a pinhead. But once it was published, the angels would fly, for Peter Abelard was a beloved progenitor of the nation.

Across a thousand years, Abelard's fame had competed with his infamy: a heretic—or a wise philosopher; a hero of modern humanism—but also the *bête noire* of anti-modern Catholicism, which only endeared him more to the anti-clerics of the French Enlightenment. Always, of course, he was celebrated—or reviled—as the inventor, with Héloïse, of modern love. They were the Romeo and Juliet, Tristan and Isolde, Lancelot and Guinevere of *la France.* But what concerned Vedette—and, centrally, the story he told—was the all-but-ignored question of Abelard's attitude toward Jews.

The improbable Jewish scholar had begun, in 1940, by isolating the anonymous texts and transcriptions likely to have come from the sacked libraries of the two Benedictine foundations that had, through all fluctuations, continued to preserve some association with Abelard—the monastery he'd founded for Héloïse, the Paraclete, and Cluny itself. Through the same methods of close analysis that had shaped his Talmudic study, Vedette identified rubrics, word choices, and original constructions peculiar to Abelard. Once Vedette was barred from the archive in 1941, and reconciled to his insistent daughter's collaboration, he instructed her in what to look for in the transcriptions—Abelard's invented words, characteristic phrases, and always the word *"Judaeus."* When those or a dozen other particular constructions leapt out at her, she painstakingly copied the entire text, to bring home yet another essential clue to the literary detective work that had come to define the life of her father, the housebound Jew.

Vedette's foray into the deep past, viewed through the lens of Jewish jeopardy, made him more attuned to the true meaning of the present, perhaps, than anyone in Paris. That was what his daughter saw, and what she insisted on advancing. It was as if, even in his isolation, her brilliant father had been lifted, eagle-like, to a great altitude, from which he looked down with rare clarity on the full moral scale of the Nazi occupation, and the Vichy surrender.

Rachel saw the thing clearly. This deadly turn in the French story did not have to be. It could have gone another way, and the pivot point, ages ago, was the place of Jews. Saul Vedette was an archaeologist of the national soul, quickening history to change the way people thought in their own astonishing time. Rachel was exhilarated to be helping him: Saul Vedette was bringing the past into the present to save lives. Of course she urged him on!

But then, only weeks ago, had come the Sorbonne verdict. Her father's mistake, in handing his preliminary draft over, was to trust a man he thought a friend—Jean-Marie Laurent, the eminent Catholic philosopher, expert on Thomas Aquinas, and chair of the Institut Médiéval. Instead of giving Vedette the informal manuscript reading he sought, Laurent convened an official academic committee to review *Abélard et Israël,* as if Professor Saul Vedette were a junior scholar up for promotion. Laurent sent word that he would be coming to the Vedette apartment, but made no mention of the committee. No sooner had the three professors arrived than Rachel sensed, from their uniformly sour expressions, that she herself had made the more grievous miscalculation—just in encouraging her father in the project, enabling it. The committee had come to make its finding official. Its procedural formality was made ludicrous, of course, by the fact that the donnish verdict could not be presented, as ritual required, in the ornate seminar hall at the Musée de Cluny, since the petitioning author was a banished Jew.

As Rachel arranged chairs for the three stoic professors in the cramped living room—after they declined her offer of tea—her grasp of their dark mood made her wonder why they hadn't just sent a negative letter. What was Monsieur Laurent up to?

Rachel withdrew to her sleeping alcove and sat on her cot to watch. Her view was half obscured by the alcove curtain, which she half used to hide behind. Soon enough, the thing was clear. The three professors, formally dressed in dark suits and ties, sat like the judges of an appellate court, lacking only white linen tabs at their collars. Saul Vedette was in his armchair, dressed in his best suit and tie. If he shared his daughter's foreboding, he did not show it. He had received his former confrères with genuine warmth, and now calmly awaited their response to his work.

Laurent took the lead. Elegantly tailored, he wore bushy but well-trimmed gray hair and a full mustache. He made a show of composing himself, adopting a neutral countenance, and stiffening his posture, the small of his back firmly against the chair. The faces of his colleagues were stony. One of them was striking in his bony leanness, and the other for the sheen on his bald pate. A mournful expression crossed Laurent's face as he reached into his valise and pulled out the typescript of *Abélard et Israël*. Its pages, Rachel saw, were vivid with pasted-on place markers of yellow and red. He put the stack of pages on the low table, which, for Rachel, suddenly took on the character of a judicial bench.

"You make a large argument, monsieur—" Laurent began.

Vedette interrupted him. "'Monsieur,' Jean-Marie? How long has it been since you so addressed me?" Vedette's tone was friendly, but Rachel heard a challenge in her father's maintaining the familiar form *"tu."*

Laurent ignored the interruption to continue with what Rachel now heard as a rehearsed statement. "—but it is deeply flawed, and insulting to the deposit of Catholic faith." Faltering momentarily, Laurent withdrew a page from the inside pocket of his suit coat and, following notes, announced what he called the definitive conclusion of the review committee. Rachel leaned forward to hear.

With clipped efficiency, speaking as to a self-deceived doctoral candidate, Laurent told one of the great living medievalists, first, that his interpretations of Abelard's known works were unsupported by any objective reading. Especially egregious was the failure to reckon satisfactorily with Peter Abelard's *Commentary on Romans,* in which, Laurent said, "The philosopher's orthodoxy on the Jewish question is clear."

Vedette cut in, still calmly. "'The Jewish question,' Jean-Marie? Is that phrase Peter Abelard's? Or is it Saint Paul's?"

Laurent blushed. "The question of Israel's replacement."

"'I say then,'" Vedette recited, "'hath God cast away his people? By no means! . . . God hath not cast away his people which he foreknew.' As I show, Abelard features that verse from Romans, chapter eleven."

"He wrestles with the verse, that's true," Laurent replied, and then added, "but not 'features.' In no way 'features.'" Laurent conveyed a sudden disdain, and Rachel sensed how her father had offended him—a Jew presuming to offer instruction on the Epistles of Paul? Laurent continued firmly, "Abelard's *Commentary* is clear on the matter. Orthodox. Israel is superseded. The Church replaced the synagogue in God's affection. A sad thing for Jews, but the truth. And from that truth, all the Jews' problems follow."

Vedette shrugged with apparent equanimity, but Rachel sensed his iron will—and his refusal to be baited. He said, "And as I demonstrate, Jean-Marie, the *Commentary* came early in Abelard's work. The philosopher's first conclusions might also have been superseded in his later writing."

"Not demonstrated," a second professor interjected, the bald one. "His conclusions were *othodox*," the man insisted.

Laurent glanced at his colleague sharply, conveying that he, as chair, was the one to speak.

But again Saul Vedette intervened, looking directly at the second professor. "You emphasize Abelard's orthodoxy, monsieur. Yet surely you know that he was condemned as a heretic at the Council of Sens. For being *un*orthodox."

"That was for his muddled teaching on the Trinity."

"Not for that alone, monsieur. The anathema was pronounced for his quite unmuddled refusal to say the Jews had sinned." Rachel marveled at her father's poise. "You will find the council's declaration in Denzinger. Shall I give you the reference?"

Laurent raised his hand. "This is not a disputation. This is a presentation of the committee's conclusions." With another silencing glance at his colleague, Laurent went on quickly with the summary: that the case for the textual parallels and stylistic echoes between settled Abelard writings and anonymous manuscripts was unreliable; simply ridiculous was the central assumption of Vedette's argument that Abelard manifested otherwise unheard-of pro-Jewish sentiments because he had intimate exchange with Jewish counterparts, even depending on texts written by a contemporary Spanish Jew.

But when Saul Vedette now raised his hand, Rachel was alarmed to see an unprecedented tremor in its fingers. For the first time, she sensed his vulnerability. He was too old for this. He was exposed, vulnerable. Perhaps his sugar level had dropped. The rush of rejection was swamping him, and there was a new uncertain note in his voice as he said, "The physician and philosopher Judah Halevi. I show clearly—"

The third professor, the lean one, blurted, "Impossible! Peter Abelard never met Judah Halevi."

"I do not say 'met,' monsieur. I say 'read.' Abelard's *Dialogue with the Jew* repeats—"

"Without evidence!" the man said.

"With plausibility, monsieur," Saul countered, reclaiming authority. *He knew this.* "The two thinkers were exact contemporaries. Abelard had correspondence with Toledo. It would be surprising if he and Halevi were *not* aware of each other. Our standard of measure across nine hundred years cannot be certitude. I assert what is plausible."

"Fantasy," said the second professor, the bald one. Laurent, having lost control, was discomfited. The bald professor went on: "A Jew's fantasy. As if Peter Abelard needed a tutorial from a Jew."

"Why not?" Saul asked quietly. "I myself offered tutorials for a quarter-century as a member of the greatest Catholic faculty in France."

"Not in sacred theology," Laurent said, hinting at an unexpected remorse.

Rachel saw that she had wholly underestimated the danger of what her father had taken on. The insult of a Jew's trespass had infuriated even his old friend, who now had neither the ability nor the wish to defend Saul Vedette further.

"Moses?" Vedette asked. "Not sacred?"

"That was before, Saul," Laurent said sadly.

"'Before,' Jean-Marie? Before what?" When Laurent did not answer, Vedette said, "My friend, I asked you only for your informal reading of what I wrote. I would have welcomed your opinion. Instead, you spring this procedural *embuscade,* like a trap of the Inquisition."

"I had no choice," Laurent explained. "You came to me because of my office. You were hoping for an institute symposium. You wanted the imprimatur. It was never going to happen. A decisive negation was required. And now you have it."

Vedette shook his head, mournfully. He made one last appeal. "Abelard powerfully lifted up the plight of Jews of his own day. There's the important point. He expressly called Jews undeserving of punishment—either in this world or the next." As he spoke, Vedette's voice began to rise, and to take on an unprecedented urgency. "Abe-lard's witness, however dismissed at that time," he continued, "could speak to the conscience of France in our time. An upraised Catholic voice! Out of the silence! To save Jewish lives! Right now! Think of it!"

"I have thought of it," Laurent said. He had retreated into his formal role. "But this is a matter of scholarship. And we have given you our scholarly conclusions." He stood, and then the other two did as well. With a flick of his hand toward the stacked pages before him, Laurent concluded, "The work is selective, incomplete, shallow."

Vedette remained sitting, holding his old friend's eyes. The Jew said quietly, "You are blushing, Jean-Marie. It is fitting. You *should* be ashamed."

Laurent turned to lead the way out, but the bald professor hesi-tated. From the door, he looked back at Saul Vedette, and said with narrowed eyes, "Are you registered?"

"I beg your pardon?" Vedette replied.

"As required. Are you registered?"

Vedette did not answer. Rachel clutched at the curtain, drew it to her mouth. She recognized the moment for the threat it was, but abstractly. She could not conjure what actual danger loomed.

When the men had departed, leaving the typescript where it was, Rachel remained on the edge of her cot, awaiting her father's signal. Instead of turning to her, he simply slumped in his chair. She realized that he had held himself upright, apparently stalwart, by an act of will. She was pierced with anguish for him, and now saw in the collapse of his posture the forecast of defeat. What would he be without the commission he had embraced for the sake of the Jews of France? Without the urgent work for which his entire life had pre-pared him?

She entered the room. He ignored her as she went to the low table that held the manuscript. She leaned to it and flipped the pages, leaf-ing through to the markers that flagged criticisms. She quickly took several in, the matter of Halevi, of Paul's Letter to the Romans, a chal-lenge to a particular word usage. She understood what had just happened: not a true finding based on the merits of their work, but the dismissal by Catholics of a presumptuous Jew. She saw, nevertheless, how the professors' criticisms could be useful. "Papa, we can use these queries," she said quietly. "We can take up these questions, one by one, and answer them in the book itself. The professors have helped us to make a stronger case. We can do it, Papa." She turned to him. He was staring at her, but his eyes were unfocused. Yes, his blood sugar level was askew. She went to the kitchen for a small wedge of chocolate and brought it to him. As he slowly chewed, she let her hand rest on his head. "We can do it, Papa," she repeated.

In the weeks since, her father had never put into words what Laurent's rejection meant to him. Because Rachel made *Abélard et Israël* seem as important as ever—and still possible—he continued his work, as she did hers. They began to take up the flagged queries, one by one. Yet it seemed fated that the grievous fatigue that warned of a worsening diabetes had begun to overcome him. Though he was restless at night, he would sleep in his chair through the afternoon. In the mornings, he still sat with his papers and dictating machine, but Rachel knew that, despite her encouragement, he was only going through the motions of work that would never achieve its purpose. He maintained the regimen of his insulin injections mostly because she supervised it. The ghost of Jean-Marie Laurent haunted their rooms. But Laurent's betrayal, Rachel slowly came to recognize, was a shadow of her own.

Only now, sitting at the window of Deux Garçons, wearing a yellow star on her breast with a suitcase at her feet, did she fully grasp what had happened, what she had done. The year before, alarmed to see her stalwart father faltering, she had rushed to shore him up, thinking she was doing so for his sake. But since she could not bear the thought of his decline, much less defeat, she had acted for herself, not him. She had so come to prize their collaboration that she could not imagine its being finished.

In truth, there had never been a chance that his intimidated Catholic colleagues would welcome a Jew's rereading of Catholic dogma. In the back of her mind, she had always known this. For more than a year, she had lied by encouraging his project. Not only that. Protecting the image of his monumental authority, which formed the very structure of meaning she regarded as her birthright, and then protecting the partnership for which she had come to live, Rachel had delivered her father into the jaws of the ancient enemy which, on a signal from the bald inquisitor, had just snapped down.

CHAPTER THREE

In the Manhattan phone book, counting "Jonathan"s and "J"s, there were more than twenty possible John Malloys. The ridiculousness of Michael Kavanagh's situation struck him at once. What? He should call each fellow out of the blue and ask if he'd ever been a Catholic seminarian? Kavanagh studied the listings, looking for clues. "Malloy John B., 405 W45, PLaza 7-6127"; "Malloy John Leonard, 656 10Av, JUdson 6-1590"; "Malloy John flags & uniforms, 209 Grand, CAnal 6-6762."

Presenting himself at the Communion rail that morning, Malloy had been strikingly tailored, so perhaps an enclave of the well-heeled—the Upper East Side or Gramercy Park. "Malloy John P., 26 Mtgomery, GRmrcy 3-4169." But Kavanagh's eyes kept losing focus as he tracked down the page. Impossible. Impossible. Ridiculous. He felt foolish.

He had always imagined that Runner Malloy would have moved promptly back to Poughkeepsie. Perhaps he did. In that case, passing through Manhattan this week, a simple spur of the moment had brought him to Good Shepherd: John J. Malloy, sales rep for IBM, say, or Mid-Hudson Electric Power, come to the big city to drum up business, and, by the way, drop in on an old pal. Or maybe he'd just chosen a church at random, wanting to receive Communion, in which case the sight of his old friend—the priest!—had flummoxed him.

No. No. Not at an out-of-the-way parish on the far tip of the island. Malloy had known. Malloy had come for him. But how would he have found him? A phone call to the Chancery? No. The Archdiocese fronted for its priests. If Runner, on the telephone, had asked for the present pastoral assignment of Father Michael Kavanagh, he would have been politely invited to send a letter, care of the Vicar for Clergy. Malloy would have had to go to extraordinary lengths to track down his onetime chum, so his showing up was not spur of the moment.

What, then?

Kavanagh shook himself for making a mountain of a molehill. Malloy had shown up—that's all. Yes, once he had knelt at the Communion rail, his declining to receive was a curveball, but why take it as a message? Maybe it was prompted by a last-minute state-of-grace scruple having nothing to do with his old friend. But why disappear, then? What the hell?

The tiny letters and numbers of the phone book blurred as an image intruded on Kavanagh's mind, the last glimpse he'd had of Malloy, all those years ago. "I'm gone," his friend had said, standing in the threshold of Kavanagh's room, an expression of rank misery on his face. He was dressed in his black suit and tie, street clothes. "I couldn't leave without saying goodbye."

Kavanagh, by contrast, was in his pajamas, his bare feet cold upon the terrazzo floor. The knocking on the door that had awakened him had been soft, but Kavanagh had bolted upright. It was forbidden for students to come to one another's doorways before Lauds, nor were thresholds *ever* to be crossed, but if what Malloy had just said was true, the rule infraction was meaningless—at least for him. Half asleep, Kavanagh registered his friend's declaration as a joke.

"Gone? What the hell? Gone where?"

"Mundus, caro, et diabolus." Runner forced a grin.

"Cut the crap, Malloy."

"No, really. The world, the flesh, and the devil—"

"What are you talking about?"

"I told you. The world, the flesh, and the devil—here I come!" Tears flashed in Malloy's eyes. "Ask Agent. He'll explain."

With that, Runner Malloy slugged Kavanagh's shoulder once, sharply. Then he turned and walked away, down the long corridor. Watching him go, Kavanagh noticed how rigidly his friend held himself, arms stiff and hardly swinging, the ramrod posture of a man exerting control over an anarchy of feeling. But all at once, Malloy broke into a run, a slowed-down corridor version of that trademark sprint that had given him his name. Smooth, fluid motion. A man suddenly at ease with himself, leaning forward, elbows angled, foot strikes perfectly in sync with the swing of his arms, but falling so lightly as to be unheard. Kavanagh recalled Malloy's having told him once that, as a child, he had only ever felt free when he was running. First it had been flight from his father's blows. Then it had been solitary play along the grassy banks of the Hudson, going with the wind, like a gull. Then, in school, winning races had been the one thing he could do to garner praise. At the far-off end of the hallway, he disappeared without looking back.

Runner, Kavanagh thought now, in the phone booth, and the simple meaning of the name hit him. Malloy had moved out and moved on all those years ago, while Kavanagh himself had stayed. Stay of proceedings. Stay of adjudication. Stay of execution. Stasis. Stayer Kavanagh.

He closed the phone book, slapping its heavy cardboard cover, and swung it back into its slot below the wall-mounted telephone. Next to the phone, a piece of taped-up paper struck him, a set of the rectory's frequently called numbers, each with its identifying word: "Convent," "Parish School," "Tribunal," "Chancery," "Residence." This last referred to the Cardinal's mansion on Madison Avenue, more commonly known as the Power House. Kavanagh stared at the numbers for a moment, like an uncomprehending pupil at a math problem. The numbers added up to something, but what? The booth stank of cheap cigars, and the peculiar odor of the unlaundered cassock—part incense, part BO.

The hell with the numbers, he all but said. As always, it was a relief to push the hinged door open and, with the booth light snapping off behind him, to step into the shadows of the rectory corridor.

The hum of the television set came from the adjacent room, the

Common Room, to which the Fathers repaired of an evening, after the bingo, the sodality meetings, the last round at the hospital, or, as in Kavanagh's case, the CYO basketball scrimmage in the school gym.

Glancing in, Kavanagh saw Frank Russell and Billy Mitchell posted like the library lions, each with his clerical collar loosened, and each holding a highball glass in one hand, a cigarette in the other. They were fixated on a newsreel television show; on the screen, a familiar figure was pounding a lectern, but Kavanagh did not take in what he was saying. In the far corner of the room, behind the fully spread *Herald Tribune,* was another priest. That would be Joe Gallen, who disdained television but begrudgingly forced himself into the corner chair for a nightly display of community spirit.

Frank and Billy were a pair of burnt-out but harmless cases, twenty years Kavanagh's senior, and thirty years older than Gallen, whom they mocked as "Suede." Since the wicked nickname derived from "suede-o-intellectual," the priests had dosed it with self-mockery, too, as if they themselves could not pronounce "pseudo." The name had stuck, and Suede Gallen, with forced camaraderie, even answered to it now and again. In fact, Gallen was a part-time doctoral student in theology at Fordham, and there was nothing "pseudo" about his brain power.

Of the three priests, Kavanagh preferred the old coots. Their ardent goodwill had long ago cooled into the chill of causing no trouble, checking off boxes on the parish duty list, ducking the sweep of Power House radar. But to Kavanagh, the thought of actually joining them in front of the TV seemed insufferable. He saw now that the newsreel featured a fulminating Joe McCarthy, whose pudgy face looked flushed, even in black and white. His arm was raised above his head; his fist was clenched. Kavanagh hated to have to watch or listen to the buffoonish Wisconsin senator, but he needed that drink. He slipped into the dark-paneled, heavily curtained room and moved to the oak table opposite Gallen. Half a dozen bottles of booze stood guard over a pewter ice bucket and a spread of glasses. He poured a couple of fingers of bourbon, dropped in some ice, then moved, sociably enough, to stand behind the two old priests.

"Howdy, Mike," Billy said, looking up. As always, a tear ran down his right cheek, where the oddly pale skin was flattened. As a young man, the priest had been a Doughboy in France, and had taken shell shrapnel to his face, losing an eye. On that reconstructed side of his face, he had no feeling. The tear duct at his glass eye regularly overflowed, making it seem that Billy was weeping, but he wasn't even aware of the tears. It was odd. The children in the school were famously frightened of Father Mitchell, but he was a sweet soul. "Catch Senator McCarthy," he said now. "Listen to this. . . ."

McCarthy, with his florid ruddiness, sweaty forehead, widow's peak, and shapeless suit, looked like an upended pile of soiled laundry. He was raucously holding forth in front of a wildly appreciative audience, declaiming, ". . . the final Armageddon foretold in the Bible . . ."

At that, Frank Russell let out a howl of approval, and reached over to slap Billy's shoulder, spilling ashes on his black shirt, a mess of which Billy took no notice.

". . . that struggle between good and evil, between life and death . . ."

Billy and Frank jostled each other—the triumph of hearing the Bible appealed to, their own vocation given sudden relevance. "You tell 'em, Joe!" Billy cried.

"We cannot survive on half loyalties," McCarthy went on, "any more than we can fight the facts of Communist conspiracy with half-truths."

Kavanagh's glance went to the corner, where Joe Gallen, having lowered his newspaper, was waiting to make eye contact with him. They smiled at each other, united suddenly in a feeling of sad embarrassment. Kavanagh crossed the room and took a chair by Gallen's. "Captain O'Blunder," Kavanagh said, raising his glass.

"Patrick O'Trigger." Gallen brought his glass up, and they clinked. Gallen added, unnecessarily, "McCarthy's a disgrace."

"Tailgunner Joe. Television's idea of a Mick," Kavanagh said.

"The Jews love to see an alcoholic Irish Catholic making an ass of himself."

The remark surprised Kavanagh, the swerve of it. He sipped his drink. Gallen started to lift his newspaper again, but Kavanagh said, "Why do you say that?"

"Because he is. McCarthy's a drunk."

"No, I mean about the Jews."

"John Cameron Swayze?" He gestured toward the TV with his glass.

"The newsman?" Kavanagh asked.

"*Swayze,* Michael. *Swayze.* They're all Jews. Television. Movies. Show business. Walter Lippmann, obviously. Walter Winchell. But all the others, too. They change their names. Milton Berle. Bob Hope. George Burns. Gracie Allen. Jews."

"Bing Crosby?" Kavanagh said, grinning above the rim of his glass.

Gallen did not answer.

"No, really. Bing Crosby?"

"No," Gallen said. "Not Bing Crosby." He lifted the paper again, hiding.

"You scared me there, Joe. What with Bing playing Father O'Malley in *The Bells of Saint Mary's.* What would Ingrid Bergman say if her lovable pastor was Jewish?"

From behind the paper came the one word, "Bergman?"

Kavanagh stared at the front page of the *Herald Tribune,* taking in the headline "General MacArthur Wants Atom Bomb for Korea." It had never occurred to him that Ingrid Bergman was Jewish, but then he thought of *Casablanca:* Philip and Julius Epstein. Peter Lorre. What about Humphrey Bogart?

He took a drink. Normally, he'd have thought nothing of a fellow priest's crack about Jews, but for some reason it cut him tonight.

Then he knew.

Gallen had made plain an intention to stay behind his paper, but Kavanagh said, "Joe, actually, I've got a question for you." In fact, Kavanagh realized, Gallen was the only one in the rectory who would have a clue to what had nagged at him all day. "Simone Weil," Kavanagh said.

"What about her?"

"Was she an anti-Semite?"

The *Herald Tribune* came down, collapsing into the priest's lap. "Don't be ridiculous. She started out Jewish."

"But she compared the ancient Hebrews to the Nazis. Said they were alike."

"I never heard that."

"In her journals, the ones still in French. Not translated into English yet."

The younger man was silent for a moment, deliberately quizzical. No priest at Good Shepherd could read works in French. Certainly not Kavanagh. "Well, if she made that comparison," he said finally, "she had a point. 'Blessed be he that shall take and dash thy little ones against the rocks.' Can't you see the Nazis doing that? Do you know how many times the Old Testament celebrates the murder of children?"

"No. But I'll bet you do."

"Read the Psalms, Father."

"I do read the Psalms, Joe. Five times a day."

"And the prophets. Jeremiah. The ancient Hebrews practiced child sacrifice. Infanticide."

"Bullshit, Joe. The whole point of the Abraham-Isaac story is to *end* child sacrifice."

"Exactly. Proves the point. Genesis can't order the end of child sacrifice if the ancients aren't practicing it. And Exodus. Passover. Hitler had nothing on Yahweh's Angel of Death. Every firstborn male baby of Egypt killed by the will of God? Please."

"*Jesus* was killed by the will of God, Joe: 'Not my will, but *Thine* be done.'"

Gallen snorted. " 'His blood be upon us and upon our children.' In point of fact, Father, that's the Jews—not God. Christ-killers. Simone Weil was right. It's not anti-Semitism to speak the truth." The priest snapped his paper up.

Kavanagh was surprised less by what the smug young bastard had said than by his own reaction to it. Theological impeachment of

Jews was run-of-the-mill. Visceral rejection of such judgment—that was new. *Blood be upon our children:* how many children died in the death camps? For the first time in his life, Kavanagh heard the phrase from the Gospel of Matthew as an incitement.

But Joe McCarthy must have further outraged himself just then, because an unrestrained burst of applause exploded from the television, echoed by the hoots of Frank and Billy. Kavanagh stood, crossed to the oak table, hit his glass with another splash, and left the Common Room.

In the corridor, by the phone booth, he stopped. "Ask Agent," Runner Malloy had said all those years ago, and Kavanagh had. "Agent," as he was known behind his back to seminarians, was Father Sean Donovan, the Church-history professor. Because he was an Irish import, the priest was stamped in the argot as "FBI," for "Foreign Born Irish." That, in the razor-sharp remaking of the compulsive nicknamers, led to the moniker "Agent." The inevitable edge of ridicule involved, in Father Donovan's case, his being badly overweight, and having the pasty flesh of one to whom athletic fields or shooting ranges would have been *terra incognita*—the polar opposite of a G-man. Yet Father Donovan, then a man of about fifty, was perhaps the most beloved member of the faculty. Still, Kavanagh remembered being surprised at Runner's reference, because John Malloy had not been one of Father Donovan's lads. He'd gone for spiritual direction to someone else—Kavanagh couldn't remember whom.

Sean Donovan was still Kavanagh's good friend, even if, for the last ten years, he had been, as one of the Archdiocese's two Auxiliary Bishops, Cardinal Spellman's left-hand man. The Cardinal had a genius for manipulating his clergy, and Bishop Donovan was the designated good cop, nicely balancing resentments stirred by the Cardinal's *right-hand* man—Bishop Alonzo Grant, who was known behind *his* back as "GI," for "Grand Inquisitor." Grant, in fact, was the power in the Power House—the enforcer. Compared with him, Bishop Donovan was a sob-sister. What stymied Kavanagh at the phone booth was a mad impulse to give Sean a call, but at this hour? The phone would ring in the Residence Common Room, where Grant could be sitting—or even Spellman himself. Calling the Power House near midnight? *Are you nuts?*

Kavanagh took his drink along the dark corridor, then up the narrow stairs, bypassing his own third floor to spiral all the way up to the heavy door that opened onto the roof. The rains of the day had passed, but the air was still murky. In the lee of the mechanicals shed, he found his battered beach chair, stowed up there since September. The canvas contraption, once he opened it, was the instrument by which he turned the remote tar-paper roof-deck into his personal refuge. He had not expected to be up there again until May or June, but the day's strange and sudden anguish compelled him. He sat, shivered, hugged himself against the November night's chill.

Kavanagh had spent the war as a navy chaplain, assigned mainly to the Navy Yard Hospital in Brooklyn, where there was a tar-paper rooftop cubby like this, to which he'd escaped at night. Thousands of the wounded and dying were evacuated from the war zones to that hospital, and his job had been to hold hands with the weeping and the catatonic alike, anoint their foreheads, close their eyelids, then write letters to their parents. Across the nearly three years he was there, the space between hospital beds went from eight feet to six, then three. By the end, even the amputees counted themselves lucky, and by then Kavanagh's nighttime escape to the rooftop had become habitual. From there, he looked out across at the Manhattan skyline, as if from the bridge of a ghost ship, but tonight, from his ghost rectory, he took in the far less glamorous, if equally familiar, silhouettes of the water towers, stairwell sheds, and stepped-back rooflines looming over Inwood. Here and there, lights were being snapped off. At last, Kavanagh took the truly hefty swallow of whiskey he'd been waiting for all evening.

Back in the day, at the seminary, Father Sean Donovan's history classes had been marked by levity. Even lecturing in Latin about the *quaestiones* of Thomas Aquinas, he'd toss off wiseacre asides—"*Carpe noctem,*" in warning about an upcoming exam—that thrilled the lads just because they got the joke: spend the night studying. Like all priest faculty, he doubled as a spiritual director, and more young men lined up at his door for counseling than at any other professor's. He was Kavanagh's Confessor—an intensely trusted mentor from whom Kavanagh kept no secrets.

That day of Runner's departure, immediately after breakfast, in the work period during which Kavanagh was supposedly mopping out the shower stalls, he went instead to Father Donovan's room on the priests' corridor, aware of a tangled knot in his breast, feelings for which he had no name. He hesitated at the door, fingering the top buttons of his cassock. Finally, he knocked.

"Come," the priest said, his voice muffled by the stout door.

Kavanagh entered. "Good morning, Father. I'm sorry, but—"

"Never mind that, Michael. I expected you." Then Father Donovan added, as always, the Irish pleasantry, "You're very welcome indeed."

At the priest's lilting brogue, Kavanagh's spirits lifted.

Father Donovan was seated at his desk, his breviary open before him. Like Kavanagh, he wore the floor-length soutane, although the hefty priest's collar was unfastened, as usual. He stood and offered his hand. The grip was strong, conveying an unexpected depth of feeling, which Kavanagh knew to take as a declaration. In the corner opposite the neatly made narrow bed stood a pair of cracked leather wing chairs. The men sat, each one knowing which chair was his.

"You've come about John."

"He's gone?" Kavanagh asked.

The priest lit a cigarette, and used the waving out of his match to dispel the first cloud of smoke. "He is, Michael. He resigned yesterday."

"Resigned? I assumed kicked out for some reason. If Runner was going to quit on his own, he would have told me."

"I gather he did tell you."

"But only this morning, on his way out the door. He left while it was still dark."

"He didn't want a fuss. And you know how the Rector deplores display when a lad is moving on." There was consoling sadness in Father Donovan's eyes.

"But it seems like something shameful is happening."

The priest said nothing to this.

"Is there?"

Again, silence. Kavanagh shuddered to think he was intruding on the seal of Confession. "Father," he said at last, "Runner told me you would explain."

"Yes." The priest nodded solemnly. "He gave me permission to explain to you. Only to you. And he expects you to keep the confidence."

What confidence? Kavanagh could hardly breathe.

The priest took a long, deep drag, not lowering his gaze. He let the smoke out and tapped the ashtray on the table that stood between them. Kavanagh sensed the pulsing behind his own eyes. He looked down at the rug, a threadbare Oriental, along the edge of which the priest's shoe tapped nervously at a comb of fringe.

"Will you?" the priest asked.

"What?"

"Keep John's confidence."

"Of course. But what gives? I don't get it. Why wouldn't he have talked to me?"

"John was struggling with his vocation, Michael. For some time."

"He loved it here, Father. Ace student, best jock in the class— who didn't like the guy?" At some point here, Kavanagh knew, there would be no holding back his tears. Father Donovan was the only one in whose presence he ever wept. "Runner wanted to be a priest more than I do."

"But you're still here, son. He's not. It was really quite simple. John felt a need of love that he could not satisfy as a priest."

"Jeez, Father, who doesn't have that feeling?"

"I don't."

"I know, but you're . . ." It took an awkward long moment for Kavanagh to add, ". . . already ordained."

"He made a prudent choice, lad. Prudence may not be the greatest of virtues, but it's the most useful one." Silence fell between them then. Excruciating silence. Endless silence. At last, Father Donovan said, "Michael, he told me to tell you something." The priest paused. He puffed his cigarette. He batted at the smoke. He said, "John made his decision because of you."

"What?"

"After much prayer and discernment, he had concluded that his feelings for you were out of bounds."

The stark declaration stunned Kavanagh, flummoxed him. Instead of reacting with the spilt rush of emotion he'd been dreading, he simply clamped down on all feeling. *Dive! Dive!* The hatch covers of a plunging submarine swirling shut, like in a movie. And dive Michael Kavanagh did, ever after.

In recalling that moment now, from the shiplike deck of the rectory roof, Kavanagh recognized what he had snuffed: the unfamiliar feeling from that very morning, what had sent him reeling through the thickets of Inwood Hill and Fort Tryon Park. Not guilt, as he'd have predicted if he could have foreseen this recollection, but grief.

Even in his mid-twenties, Michael Kavanagh had been a callow boy, far younger than his years. He now looked back on the lad he'd been through the distorting lens of a parish priest's long experience of the Confessional, listening to ugly secrets, but he still recognized himself as that tenderfoot. In being green, naïve, unaware, young Kavanagh had not been special, but typical of the kind of Catholic kid who welcomed the chance to sublimate the deepest, but also most frightening, specimens of desire.

Beginning with his mother, who'd lullabied him, a chosen child, Kavanagh was raised to a status apart. Wasn't he blessed with a heightened sensitivity to the substance of things hoped for, the evidence of all that is unseen? Wasn't his a capacity for depth of which his brothers and sisters, through no fault of their own, knew nothing? So went the story told to young Michael. He had the feel not just for God, they said, but for God's grandeur in all that is. He was born to be a priest.

Well, he thought now, they don't call it parochial school for nothing. Ignorant of boundaries—so what was "out of bounds"? He had not known in particular what Father Donovan might have meant by that phrase, and, actually, he had not known in general, either. If, in Kavanagh's own personal bubble at Dunwoodie, the love of women was remote, the erotic love of men for men was simply unimagined. Such a totality of denial suggests what terrors the homoerotic held for the seminary culture, and that culture had fit Kavanagh like a glove. His affection for Malloy had been as absolute as it was unself-conscious. Kavanagh would have said, if the question had ever come up, that his feeling for Runner was absolutely chaste.

But all at once, in the priest's room, that bond had somehow been made to seem sinful. Filthy.

Malloy, by leaving Dunwoodie like a thief in the night, had him-self declared it sinful—a moral flip of which Kavanagh had known nothing. Yet that not-knowing, he understood now, was its own offense. Such innocence—here was the lesson—is not a virtue, and at a certain point, for sure by the time a man is shaving every day, it becomes mere self-deceit. Looking back at that moment, Kavanagh saw in a flash how his entire youth had been fraudulent. And now?

His world—beginning when the nuns joined his mother in the conspiracy of "vocation," but continuing right through the seminary equivalents of college and graduate school, with black-robed profes-sors affirming him—was an enclosed terrarium that pretended to be the unfenced frontier. How hedged in were they? If the word "semi-nary" shares a root with "semen," the linguistic joke was not one the lecturing Father Donovan would have tossed off in class, nor would his precious lads have found it funny.

But all of this, oddly, was key to what had made John Malloy attractive in the first place. Without the seminarians' being aware of it, one effect of the implicit but potent restraints on feeling that defined experience at Dunwoodie—the wages of repression—was to paint the tone and tenor of the place with the gray that makes war-ships invisible at sea. But Runner Malloy, by personality and force of will, had been color itself—with no one more attuned to his standing apart than Michael Kavanagh had been. Malloy had carried himself with a lighthearted flair that—in the haunted house on the hill in Yonkers, with its dark hallways, musty stairwells, gloomy dining hall, and faux-Gothic chapel—seemed forbidden. His easy masculinity was marked by small notes of personal style: black leather belt worn with buckle to the side; watchband a loose-fitting Speidel of stainless steel, which hung on his wrist like jewelry; slip-on shoes that flapped slightly at his heels when he made the genuflection during Mass. In fact, his genuflecting way of touching his right knee to his left heel displayed an unselfconscious grace that seemed akin to the astounding moves he routinely made on the basketball court. There was, that is, something princely about Runner, a smiling tough guy who, in making a point, could rest his hand effortlessly on Kavanagh's shoulder, an intimate gesture that, because it couldn't be helped, couldn't be wrong. How could any of this—then or now—be "out of bounds"?

"Because of you." Father Donovan's words hovered in Kavanagh's head.

Runner's laugh could roll across a room, clearing whatever clogged the air. When Kavanagh, in literature class, had learned about irony, he understood how Malloy's regular bemusement at the many incongruities of seminary life fell short of mockery. Kindness, manliness, intelligence, and beauty had come together so easily in him that it seemed everyone should have been kind, manly, intelligent, and beautiful like that—but no one else was.

"Because of you."

After that day, Sean Donovan, as Father Donovan and then as Bishop Donovan, had never again mentioned John Malloy to Michael Kavanagh. Nor had Kavanagh to Donovan. Kavanagh, sitting now on the midnight roof, swirling what remained of his ice cubes, saw how absurd that was. And how inhuman. As Bishop, Sean Donovan was no longer Michael Kavanagh's Confessor, but he was still as good a friend as he had on Planet Earth. And they had never discussed Runner? Kavanagh saw the rough outline of what he had deflected all these years: that, if Runner Malloy had been thrown off course by some inchoate, wrong-seeming feeling of love for him, he, Kavanagh, had mercilessly stayed that course, which then took him into a life with a hole at its center. He had successfully papered the hole over, but it had been there always, a hollow void where once had pulsed a pure feeling of lift.

When Runner so suddenly disappeared because of a dread attached to him, Kavanagh had found it the most natural thing in the world to shut off instantly the youthful lightness of heart that had attracted Malloy in the first place—the lightness that their friendship had intensified, and that had defined, for Kavanagh, the meaning of the State of Grace. Across the years since, Kavanagh had unconsciously refrained from thinking of Runner, but on this night he had to admit to having forgotten nothing. Yes, this was grief. Raw, unfinished grief—not just at the long-ago loss of a friend, but at the loss of nothing less, despite appearances, than his own—what to call it?— wholeness? *Integritas.*

Kavanagh sipped. He'd been shivering all this time. He let his eyes drift across the nightscape, acknowledging the wish to be somewhere else, as if the looming tenements could be the walls of canyons; the squared-off silhouetted rooflines the buttes and flat-topped mesas of a John Ford location, shot with blue tint. Indeed, the walls of the buildings opposite could have been prehistoric rock faces, with each lighted window the marker of a cliff dweller's fire, a scene thick with primitive humanity. *Fort Apache.* But this was not the West. The people whose cramped rooms were across the way—dozens and dozens of them—were the furthest thing from exotic aboriginals. They were post-office clerks and grease monkeys and widows and meter readers and bus drivers. They were all clinging to hopes of which they spoke in whispers to no one but their beloved priest, their kind Confessor, their Father Mike.

Kavanagh felt a rush of worried affection for his parish, and, becoming more kind to himself, acknowledged his satisfaction that, whatever the celibate's clamp on warmth, tenderness, desire, and longing had done to his capacity for true intimacy with another, still, he had somehow emerged from his years of disciplined pastoral service as a priest on whom the people could depend—not to mention God, whoever that was. He was a connoisseur of other people's moral complexity, but what of his own?

"Oh, the hell with that," he said out loud. Kavanagh raised his glass toward the darkened tenements, a toast to the fact that, yes, as he insisted silently, the widows and clerks and telephone operators, and all their raucous kids, were enough for him.

But then Kavanagh's gaze lifted to the ink-black shape of the distant landscape, a subtle backdrop against which the foreground buildings took form—Inwood Hill, and beyond it Fort Tryon Park, of which he'd hardly ever taken note from his rooftop aerie. He saw jutting above the trees the barest upper edge of what he now could note as the monastic bell tower, The Cloisters, which promptly brought the image of the woman to mind.

Grief. Runner Malloy, yes. But also her. "You should complete your obligation, Father." Her last words to him. But what obligation? Was there an obligation to an unfinished grief? There it was—the feeling that *she* had sparked in him and which, even now, he'd only partially fathomed. Rachel Vedette. Simone Weil. "Her refusal to be modern. Her empathy with suffering, which was limited, but quite real."

Kavanagh's mind went back to Gallen, and his sanctimonious contempt for Jews. Suddenly, Kavanagh realized why that routine Catholic denigration had cut him: the Passover Angel like Hitler? Ancient Hebrews like Nazis? Kavanagh took offense because he had heard Gallen as if he himself were Rachel Vedette. A Jew.

So, naturally, her voice was coming back to him: "In French, we say *'cloître.'*" Gaunt. Stern with herself, but not with others. He thought of the ease with which she'd let her hand rest on the upper ledge of the arcade column, the natural pose that suggested not just authority, but proprietorship. The exotic place was hers. The Cloisters were a last vestige of Christendom, but what had Christendom just done, in the Europe from which Rockefeller's medieval relics had been so timely plucked, except destroy itself? After the obliterating war, the already set hilltop museum in New York, without any reinvention of its own, had become a memorial to an entire culture's suicide. In her identity with the place, the woman—who might otherwise have been a simple witness—had herself become a mode of remembering. Her pallor was the clinging shadow of some other angel of death than God's, but she had refused to die. And that, he suddenly understood, was what had drawn him to her.

CHAPTER FOUR

The sport of bicycle racing, too, was conscripted into the Hitler-driven campaign against the Israélites of France. The Winter Bicycle Track was a huge indoor racing arena designed to accommodate nearly thirty thousand spectators. Now it held the Jews of Paris. They were brought there not in trucks or prisoner wagons, but in the ordinary green-and-cream-colored municipal buses that most had ridden every day of their lives. One of those Jews, thrown into the Vélodrome d'Hiver within two hours of Monsieur Beguin's phone call, was Rachel Vedette, for whom the sudden horror of the ordinary Paris bus onto which she'd been violently dragged by a former ticket taker seemed a defining measure of the day's meaning.

The Vél' d'Hiv stood on the Left Bank, in the 15th Arrondissement, not far from the Eiffel Tower. Indeed, the arena had been built for the World's Fair in 1900, when Eiffel's soaring pylon of girders served as a focal point for the festival grounds. Ever since, the massive shell-like rink had been the scene of great spectacles—not just the match sprints and team pursuits of cycle racing, but also boxing matches, ice shows, including several starring the Nazi-friendly Sonja Henie, and, throughout the 1930s, great rallies of the French fascist parties.

But free-wheel, brakeless bicycles whizzing along at ninety kilometers an hour were what brought frenzied Parisians to the place again and again. Speed and, with inevitable crashes, blood; who didn't love the Vél' d'Hiv? A steeply banked oval track made of wood encircled a large infield. Above it all hung two severely raked tiers of seats, which loomed like mountain ledges over a valley. The velodrome roof was made of a great patchwork of glass and girders, but the glass had been painted black two years before because of air raids, and a cloud of gloom enshrouded the place even before the terrified and disoriented Israélites arrived.

The Vél' d'Hiv was where the French National Police brought their prisoners, but it was the so-called Gabardines, the Germans in civilian clothes, who'd instructed them to do so. The arena had been requisitioned by the Gestapo a year ago, but for a purpose coming clear only now. By midnight on July 16, something like eight thousand people had been herded into the vast open space, then left to their own devices behind locked and guarded doors. They would be joined within a day by half again as many. Gendarmes could be seen amid the throng, with their batons and holstered pistols, but no one was pretending to bring order to the anarchic scene. Children wailed in corners by themselves, ignored. Family groups fought one another for cleared places by the wall. Circles of Orthodox men, wearing yarmulkes and wrapped in prayer shawls, davened away. Their rhythmic dipping motion, like birds dropping beaks into fountains, was a declaration of detachment from the horror around them. But they were aged. Because the Jews of Paris had long assumed that only able-bodied males were vulnerable, and because Jewish men had therefore made themselves scarce, most of those arrested that day were women, children, and the very old. They clutched bundles, boxes, suitcases—whatever they'd been able to grab before being seized. They appeared to fear their fellow prisoners as much as the mostly unseen police. A great stench filled the place, and it shocked the prisoners to realize that they themselves were its source.

Like the others, Rachel held fast to her suitcase. To her, the scene was like a dream of hell, the kind of vision conjured by self-tortured medieval monks, lacking only personified red devils leering from the margins of illuminated vellum. Herded into the arena like animals into a vast slaughterhouse pen, the prisoners now sat in clusters, holding on to one another; or they wandered about singly, stupefied and lost. Pairs of children shuffled aimlessly, clinging to each other's hands. Some had cardboard tags attached to their shirts, with names. The arena toilet rooms had been locked, because, as the Gabardines saw it, their windows made escape seem possible. So heaps of human waste had begun to accumulate in the back row of the lower-level tiered scats. That an ad hoc latrine had somehow been defined by the prisoners themselves was the only semblance of order, and most—but not all—headed into that remote shadow to defecate and urinate.

Rachel was looking every person she passed in the face, hoping for a flash of recognition. Hoping, of course, for her father. She had applied a fierce clamp onto her emotions, and channeled all feeling, thought, fear, and bewilderment into the act of focused observation. Finally, she came upon a passing blue-uniformed policeman, and when he looked toward her, she stepped directly into his path. He drew back, startled. He was young, perhaps as young as she, showing no sign, for example, of needing to shave. On his shoulder, the patch read "Préfecture de Police de Paris." Therefore, he was not a member of the Gendarmerie, the far more powerful national police force, which was, in fact, in charge of the arrest of Jews. Rachel had already accommodated the startling discovery that French officials were doing the savage work of the hated Germans. But the gendarmes wore brown uniforms; this *flic* was in blue. Was he a local cop who'd stumbled into this madness? And did the disoriented expression that came across his face now suggest that his uncertain will could be bent to her will of iron?

The young cop was clearly a man of no rank, yet she addressed him as if he were. *"Sergeant, s'il vous plaît."*

Reflexively, he tipped his hat. Rachel was pleased to see a rush of blood to his face. "Mademoiselle," he said.

"I am searching for my father." As if she were a connoisseur of the tricks of flirtation, she let her glance fall shyly, then brought it up again, while biting her lower lip. She could feel water pooling in her eyes, the first counterfeit of such affect she'd ever accomplished. She pushed her shoulders back slightly, but enough to bring her bosom forward. Her free hand went first to her hair, where the once-severe bun was in disarray, as if drawing attention to the fact that most of the other women wore carefully knotted headscarves. Then her hand went to a button at her throat, which she undid as if from pure nervousness. The loosened collar fell from the hollow of her neck toward the upper curve of her breast, showing a small but potent strip of flesh that had never seen the sun. She began to speak once more, then stopped. She let the tip of her tongue slide across the edge of her lower lip, just visible to the policeman: she knew when his stare settled on her mouth. Thus, in a matter of seconds, she had drawn on previously unknown wiles to put her offer in the air—the promise of exchange. She said, "Will you help me?" But she was thinking, once more, *Who am I now?*

THAT FIRST AFTERNOON, the young *flic* had escorted Rachel in a spiraling circuit of the sprawling arena infield, breasting through the crowd of stunned Jews, needing only the occasional rough show to clear the way when some crone refused to move. *"Déplacez! Déplacez!"* he barked, but his menace was fake.

At one point, the cop had grasped Rachel's free hand. She let him hold on to it, but noted that he shyly pretended that clutching her fingers was necessary to leading her through the press. He was anything but domineering. Soon enough, he had become almost as invested in finding her father as she was.

Even before dusk outside, the vast interior space beneath the blacked-out glass roof had become awash in shadow, and the upper levels were entirely unlit. Climbing to the first balcony brought them into the pitch dark, which Rachel welcomed, because when the cop unhooked a pocket torch from his belt he dropped her hand. As she asked him to, he shone the cone of light into the face of every old man they passed, until, in a corner on the second balcony, they came upon him. He was a semiconscious hulk, like dozens of others, collapsed upon himself, yet she knew him at once. "Papa! Papa!" she said, dropping the suitcase to kneel beside him, enclosing her father in her embrace.

The policeman leaned to her and whispered, "Do not let them see that he is sick."

"He is not sick," Rachel hissed in reply. "He is only tired."

She pulled her father up, clutched his face, and drew it close to her own, "Papa! Do you see it's me?" His eyes were open, but swimming, and when she saw that he could not hold his head erect, she let him down again. To the policeman she said, "Shine the light here," as she opened the suitcase. He did so. She withdrew the brick of chocolate and efficiently proceeded to unwrap it, exposing the knife. She unfolded its blade and shaved slivers of the chocolate into her hand, perhaps fifty grams' worth. Then, propping her father up, she fed the bits into his mouth. He was conscious enough to cooperate, and took the pieces in hungrily. When he'd eaten the chocolate, she took one of the bananas, peeled it back, and placed several of its slices into his mouth as well. He swallowed with difficulty, but he took what she fed him.

Then, again, he leaned against her. She reached into the suitcase, for his yarmulke. She placed it on his head.

"He should not wear that," the cop said.

Rachel said, "You think they don't know he's a Jew?" The bitterness in her eyes made the *flic* withdraw, leaving Rachel and her father alone in the dark corner. Nearby, there was a mother nursing an infant, and a trio of boys squabbling. Old women had arranged themselves in circles of quiet lamentation, and, closest at hand, a clutch of men were davening at a candle. Someone was sobbing.

Within perhaps half an hour of eating, Saul was able to sit up. He squeezed Rachel's hand, then released it—which was their signal that he was well. She turned back to the suitcase and withdrew the Nachmanides commentary on Job. He received it gratefully, pressing it to his breast. She handed him his glasses, which he put on—and looked like himself again. At home, apart from sleeping, he was never without his glasses, although he had no need of spectacles for this particular book. Only to hold it was to take the wisdom in.

Her father sensed Rachel's blatant air of territoriality, as she snapped the suitcase shut and propped it as a barrier between them and the old Jews reciting Kaddish, only a bare meter away. The folding knife had fallen to the floor. Whether she intended it or not, there was something threatening in the way she picked it up, half flourishing the blade as she closed it back into the bone handle. Saul leaned close to put his mouth at her ear. He whispered, "Do not treat the stranger as the enemy. If we do that, the Germans have won."

"And the French?" Rachel said, a comment she regretted at once—as if the horror of what their countrymen were doing might be lessened if it were not actually referred to.

He had no more wish to speak of their neighbors than she. He recited quietly, "'I am the man who obscured your designs with empty-headed words . . .'" She recognized the verse from the book of Job. It was like her father to express his feelings in such a citation. He continued, "'I retract all that I have said, and in dust and ashes, I reproach myself.'"

"Do not reproach yourself, Papa."

"I should have made you go last year."

"We should both have gone," she said so simply, fending off an impulse to apologize. "But that's the past," she said. "Now we have the present. Let us be thankful for the present moment."

"The future will only be worse."

"All the more reason to be thankful, then," she said. Indeed, she was still filled with relief—almost happiness—to have found him.

He looked at her, marveling. Then he asked, "Did they come for you at the institute?"

"No."

"Where, then?"

"Deux Garçons. Monsieur Beguin called the police."

"*Connard!*"

She knew better than to tell her father that she had asked the man to place the call. She shifted, and drew him closer, aiming to break the line of his thinking. He fell silent again, leaning in to her. She held him, stroking his back. As soon as she could, she would have to give him his insulin shot, but the needle-barrel measurement had to be exact, and in the dark she would never get it right.

Relieved as Rachel had been when the policeman disappeared, she welcomed it when, perhaps an hour later, he came upon them once more. She raised her finger to him, and he drew close. "Your light. I need your light again." He dutifully shone the beam where she needed it as she prepared the hypodermic needle. Her father offered the pinch of his flesh just as if they were home, and the shot went in. The policeman snapped the light off, and, understanding that the procedure was complete, he drifted away. Soon Saul was asleep, with his head resting on the pillow with which Rachel had cushioned the medicine inside the suitcase.

She was not surprised when the policeman returned. She made room for him. He sat beside her and removed his hat. He lit a cigarette. When he offered her one, she took it. The prolonged noise of the arena achieved a kind of monotonous din that fell on the ear like silence, out of which he told her his name—Maurice. He told her that he was from the country, and that, through a cousin's influence, he had landed a position with the Préfecture de Police de Paris as a way of avoiding the German labor conscriptions. "I am nobody," he said, and laughed, picking up his hat. "But this hat makes everyone believe I am a god."

"To some of us," Rachel said quietly, "you are a god."

Her statement startled him. Even in the shadows, his face displayed the befuddled wonder with which his situation filled him. Surrounded by misery and dread unlike anything he had ever beheld, he yet felt powerful in a way he never had before. His eyes were wet with emotion.

Rachel did not lower her gaze from his, even as she put her cigarette to her mouth, inhaled, let the smoke slide out from her lips. "Maurice . . ." She paused.

He leaned toward her.

She completed her sentence. ". . . I need you."

Not breathing, the young man only nodded. Rachel reached out to touch him, which sent a bolt of tension through his shoulders and neck, an involuntary shudder. But her hand went to his belt, where she unhooked the pocket torch. "I need this."

He did not move as she put the gadget by her side, away from him. She stubbed out her cigarette on the cold, hard floor. He did likewise. When he looked at her again, her eyes were waiting for him. "Thank you," she said.

Once again, he nodded. Then he stood and left.

. . .

FOR THE DAYS that they were in the arena, the policeman took care of Rachel and her father, bringing them water, bread, strawberries, and carrots. When she asked for lemons and a ration of sugar cubes so that she could concoct the sweet drink her father needed, he supplied them. For others, the permanent shroud of near darkness multiplied the horror, but not for her. She understood that the cop was right about not letting the Gabardines see that her father was infirm. In the dark, using the pocket torch, she could inject the insulin without being seen.

Two days in, when she had no way to sterilize her father's insulin needles properly, the cop was able to bring her a bottle of Cognac, in which she let the needles soak. He had no need to make his reciprocal demands explicit. Her initiating flirtation had, as intended, made her seem receptive, and she knew better than to cut him off.

In the quiet of successive nights, he showed up at their corner, and waited mutely for her to stand and face him. If her father was awake, she simply shook her head, and he withdrew into the shadows. When he returned and her father was asleep, she knew to stand. He led her to a cubicle in the eaves of the arena, a closed-off space that served as a utility vault, a closet jammed with transformers, circuit panels, and bundled electrical wires. She did not resist as he backed her against a waist-high horizontal pipe, where he pressed himself against her.

At first, he made his tentative moves apologetically, and she realized he was as inexperienced as she. The first night, he was content to kiss her and fondle her breasts through the fabric of her dress. The second night, because of the way he thrust himself at her midsection, she was aware of it when he ejaculated inside his trousers, groaning softly, and then backing away at once. She sensed his embarrassment, and, as if to explain, he began to speak. "From a young age, I was a seminarian. I never—"

She put her finger to his lips, silencing him—a move he welcomed. Realizing her advantage, she realized, further, that her advantage could apply with other men, too. The young policeman had given her the strategy she needed. She then employed it with him on the nights that followed. Once her father was asleep, she was ready for his arrival. In their cubicle, she took the lead in kissing with her tongue. Using maneuvering skills she had not known she possessed, she massaged his penis through his trousers, bringing him to arousal as quickly as possible. When the sperm shot into the cup of her hand, but still inside the rough serge of his pants, she could feel the bursts, which, soon enough, were reliable signals of her success—and her safety. The cop took such release as all the climax he could want. He would mutter an embarrassed word of thanks, back away, and kiss her again, but now as a sweet *bonne nuit*.

Rachel, with moves that came as naturally as opening a book, had claimed her place in the realm of feminine power. The trick, with this poor sap, was to get him to peak before he wanted more from her. How had she known that?

As they were about to part, after their fourth time together in the cubicle, he stopped her. "I must ask."

Rachel responded only with a cold, dead look. She thought he'd understood that the last thing she wanted was talk.

But he pressed her, saying again, "I must ask."

"What?"

"Why do they hate the Jews?"

"They?"

"The Krauts."

"Are there Krauts here?"

"Yes. In suits."

"How many?"

"Eight. Ten."

"And how many dozens of you? Police? Gendarmes? Frogs?"

He had no answer.

She shrugged, "Because they say we killed Christ."

"That can't be it."

"Of course it is."

"No."

"But what they say is true, Sergeant." She put her fingers lightly on his cheek. "For sure, we killed Him—knowing all that would be done to us in His name. We killed your God. *Our* God told us to do so. We would do it again. The anti-Semites are right about us." She tapped his cheek, once, as if from fondness. Then she turned and walked into the dark.

The seven days that Rachel and her father spent at the Vél' d'Hiv were a brief initiation, yet long enough for her to work new muscles and, as it were, let them flex. She stopped being astonished by their situation, and her responses to it.

By the time the throng of Jews in the bicycle arena began to be herded once again to vehicles—now onto canvas-covered lorries, not the cushioned seats of municipal buses—Rachel knew what, besides clutching her father and holding on to her precious suitcase, she had to do. Thanks to her *chouchou,* her uniformed pet, the necessary shell around her heart had begun to calcify.

When she and her father, in a knot of Jews, were being pushed by other French policemen out into the harsh light of day and toward the next truck, she glimpsed Maurice standing under the narrowed eyes of a pair of Gabardines. He saw her. She recognized the expression of sick longing on his face. She felt nothing.

Her father was clutching the *Historia Calamitatum.* When he stumbled while making his way up the makeshift stepladder onto the bed of the lorry, one of the Gestapo watchers lurched toward him, swinging a cudgel. Rachel reacted more quickly than the German moved. She came between them, so that the blow fell on her head, not her father's. It knocked her forward, savagely, and she might have passed out, but her mind was too intent for that. The German laughed loudly, but the triumph was hers. She was able to steady her father—"Up, Papa," she whispered, "up!"—until he crumpled into the truck. He had dropped the leather-bound book, but Rachel, stooping quickly, was able to retrieve it. Once she was on the truck herself, supporting him again, Rachel glanced back at Maurice, whose expression had changed to one of guilt and horror. Toward him, still, she felt nothing.

She clung to the Abelard. Her former question—*Who am I now?*— had its answer. *I am the safekeeper of Saul Vedette. That's all.*

CHAPTER FIVE

"You flout doctrine!" came the frenzied cry from the rear of the packed-full refectory, sparking a burst of derisive hoots, whistles, catcalls—some to defend, some to ridicule. Epithets were thrown more in the vulgar tongues than in Latin: the guttural Frankish could be heard, along with Romanic, Burgundian, Norman, and other alien modes of speech.

At the lectern on a platform that lifted him three or four feet above the crowd, Peter Abelard simply stood with his left arm raised, the soul of patience, waiting for the howling to subside. He was tall and slender, a man in his thirties. His face had a chiseled look, its features organized within the vertical brackets of a prominent, strong chin and flashing blue eyes. Strong, yes: a demanding visage. But his expression just then was bemused, as if he took kindly to being called to account. With his right hand, he absently stroked the edge of the lectern, the smooth wood. All at once, he looked down upon that edge, as if his caressing hand were taking satisfaction in carving he had done himself. He was a supremely satisfied man. The fellows before him had come here to Paris from as far away as Britain, or beyond the Pyrenees, or below the Alps. Each lad had his native lisp, stutter, cluck. More than three hundred young men, most cloaked and tonsured as novice clerics, were crowded onto the benches and long narrow tables; others

perched on the ledges at windows from which had been removed the
framed and stretched hides that, in rougher weather, kept out the rain
and chill while admitting a shadowy light. This afternoon, the fresh
light of early spring washed into the room, bathing, especially, those
near the openings.

The initiating indictment, called out in proper Latin—*"Contemnis
doctrinam"*—had come from one of the dozen Masters clustered near
the large fireplace in the back of the room. They were garbed like the
students, only more so: long woolen robes, black in color, but belted
or trimmed with animal fur; some with their heads covered by caps
or cowls. Flames licking from the small fire behind them cast a net of
shadows, the brighter flashes of which illuminated their faces. Yet
the Masters might have been masked, such were their set expressions.
That gave them the air of a disapproving Delphic chorus. The one
who'd hurled the gibe could be distinguished from the others by his
flushed, ruddy checks and sparking eyes—a show of anger that was
more open than he wanted, leaving him exposed. But he'd said his
piece, and was silent now, like the other Dons. It was the host of
students who were making the noise, a cacophony of varied tongues.
For as long as the outbursts lasted, the scene might have been at the
cursed base of the Tower of Babel, instead of at the feet of the greatest
teacher in Paris.

Normally, sessions of the Cathedral school were held in the chambers that opened off the large Cloister, on the upriver third of the
island, just beyond the curving wall of the apse—a villagelike maze
of ad hoc quarters into which the rowdy young scholars routinely
pressed themselves. But the lectures of the legendary Master Peter
required the largest space on the close, excluding the massive five-
aisled nave itself. That left this refectory. On three sides, close to the
ceiling, perhaps two dozen lads clung, like monkeys, to the narrow
clerestory shelves that projected into the air at twice a man's height.
Yes, monkeys—a congregation of monkeys and baboons, snorting and
hissing from perches. And stinking like simians, too—or so the male
aromas struck the nostrils of one of the other cloaked figures observing from the rear, also near the fireplace, yet somewhat apart from the
clique of Dons.

Finally, as the mob noise fell off, Peter Abelard said in decisive—if not quite rebuking—Latin, "Well, then, dear brothers, I put it to you. We'll have a case. You be the judges." He extended his raised hand farther, his arm gracefully curving toward the students, a benign gesture of blessing. "You have heard it said recently that Count Baldwin of Boulogne was taken captive by the Turks at Harran in the Principality of Antioch." At this, the last hoots fell off. The Master let a silence build, severe and grim. He could be certain that when the boys before him had initially heard this news of the first defeat of Frankish forces in the Holy Land, they'd have fended off an impulse to take the cross themselves. Now they'd be feeling guilty about their failure to have done so, confused whether to dread a conscripting martial summons from the Pope, or to long for it. Peter Abelard wanted their complete attention, and by raising this question he got it.

The implications of his dare, however, were heavy not only for the students—and they knew it. After all, they could do arithmetic. When Pope Urban's great war for Jerusalem had been launched to begin with, sending Baldwin and his army east years before, Peter Abelard himself, at seventeen years of age and the eldest son of a knight, was primed to mark his tunic with the cross and raise a sword for Christ. Indeed, he was all but required to. Yet, instead, he had said no to the sword, bowing his head for the tonsuring blade and donning a cleric's robe. Faced with the bellicose fervor that had swept all of France, young Peter Abelard had stood against it—simply by refusing the war of God's will in favor of the battles of philosophical disputation. His "no" to the Militant Christ had been "yes" to the Prince of Peace.

"Let us suppose," he continued, "that two of the young men in this very fraternity, moved by the Paraclete Himself, resolve to join in the rescue of Baldwin, the revered King of Jerusalem. You, Rudolph of Lyons, for example. And you, Tomas Clare." Abelard pointed at each one in turn. "Are we all agreed on this diegesis?" he asked. "Rudolph and Tomas set out on the great adventure, in the name of God and all goodness. Knights of Christ." His hand lifted once more, a gesture inviting howls of assent, and the noise came. When Abelard's hand fell, so did the sound. The throng of students, one creature

now, were his *schola cantorum*, an instrument willingly being played.
He was broadly grinning. He tossed a quick glance back toward the
knot of his cowled deprecators, reading their jealous minds: *How does
the varlet do this?*

"Which of our boys is virtuous?" he asked.

"Both are," came the answer from several.

"Aye. Both are virtuous, because both aim for virtue. At risk to
themselves, and cost to their fathers, Rudolph and Tomas wrap themselves in the mantles of selfless rescuers. They swear their solemn vows,
stitch their tunics with the horizontal-vertical sign, and set out, each
thereby earning the plenary indulgence." The two named lads were
alike in blushing. One was sure he was being mocked, and the second
was terrified that he'd be called upon to speak. As for the others, an
air of excited agitation rose from them, and also of not a little intimidation. Was the Master slyly recruiting for the much-spoken-of armed
pilgrimage, the overdue successor to the storied uncles' campaign that
had banished the infidel from the Land on which the sacred feet of the
Lord had trod? Land that was now, with Baldwin's capture, in danger
of being lost to the Saracens once more.

Abelard continued, with the solemn air of one reciting an epic.
"But Rudolph, en route to Jerusalem—let us propose this, to illus-
trate the question—is waylaid by robbers, far short of his goal. Poor
Rudolph's company is routed, his horses are stolen, his squires, arms
bearers, and bowmen taken away, captive. He is required to pay the
total of what remains of his father's purse just to stay alive. He returns
to Paris." Abelard fell silent for a moment, just long enough to drive
home that no one hooted at this turn in the story.

Everyone in the refectory was staring at Abelard, rapt. He went
on: "Tomas, meanwhile, succeeds in fording the Strait of Constanti-
nople, crossing Anatolia, reaching the Principality of Antioch, laying
siege to Harran, and obtaining the freedom of the King of Jerusalem." Silence again. Abelard waited. No one cheered. No hooting. The
students listened as to the report of a monumental turn in history.
"Now," Abelard intoned, "who is virtuous?"

"Tomas!" A dozen voices called out the name.

"Not Rudolph?" Abelard opened his hands, quizzically.

"Tomas! Tomas!"

"But Rudolph's purpose was the same as Tomas's. Wherein does virtue lie if not in purpose?"

"In freeing the King of Jerusalem," came the reply, followed by grunts of agreement.

"Heroism, perhaps. Success in battle is a mark of the hero. But is goodness determined by success? Was it heroic of Tomas that he had the good fortune *not* to be waylaid by a superior force of bandits? Was it owing to a lack of virtue that Rudolph found himself on a particular stretch of road just when a superior force of bandits showed itself? What if Tomas *instead* had been on that road at that hour? Would his righteousness be any less if the pure misfortune that befell Rudolph had, rather, befallen him? Or what if *both* had been waylaid? Does their having taken the cross, and offered themselves as God's men-at-arms, count for nothing? What does God see when He looks into the hearts of men?"

"God sees Jerusalem! Holy Zion!"

"But what of our two examples? Turn the case another way. What if the aim of our hero Tomas was not to secure the well-being of the Count of Boulogne, or even to secure the protection of the Land upon which the Lord Christ trod, but, rather, to secure the glory, fame, and wealth that would come to him, Tomas, if he were to be the instrument of Baldwin's rescue? What if, instead of piety, Tomas was moved by vanity and greed? Is that virtue?"

"And Rudolph"—this from one of the acrobats clinging to a clerestory ledge—"rightly intended, yet in a ditch by the road."

"Yes," Abelard answered, "the one victorious, but badly motivated; the other defeated, but wanting only the true will of God. Which man is the man of virtue now?"

"Rudolph! Rudolph!" The cheer went up, the lads raucous again. This was the victory they'd awaited—the turnabout trick of mind that Master Peter always accomplished. Those nearest Rudolph of Lyons slapped his shoulders, cuffed his head. "Rudolph! Rudolph!"

Abelard raised his arm once more, waiting. When the shouting subsided, he turned his hand with a peculiar motion that those who'd studied with him recognized as the sign of winding up, the drawing of a conclusion, the syllogism coming home. But the Master surprised them with yet another question. "So—do we conclude that virtue resides in the intent," he asked, "not the deed?"

The silence of the lads now was mulish. Abelard waited them out. They knew that he would not speak again, ever. Not until one of them had ventured a word. And so, finally, it came. A boy near the back, not far from the corner in which the other Masters stood, lifted up, cautiously, a phrase he had from Peter Abelard himself, just uttered. "Virtue resides in the true will of God."

"Which is?" Abelard fixed his glare on the one who spoke, and once more waited.

"The rescue of Jerusalem," the boy said, uncertainly.

"But rescue from whom? The Ishmaelites say that from Jerusalem their Prophet ascended to heaven, making the city holy to the Saracens, who assert that God therefore wants it for them. To Saracens, *we* are the infidels. Who is right? And how do we know? The true will of God? Which is?"

It was the silence of the throng that now seemed eternal.

Finally, Master Peter rescued them, as he often did at such moments, by turning the matter, yet again, in a wholly different direction. "Saracens," he said. "Why are they called with such a name?"

Silence still, thickening.

"What, has no one here read Jerome?" Abelard asked. "The sons of Ishmael. Why do we call them that?"

"Because they spring from Abraham's older son."

"Indeed! What's your name, good lad?"

"John of Cologne."

"And who, my dear John, was Abraham's wife?"

"Sarah."

"Yes?" Abelard's hand curved in a small circle, a kindly gesture of coaxing.

"Therefore," the boy offered, but tremulously, " '*Sara*cens'?"

"Precisely." Abelard threw his arms wide. "Saracens! Because they claim descent from the *wife*, Sarah, not the concubine, Hagar. Legitimacy is at issue here. 'Saracen' is a claim to righteousness. And our

colleague here cut to the core of it. Where is his acclaim? Where is
the acclaim for John of Cologne?"

With that, the boys resumed their hooting and stomping, now
elaborated by the clapping of poor John about the head. Peter Abelard
grinned down at them as they cavorted. An observer, even looking
on from the far-off corner of the refectory, could sense the teacher's
profound affection for his pupils. He loved them for their unruliness.
He *believed* in their unruliness. He channeled its energy into his own
purpose.

At last, Master Peter raised his voice, along with that wafting arm
of his. "And what?" he called. "And what?" He waited for the settling
down, the attention. When he had it, he resumed: "And what if the
Ishmaelites *are* righteous? True progeny of Father Abraham. Legiti-
mate! What then? Turks, Saracens, sons of heaven, all! What then of
'God's true will'?"

The group fell absolutely still, stunned by these words, as by the
blow of a log to the head. After a long time, Abelard asked quietly,
"How do we, exiles in this vale of tears, know what the great and
Almighty God, in His eternal wisdom, wants for Jerusalem?"

Out of the silence, from the back, came the stout voice of another
of the skeptical Masters. "Holy Mother the Church tells us, through
her spokesman, the Holy Father."

Abelard's gaze lifted, and engaged. He had the air, suddenly, of
a man who, having carefully pulled on a thread, had found its knot.
"We know by listening?" he asked. "Not by thinking?" He waited, as
if there would be an answer. There was not an answer, of course. He
said, "Listening to what we are told? Are we made for our ears, and
not our minds?" Again he waited. No answer. He opened his hands
wide, shrugging slightly. "What is the point of all this trouble, then?
The way we parse subtleties, compute partialities, unpeel the skin of
paradoxes, arriving eventually at a place where we can draw contingent moral and intellectual conclusions, based on thought? What is
the point of troubling to construct an argument, and to follow where
it leads, if all we need, *a priori,* is the answer from above?"

But the reply came back, ringing across the room, sure and well said: "The answer from above is certain. What you offer is uncertain. You trade in half-truths, not the Truth."

"Ah, Truth!" Abelard replied, "What is Truth?"

"Pilate's question!" shot back the disputing Master, a resounding rebuttal from beside the fireplace.

"Indeed so, dear brother," Abelard said, but without looking toward his interlocutor. Abelard was on his game, like a monk playing a leather-bound wad of horsehair against the Cloister wall. He went up on his toes, leaned across the lectern toward the crowd, and shook his head, declaiming, " 'Pontius Pilate saith unto him, What is truth? And when he had said this, he went out again unto the Jews, and saith unto them, I find in him no fault at all.' " Abelard raised his fist, and repeated: " *'I find in him no fault at all!'* What does the Evangelist tell us here? Pontius Pilate *alone* saw the truth of the Lord Christ's innocence. He saw that single truth, and, for a moment, insisted upon it. Not a 'half-truth,' but a particular truth, a precious jewel of a truth: *'I find in him no fault at all!'* So said the Imperial Procurator of Syria Palaestina, Pontius Pilate. A golden moment. If the heavenly chorus did not sing at that assertion, what are the pristine voices of angels for? *My* earthly chorus, by contrast"——here, finally, Abelard flung his articulate arm toward the back of the room, a gesture of contempt for his critics——"squeaks of 'half-truths,' and misses the point that even a brutish Roman pagan grasped. Pilate knew to care nothing for access to the disembodied 'Truth.' Pilate was right to ask, 'Truth? What is Truth?' There are only grounded truths, and Pilate saw the one that was right before him. The grounded truth of one man. The Word become flesh. *One man!* Here is the point, my brothers! Flesh! Flesh! God in one thing——not all things——God in one body. One man. One cut of meat! The meat of the reasoning human mind. Jesus Christ, yes. Of course. But not only Him!"

Abelard pressed his hands to his head. "This! This! A particular thinker, with his particular thoughts! Yes, we listen! But then we think! With *this*!" He pressed his head between his hands, and turned slowly, showing himself to the crowd of students, as if to put the organ of rationality on display for the first time since the fall of Adam. "*Here* is the Word made flesh. In every one of us! Each person, particular, and alone. One. *Here* we have the Incarnation in all its glory. The conscious human mind, the knower aware of his own knowing. And in the conscious human mind, aware in the moment only of *this,* never of *that*—of the individual only, never of the general—what do we have but the Real Presence of the ineffable God—who, by virtue of this Incarnation, is no longer ineffable!"

Now he was rolling, like a horseman heading downhill, toward the home corral. His voice had that gallop to it, that pitch. "What else does the Apostle mean when he says that God *emptied* Himself! Emptied Himself of all that is abstract, ideal, and universal. The Truth, if you will, emptied itself into, yes, *half-truths.* Call them what you will. In the banishment from Eden, half-truths are all we ever have. The reasoning human mind puts them together into something larger, but even larger—they are always and forever elements of the next computation. We poor humans do not *possess* the Truth. We are pilgrims, ever on the way to it. And the mode of our pilgrimage—investigating, assessing, judging, deciding—is thought."

"No! Faith!" cried the Master from the rear.

"Faith that thinks!" Abelard shot back.

"But God's will!" Now another of the Dons joined in, this one with the trumping tone of an Inquisitor's *accusatio:* "Where is God's will in your scheme? God's will is the Truth. The Church asserts it. The Church reveals it."

Abelard shot back, "God's will is known completely to none but God. If there is 'the Truth,' it resides with Him, not with us. *That,* dear brothers . . ." Here Abelard's entire physical appearance changed. The tension in his shoulders relaxed, like the King's guard given leave to rest. He seemed to shake himself, as if throwing off the bad energy of combat. He turned back to the students, as if, having provoked his envious fellows in the back of the room to take his bait, he could at last complete the thought with which he had begun. ". . . is why the interior intent of the moral agent is the key to virtue. We return to Tomas Clare and Rudolph of Lyons." Abelard quickly touched the gaze of each boy, showing fondness. He continued, "It is human to err in knowing God's will. Therefore, your act in its pursuit can be wrong, but you can still be virtuous if your aim is pure. The intent defines, not the deed."

"But the Jews!" the Inquisitor called out from the rear. "Pilate declared the Lord's innocence to *the Jews*! And the Jews cried, 'Crucify him!' What of *that* deed? What possible virtue was there in deicide?"

Abelard stood firm, upright, moving only the muscles that controlled his eyes, to find the one who'd so challenged him. The look he cast now, in contrast to the teacherly affection he had just displayed, landed as dead weight—a blow. When he spoke, it was slowly, each word a millstone. "If the Jews believe they are enacting the will of God when they cry out 'Crucify!,' then theirs is an act of virtue."

"You lie! If the Jews are not guilty, no one is guilty!"

"But are they damned?" Abelard asked. Still, he spoke with exquisite precision, wanting to be understood. "If the Jews believe God wants them to kill Christ, then, however gravely mistaken, their intention saves them." The smallest smile crossed Peter Abelard's face, and, given what he had just said, it added heat to the fire of his sacrilege. The silence broke only when, moments later, the teacher himself, still addressing his unnamed antagonist in the rear, said, "Guilty, yes. Certainly. But also redeemed. Thank you, esteemed brother, for drawing us to the conclusion of our lesson."

But Abelard was not finished. His habit, after such a joust, was to greet his antagonist, and wish him well. William of Champeaux, his great rival in Paris, had decamped from the city after being repeatedly bested precisely on the question of virtue's meaning. The hecklers today were Champeaux's disciples, and graciousness toward them was one of Abelard's ploys. Therefore, in the general bustle of adjournment, he plunged into the crowd and made his way toward the fireplace, where the Masters had clustered.

But by the time he was through the press of boys, the critics were gone. Almost alone beside the fireplace stood the Cathedral Canon, one Fulbert, whom, until now, Abelard had not noticed. Fulbert was the man appointed by the Bishop of Paris to preside over the College of Canons Regular and to maintain order in the Cloister, lest the unruly pupils of the school utterly destroy what was essential to contemplation. But the Canon's sway as enforcer of discipline in the Cathedral precinct went further than students.

In effect, Canon Fulbert was to the Bishop what the constable, cofferer, steward, and Grandmaster were to the King; he performed, that is, a great mélange of crucial roles. Fulbert's gift was to sense what His Lordship needed before His Lordship did—and to supply it. Still, he was not given to study, cared nothing for the dialectic of lessons, and rarely attended symposia. He was a stout cleric, his ample girth and ruddy face contradicting the ascetic zealotry with which he policed his realm. His bald head was uncovered, and the pale flesh running up from his brow glistened with perspiration, as if for Fulbert the simple act of breathing was exertion. As always, he carried a staff, which, when walking, he habitually banged on the floor to the rhythm of his stride, a sound that the intimidated students took as warning of his approach, exactly as he intended. With that staff, Fulbert was known to have knocked unconscious men larger and more robust than he, and he was said to have killed some. When he was confronted with wreckage, his way was to stride through it and leave more behind. The young scholars were long accustomed to being beaten for mistakes in their letters, sums, and recitations; more grievous rowdiness could be a matter of mortal danger. As they left the refectory, therefore, they gave the Canon a wide berth.

Immediately behind Fulbert was his so-called Brother Thrall, the Canon's personal *servus.* A young man with a wispy beard, clothed in a rough woolen smock and leggings, the thrall was short and slender, with a dark face so unmoving and expressionless as to seem a mask.

Thralls were disenfranchised persons of uncertain origin, the bastard sons of battle captives, fugitives, or vagabonds—rank outsiders in a ruthlessly structured feudal society. Snatched by priests from birthing beds, such male infants were, so it was said, rescued by the Church from the vale of sin, to be protected and raised in rectories and monasteries—but at the price of growing up as Church slaves. A major ecclesial institution like the Cathedral could count a dozen such *servi,* attached to the Cloister in perpetuity. Mostly, they were degraded laborers—rat catchers and gravediggers. Unlike even the lowliest serf, a man of the thrall could never expect to marry, work for himself, own a plot of land, or pursue a life outside his holder precinct. But some thralls, beginning as favored children, became personal servants to prelates, and such was the case with Canon Fulbert's *servus*. He was always at Fulbert's elbow, ready to clear the way ahead with the short, stout cudgel he carried; saddle the Canon's horse; test his food for poison; sleep on the floor beside his bed—ready, for that matter, though this was not spoken of, to be drawn into that bed for the fondling he was taught to perform as a very young boy.

Coming up behind Brother Thrall and Fulbert was a monk, his cowl drawn forward over his head, leaving his face obscured in shadow. In contrast to Fulbert, he was a slender figure, and taller. The monk's hands, apparently joined at his waist, were hidden inside the bag sleeves of his habit. Fulbert turned and gestured him forward, and it was suddenly apparent that the monk was in the Canon's company.

Abelard bowed slightly to Fulbert. "My lord, your presence at my lecture honors me."

"As always, Master Peter, your presence honors the school." There was something tight-lipped in Fulbert's statement, as if he disliked having to acknowledge Abelard's eminence. If Paris was lately outdrawing schools at Chartres and Orléans, it was due to this self-important genius, and the Canon knew it. Not only students flocked to the Cathedral environs, but merchants, dressmakers, woodworkers, wine sellers, and goldsmiths.

Three new stall markets had sprung up on both sides of the Seine in the last year. Houses were being built as quickly as cut lumber could be brought in from the mills. All of this redounded to the Cathedral, therefore to Fulbert, who was the collector of tithes and manager of money. His standing depended on the growing prestige of the school, which led to the profits of the Cloister trades, and therefore revenues to the Church that the King did not control. The Bishop was prospering because of Abelard, although His Lordship seemed ready to credit Fulbert instead—an impression the Canon happily encouraged. Therefore, Fulbert had to be careful with the school prodigy. Yet he could not fully stifle his discomfort at what he had just witnessed. "The Jews as exemplars of virtue, brother?" Fulbert said. "You provoke as much as you enlighten."

Jews were no mere theological abstraction where Fulbert and Abelard stood. The small island in the Seine was divided into three realms of influence: the Cathedral to the east, the Royal Palace to the west—and in the dead center the lively marketplace, which had become the pulse not just of the island, but of the city. And that center had been known for more than a century as Vicus Judaeorum. The Jewish Village.

Abelard smiled easily. "I provoke *to* enlighten."

But the monk beside Canon Fulbert now spoke up, abruptly. "What nonsense."

Abelard faced him, taking in his appearance for the first time. The monk's voice was high-pitched, but the Latin phrase—*Quod deliramentum verba*—was perfectly constructed, asserted with authority. "I beg your pardon?" Abelard said.

"That business about the Saracens. Just because the venerable Jerome was misinformed, that does not justify repeating such flawed etiology."

"You know Jerome?"

"His *Life of Saint Hilarion,* the anchorite in Palestine. The myth of Sarah, wife of Abraham, as the source of 'Saracen.'" The monk's self-assurance verged on cockiness. He continued: "Jerome was being fanciful. And Jerome, of course, predated Muhammad by more than two centuries. 'Saracen' refers to Arabs, not, as you call them, to Ishmaelites. And certainly not to Turks. Surely, you know this."

"In that case, dear brother, where does the word 'Saracen' come from?"

The monk, aware of being tested, did not reply. The young scholars were gone from the refectory by now, and the three were alone.

"Please," Fulbert said. He put his hand on the monk's arm, but tentatively. It was unusual for the Canon to betray insecurity.

Abelard said, "Jerome gives us the simple explanation of 'Saracen.' Simplicity is the way to knowing."

"'Sahara,' Master Peter," the monk replied. "The great desert. Known to reach from the Red Sea to the far ocean. Not one, but many deserts. Therefore, 'Sahara,' which is the plural of the Arabic word *sahraa.* Desert. 'Saracen,' speaking of simplicity, means 'people of the

desert.' That is all. Abraham's wife has nothing to do with it. Neither
does a claim to legitimacy. The infidel is the infidel, descended from a
whore." At this, the monk's hands went to the cowl and drew it back,
exposing a plaited crown of brown hair, and fully showing the delicate
features of a young woman. Her dark eyes were large, and her face was
sharply defined by pronounced cheekbones, a thin nose, a small chin,
and full lips, which took their rest in an easy smile. A face impossibly
well proportioned—a finished composition.

Fulbert glanced about, to be sure they were alone, then hastened
to explain. "This is my late brother's daughter," he said anxiously.
"Her mother was cousin to Gisela of Bourgogne, the mother of Ade-
laide, the Queen Consort, one of whose ladies sent her to me." A
sudden perplexity in Fulbert's demeanor hinted at his dilemma. To
be pressed by a member of the Royal household was a nightmare for
a man whose first duty was not to the King, but to the King's main
rival, the Bishop.

"And I am looking for a teacher," the young woman said. She was
not twenty years old.

Abelard channeled his surprise into the imitation of offense. "A
woman? In the sanctuary of study?" He turned to Fulbert. "My lord,
does the Bishop know of this?"

Fulbert blushed. The Bishop was known to whip women out of
Cloisters reserved to men. "On matters of familial charity," Fulbert
insisted, "the Bishop would counsel deference. I cannot disrespect the
memory of my brother. My niece here has been expelled from the
convent at Argenteuil, where she defied the Prioress."

"Not expelled, dear Uncle," the young woman said. "Not defiant.
It was Mother Prioress who insisted on my further education, which
was impossible at Argenteuil, where I learned all there was to learn."

"You pilfered candles from the sacristy."

"So that I could read at night. It is ridiculous that no one reads
at night."

"Candles are a luxury," Abelard put in.

"But reading is a necessity. Fewer candles for the altar, I say. More
for the *scriptorium*."

"You see?" Fulbert said, opening his hands.

"Dear uncle," the young woman said, sweetly now, "Mother Prioress knows of your great influence. She sent me forth with a blessing, knowing you would provide. And my dear mother's cousin, Lady Gisela, redoubled the blessing." She looked directly at Abelard. "I need a teacher."

"So you were assessing me, in your disguise."

"I was."

"And you find me overly simple, like Jerome."

"There is more to learning than the Church Fathers."

"Yes, there are the philosophers. You have Greek?"

"*Oute o Theos mporei na allaxei to parelthon.* 'Not even the gods can change the past.'"

"Besides Agathon, what philosophers do you favor?"

"Boethius. *The Consolation of Philosophy,* which, as you know, is an interchange between a disillusioned Boethius and the true spirit of philosophy, who appears in the work as a woman of erudition and tenderness."

Abelard shook his head, a negation. "Boethius was condemned as a Hellenist. A martyr to thought. You keep dangerous company, sister. The school of Paris is timid compared with that. Why would you study here?"

"Your subject. Virtue. What makes a person good? It is said you draw on the Greeks, who come to us now from the Arabs and the Jews."

"It is true. There are texts coming from Toledo."

"Virtue lies in purpose more than in deed," she said evenly. "I accept your argument, even if your logic fails."

"You use my own thrust against me." Abelard felt a rare unease stirring in his chest. It was not the unease of debate. He stifled it, asking, "What failure of logic?"

"The *deicidii* are still the *deicidii,* no matter the intention. The murder of God stands alone. What you said about Jews is absurd, on the face of it."

"So—your case is made," he replied. "The infidel is still the infidel. The Jew is still the Jew." Abelard paused, then added, "The woman is still the woman." Again a pause. His gaze fell ever so briefly down the length of her hidden body. Under the loose-fitting monk's habit—there—he saw the faint curve of her breast, a line at her hip. With counterfeit dash, emphasized by a sweep of his hand, he said, "On the face of it."

She smiled again. "Infidel. Jew. Woman. If, in the spaciousness of your thought, there is room for the first and the second, there must be room for the third. 'What is the point of troubling to construct an argument, and to follow where it leads, if all we need, *a priori,* is the answer from above?'" The trap of her mind had caught his words, and now, released, they'd snapped back to hit him. "*Your* logic," she added. Her smile now conveyed her savoring.

Abelard nodded, but slightly.

She went on: "My uncle has permitted me to be here, in the rear corner of your lesson hall, for three days now. I find you unconstrained in your thinking. You go where it takes you. I have learned the rules. Now I would learn to break them."

"Keep the rules, dear sister—"

"—and the rules keep me. I know that. Would you teach me, or not?"

"How would that work?" Here it was. Abelard felt ambushed—not by her request, which he had seen coming, but by the resistance he felt. Not to her mind, which beckoned as an open sky beckons the bird, but resistance, rather, to that bare suggestion of her breasts beneath the monkish garb. Resistance, therefore, to her body. No, to her body in perfect combination with her mind, the joining that so enlivened her amazing face. It was a rare thing for Peter Abelard to feel the stirring in his loins, but there it was. A man of continence, long without women, he had a fine-nurtured habit of turning efficiently away from such feeling, but now he did not. Still, he was like a war dog, tensed for danger. He glanced at Fulbert, as if it were the Canon to whom he had put his question—not himself.

"You would take up residence here, on the close," the stout cleric answered. "I would have you named to the College of Canons Regular." Fulbert paused. The Canons Regular at Notre-Dame lived a quasi-monastic life, under the rule of Saint Augustine, a reforming impulse aimed at retrieving the ecclesiastical discipline of the early

Church. Abelard did not react. Fulbert shrugged. "Or, once named as a Canon, you could simply join my household, a sort of chaplain. As a courtesy to me, you would offer a private tutorial, now and again, to various members of my domestic sodality. No one need know to whom, precisely."

"The Bishop?"

"No one need know," Fulbert repeated. It would not serve his purposes for the Bishop to know of his kindness to the cousin of the King's wife, but the King's wife would know, which might, in a time of intrigue, prove useful.

Abelard shook his head. To be in conspiracy with the unscrupulous and self-promoting Fulbert was a further risk. Abelard cast his eyes about, to be sure they were unheard, and he was startled to see in the shadow the expressionless Brother Thrall, whose gift, clearly, was for making himself invisible. Within earshot of all that the Canon had said, the *servus* held himself as if he had heard nothing. But to Abelard, the jeopardy was clear. Prudence presented its mandates: One, stay out of intrigues between Bishop and King. Two, *cavete feminam.*

Females were excluded from Cathedral study, and for good reason. *For this reason.* Out of the question. Forbidden. Such violation of the order of the school would be dangerous for a man of Abelard's prominence, whatever it was to the conniving Canon. But in the brief joust over Saracens and philosophers, Peter Abelard had just been bested, and that set the old, beguiling impulse of contest moving in him. Plus, the young creature was beautiful.

"What is your name?" he asked.

"Héloïse."

He saw her, he loved her. And so likewise Héloïse, him.

CHAPTER SIX

Since 1948, the Chancery of the Archdiocese had been in the south wing of the Villard Houses, a sprawling Roman Renaissance palazzo on Madison Avenue immediately behind St. Patrick's Cathedral. The place had been built by a nineteenth-century railroad tycoon, whose heirs were taken down by the income tax, the market crash, and the dislocations of two wars, making way at last for Francis Spellman, the shoemaker's son who secretly believed himself to be a prince— a Borgia one at that. The stately complex featured Tiffany glass, La Farge murals, and bronze fixtures by Saint-Gaudens, but those names were merely names to Michael Kavanagh. Enough for him that the palace splendors were of another order entirely—not his.

He tried not to judge, but really.

As he mounted the grand staircase, with its polished pink marble under flashing chandeliers, its Oriental runners with brass fasteners, the elaborately carved oak wall capped by the huge seal of the Archdiocese—the tasseled Cardinal's hat, the Greek cross, the flame, the motto *Fiat Voluntas Tua*—he felt as out of place as ever. The effort simply to carry his weight up the staircase, one raised foot at a time, registered as a coming headache. He shook it off and chastised himself for this smug alienation.

The good works of the Church were focused on parishioners like his own, including the poorest people in New York. Offices in this building—the Catholic Guardian Society, the Hospital Apostolate, Catholic Relief, Catholic Home Bureau, Catholic Schools—made that service real. And the people themselves would love this lavish place for belonging to their Church—an immigrant's revenge. So who the hell was Michael Kavanagh to be put off by its showy indulgence? The Villard Houses were a celebration of Irish Catholic arrival, even if the arrival belonged to one man alone: Spellman, the self-styled American pope. The building was as close as His Eminence would get to the Apostolic Palace in Vatican City. To come here was to risk running into him.

And, yes, a headache was coming.

On the second floor, under a barrel-vaulted ceiling and opposite a row of large windows opening onto a courtyard, the left wall of a long corridor was hung with portraits of crimson-clad Irish warlocks—Spellman's predecessors, Farley, Hughes, Hayes—as well as of beati-fied New Yorkers—Mothers Cabrini and Seton, and the Jesuit martyr Isaac Jogues. Beyond a large, sterile fireplace with a flamboyant mar-ble mantel, Kavanagh came to a set of double doors, on one of which was a small brass plate stamped with the words "Episcopal Vicar for Clergy." He entered.

A plain woman of indeterminate age looked up from a ledger on her desk. She wore rimless spectacles, her lank hair in a school-marmish bun. With an unfriendly expression of surprise, she took in the sight of him—his black suit and clerical collar, the omnipresent breviary under his arm. On the wall behind her was a Baroque paint-ing of the Risen Christ. Below that was a file cabinet. That Kavanagh did not know the woman made him realize how long it had been since he'd come to Sean's office.

"I am Father Michael Kavanagh, hoping to see Bishop Donovan."

By way of reply, the woman glanced at the ledger, an appointment book.

"He's not expecting me," Kavanagh said.

"One moment, Father," she said. She stood, and disappeared

behind a further pair of walnut doors. A moment later she returned, and, without disguising her disappointment, said, "His Excellency will see you."

Bishop Donovan's office, in contrast to the opulent public spaces of the Chancery, was sparsely furnished: an uncluttered U-shaped desk in the window alcove, a tired leather couch adjacent to an off-kilter butler's table, and a Windsor chair that had lost its sheen. Against the distorting glass of the leaded window, spindly bare branches scratched like fingers in the November wind. On one side of the alcove hung a simple crucifix, and on the other was a photo of the Pope, his familiar gaunt profile, spectacles glinting.

Bishop Donovan came toward Kavanagh with his hand extended. He was well into his sixties now. His hair was white, his skin ruddy. His black cassock and purple cincture hung loosely on a frame made for more weight than he was carrying. A gold cross swung from the chain at his chest. "Father Michael Kavanagh, what a pleasant surprise!" The man's happiness was unfeigned. "You are very welcome, dear Michael."

Only now did Kavanagh allow himself to feel that his odd waking impulse to come downtown was right. "Thank you, Bishop," he said.

"Cut that out, Michael."

Kavanagh grinned. "Thank you, Sean."

"Not 'Agent'?"

Kavanagh laughed, then so did Donovan. In truth, the old priest was proud of his long-lost nickname.

They sat, Kavanagh on the sofa, the Bishop on the chair. Kavanagh placed his breviary on the cushion beside him.

"It's been—what?—most of a year?" the Bishop said. "I thought I'd see you at the Holy Thursday Gaudeamus."

"I was at Tenebrae, of course, in the Cathedral, in the shadows. Who doesn't love the extinguishing of candles? But I couldn't stay for the reception."

The Bishop nodded pleasantly. "Tenebrae is my favorite liturgy of the year. Shouldn't say that, since it's all about the death of the Lord. But I love getting the fellows together afterward. *'Gaudeamus!* Let us rejoice!' Some take offense at the priest party I throw on the eve of Good Friday."

"Not me. Just couldn't get there."

"What about next week? My Thanksgiving shindig for the fellows. Wednesday night. I've lined up Patricia Murphy's. Swell place. Candles galore. You coming?"

Kavanagh hesitated. Once, he'd relished the lubricated company of his fellow priests, but the edgy banter of such gatherings had gone stale for him. What was the Latin for "Let us trade barbs"? He said, "I don't imagine so, Sean. Wednesday nights are tough. You know how it is."

"A busy parish priest. Right. I have the impression, speaking of candles, that you're burning yours at both ends. I hear from Frank that you're working too hard, Michael." Bishop Donovan picked up a pack of cigarettes from the coffee table, shook a pair up, and made the offer. Michael took his. He supplied the light, a match.

Waving it out, Kavanagh said with abrupt solemnity, "What else do you hear, Sean?"

"What do you mean?"

Kavanagh's mood had come between them. His headache was full-bore by now. "From Runner Malloy. John Malloy."

The Bishop did not reply, but neither did he lower his eyes.

Kavanagh said, "John Malloy came to Good Shepherd yesterday. To the early Mass. He disappeared before I could speak to him. I was left wondering how he knew where to find me."

Still, the Bishop said nothing.

"Then it occurred to me. You told him. Before he came to Good Shepherd yesterday, he would have come to see you. I haven't seen him in all these years, but you have. You're in touch with him." Kavanagh waited. Then he added, "Am I right?"

The Bishop took a drag, then leaned forward to roll the tip of his cigarette in the ashtray. "It's true," he said, but carefully.

"And you told him where I was."

"It didn't occur to me that he was of a mind to contact you."

"He didn't contact me. That's the point. He was at the Mass. He came forward for Communion but didn't receive. It threw me, a kind of message: showing up, out of nowhere, but also kneeling at the rail, then shaking me off when I offered him the Host. What was that?"

"I have no idea."

"Then he stalked away."

"That *is* odd."

"But you've talked with him. You're in touch with him."

"Not 'in touch.' I had a letter from him—Special Delivery, out of the blue. Then he came to see me, the day before yesterday. First time I've seen him since he left Dunwoodie, what . . . ?"

"Fourteen years ago."

"Yes."

"It hit me yesterday, Sean . . . how in all these years, you never mentioned him to me."

"I'm aware of that, Michael. I'm also aware that you never brought it up."

"You made it seem like the Seal of Confession. The private forum. How could I?"

Instead of answering, the Bishop drew in smoke.

"But yesterday . . . last night . . ." Kavanagh had to search for words. "I realized how strange the whole thing is. . . . Back then, you told me Runner left the sem because of me."

"Not because of you."

"Yes. 'Out of bounds,' you said. Feelings for me that were 'out of bounds.'" Kavanagh channeled his sudden agitation into the smashing of his cigarette into the ashtray. "And you never discussed that with me? Out of bounds? For years, I thought I'd done something horribly shameful. A guy kicked out of the seminary because of me?"

"Not 'kicked out.'"

"He *would* have been. He confessed his feelings to you, and then you convinced him to leave. But if he hadn't, you'd have seen to his being tossed."

Bishop Donovan only eyed the tip of his cigarette.

"Then I'd have been tossed, too," Kavanagh said, with the sudden spleen of a man seeing a thing for the first time.

"No, Michael—"

"Good God, Sean. You got Runner to resign as a way of protect-ing me. They'd have come after me! What's his name, the Rector—"

"Tobin. Peter Tobin."

"Right, Tobin! He wouldn't have thrown out just *one* guy for being . . ."

"It *was* feelings, Michael. But only feelings."

"Damn right! Feelings are what brought me here this morning. Feelings I've never gotten free of . . . something *in me* that was out of bounds. Obviously, I knew exactly what you had told me about Runner, but as for me . . . What the hell, Sean?" Kavanagh checked himself.

"The love of men for men," the Bishop said quietly.

"We cannot even say the word, Sean."

"Yes, we can, if necessary. Is it necessary?"

Kavanagh shrugged. "'The love that dare not speak its name'? Don't be ridiculous. I was in the navy, remember? 'Why do they let Marines on ships? Because sheep would be too obvious.' But there's the point. Jokes like that are the big deflection. The navy has nothing on the Church: sailors terrified of the blue discharge. And priests? You said it: burning the candle . . . CYO . . . basketball drills . . . hospi-tal rounds . . . parish school . . . hearing Confessions . . . Keeping at bay . . . what? Feelings that are 'out of bounds'? My idea of hell is an afternoon without appointments."

"The people love you."

"I'm not talking about the people, Sean. Or about John Malloy, for that matter. I'm talking about you. You told me that my friend's first dream of himself was crushed because of me. From then on, *my* dream was sullied. And I was to pretend it never happened. Which, God forgive me, I did."

"You're right. I protected you."

"From what? Tobin? Expulsion? No! From feelings I should have acknowledged. Feelings that were *not* out of bounds. Runner was my friend, my *particular* friend. And you made me the means of his betrayal. You betrayed us both."

"You should have talked to me."

"How could I? You hid behind the Seal of the Sacrament of Penance. John Malloy was an occasion of sin! *That* is what you made me think. So I blanked it out. All these years, Sean, you . . . who knows me better than anyone . . . and who . . ." Kavanagh's voice trailed off. He wanted to say "who cares about me," but *that* seemed out of bounds. He let his silence make the point. Sean Donovan was no friend.

The Bishop did not pick up the thought.

Finally, Kavanagh asked, "Why did we never discuss what happened to Runner? Why did we never discuss whether I am a homosexual?"

"Are you?"

"No. No. I am not a homosexual. It took me the war years at the Navy Yard to understand that. Three years of loving men, actually. Men dying in my arms. Men whose cheeks I kissed . . . whose hands I held, hour after hour . . . whose faces I still see in my sleep. I loved those men, every blessed one of them. Homosexuality had nothing to do with it. But so what if I *was* homosexual? Is that what you thought to protect me from? 'Particular friendship,' Sean? The great crime at Dunwoodie? We were warned off it in a thousand ways. The threshold rule. No after-lunch walks in pairs. But what is friendship if not particular? What other kind of friendship is there?"

"Michael, you're not making sense."

"Maybe not, but that's because talk of this is branded as dirty. Sealed off behind the Seal. I don't buy it. Haven't bought it for years." Kavanagh stopped. Indeed, it surprised him to realize he'd stopped to catch his breath. He'd gotten ahead of himself. But he'd just caught up with something, too.

The Bishop eyed him warily, and that also seemed an affront.

Kavanagh was far from finished. "In the navy, I told guys to relax if they felt guilty for getting laid. I tell Inwood plumbers the same thing, and also their wives, if they can't handle getting pregnant again. What is it with us and sex, Sean? God isn't sending people to hell over the rhythm method, no matter what the Pope says. Not over masturbation, either. The people love me? Of course they love me. I tell them to relax."

"What you tell people in the Confessional is not my business."

" 'Out of bounds.' What *was* that? I'll tell *you,* Sean—exactly what it was. 'You are on your own, bud.' That's the message, and I've been hearing it all these years in a voice I've always known, but could never quite identify. 'You are on your own with feelings of grief and confusion and loss and loneliness.' I saw it yesterday. I have not had a 'particular friend' in all these years . . . not since Runner Malloy. That's why the sight of him threw me so. Simple friendship . . . that's what's 'out of bounds.' You made it an issue of homosexual love. What's the phrase in Canon Law?—*crimen pessimum?* The 'worst crime'? No. Wanting not to be alone—that's the 'worst crime.' "

"Michael, you need to stop this—"

"Right! Stop the feeling. Shut up about it. Sit on it. Bury it. How? Why, light the candle at both ends and let the mother burn. 'You are on your own, bud.' And what I've just realized is that the voice telling me that all these years has been yours."

Donovan shook his head sadly. "Nothing wrong with wanting not to be alone. Who wants to be alone? That's why we have the Common Room in every rectory."

"Each with its bottomless bottle of Chivas."

"It's not for Chivas that the fellows come to my shindig on Holy Thursday, the one you are too busy to attend. It's for the friendship you claim to want."

"No, Sean, it's for clerics cutting each other down to size. What passes for chummy humor, priest to priest, is sarcasm, and you know it. I bailed out on that bullshit years ago."

"My goodness, Michael. This bitterness is so unlike you."

"It is me, Sean."

"You are remembering your friendship with John as something golden, beyond compare. . . ." Bishop Donovan leaned to the ashtray and tapped it, without breaking the practiced rhythm into which his speech now fell, a stilted rhythm, pretending to be easy. "A beautiful nostalgia . . ." He had assumed the mode of pastoral counselor. "But perhaps that feeling of intimacy was—don't misunderstand—a bit of a boyish infatuation. That you have nothing like it in your life now . . . could that just be a simple measure of manly maturity?"

" 'Boyish infatuation'? 'Manly maturity'? What are you saying?"

"I'm saying the life is hard, Michael. Toughen up."

Kavanagh laughed abruptly, even as blood rushed to his face, and his headache spiked. The Bishop's rebuke surprised him, yet so did his own readiness to be chastised. Self-doubt loitered in Kavanagh, like a tumor in his lung. He knew that what Bishop Donovan said was true. He was prepared to think ill of himself, and here was another reason to do so. Toughen up, indeed. His skull was cracking.

For want of something to say, he turned to his breviary, opened it and took out one of several printed bookmarks. He read, " 'To live in the midst of the world with no desire for its pleasures; to be a member of every family, yet belonging to none . . .' Like that, you mean?"

"Lacordaire," the Bishop said, and he recited from memory, " 'To daily go from men to God to offer Him their homage and petitions; to return from God to men to bring them His pardon and hope . . .' Not a bad vocation, that."

" 'To bless and be blest forever,' " Kavanagh read. " 'O God, what a life, and it is yours, O Priest of Jesus Christ.' " Kavanagh slipped the bookmark back between the pages and put the book down again, an act of punctuation. For a long time, the two men sat in silence.

Finally, Kavanagh asked, "So what is it with John Malloy?"

"I can't discuss that."

"Seal of Confession."

"Or that."

"What can you tell me?"

"He's a teacher. A school in New Jersey. A coach."

"He was dressed like a stockbroker."

"It's that kind of school."

"Why did he come to Good Shepherd?"

"Beats me, Michael."

"Did he talk about me?"

"Not really."

"Not really?"

"I can't discuss it, Michael."

"Can you put me in touch with him? I'd like to see him."

"If he gets back to me, I'll ask him. Otherwise, it would be a violation."

"But you felt free to point him to me."

"Not the same." Now, when Bishop Donovan stubbed out his cigarette, it carried the meaning that the session was over. Session. Not old friends together; not even counselor and client, Kavanagh saw suddenly, but employer and employee.

Both men stood. Kavanagh's gaze went to the crucifix on the wall, then to the portrait of Pius XII. "Something else, Sean," he said.

Bishop Donovan smiled, a full display of official, but still genuine, benevolence. He was a good boss. "Anything, anything at all."

"Simone Weil."

"The French saint?"

"Was she a saint? I've been reading her book. She was never baptized. She wouldn't join a Church that claimed the right to say *'Anathema sit!'* "

Donovan snorted. "We don't say it that much anymore."

"You said it to Runner."

"No, I didn't."

"I told you, at Good Shepherd yesterday, he knelt there but didn't receive Communion. As in 'excommunicated.' That's what you'd done to him. That's what he was telling me."

"I protected you."

"What did I need protection from, Sean?"

Bishop Donovan did not answer. The silence grew, becoming a kind of presence in the room. At last, Kavanagh bent over to pick up his breviary. Straightening, he asked, "Was Simone Weil an anti-Semite?"

"Good God, no. She was a Jew."

Kavanagh nodded, and turned. That he left the room without a word of farewell was, he knew, quite rude. He did not understand what was happening to him.

The morning sun washed down on Madison Avenue. The sidewalk was crowded with workers and shoppers, all happy, all moving briskly in the November chill. Kavanagh stepped into the rush. He was wearing neither a topcoat nor a hat, and this emphasized his clerical suit; passersby, as always, made way for him. Normally, aware of the impression he made as a priest in public, he would return the nods and smiles that the clerical collar drew from strangers, but not today. By the time he reached the nearest corner, he had to move out of the human current. *What's happening to me?* He pushed to a lamppost and leaned against the stout, grooved metal, clutching his breviary, indifferent to appearances. His breath was short again. He looked skyward, as words came unbidden into his mind. Perhaps he spoke them: *"Non credo."*

CHAPTER SEVEN

And, can you believe it, Philintus? Canon Fulbert allowed me the privilege of his table, and an apartment in his house. . . . You, my dear friend, know what love is; imagine then what a pleasure it must have been to a heart so inflamed as mine to be always so near the dear object of desire! I would not have exchanged my happy condition for that of the greatest monarch upon earth. I saw Héloïse, I spoke to her: each action, each confused look, told her the trouble of my soul. And she, on the other side, gave me ground to hope for every thing.

That first morning of what became their articulated attachment was, in fact, their eighth time together. They were in the cubicle off the main *scriptorium,* the large room in which the copyists tended to the Cathedral's collection of ancient texts. Abelard routinely held his tutorials there during Terce, when the Cathedral scribes, bound to the Hours, would be at choir, and he could offer instruction without an audience. Through a single small window cut a wedge of light that illuminated, for the necessary period, just the square of space the Master and his pupil needed to do their work. In the bright air stood a small table and a pair of chairs. Their table. Their chairs.

In truth, Peter Abelard's condition was not as happy as, much later, he made out to Philintus—as no one knew better than Héloïse herself. His infatuation with her had come at him like ambush, an assault of feeling made worse by the feeling's being necessarily and absolutely secret. In the early weeks, he had thought it secret from her, but wrongly. It had not occurred to Abelard that she could match him in fixation, even if she was made less distraught than he. A man of no carnal experience, he was far more afraid than he was delighted.

In what became his famous letter to Philintus, as in much-sung lyrics he himself went on to compose, he described a storm of exuberant lust that promptly blew through the wills and consciences of a pair of formerly disciplined ascetics. *The same house, the same love, united our persons and our desires. How many soft moments did we pass together! . . . We made use of all the moments of our charming interviews. In the place where we met we had no lions to fear, and the study of philosophy served us for a blind.* Héloïse well knew it was not like that, although she, too, would later look back through a scarlet lens. In fact, they were a pair of timid neophytes, gingerly circling each other.

Abelard and Héloïse now sat across from each other, as they had been doing, at this hour, twice a week for a month. They had fallen into a routine of stiff formality, a proper custom, and each assumed it must continue. Between them was a small stack of wax tablets on the likes of which Héloïse had been presenting her translations of Cicero and Ovid into Greek. At first, she had protested this novice exercise. Rome had surpassed Athens, and Rome's language—her own language—was the pinnacle of expression. She assumed that Master Peter was simply testing her knowledge of Greek, but she was wrong, as she began to understand this morning. He had come to his real subject aslant.

"*Metamorphoses,*" he said. "Ovid gives us the word for the transformation of essences. An ingenious coinage in our tongue, yet he has the word from the Greek."

"*Metamorphoses,*" she said, speaking the word not in Latin, but in Greek, with its proper accent. "Change of form."

"Precisely. But is 'change of form' possible? When 'one thing' becomes another, does it not cease to be 'one thing'? Can it really be 'another'? Translation is the case before us."

"*Anima* into psychē?"

"Good. The 'soul' in one language, yet something more like 'the mental faculty' in the other. Shades of distinction. Distinctions lost in the handing over from tongue to tongue. In your translations, sister, you do not succeed in carrying the full meaning of Ovid's thought from Latium to Attica." Master Peter indicated the tablets between them. "I find no equivalence."

"My translations are accurate," Héloïse said quietly. She picked up the stylus, to stop her hands. It looked like an oversized needle, a sharp-pointed utensil carved from the leg bone of a cow, the color of charred wood.

"Yes. Wonderfully so," Abelard said. "But accuracy is not equivalence. That is my point. No equivalence. Translation claims to be a kind of metamorphosis, but is not. No idea ever remains the same when it is translated. Not even when translated with such brilliance as yours. Give me an example from today's passage."

"An example?"

"Of metamorphosis."

"Actaeon, the hunter, into a stag, the hunted."

"Yes, good," the teacher said, but he could be seen to stifle a pang, and Héloïse supplied its source. Actaeon, the Theban hero, wandering through a forest, comes upon a sacred grove in a small lake of which the goddess Diana is bathing. Actaeon beholds her nakedness—the mystery of her maidenhead. For this violation, he is—snap!—changed into a four-legged animal. At the evocation of that pool, with its attendant nymphs, Héloïse, knowing more than Abelard, sensed how both of them were seized by an image of the goddess in her glistening wet flesh: Diana's arms raised to gather in the spray of her hair, her flawless breasts all the more alluring for being so innocently on display. As if to deflect an actual vision, Abelard's eyes fell, but Héloïse saw them settle upon the embroidered yoke of her own gown. Above a tightly laced bodice, the gray tufted fabric rose with her breathing. Despite having no experience of men, she knew that his mind, thus set loose, would conjure her breasts, too: tumescent, erect, like the breasts of striding female figures in marble, Minerva, Juno. Surely, the classic statues of Lutetia would have been his only points of reference for the womanly nude. But at that moment the flesh to be seen of Héloïse, in all apparent modesty, was nothing more than the hollow of her throat, set off by a thin golden chain. Her fuller neck would be a deep red, pulsing with life.

He composed his voice to say, placidly, "Still, identifying the animal with the prince, we are expected to regard the stag's fate as tragic."

She said, in her best pupil's voice, "Actaeon's own hounds kill the stag, not knowing it is Actaeon."

"But there's the point," he declared. "The stag *was* Actaeon, but *is* no more. Our identification is in error. The tragedy is false." Abelard tapped the topmost tablet, a teacherly gesture. He was now enacting a role, controlling himself. "The power of the myth," he continued with apparent calm, "lies in this deception. We grieve the slaying of the prince, when, in fact, a mere animal has met an animal's proper fate. By offering us one such instance of metamorphosis after another, a Roman, Ovid, not just drawing on the Greeks but mocking them, is showing us that there is no such thing as metamorphosis. Essences are not mutable. Things are what they are. That is all. It is an *urgent* point—a rebuttal, in anticipation of the mistake that comes later with Plotinus, the confusion of matter and form."

"But the chaos of primeval origins is transformed into the order of Rome." Héloïse, too, could perform. "Is that not the poet's true subject?"

"Indeed. You perceive the depth of things, girl."

"Why do you call me 'girl'? Why not 'woman'?"

"Why did you choose Actaeon? Of all the myths?"

Héloïse lowered her eyes, as if found out.

"Diana threw water in his face," Abelard said quietly. "The curse that changed him into a beast. Why?"

"Because he spied her."

"And saw?"

"Her body unclothed." Héloïse had the stylus now firmly between her two hands, pressing the thing as if to snap it in half, staring as if to see the exact moment of break. Then, all at once, she raised her face and brought her gaze directly to Peter Abelard's. Each of them was blushing. She said boldly, "But is there shame in a body unclothed, Master?"

"I would think not. 'And God saw every thing that He had made, and, behold, it was very good.'"

"But that was before the sin of Adam."

"Adam's sin was in loving Eve too much, nothing more."

"But the sin falls upon us all, so the Fathers instruct. We are 'the mass of perdition,' soul-wounded children of Eve. We come into the world naked, and our nakedness makes us ashamed."

"What norm of justice is it that accuses an innocent child in the presence of God, our most merciful judge, of the sin of the parents? That norm of justice would not stand in any court of man. Therefore, neither will it stand before the Judgment Seat of God. If the Doctrine of Ancient Sin means the innocent are doomed, then the doctrine is wrong." Abelard's words took on a sudden heat, as if he had debated this question in solemn disputation. "Is God cruel?" he asked. "Does God will the destruction of lives rather than the fulfillment of what He has created? What sort of God is this?"

"How do you renounce settled doctrine?"

"By thinking," he said quickly.

"About God?"

"About the simple question: who would sit blissfully for all eternity in the presence of a monster?" Peter Abelard challenged her with a fierce look.

Héloïse stared at him, her mouth agape.

In the great legend of their romance—*Under the pretext of studies, dear Philintus, she and I totally abandoned ourselves to love . . . there were more kisses than considerations of grammar*—concupiscence determined their fate. They were a lascivious pair who gave in to "hurtful desire," with dread consequences—the "calamity," in Abelard's own word. This was the lecherous story that a mutilated man later told, to appease his disapprovers and to assuage his guilt. In the story, he was the prime mover, the willful seducer; she the guileless quarry, though once incited to mad ardor she never recovered. But that trite saga of Eros explosively ignited, composed in the aftermath of an unspeakable punishment, deletes what was essential in the passion that first defined each of them, if separately.

For Héloïse, true, the manly beauty of her teacher, in combination with the physical charisma that drew legions to his lectures, was the beginning of attraction, but it was the free play of his *mind* that astounded her. He was unfettered not only by precept, but by power. "How can you say that?" she asked him more than once. His reply was constant: "I can say it because it is what I think." A savvy young woman, Héloïse sensed that, despite the self-assurance with which the Master carried himself, he was desperate for the praise of scholars. He would sacrifice, for reputation's sake, almost anything. But that "almost" was key, for the one offering he would not make in exchange for fame was the truth of his own thinking. And that, of course, was what brought him fame.

But now, in her presence, another force was at work, and she understood it before he did. Abelard came most fully into a towering intelligence when, for the first time in his life, he felt its engagement *physically.* The body of Héloïse, as it were, gave Abelard *his* body, and only then did he grasp the one proposition toward which he had been groping, even in philosophy, for years—namely, that the hard distinction between body and soul is false. Therefore, also, between ideal and real; between substance and form: "because it is what I think"! But thinking in this woman's presence was not what thinking had ever been before. Thus was fulfilled and released what had been an implicit, unadmitted impulse from their first meeting, in the Cathedral refectory, hemmed in by obnoxious young scholars, with Canon Fulbert standing by. Yet the first true coupling between the storied Abelard and Héloïse—and surely for these two it had to be like this—was *of the mind.* The furthest thing from profane desire, their connection was the sacred revelation of word become flesh— *incarnatus est.*

Abelard was hardly breathing, rock-still. Yet she sensed full well the new meaning of it when he circled back to the lesson. "Translation," he said at last, "is never fully true. There is no such thing as the total transformation of essences. A thing is only what it is."

Héloïse remained fixed upon the stylus between her fingers. "But what of the bread and wine?" she said, so quietly. "Transubstantiation. In Greek, *metousiosis.*"

Abelard did not reply. This was a swerve, as she knew it would be, for which he was not prepared.

She said, in her recitation voice, " 'But if the word of Elijah had such power as to bring down fire from heaven, shall not the word of Christ have power to change the nature of the elements?' That is Father Ambrose." She paused. She was in earnest, yet she was also extemporizing. " '*Hoc est enim Corpus Meum,*' " she said. "Bread into flesh. Wine into blood. If that is not metamorphosis, what is? The bread is no longer the bread. The bread has become the body of Christ. Christ Himself said those exact words—'*Hoc est enim Corpus Meum*'—which is why the priest must repeat the exact words. The words must be fully true to have such power. The exact words effect the change of substance . . . of essence."

"No, dear girl. *Not* those exact words." Abelard took refuge, again, in teacherly condescension. "The scrupulous priest, pronouncing each syllable for efficacy, is a superstitious fool, playing at magic. The Lord did not speak those exact words for the simple reason that He did not speak Latin. Saint Jerome spoke Latin. Father Ambrose spoke Latin. Not Jesus."

"Well, the Greek, then. The words Jerome translated. The meaning is the same."

"Not Greek, either. The Gospels are Greek, but Jesus was not. He spoke the language of Jewish peasants. A local dialect—not even Hebrew. Jesus spoke, and His words were translated by those who loved him. The translation was then translated again—still with love, yet with shifts in meaning at each point. Shifts in meaning not only in His words, but in the matter of the sacrament itself. This is not a trifling matter." Peter Abelard's gaze had fixed her, sternly. He went on, launched now in a serious discourse. "The bread He held up before the Apostles was not what we think of as bread, even at the Holy Mass. It was matzoh, of which we read in Exodus, the unleavened festival food of Jews. The Last Supper, before it was a Mass, was a Passover meal. Before it was Catholic, it was Jewish. Does that fact of the past change meanings of the present? How could it not? *Pascha. Missa.* The two things are not the same. Only in seeing that do we see the separate truth of what each one is. Was Jesus saying what we think He was saying? We cannot know with precision. The faith involves not meaning, but *meanings*. As for 'transubstantiation,' that high-flying word owes more to pseudo-philosophers than to the Lord. To Him, if He were here today, the word 'transubstantiation' would be babel."

Abelard reached across the table and closed his hand around her joined hands, the stylus. "Things are what they are. This writing instrument," he said quietly, "is only a writing instrument."

Héloïse shook her head. "No. Not now." She, the one who knew, met his eyes. "It is the instrument of our intimacy."

He rose from his chair, leaned forward, and placed his mouth upon hers. Surprising herself, she brushed the tip of her tongue against his lips, which opened. At that, she pressed the bone stylus against the pivot of her thumbs, but it did not break.

EVEN IN HOLY *places before the altar I carry the memory of the guilty loves I shared with you, Dear Peter . . . and, far from lamenting for having been seduced, I sigh for having lost them. I remember (for nothing is forgot by lovers) the time and place in which you first declared your love to me, and swore you would love me till death. Your words, your oaths, are all deeply graven in my heart.*

In the *scriptorium,* after that first kiss, they found themselves again and again embracing, bringing their clothed bodies together, a pair of novices whose moves were marked, soon enough, by an instinctive proficiency. Peter pressed his hands against her bosom, but, in that schoolroom, dared not unwind the back laces of her bodice, or push into the linen bands that kept her breasts high. For her part, Héloïse, acting on instincts she didn't know she had, pressed him through his rough woolen tunic, first at his shoulders and sides, then into his lap, below his cincture. She was startled to feel him aroused and stiffening there—startled and transported. When, once, her clutching hand sensed a throbbing inside the cloth, she recognized an instance of the storied ejaculation, even as his groans announced it. She was appalled that she had herself caused this animal response, but at the same time felt a thrust of her own feelings that was not so different. She was shy with this initiation, virginal. And she was afraid. Yet she found herself rubbing him like that again, and when he reached into the underskirts at the delta of her legs and pressed, she followed him up successive hills of sensation, unsure what was happening, but giving herself to it. Only when he pressed his hand against her mouth did she realize that she, too, was making dangerous noises.

In those first weeks, each time they arrived at the point where the only way forward was through the full stripping off of robes, skirts, and underclothing, they stopped. Rather, she stopped them—for her terror continued to outweigh the longing she was not prepared to acknowledge as lust. Only much later, in looking back, did she understand that that combination, dread and desire, defined the euphoria that had taken them captive.

The fullness of time was bound to come, and, with the Great Compline on the Solemnity of the Annunciation, with its prostrations, litanies, and venerations of icons, it did. The ceremony was followed by the festal night-collation of wine and cakes, an exceptional revel, which they knew would send all the Cathedral fellowship into the deepest of sleeps. After the Canons, choristers, acolytes, servants, and members of Canon Fulbert's personal household retired for the night, Héloïse and Abelard, separately, waited in their chambers, while the silence settled upon the Cloister. To that day's lesson, in the schoolroom, Abelard had brought a pair of small candle stubs, each the exact length of the other. He'd opened his palm, so that she could see them, and she'd understood at once. She had sensed his uncertainty—his hand was tremulous—but passed it by, taking a candle stub without comment. She quenched her own uncertainty by pretending not to feel it. This deliberate setting of a plan was blatant, and part of her marveled at her readiness to embark upon it. The other part simply trembled, whether with fear or anticipation she neither knew nor cared.

After the collation, they went to their separate quarters. Immediately after the Nunc Dimittis, the night dismissal chanted by the porter through corridors, hall, and dormitory, the Master and his pupil, before dousing their oil lamps, used them to light their small candles, and, hiding the glow, separately watched them burn to the point of extinction, which was the signal.

They quietly left their chambers to meet in the Cloister garden, where, beside the singing fountain, they embraced and kissed. Héloïse was cloaked and veiled, but, with his hands at her face, Peter jolted back at the realization that her long brown hair was unpinned and flowing, a downpour to her shoulders, the first time he had ever seen it so. He pushed the hood of her cloak down, exposing her head. He clutched fistfuls of her hair and roughly pulled her face to his. Overcome with trepidation, she turned her head away, but nevertheless clung to him. She yielded as he led the way toward a corner of the arcade, where there was a broad bench. But the wind was howling off the river. It was too cold. Peter stopped them, held Héloïse briefly at arms' length, then took her by the hand, saying, "Come."

Again, she yielded. He knew the way. His eyes were better in the darkness than hers. He led her into the gallery that brought them to the Cathedral porch, where he found the heavy door that opened into the downward spiral staircase. Their blind hands rode, as guides, on the rough stone wall as they descended into the crypt, where their eyes opened to the faintest light as they entered an eerie be-columned, low-vaulted chamber. Off the multiple stout pillars and ceiling groins, shadows bounced, thrown by the winking flame of the vigil candle that was kept burning in the distant chapel of our Lady of the Undercroft. The chapel nestled in the curved ambulatory, at the far end of the crypt, below the high altar in the apse of the Cathedral above. On the chapel walls, barely visible in the candlelight, were frescoes well known to show the great scenes of Mary—her Annunciation, Visitation, Nativity, and Assumption. Wall niches and shelves held clay vessels of sacred oil, and golden reliquaries. In the center of the chapel was an altar before which was spread, on the rough stone floor, a plush violet-hued woven fabric, a Moorish wall covering far too precious to be laid on the floor except here, in the sacred place reserved for priests and bishops. Embroidered with threads of gold and silver, the carpet was one of several that the Poor Fellow-Soldiers of Christ had brought back from Jerusalem. It was to the luxury of that soft, knotted pile that Abelard brought Héloïse.

What most surprised Héloïse was her own feeling of serenity. The few moments it had taken them to move from the Cloister garden, along the arcaded gallery, and down the spiraling stairs defined, for her, a great passage. True, Peter had been her guide in that climactic sojourn, but she had come to this brink of womanhood of her own will, so that she was ready for whatever was coming now. Having led her to the edge of the carpet, Peter began to pull her into his arms, but she turned away from him. She moved toward the wall, beside the sanctuary candle, which was as tall as a man, as round as a bread loaf, and giving off the sweet aroma of beeswax. Its flame danced above her, illuminating the ceiling groins, while leaving most of the chapel, with its stand of stout columns, in a web of interlocking shadows, which was all her modesty required.

Indeed, she was plainly visible as, with her back to Peter Abelard, she began to disrobe. His eyes were upon her, transfixed, and she knew that, to him, her clothing would be a mystery shrouding the further mystery. In methodically shedding it, she was being practical, not coy, yet her moves amounted to an instinctive heightening of anticipation—hers as much as his. She stepped out of her sandals. She tossed away her hooded surcoat. She unclasped the first of her two tunics, a dark red woolen garment, sashed with a golden cord, and draping only as far as her knees. It fell to her feet, a bloodlike pool. Her unbleached undertunic had a row of buttons running from the hollow of her throat to below the flat bone at her chest, and, though Peter could not see it, her fingers trembled to unfasten them, as much because of the cold crypt as in nervousness. Foreseeing this moment, she had not swaddled her breasts with linen bands, so that when, with one brisk movement of her arms and shoulders, she shrugged the tunic off, she was all at once naked.

She turned to face him. Later, she would wonder at the moral ease with which she so made a display of herself, yet that moment was an instance of nature's plain goodness—her own goodness. Without breathing, she watched as Peter Abelard, with his gaze never leaving her, removed his clothing. She sensed that her own calm had cued his. Having removed his boots and stood straight again, he, too, was naked then. He, too, was still. They were like a pair of pagan statues, unmoving, separated by the width of the carpet that came from Solomon's Temple. It was as if their only purpose was to behold each other. What Héloïse saw in Peter, more clearly than before, was love.

Which of them moved first? They would never know. They stepped forward at the same instant, and came together, flesh against flesh at last. At his touch, her skin itself snapped alive. Peter's arms encircled her waist, his fingers cupped her buttocks, his chest pressed hard against her breasts. His lips took her lips, she took his tongue again, the rough taste of wine. He lifted her high off the floor with strength that gave her a first physically felt perception of his manly vigor. He swung her up into the cradle of his arms, his mouth never leaving hers. She clung to him. He rocked her. She floated. But then, sinking, she half fainted, suddenly at the mercy of a mystical weightlessness, only to realize that he wasn't falling, but genuflecting, his right knee to his left heel. Leaning over, he placed her with exquisite tenderness on the soft woven fabric before the Virgin's altar—an offering. Her gaze snagged on his tonsure, the cap of flesh that marked him for a man of Holy Orders. A vowed cleric! The word "sacrilege" leapt into her mind. To banish it, she looked away, only to find herself caught by the sight, on the near wall, of the Blessed Virgin kneeling before the angel Gabriel, and now the word was Mary's: *"Fiat"!*—"Be it unto me!"

On her back, arching up, she opened her legs for him, and, with his muscled naked torso, he slid between them, a river vessel into its slip. Clamping his waist with her knees, she joined her ankles. Somehow, so it seemed, they both knew just what to do—until they didn't.

With his groin, he pushed at her groin. He grew rough, sawing back and forth. The grip of her legs slipped, and she rewound them. He startled her with a foul grunt—the animal again. He had tried to enter her, but she was certain that he had failed. He pulled his face back to look in hers, and when she sought the caress of his eyes, what she found instead was the twisted expression of a stranger.

"Oh," he said, "Oh!"—an ugly, guttural sound, but she recognized a plea. Reaching down to him, she found a way to help, and he began to push her along the carpet. An excruciating pain sliced through her. For an instant, she felt herself pulling away in her mind with a feeling of disgust, for he *did* seem an animal. She tossed her face aside, rejecting his mouth. But then pain gave way to an expansive wave of tingling as, well inside her now, he found his rhythm. She found hers. She looked at him, and he was looking back at her. The stranger was gone. This was Peter, her dear Peter.

Later, they lay together, with Abelard leaning up against the cold marble of the altar, and Héloïse leaning against him. They were covered only with his ample cloak, a cleric's cope. The candle-thrown shadows danced around the vaulted crypt. " '*Quod factum est, in ipso vita erat,*' " he said. "We have it from the Gospel of John." Abelard had only to whisper now, so close were his lips to her ear. " 'Whatever was made, there was God's life in it.' "

"It says not 'God's,' " she replied. "Where in that text find you 'God's'?"

"That is the meaning of 'life,' dear one," he replied. "Wherever there is life, there is God. 'I am come that you may have life, and have it more abundantly.' And when have we had life if not here? In this?" His hand, beneath the cloak, was cupping her breast.

"I need not God to know life's abundance," she said, "or to love it."

"But life here points to life there. And so with love. Our love is a sacrament of God's presence. Therefore, not profane."

"You muster an argument against yourself, brother, not me." She laughed. Having been slightly embarrassed at the discovery of their sexual competency, she was embarrassed now at his urge to sacralize it. "What need have we of the sacrament here?" she asked. "Isn't the love enough?" Under the cloak, his hand was moving toward her waist.

"But, surely, dear one . . ." He hesitated.

She sensed the return of his interest.

He continued, ". . . our presence here, in the Virgin's sanctuary, requires a rebuttal to that long history of denial. To all who would take offense, I simply want to say, God takes no offense."

"God's offense?" To her astonishment then, she realized that offending God had yet to cross her mind. She was satiated. What had God to do with this? Years later, looking back, she would express this sensation of pure carnality—carnality's purity—with robust language, an affirmation that would strike some as liberating and others as lewd. But not now. She was shy still—yet a stranger in the realm of lost virginity. Her happiness was full enough to include the necessary pang of sadness; her womanliness enough to include how she was still a girl. The moment was enough.

He was missing her mood. He shrugged. "I only mean to say that the Church made a terrible mistake in opposing the physical and the spiritual . . . body and soul. . . . We reverse that mistake, you and I. This is . . ." His hand now was between her legs. His breath caught. ". . . the sanctification . . . of desire."

As she moved her mouth toward his, she said, "Perhaps so, dear Peter. But also . . . this is just a kiss—a wanton kiss."

CHAPTER EIGHT

After their arrest, Rachel Vedette defined her father's survival as her only purpose, and came to understand that if she did not succeed in getting him through whatever befell them, then he would never not be the ghost at her elbow, the opaque figure blocking light, a permanent companion; pure shadow. And it came to be so.

She'd failed him; no, worse. Horrors followed for her, but nothing to compare to his loss. A barred door swung closed on the deepest part of herself, which isolated her, but protected her, too—if a wall of numbness can be called protection. Eventually, she knew that, unlike her father, she would live, but she also knew that she would not live long enough to see that barred door open, ever. Survival, too, would be imprisonment.

Her father's evanescent presence had come to form the core of her condition: him, with his yarmulke, his pipe, his bowl-stained fingers, his glinting spectacles, his shirt lifted above a pinch of flesh at his waist, his benign expression of gratitude, his mute refusal to look at her at the end. He inhabited her.

Here he was on the tattered daybed in her fifth-floor walk-up room in Hoboken, New Jersey; beside her on the seat in the bus coming through the Lincoln Tunnel; at the next strap on the A Train; at her elbow on the path through Fort Tryon Park; on the stone bench in the Chapter House of the Cloister from La Chapelle-sur-Loire. What fellow commuters and museum co-workers, what ladies in from Westchester, even what lilting chants and luminous tapestries Rachel Vedette found herself surrounded with every day—it all registered only at the glinting surface. The presences of persons and things were chimerical compared with his. In the greatest part of herself, she was simply never not back there, with his head hazily on her shoulder; and therefore never not back even further, to the time that had given him hope—the time of the Latin letters she carried, tokens of remembered hope.

By the end of July, two weeks after the initial arrests, about five thousand Jews of Paris had been transported from the Vél' d'Hiv to someplace less than an hour's ride, in traffic, from central Paris. In that transit, in the dark of the shrouded military truck, Rachel had paid attention, counting the stops and starts, trying to sense where they were being taken. She willfully clamped down on any other sensation so she could stay alert and cling fiercely, all the while, to her father's arm with one hand and to her suitcase with the other. When the truck halted at last and the canvas was thrown back, Rachel saw that their truck was one of dozens lined up in the center of a vast horseshoe-shaped housing complex made of huge, linked concrete buildings the shape of tissue boxes. Judging from haphazard scaffolding, flapping canvas, and boarded windows here and there, the multistory apartments and commercial structures were unfinished, but legions of bundle-bearing Jews were being herded out of the trucks, lined up, and directed into one block or another. French policemen were again the enforcers, and, again, men in dark civilian suits were supervising. Germans.

Rachel, assessing quickly, saw that the males among the prisoners, from her truck and others, were being channeled in one direction, while women, children, and elders were being driven in another. With alarm, she saw that girls and young women were being singled out, and corralled. All across the yard, inside an enormous ring of barbed wire, orders were being barked loudly, more by the Germans than by the Frenchmen. The ugly language hung in the air, along with the noise of truck engines, the clatter of pushcarts, and bursts of static from ill-functioning loudspeakers. Helping her father down from the truck, Rachel was unable to prevent him from stumbling again. This time, his yarmulke fell from his head. Before she could retrieve it, a gendarme stepped quickly forward to bring his stout polished boot down on the circle of cloth, crushing it. Rachel fixed him with her stare, and waited for his eyes to find hers. Her contempt outweighed his. He was barely older than she. His loutish smile faded, and, despite himself, he stepped back. Saul bent over to pick up the skullcap, muttering as he did, *"Kiddush Hashem."*

Once, her father would have had no need of reinforcement against such a crude fool. Saul Vedette's resolve had not faded, but the strength needed to act upon it had drained almost entirely away. Rachel pressed forward to confront the gendarme. "Thank you, sir, for giving us the occasion to bless God's name."

In the face of her ferocious expression, the *flic* blushed, which passed, in that circumstance, for an unwilled apology. He pointed the way toward the muster point where prisoners were being sorted, and Rachel, holding her father's arm, pushed into a knot of old women. As Rachel hoped, they registered as a group more by age than gender, and so her father blended in as just another elder, and he was not taken off with the other men. Soon they found themselves in a halting procession—more like circus animals than vested clerics or marching soldiers—that took them ultimately, two and three at a time, through the narrow door of a seven-story apartment building, into a stairwell where the dusky air, shut off from daylight, was moist with heat. They climbed to the third level, followed a dark corridor, and filed into a large, open room, well lit by windows, crowded with double- and triple-stacked bunks, and divided by two aisles.

Rachel quickly put the count of aged couples, mothers with toddlers, widows, and a few stooped old men, some with canes, at seventy or eighty. The terrazzo floor of the space was littered, she saw, with tiny black specks, and only as she crushed them underfoot, with crackles, did she recognize the carcasses of flies. She pushed ahead, dragging her father, to claim their space with the toss of her coat and suitcase—a two-tiered bunk in the far corner of the room. She chose it for its relative isolation, hoping for distance from the general disorder, and for safety.

Later, after a plump but dignified woman in a rumpled, once-stylish tweed suit helped them negotiate the unswabbed latrine, Rachel helped Saul into the lower bunk, a plank bed with a thin straw mattress and a single threadbare blanket. She removed his shoes, retrieved the cushioning pillow from her suitcase, and arranged it for him. She covered him. Then, discreetly preparing his needle, she injected him. She kissed his forehead. Almost at once, he was asleep.

When he woke, she was sitting beside him, stooped under the upper bunk, and she told him part of what she had learned in her quick scouting of their new quarters. "This place," she whispered, "was built to be a modern planned city, apartment towers and businesses. The war came before it was finished. When the Germans moved in, they used it as a barracks; then for British prisoners. Now us." She smiled, as if the irony of their place in this sequence pleased her.

What she was not telling her father was that, on the fifth floor of this very block, two flights up, she had found a dispensary, which was still in the process of being assembled. That the medical unit, a long trek up a nasty stairwell, would hardly be accessible to the general population was a signal more of deliberate callousness than of bad planning. She had met the nervous young medic who was assigned as its clerk, and whose duties, he said, would include obtaining neces- sary medicines. She was in his presence only briefly. As she left the dispensary, she had pretended to stumble, brushed against him, and hurriedly moved away, but not before sensing his interest. She sensed, also, how his eyes followed her as she walked away.

Her father, she saw, was listening carefully when she said, "We are less than twenty kilometers from Île Saint-Louis, a place called Drancy, in the district of Seine Saint-Denis."

He stirred. "Ah! Saint-Denis. So named because of the monas- tery." He half sat up, clutching her sleeve. "His monastery."

"Whose?" Rachel asked.

"Peter Abelard's," her father insisted. "Peter Abelard's! After the catastrophe at Notre-Dame, Benveniste brought him here! Benveniste saved his life by bringing him to the monks of Saint-Denis."

"A good omen for us, then, Father," Rachel said. "We, too, will be saved at Saint-Denis."

Saul let his head fall back on the mattress. Unconsciously, he reached to adjust his yarmulke, then remembered. He removed the skullcap to look at it, the smudges of mud. He kissed it, then placed it beside his pillow.

"HELLO."

Rachel looked up from her book. A man was standing only yards from her, in the center of the Chapter House. She saw at once, from his getup, that he was a priest. Then she realized it was the man from the day before, only now dressed in his black suit and Roman collar. As before, his breviary was under his arm. His other book—Simone Weil?—was gone. How long had he been positioned there? "Good day, Father," she said quietly.

"I was just coming back to Inwood from downtown," he said, "and I thought I'd stop in to my new memory palace." He grinned, but unconvincingly.

Rachel sensed an edge of sadness in him. Or was that her own projection, an imposition on a passerby of the desolation he had interrupted? Coming back to herself, she retrieved the sensations of her actual situation: the queasiness in her belly; the cold beneath her buttocks from the stone bench on which she'd been seated through her lunch hour; the chill in her shoulders from the stone wall. That her stomach was queasy might have been a symptom of the culprit-angst that had seized her years before, and never yielded, but, really, it was only an effect of not having eaten. She never ate during the day. Hunger was so much a part of her normal state that, apart from an arid intestinal hollowness, she did not feel it.

"The Cloisters," he said, casting his eyes about. "I'm embarrassed to have ignored this place all these years."

"I am glad for you, Father, that you found the museum. Glad also for us." She spoke formally. Her mind was still partly tethered to that room crowded with tiered plank beds; its air of fear and despair; the metallic gray wash that, in her recall, always veiled the scene like an antique etching of Dante's netherworld. Only by a concerted act of will was she able to return here, a transition through time and space that, whenever she accomplished it, marked her as a woman still capable of hope. To come back from memory was, in some way, to believe that its injury could be left behind. Yet whenever her current life took precedence over the past—the mundane over the terrible, strangers over Papa—she had, first, to shake herself loose from shame.

She forced herself to focus on the figure before her. That this New York priest was an altogether impressive-looking man surprised her. Yesterday, in his plaid shirt and windbreaker, he'd seemed smaller, uncertain. Now he appeared as a man of authority. His black suit emphasized the sharp black of his hair, a lock of which hung as a ringlet on his forehead, an accident. Yesterday his hair had been matted from the rain.

"Yes. I'm glad, too," he said absently, still glancing here and there. He *did* seem somewhat awed, but he said only, "I've been thinking about this place since yesterday. The surprise it was. Hard to explain, but a feeling from the past had brought me here, and then, lo and behold, the past is the whole point. What you said about being consoled, the museum as a sanctuary."

"That sounds pompous. Did I say that?"

"Something like it."

"'Memory palace'? Surely, I did not say that."

He smiled, but again thinly. A grimace, really. "No, I guess I did," he said. He made as if to join her on the bench, then stopped himself, saying, "I have the feeling I owe you an apology, but I'm not sure why."

"Apology? That is not true, Father. For one thing, I am the one who rudely walked away."

"Because I was about to overstep? Am I overstepping now?"

"You tell me."

He turned to watch a pair of museumgoers pass by, guidebooks in hand. Then he faced her again. "I'd had an odd experience yesterday morning, at Good Shepherd. Somehow, it brought me here. And then you. You made me think of Simone Weil, as I said."

"Because Simone Weil, also, was odd?" Rachel Vedette heard the harsh note in her question, and of course, as before, she'd corrected his mispronunciation of the philosopher's name—"vey" instead of "wile." She did not understand why this priest was grating on her. Yet his forwardness was forced, and came as a kind of plea.

Harsh note? He did not seem to hear it that way. He said, "She challenged the faith of the Church—not faith in Christ, but in itself. Her refusal to be baptized called the whole thing into question. I think that's why we can't shake her. We Catholics, I mean. I'm not sure about other people."

"Like Jews."

"No. I meant the others who go on about her, the magazine writers, the New York intellectuals."

"Jews."

The priest took a while to answer, long enough for Rachel Vedette to regret how she was reacting to him. Standing before her as he was, he seemed almost a supplicant, which made him, perhaps, a bit resentful. She wished that she'd invited him to sit, but it seemed too late for that. They'd fallen into the rhythm of debaters—not at all the way she normally responded, especially to museum visitors whose claim on her deference was absolute. Something else was at work.

He said, "I'll admit that your being Jewish did strike me . . . struck me as, well, yes, odd. But that's because of where we are, where *you* are. Given what this place once was, a Catholic monastery." Kavanagh let his eyes drift to the girdered glass canopy that stretched above the Cloister garden. "It's different in here," he said, "when the sun is shining." Lifting his book, he gestured with it, sweeping across the light-splashed quadrangle.

She clutched her own book to her chest. "Do you add that thought to avoid talking about my being a Jewess?"

His head jolted at her blunt question. "I thought that was an offensive word."

She shook her head no. "Jewess," she repeated. Shifting away from debate style, she struck her docent tone, the one asserting that she was in possession of explanations. "The word 'Jewess' is, how do you say, *archaic* in English. Not so in French. *Juif. Juive.*" She shrugged. "The offense is in the intention. In your language, leaving 'Jewess' aside, the very word 'Jew' can be offensive."

"How?"

She shrugged again. " 'Jew lawyer.' 'Jew down.' "

"Is it different in French?"

"In French there is blood on the word, buckets of blood."

Kavanagh hesitated. "I thought . . . German."

"French also. *'Youde'* is an *insulte raciale*. But, Father . . . ?"

"Kavanagh."

"Father Kavanagh, how quickly we came to this thicket. 'Complications of being Jewish,' you said yesterday. Is this what you meant?"

"No. Not at all. I meant nothing. But I'm surprised you remember the phrase I used."

Rachel, too, was surprised—that these after-impressions of their first encounter had lingered. As if to change the mood, she shifted her weight on the bench, adjusting her long skirt, crossing one leg over the other, laying her book to the side. The priest, even standing, unconsciously imitated her, letting a nearby column take half his weight. He put his book down on the ledge. His pose became more casual, hands in his pockets. If she had not thought of him since the day before, she recognized now, neither had she quite dispelled the uneasiness he had stirred in her—uneasiness she was fending off by being uncharacteristically brisk and curt.

She had few interactions with men, which was, in fact, a consequence of how she'd arranged her life. Except for the Director, whose main office was downtown, her colleagues at The Cloisters were women, as were most of those museumgoers who showed up for her little tours. Was it also, though, that to her, inevitably, a priest was in a category apart? A man, yes, but not a man to be taken as such.

Which, it now occurred to her, was just the point. Simone Weil's priest, the epistolary interlocutor in her most famous book, was apparently the only man she ever trusted—and wouldn't that have been for the obvious reason? Rachel Vedette realized that this American priest, just by pairing her with the self-punishing French misanthrope, had set this current of negative energy flowing. But was that his fault?

If she was bugged by something, so, apparently, was he. Instead of letting the subject go, he said, "It bothered me, what you said about Simone Weil's anti-Semitism. I found myself repeating it to others."

"Why?" she asked. She was struck by his mispronunciation, again, but this time let it go, to add, "Anti-Semitism is a fact."

"I know that," he said firmly. "As a Catholic, I am surrounded by it. I'm probably guilty of it."

"That, actually, is not the sentiment of an anti-Semite. But, Father, we have done the thing again. This is not the conversation of people passing one another in a museum. I promise you, I never discuss being Jewish here. It is never a subject." At that, even she heard the relief in her voice. She could have said, *Avoiding such subjects is why I came to America . . . why I live as a recluse . . . why no one knows anything about me.*

"So I *do* owe you an apology." Kavanagh laughed. "I knew it. I knew it."

In saying this, he was so wholly ingenuous that, to Rachel's amazement, she, too, laughed—laughed out loud.

As a way of doggedly perfecting her English during her first year in New York, she had gone to the cinema every chance she got, and suddenly she realized that he reminded her of one of those Jimmy Stewart characters, which made her laugh harder. *Yes, that's it. Jimmy Stewart.* Even the way he was leaning against the stone column, with his hands in his pockets, the fugitive curl so unselfconsciously on his forehead, that slightly doltish but compelling American masculinity, laced as it was with an essential innocence—a goodness.

Aware of her own sudden sparkle, and wanting to explain it, she said, "When you say, 'I knew it. I knew it,' like that, you make me think of those fellows in movies, although in movies they add nonsense phrases like 'By golly' and 'Gee whiz.'"

Kavanagh welcomed her turn toward levity, and he matched it, saying, somewhat goofily, "Slang toss-aways designed to avoid taking the Lord's name in vain."

"You are not serious."

"Sure I am. 'By golly' is 'By God.' 'Gee whiz' is 'Jesus.' "

At that, they both laughed again, harder, handing themselves over to the absurdity of such nonsense. And then, within a matter of moments, recovering themselves, they both fell awkwardly into silence. Rachel felt foolish, and sensed that he did, too.

Seeking to swat the awkwardness away, she said, "In French, we just say *'Mon Dieu'* and refuse to worry about it. You Americans are a nation of delicate conscience. We French know nothing about conscience."

When Rachel saw the priest's expression display a moment's confusion, she guessed that it disoriented him to think of her as French instead of as Jewish. Or had he made the switch? Not so long before, in Rachel's world, the categories were mutually exclusive.

But he knew no more of that contradiction than a Jimmy Stewart character would have. And, sure enough, with an air of "Aw shucks," he said, "As a priest, of course, I know everything about conscience."

The statement was meant to be self-mocking, but it fell flat. The silence settled once more. He took his hands from his pockets and stood up straight, away from the column. He retrieved his breviary from the ledge, turned slightly toward the garden, and looked up. Clouds had crossed into the sky above the canopy, and a chill had returned to the space, which was neither outdoors nor fully in. Rachel, who almost never noticed the loop of Gregorian chant that ran endlessly in the Cloister air, heard it now—a choir of monks, of Catholic clergy, men like this one.

"Yesterday," she said slowly, "when I turned to walk away, you had indicated that you wanted to tell me something."

"Which was why you turned."

"Yes."

"You saw how I'd arrived here. Driven by the rain, half lost, strangely defenseless. Are you inviting me to return to that moment?"

Very quietly, she answered, *"Peut-être.* Perhaps." And immediately she asked herself why—*Why am I doing this?* But then she knew. Only fifteen minutes ago, in her memory, she had been cradling her father's head in the lower bunk at Drancy, fully aware of what she would willingly do to give him a chance to live. Simone Weil's self-loathing was nothing compared with hers. Now she said, "Is that not the magic of your Confessional box—unburdening oneself to a stranger?"

"Golly," Kavanagh said, but without a hint of mockery now. He looked directly at her, and she found it possible not to look away.

They were still alone. She was still seated on the stone bench, against the stone wall of the Chapter House—the place of monastic self-abnegation. He was upright before her again, like a medieval sup-plicant, yes—presenting himself to the Abbot? But who was she to have such an association?

He said, "Unburden? The truth is, yesterday the question was simple. Today it is vastly more complicated."

" 'Complications.' "

"Miss, I wouldn't have a clue how to speak of what . . ." He let the sentence hang. Finally, he went on, "But if I did, something tells me—forgive me—I could speak of it to you."

Rachel wanted to nod, or offer some gesture of acceptance. But she did not. She had no idea where the impulse to invite his con-fidence had come from, nor was it followed now by anything else like it. She was relieved—grateful—that he was incapable of saying more. If one confides . . . complications . . . in a stranger, does the stranger not become a friend? If a Confessional box offers immunity from unwanted intimacy, why not a Chapter House—the place, as she routinely explained to tourists, where, chapter by chapter, the viola-tions of Saint Benedict's rule were confessed, punished, and forgiven? She was a connoisseur of the setting, and it might indeed have made it possible for her to offer some gentle word, something personally noncommittal, but nothing came to mind.

CHAPTER NINE

At the end of a garden, the wall which I scaled by a ladder of ropes, I met my soul's joy, my Héloïse. I shall not describe our transports, they were not long; for the first news Héloïse acquainted me with plunged me in a thousand distractions. A floating Delos was to be sought for, where she might be safely delivered of a burthen she began already to feel. Without losing much time in debating, I made her quit the Canon's house.

It was Peter Abelard, not Héloïse, who needed some sort of objective confirmation of her condition. By the time of this garden encounter, she had resolved the womanly riddle for herself, but what could he know of such things?

The absence of blood flow from between her legs, groin-fire, nausea, painful tenderness and discharge in her breasts—Héloïse had come to the understanding with trepidation. She took to pressing against the folding door of her vulva the small purse of silk that held a sliver of the veil of the Virgin Mary. Her own mother had, in that way, applied the relic to herself during many confinements, but Héloïse shuddered to recall that, in the end, the holy object had done no good. Her mother's eighth child had become impossibly lodged in the channel of her womb, and both the child—a boy—and her mother had died. Héloïse, as a girl of thirteen, had stood by, pressing damp cloths against her screaming mother's forehead—until she cried out no more.

As for Héloïse tonight, her screaming was silent. God's Mother might have been expected to mock one whose conceiving had had more to do with transports of grunting flesh than with angelic visitation, but God's Mother, too, was husbandless, ready for shame. Indeed, Héloïse chose to believe that God's Mother would be more stirred than vexed by the *secretum secretorum*. Héloïse, for her part, was vexation itself. And now, as this meeting approached, there had been not only God's reaction to fear, but Peter's.

Yet, once again, when she finally turned to him, his large heart took her by surprise. He was waiting for her at the garden wall, expecting something else. She went into his arms, but there was no question of yielding to him—or to herself, for that matter. "My darling Peter," she said with forced calm, "tonight we must do our talking at the start, not the finish. I have things to say to you."

He pulled his face back from hers, holding her then with his eyes more than his arms. She sensed it as he read what was written in her expression. "What, my dear one?" he asked quietly.

Beside the wall was a stone bench, and they moved to it. It was a midsummer night, in the stretch of time when all in the Cathedral close were hard asleep, well before the sounding of Matins. An ample moon was high in the sky, and in its light the settle stone glistened with the film of river dew. The air was cool. Each wore a woolen cloak, and each drew it close as they sat, ignoring the moisture on the bench. Héloïse spoke of her circumstance with measured cadence, a report she had rehearsed in her mind. Peter allowed her to complete her explanations. Then he simply drew her into the shelter of his arm. For a long time, they clung to each other.

Finally, he said, "We must be sure."

"I am sure."

"Hippocrates recorded cases of phantom parturition."

Héloïse laughed, though she was in no way amused.

Peter blushed. Even he saw the obtuseness of what he'd said, the cowardice of it. "I did not mean that," he offered. "The first reaction of a dolt. Let me say instead what I truly mean . . . what matters most and first. We must see that *you* are properly cared for. Your uncle—"

"My uncle will regard you as the source of mortal dishonor." Suddenly, Héloïse pulled herself away from him, turning to clutch at his tunic, making fists around the fabric with which to shake him. "He will be terrified of my cousin's reaction; he will grovel before the Bishop, to deflect the loss of his benefice"—such was the litany of dread to which, night after night, Héloïse had submitted; it poured from her now—"while the Bishop, imagining me as more Royal than I am, will fear for the King's honor. For all of this, my uncle will be deranged with anger, but that is the least of it. Our child will be deformed—"

"Héloïse—"

"No! Listen to me: 'Corrupt unions produce corrupt children.' You know that."

"I know no such thing."

"It's the *Decretum*."

"The *Decretum* be damned. Is our union corrupt?"

"If the child is whole, the Church will seize him as its slave. *Filius nullius.* The son of one tonsured is the 'son of no one.' He will be a thrall, and you've seen even *here* how such poor bastards are treated." Héloïse's fear was well founded, for in the wake of the Gregorian Reforms, the Church was just then imposing fierce new disciplines on clergy. This was happening in the name of chastity, but even Héloïse knew that the real issue was lucre: when the ordained men died, their putative wives, sons, and even concubines were laying claim to the properties over which the tonsured class presided—from Pope, Bishop, and Abbot down to parish priest and oratory chaplain. Therefore, clerics and monks had to be universally reined in, the entitlement of ecclesial heirs eliminated. The most efficient way to do that was to enslave the sons of all who'd undergone the laying on of hands. Enthrallment was a present solution and a future deterrent.

"If the child is female," Peter insisted, "the Church will care nothing for her, whether I wear the tonsure or not."

"The child is male."

"You cannot know this."

"But I do. Joanna showed me."

"Joanna knows of your condition?"

"She is my maidservant. Of course she knows."

"What did she show you?"

"A drop of leakage from my breast, into a bowl of water. If it floats, a girl child. But in my case, it sank. A boy."

"In what text does Joanna find such a method of assessment?"

"The text of what women know."

"There are other texts, my lady." Peter silenced her by drawing her face into the hollow of his neck. "And for tonight, our concern is not with the child, but with you—and you alone." A burst of feeling stopped her lover from speaking more, and Héloïse read it. Unspoken between them now was the fate of *her* mother, but Héloïse had described that horror to Peter, and he knew that she had never put it out of her mind. For them, it was the particular instance of the general condition—that bringing a child into the world was the most dangerous thing a woman could do, a brutal God's punishment of baneful Eve.

Abelard collected himself, and said, "We must learn what you need. We must be sure that you are well."

With her face closed into the cleft of Peter's throat, the dolors of Héloïse seemed wholly private, and she wept. That she was carrying a child conceived in sin—a humpback child, an imbecile—brought implications she could not openly acknowledge. In truth, the near-certain deformation of her child defined her fear as much as the dangers of delivering him. The only reprieve from her anguish came from this fresh taste of Peter's love, which alone outweighed her worry. His love—pure, constant—redeemed the iniquity of what they had done.

After a time, he said, "Come now." He stood, pulled up his cowl, less for warmth, she sensed, than to cover his tonsure. He still could not be seen with her alone, even in the night. Especially in the night. She let him adjust the hood of her cloak, so that she, too, was covered. Nor did she resist as he led her out of the garden, through the horse-gate, into the lane that ran along the north wall of the close. Because of the moon, once they were out of the shadow of the looming Cathedral, the hooded pair could make their way without a torch, and Peter moved them along as if he knew just where to go. She let him lead her, consoled to have, finally, yielded her will.

Soon they were in the ghostly warren of shuttered market stalls, a silhouetted salmagundi of vacant lean-tos and booths, where rats scurried away at their passing, and where the stench of melon spoilage and butcher's offal rose from the runnel that divided the street. Peter nudged her away from the scummy puddles, while Héloïse, leaning into him, carried her skirts. At one point, an upended miller's cart blocked the way, and for a moment Héloïse feared the obstacle as the trick of thieves, but Peter, releasing her, simply hoisted the cart up and, with a grunt, pushed it aside. No thief would challenge such a man.

When he took her by the arm again, she asked, "Where are we going?"

He said, "To one who knows."

Again she yielded to him. When they left the market labyrinth behind, the street narrowed even further, now hemmed in on both sides by huts made of woven sticks and dried mud. As they went deeper into the quarter, huts yielded to timber-framed houses with second stories. The structures loomed over the street, blocking the open night sky and its moon, plunging the couple into a tunnel of shadows. Here the stench of the market gave way to aromas of curdled milk, boiled roots, and dampened ash. Héloïse felt a wet breeze on her face—the river again. Therefore, they were not far from the north bank of the city island.

"Wait," she said. "Where are we?"

"Just come," Peter answered.

"No." She stopped and pulled away. "Where are we?"

"Vicus Judaeorum."

"The Jews' quarter!" Now she understood her discomfort. The district between the market and the river was forbidden to Christian ladies. She had never entered it. "Why are you bringing me here?"

"Prince Isaac ben Joseph Benveniste. He has what we need tonight. Wisdom and science."

"Prince? What prince?"

"Prince among the Hebrews," Abelard muttered. "They say *'nasi.'* We say 'prince.'"

Benveniste was the Elder of Elders, a sage from Toledo, in the Kingdom of Castile. He had come to Paris to establish an academy for the study of Talmud, but holy books were only part of his expertise. Among Jews, he was a legend on both sides of the Pyrenees.

"And he receives intruders in the depth of night?" she asked.

"Shh . . . shh . . . dear woman. We are not intruders."

"Peter, we cannot do this."

"We are doing it. The depth of night is the best hour. No one will know of our meeting."

"Meeting? Where?"

"Here." At that, he turned and rapped softly on a nearby door.

"We cannot do this," she hissed.

But Peter Abelard did this once a fortnight. With all discretion, he regularly presented himself to Benveniste for instruction in the texts coming from al-Andalus, and for tutoring in the language of the Moors. But on this night, medicine was the point, and Prince Isaac was a master there, too, knowing the herbals and the lapidaries; knowing the four humors, and the course of blood. But Héloïse was still resisting, pulling back from the door. Abelard held her close, to whisper, "The King—*our* King—has given him the Physician's Privilege."

"Physician! My condition is a matter for midwives, not physicians—women, not men."

"I honor your superior knowledge, dear Héloïse. I admit my ignorance. But on matters of the body's well-being, Prince Isaac is the wisest man in Paris. From birth to death."

"How do you know him?"

"He is my tutor."

"He is your Jew? What they say of Abelard and 'his Jew' is true?"

"Perhaps, depending on what they say."

"That your mind is turned," she said. "A Jew has twisted your thought. Your enemies say that."

"Would that my mind could be turned by such a one. It is true, I entrust my thought to Prince Isaac."

"And now you would entrust me?" She clutched at his garment, insistent.

Abelard reined in his impatience. He well knew that the Iberian Moors had opened the secrets of medicine to the Jews—secrets of Hippocrates and Galen and Ibn Sina. Secrets that did indeed have to do with childbirth, whatever women said. Still with his voice lowered, though it was now laced with impatience, he said, "I will not have you burning incense to planets and frogs. . . ." He might have added, such was the wisdom of the women, *and sucking on the severed right foot of a crane.* Instead, he said, "When your time comes, I will not have you clutching a piece of the toenail of Saint Mary of Magdala."

"Of Saint Margaret."

"Who died a virgin. Why should a virgin be the patroness of the pregnant?" He covered her hands with his, pressing them. "Rationality, dear Héloïse. That is what we need. You know this of your own experience. . . ."

Héloïse buried her face against him.

Peter stroked her, saying, "I am thinking of your dear mother."

Her voice was muffled when she said, "I think of nothing else."

"Then it is settled," he told her. "We must know what your well-being actually requires."

She pulled back, looked at him, and began, "You are the only man to whom I reveal myself. You must—"

Before Héloïse could object further, the door opened. A white-bearded man appeared, his craggy face illuminated by the flame of an oil lamp he held at his breast. On his head he wore an odd three-pointed cap. He stood in what she now saw as an exceptionally solid door frame, to one side of which was nailed a small tube of parchment. Protruding from above the door was the timbered overhang of a second story. Héloïse took a step back and lowered her head, hiding her face in the shadow of her hood. Yet she saw it when the Jew lifted the flame before Peter, to make him visible.

"Master Peter Abelard," the Jew said.

"Your Holiness." Peter half bowed. "Forgive this violation of the peace of your household. We are in great need of your counsel."

For a long time, the Jew was silent and impassive. Finally, without a word, he stepped aside. Peter led Héloïse into the house, and the Jew pulled the door closed behind them. In two corners of the first room, barely more than a vestibule, were blanketed sleepers. They did not stir. Servants. If the Jew had family, they would be on the warmer floor above, in the eaves.

Peter seemed to know where to go, and he crossed into a second, larger room, where a pair of benches flanked a hearth in which embers smoldered. In from a third room washed a cone of yellow light, and Peter went directly there. Héloïse followed. A slightly elevated ceiling accommodated an arrangement of shelving that covered two walls. The shelves were made of hewn lumber. One set held a hodgepodge of vessels—earthenware jars and pots, some large. The other, she saw with astonishment, held pyramids of scrolls and stacked codices, books—a rich man's library. Running the length of the third wall was a single low shelf of doubled planks on which rugs and animal skins were haphazardly spread; a sleeping pallet—the Jew's?

In the room's center was a rectangular table, on which the candle-stick stood. Fresh-cut rushes, intermingled, judging from the scents, with lavender, lemon balm, and thyme, were spread on the hard-caked mud of the floor. The table also held a stripped feather quill, a knife, a horn of carbon ink, and a fan of vellum pages on which could be seen the small angled marks that Héloïse recognized as Hebrew letters. The Jew placed the oil lamp on a shelf, then began efficiently to clear the table, shifting its material to the bench. From the easy agility with which he moved, Héloïse saw that the man was not as aged as the white of his flamboyant hair and beard had suggested. The skin around his eyes and mouth was smooth.

Once the table was clear, the Jew drew himself up to his full height, touched his cap, and bowed to Héloïse—his first acknowledgment of her. In return, she nodded.

The Jew then stooped to pull a stool out from under the table, and Peter, opposite, knew to do likewise. The Jew sat. Peter arranged the stool for Héloïse. She collected the drapery of her gowns and cloak, and sat. Peter stood behind her. "We come to you with secrets," Peter said.

The Jew's almost imperceptible nod seemed the appropriate reply. His hands were folded on the table.

Peter continued, "We have reason to believe that we have conceived a child."

The Jew showed nothing. His gaze went to Héloïse, who, to her surprise, sensed in him nothing but kindness. She said, "It is true. I am certain."

The Jew said, "No one can match you in this knowledge."

Peter said, "But is there a way to be *more* certain? Secrets of the Talmud? The Moorish texts?"

Though the Jew spoke in answer to Peter, he did not take his eyes from Héloïse. "The way to stand beyond question is to listen to the one who knows. Neither the Talmud nor the Canon of Ibn Sina compare to that. Is it you, my lady, who seeks my counsel?"

"I yield to Master Peter Abelard," she answered. "He has set us in flight from superstition. What would you do to confirm my condition? With your science, I mean."

"There are measures."

"What measures?"

The Jew stood and turned to the shelves behind him. He opened a metal box and, with pinched fingers, carefully placed something in his cupped hand. Then he turned back, to sit again. He spilled onto the table a small quantity of seeds, and a single shoot of wheat.

"In the privacy of your place," he said, "if you chose to adopt this method, you would keep these moist with your *urina,* the fluid discharge from your bladder. These are barley seeds; this is a spike of emmer wheat. If, after two days, either the seeds failed to sprout or the emmer failed to germinate, then you would know that you are not with child. It is possible. On the other hand, the quickening of either the barley or the wheat would mean that you are indeed with child. With a high degree of certainty."

"And as for the"—Peter hesitated—"state . . . of being male or female?"

The Jew answered solemnly, "Some say that if the barley sprouts before the emmer the child will be male. Vice versa, female. This part of the measure is also reliably accurate" all at once the Jew smiled—"about half the time."

Héloïse did not match his smile. She said soberly, "For the knowledge of my son's gender, I was instructed to let a drop of discharge from my breast fall into the water."

"Yes," the Jew said, "to see if it floats. Also reliably accurate . . . about half the time." Again, a smile.

"But my knowledge does not depend on experiments," Héloïse said.

The Jew shrugged.

Peter asked, "And what of my lady's well-being?"

The Jew opened his hands. "God in His wisdom has prepared the woman magnificently for this miracle." Addressing Héloïse, he said, "You are a healthy girl. I see that. Good color in your face. The proper pink in the cuticles of your fingernails. Robust posture. Hips. You have come into womanhood with grace. Is this your question, or only his?"

"It is mine."

"Then may I ask questions of my own?"

"Yes."

"Is there pain in your abdomen?"

"No."

"Difficulty in emptying the bowels?"

"Some. Yes."

The Jew nodded. "The body adjusts, as your digestion now must feed two stomachs. If that difficulty persists, have your kitchen prepare squash, boiled in ale. Take it in with mustard. What of your blood flow?"

"It was regular, until now. I should have had the monthly flowers three weeks ago."

The Jew nodded. "The body economizes with blood now, supplying the coming child. In these weeks, are mornings difficult for you?"

"Yes. Biliousness."

"Also as it should be. The body purifies itself, expelling malignant humors. The Lord is making you ready. You will be formidable at this. You were made for it."

Héloïse was stunned to find tears welling in her eyes. "My mother died while giving birth." She blurted this, having never meant to refer to her poor mother's fate, the trauma of her own witnessing of it.

"I am sorry. But that unhappy outcome . . . it was not when you yourself were born?"

"No."

He moved his head up and down, slowly—indicating a conclusion. "You will die, my lady," he said. "But not of this child. Not of this birth. You will live a long, good life." The Jew said this as if his knowledge were certain, and Héloïse thought of Simeon, the just man of Jerusalem who consoled the Mother of Jesus. The Jew continued, "Still, it is true that the birth will be difficult, and you are right to be afraid. It is fear that I sense in you, is it not?"

The tears spilled out of her eyes. Héloïse nodded yes.

The Jew reached across the table and took her hand. "But you were made to bear the difficulty. The fearsomeness will be nothing when your child is placed in your arms."

"Saint Paul says as much," Peter put in, but neither the Jew nor Héloïse acknowledged him.

"I repeat . . ." the Jew began. Now he covered the hand of Héloïse with his second hand. "You will be formidable."

"And between now and then?" Peter asked.

The Jew waited for Héloïse to ratify the question with her nod. He said, "What you eat will affect your unborn child. Dry food. Avoid fluids that are cold. Avoid acidic fruits like pomegranate, or mix them with wine. Dry and crush the flowers of fruit-bearing plants and brew them into tea. As the time progresses, confinement is appropriate, as if you yourself were returning to the womb. When the child is coming, you will do well to have your flanks rubbed with rose oil, but only for comfort. Your body will supply what you and your child need. Trust that."

"Will the child be deformed?"

The Jew shrugged. "No more than all the sons and daughters of Adam are. Some deformities are of the body, some are of the spirit—but no one is spared, which is why we must be kind to one another. Caring for yourself is the way to care for your child. Leave the rest to the Holy One, who watches you. Nay, who abides in you right now. It is the Holy One you are carrying. Blessed are you, my lady."

The Jew stood. When his glance went to Peter, Peter said, "You know that, for us, there will be particular troubles."

The Jew nodded. "Your privilege, Master, is to protect her from the troubles. Protecting your woman is your privilege and solemn obligation."

Héloïse stood, but she leaned forward. "The barley seed," she said. "The wheat."

"Yes." The Jew turned and took a small square of purple velvet and a cord from a shelf—material prepared for such a purpose. He placed the square in the palm of one hand, then, with the other, swept the seeds and shoot onto the velvet, folded its corners up, and deftly tied them with the cord—a pouch. He handed it to Héloïse.

She said, "I will do as you said, but for Master Peter's sake. I know I have a son."

The Jew nodded. "I believe you do."

In the moments it required to pass out of the Vicus Judaeorum and through the jumbled market stalls, neither Peter nor Héloïse spoke. Finally, as they approached the wall of the Cathedral close, they halted in sync and faced each other. Héloïse went up on her toes to lose herself inside the cave of his hood, to kiss him. Peter encircled her with his arms and returned her kiss. The intensity with which they clung together was, even for them, unprecedented. Héloïse thought she would break with feeling.

Pulling back at last, she said, "Thank you for bringing me to your prince."

"My darling, we have only just begun. I will protect you. I will marry you."

She laughed. "Marry me! What is that? We cannot get married."

"Of course we can. We must."

"Why?"

Abelard was thrown. "The question of honor," he said.

"I care nothing for honor," she answered.

He shook his head, scrambling to keep up with her. "Consider your uncle, then. Honor is all he cares for. Fulbert will see a grievous breach of honor. His honor. The honor of your mother's family. The honor of the Queen Consort. Therefore, the honor of the King! To say nothing of yours!"

"Mine! My honor is to be your paramour. That is enough for me. Were we to marry, your rivals would drive you from Paris; your license to teach would be revoked, your clerical status nullified." She was speaking as one whose thoughts on the matter were well laid out. She had already aligned this furrow of the field they were crossing. "If you were reduced to the lay state," she continued, "your career as a philosopher would be finished. You! The most esteemed philosopher in Christendom! Ruined! Because of me! I will not hear of it."

"But without marriage—"

"What is marriage to us? Are we not already bound for life? What need have we for the matrimonial cult? We are sworn already, are we not?"

"Yes."

"Then we are married already."

"Yes, but—"

"No one need know, dear Peter. Our secret marriage, by being secret, secures your place at the pinnacle of scholars."

Now it was Abelard who laughed. But he stifled himself to whisper, "You are carrying a child, woman! That secret will be kept for one month more—two at most. Then, as Prince Isaac said, you will need protection. *Only* sacramental matrimony protects you—protects our child. What is philosophy to that? What is Paris? I care nothing for either. I care only for you."

She cupped her hand at his mouth, to silence him. She, too, whispered, "I speak not of the mere vanity of the school, but of what you are embarked upon there. You are teaching a new mode of thought . . . thought itself, how to follow the chain of reason, to go wherever it leads."

He pulled his mouth free. "Not if it goes against God."

"But there's the point! The point of your every lecture. Reason *cannot* go against God, since reason is God's gift." To Héloïse, Peter was God's gift—pure and simple. God had put him in Paris. God had licensed his teaching. God needed him to carry on his new philosophy. With God at its center, why else should he not have invented a word for it: "theology"!

Abelard cast his eyes about. The faint glow of the coming dawn was in the air. "This is no time for talk about God."

"I am talking about you. *Your* teaching. Its importance. *Your* God."

Through her cloak, he gently squeezed her upper arm. "It is only Christ's God whom we worship."

"Yes! I have heard you speak boldly of Christ's God, the One who sent His Son not to die, but to live!" That was indeed the watchword of his teaching, as she knew better than anyone. Peter Abelard held that salvation need not be won by appeasing an angry God, as the Fathers had it, because salvation *already* abounds in a loving God's economy. "Life, therefore," she insisted now, "not death! Mercy, not judgment! *There* is your teaching."

"You learn well, woman," he said quietly.

But she was impassioned now. "You are rewriting all that has been written. Sacraments do not save us; they merely celebrate that we are saved. Your ideas are great, and they are dangerous."

It was true: dangerous to the established order of hierarchy. The Church-empowered gatekeepers of grace posed a threat to Peter Abelard of which Héloïse was more aware, perhaps, than he. If God's salvation was universally on offer, what need was there of priests? Of bishops? Of Popes? Abelard's enemies, muttering in the shadows of the Cloister, were poised to encircle him—to do more now than shout about flouted doctrine. Her ferocious rejection of marriage was rooted in an absolute determination *not* to be the instrument of Peter Abelard's defeat by such dolts.

"But dear, sweet Héloïse . . ." Again he cast his eyes about. Were they being overheard? Were the morning servants soon to appear? He began to tug at her, to draw this contest to its close.

But by now, her only impulse was to warn him. "No, Peter," she whispered intensely. "Listen to me. I know of the upcoming Great Chapter meeting of the so-called reformers at Chartres, where your teaching will be challenged on behalf of William of Champeaux."

"How do you know of that?"

"The schoolboys know of it. Why shouldn't I?" Peter famously kept his distance from the gossip that fueled the chatter of his students. They sat at his feet, but they also longed to see him in high-stakes verbal combat, never imagining that he could be vanquished. Yet Héloïse understood that even verbal combat could be deadly. His critics were arming themselves against him. She said, more quietly, "All the talk is of this upstart White Monk, your self-anointed inquisitor."

"A nobody, but not self-anointed. He is commissioned not by Champeaux, but by the toothless old lion, Anselm."

"Anselm is your nemesis—the great defender of the monster-God you repudiate. Old lions are dangerous when teamed with young jackals. 'The White Monk'—why is he called that?"

"He is too pure to wear the black robes of Saint Benedict, like the rest of us. The white habit is his claim to righteousness. His name is Bernard."

"If purity is his shibboleth, he threatens you doubly now. When he mixes illicit love into the cauldron of charges to be brought, Bernard will boil you. You will be scorned, and your reading of the Gospel will be lost—a catastrophe!"

"Do not puff up my importance, woman."

"Do not deny it, man! Your work is only just begun. You promised the prince of the Jews that you would protect your woman. You protect her by protecting the truth of your work. That is all."

"No, listen to me!" he demanded. He released her and stepped back. He steepled his hands before his chin, a posture of supplication. He spoke urgently, but still in a whisper. "Suppose all that you say is true; even so, your words are mere bubbles in the air. Come down to earth with me. You yourself said it. I wear the tonsure. The rule of clergy applies to me. The bishops are ruthlessly enforcing it. If I remain as I am, a Canon of the Cathedral, our son, if such it is, will be seized from us—'*Filius nullius*,' yes—to be a slave of the Church. And you—you will be a scorned woman."

"I will not openly marry you. Nor will I remain in Paris. You protect me by protecting the pulse of my heart, my Peter Abelard—who is also the creator of a whole new way of thinking and learning and believing. Who am I to that?"

"You are the absolute to me," he said firmly.

"Good. Then my will is absolute. You must obey it."

"But how——?" He opened his hands, a gesture of helplessness before her fierceness.

"I have thought this through, using the train of logic I have from you." She spoke with unrelenting earnestness. "My uncle's honor, my health, the safe delivery of our son, the secret of our love—all of this is secured by my return to the convent at Argenteuil. Not as its orphaned ward, as before, nor as a senior pupil, but as a sister under the vow of postulancy——"

"What?"

"No, let me! I have thought this through, I say! Listen! I will enter the convent at Argenteuil. Once initially professed, I will be sent away for the year-long postulancy in the remote novitiate. Such claustration is a mandate of the Rule. All sisters begin by dying to the world, and so will I: the prescribed one year and one day. Gone. At my disappearance, my uncle, instead of humiliated and enraged, will be credited with my religious vocation. Not to mention his relief at being freed of responsibility for me. And Lady Gisela, the cousin of my mother whom he so fears, will be edified. Mother Prioress, because of my flimsy tie to the Royal household—and because she loves me—will protect my secret. All of this will unfold soon—at once!—apparently under the urgent inspiration of the Holy Ghost. So no one will know the truth of what I bear."

"But under vows? You? A false oath? This is violence. Violence to the absolute will you just declared. Violence to our love."

"You have vows," she said.

"I told you. I will renounce them."

"So will I, when the child is safely delivered. I will resume my life, my 'formidable' life, as Prince Isaac put it. I will 'discover' that my vocation lies elsewhere than in vowed consecration. Perhaps I will become one of those useful unmarried women of the Court who take care of the neglected children of the Royals. Perhaps one of those could be our own child, a ward of the household . . . whom I could love as my own child. As indeed I would." Héloïse paused before going on with sudden gravity: "The only thing 'formidable' about me, Peter Abelard, is you. If we proceed in this way, our child will be safe, and our hidden bond can quicken once more, and thrive again, as it has until now."

"Never. Never," he said. His face had darkened with a look of disbelief—that this woman could so surprise him, so shock him. "You would make a solemn vow, consciously intending to forswear it? Never!" Peter Abelard took her by the shoulders, gripping her more fiercely than he knew. "My violation of Holy Orders is a mistake," he said. "An accident. I repent of it, and will seek dispensation. Your violation would be deliberate, a knowing falsification in advance, before God Himself. Solemnly sworn! A sacrilege, woman."

"You care nothing for philosophy. I care nothing for vows, and neither does an all-loving God. Don't you see, I am carrying *your* logic to its conclusion. We are beloved of God whether we are in vows or not, and if the false swearing of an oath saves a life, or protects the greater truth—then Christ himself would swear it."

Peter Abelard, for a moment, could not speak. How was this unfolding before him? Who was this woman? Finally, with rare ferocity and still gripping her, he said, "This is no teaching of mine."

"Dear Peter, it follows from your teaching."

"Then my enemies are right."

"Do not say that. I beg of you. Do not say that."

"You would not be *risking* your soul, woman! You would be *damning* it for certain. I will have nothing to do with this. I will not permit it."

"I am not asking your permission."

"How dare you! The child is ours *together*. The solution to our dilemma must be won *together*." He roughly released her.

Héloïse had never seen Peter so angry. But then she realized—this was not anger. This was passionate protection, his protection of her *soul*. That she cared not one whit for some supposed eternal doom surprised her as much as him. She simply did not believe in the demon God who would make it so. In any case, her soul's damnation in an imagined afterlife was pure abstraction, whereas the present destruction of Peter Abelard's thought, the silencing of his voice, the reduction to ash of his rare wisdom—all because of her—this was Hades here and now.

Chastened, she asked, "Then what is there for us?"

The last hour of night, with its dampness, weighed upon them.

Finally, Peter said, "Lucille. Nantes."

"What?"

"My sister, her Breton village. A simple journey on the River Loire. We will go there. She will care for you. She has four children already underfoot. She is a masterpiece of motherhood. She will see you through your confinement, and she will see you safely delivered. For your sake, I will continue to meet my obligations at the Cathedral school, but I will manage to be with you for days and weeks at a time." Peter did not say it—or need to—but her going to Nantes would mean that she had not falsified a sacred vow, or jeopardized her immortal soul. She would not have blasphemed, which, on his scale, was the weight that mattered most. He added, "In these months, our child will healthily come to term, but so will our mutual knowledge of the way forward. I say again: the child is ours *together.* The solution to our dilemma must be won *together.* We will find it. There's my marriage vow, dear wife of mine. I will take you to Nantes as soon as a keel can be readied."

"But my uncle . . ."

"Your uncle, the fool, is easily handled. The Loire borders Bourgogne, the realm of your mother's cousin. Use the available truth: the Loire! You've been unexpectedly summoned, which is, of course, the case! Imply that Lady Gisela has sent for you, a matter of your coming-of-age homage among the Ladies-in-Waiting in that distant retinue. The business of women tending to women at the court of the Duke. Imply that the Queen Consort will be there. All of that will silence your uncle." Again Peter Abelard encircled her with his arms, and, again, she yielded to him.

After a moment, she pulled back, just enough to whisper, "Meanwhile, I will soak the barley seeds in piss, and if they fail to sprout, I will signal you."

"I pray to God for the germination," he said. They laughed and hugged, now with relief and delight.

Neither knew it at that moment, although both would come roughly to the recognition later, but Brother Thrall, Fulbert's *servus,* was watching through the boards of the garden horse-gate.

CHAPTER TEN

"Complications," he'd said, trying to explain himself, but he could tell from Rachel Vedette's quizzical expression that the word epitomized his fakery.

She repeated, " 'Complications.' "

Michael Kavanagh stood mutely, not moving a muscle. Finally, at the mercy of rank physical sensation, he blurted, "Forgive me. I've a splitting headache." On Madison Avenue, two hours before, he had thought, *A stroke: this is a stroke!* But that piercing pain had eased off, leaving, as a residue of his meeting with Bishop Donovan, a mundane but still-screeching hurt behind his eyes. "Do you mind if I sit down?" he asked.

"Of course not," she said, clearly surprised at his acknowledgment. Even in that brisk phrase, he heard her French accent, still exotic. She said, with a gesture at the stone bench running the length of the wall, "Although, from a thousand years ago, the place is uncomfortable"— she smiled thinly—"where they confessed infractions of the Rule."

Kavanagh stared at her for a moment, feeling put off, yes—but also struck again by her erudition. The woman knew so much more about this world than he did, and yet this world was his. He had come here from the Bishop's office, like a pigeon hurtling its way home.

Unlike the day before, when it had seemed only alien, the faux monastery today was an accidental refuge.

He crossed to the stone bench and took a place a couple of yards away from her. He put his breviary down. "What a stupid thing I just said. Sometimes I amaze myself." He dared to look at her, and was surprised to see that, as she returned his gaze, she seemed not cold, as before, but kind.

She said, "What stupid thing?"

Perhaps it was her lush accent that made her seem kind.

"About conscience," he explained. He was afraid that she'd taken his "Aw shucks" attempt at self-mockery literally. "My knowing everything about conscience. The truth is, I know very little."

"That cannot be true, Father."

Kavanagh exhaled a little laugh. "No. You're right. But if I knew everything, I wouldn't have come back here today. I've been thrown for a loop." He stopped himself. He could not describe what had happened on the avenue. He said only, "I was downtown at the Cathedral. Or, rather, the Chancery. Seeing the boss."

"The Cardinal."

"No. The Vicar." He laughed. "A lowly parish priest is not important enough to have business with Cardinal Spellman. Coming back to Inwood, I don't think I actually decided to return here. I just did. Got off the subway one stop early, and headed into the park. Next thing I know, here I am. If I've intruded on you again, it's not deliberate." Even as Kavanagh said this, he realized it was untrue. Only partly conscious, perhaps, but he *had* come here on purpose—for this stranger.

But his headache clawed at his sinuses. The pain—was that what was making him nuts?

"Not 'intrusion,' Father. I am here for the public."

"But I interrupted your lunch break."

By raising her book slightly, she conveyed that her break was given over to reading, not eating.

Kavanagh eyed the thin, worn leather volume. She had been carrying it yesterday. He touched his breviary, and repeated what she had said: "You have your book. I have mine." His question was implied: *What are you reading?*

As if in answer, she drew the book flat to her chest, concealing it.

"*Le Moyen Âge?*" he asked. "Is that the phrase?"

"*Très bon, mon père.* Yes. *Des lettres.* Some letters."

"So you're studying."

"Not precisely." She shrugged. "I know these letters very well. My book, *peut-être,* is like your book. A friend."

"Something to carry," Kavanagh said, and picked up the breviary, letting its soft leather covers flap, to add offhandedly, "a priest's swagger stick."

"A what?"

"Swagger stick. What a Marine Corps colonel carries."

"Ah, baton. The marshals of France carry the baton. For fending off peasants, I believe."

Kavanagh gestured with the book. "In public, one can indeed fend off with this thing, burying one's face in it, pretending to pray. I do it all the time."

"I doubt that, Father. You do not pretend. Nor do you fend off."

"Actually, I'm rarely this forward. My headache, for example. Normally, I would never refer to it."

She lifted her shoulders, pleasantly. "Revelations of the Chapter House."

Kavanagh looked around: the rough stone, the iron sconces and wall sculptures, the triptych Golgotha, which gave as much prominence to the two thieves as to the crucified Lord.

As if her remark had been the Abbot's call to *examen conscientiae,* he let his gaze settle on the floor. *What,* he wondered suddenly, *am I doing here?*

Kavanagh sensed her falling into silence, too. *Magnum silentium,* she had said the day before, a phrase he had not used himself in years.

When the Great Silence fell each night in the seminary, students were supposed to be in their rooms, with the doors closed. One time, after the forbidden hour, someone had rapped softly on his door, and the bolt of alarm Kavanagh had felt at the sound came back to him

now. When he'd opened the door, there was Runner, looking abashed.
A major term paper was due the next morning, and he was stumped.
He had his notebook. He needed help. Kavanagh had let him into
his room briefly, but had been so obviously worried by the infractions they were committing—not only breaking the silence, but also
the threshold rule—that Runner had hustled away, leaving Kavanagh
feeling foolish and guilty.

He pushed the memory away, but the feeling stayed. He leaned
forward to lower his head into his hands, not out of embarrassment
that he had shown up here, or perplexity at why, although he felt both,
but simply because the pressure at his temples threatened to burst.

"Jesus, Runner—it's the Great Silence, what the hell!"

With poised fingers, he pushed back against his pulsing veins,
but now what he recalled were those moments on Madison Avenue, a
little while ago. *"Non credo!"* Not a stroke, okay. But something . . .
something . . . *What is happening to me?*

Though he was obsessed with himself just then, Kavanagh was
aware of it when the woman stood and walked away, her footfalls
fading softly as she crossed the stone floor, out into the arcade, to the
building beyond.

And that was that, he thought. She had done to him a version of
what he had done to Bishop Donovan—just walking out. She had
sensed his trouble, and wanted no part of it. But what *was* his trouble?

"Here, Father."

He looked up. She'd returned without his hearing, and was standing before him with a glass of water in one hand and, in the other, a pair
of white pills. Her book was wedged between her elbow and her side.

"Aspirin," she said.

Her fingers struck him again, long and spindlelike. The white
of the pills emphasized the pallor of the skin that stretched tightly
across her palm. The cuff of her white sleeve was tightly fastened—
not buttoned, Kavanagh saw now, but gathered at her wrist with an
elastic band.

He took the pills, and then the water. "Thank you, miss. You're
very kind."

"I hope it helps."

"It helps already."

They were quiet for a moment, not moving. Finally, the woman said, " 'Thrown for a loop.' A strange expression."

"A stranger feeling," he said, surprised that she'd steered back to his admission. "Unsettled," he said. "Caught off guard. What would you say in French?"

"Pris au dépourvu, bouleversé, perhaps. *Peut-être."*

"Yesterday," he said slowly, "when I came here, it was because someone I knew well once, but hadn't seen in years . . . he came to the early-morning Mass. He knelt for Communion, but then wouldn't receive the Host. He gave me the strangest look, then left. I followed him. I saw him come into the park. So then, later, I did, too. I never found him. Then it started to rain. I ducked in here."

"And we met."

"Yes. And now I find myself starting to explain . . ."

"You started to explain yesterday."

"And you walked away."

Standing before him, she had her arms folded now, like a woman to whom some accounting was due. She asked, "Why did you come back?"

"Because of something else that happened, just this morning. In my meeting with the Bishop." He hesitated. He didn't want her thinking he'd returned because of her. He raised his eyebrows, indicating the Chapter House, the arcade, the Cloister, all of it. "I guess I needed some quiet in which to collect myself."

"Yes. The Cloister is good for that." With a glance back toward the arcade, she said, "At the front desk, a group is waiting. It is time for my tour."

"Of course," Kavanagh said, and he felt heat rush into his face. Again. The madness of his being here. The rudeness.

" 'Memory palace,' " she said, with a sweep of her hand around the Chapter House. "Your phrase. Perhaps I will use that in my little talk. May I?"

Kavanagh laughed, and then so did she, which prompted him to say, "That fellow from my past showing up like that yesterday opened memories I haven't thought of in . . ." His voice trailed off.

"He is what threw you 'for a loop.'"

"Right."

"Which you mention to me because you will not see me again."

"And the same for you, right? You're being nice to me because I am a museum visitor, not a monk in the Chapter House, reviewing the Rule, accusing himself."

"Nice?" She shook her head. "Aspirin is not so much." The skin at her cheeks was tinged with pink. She, too, was blushing. With the glass in her one hand, she hugged herself, the book to her chest.

"Unless," he said quietly, "there is another time, another place."

She took a step back. *"Impossible."* She muttered the word in French, and he understood it. She turned and walked quickly away.

Kavanagh watched her go, his foolishness confirmed. He wanted out of the place as quickly as possible, but forced himself to wait a moment. Then he, too, left.

In the central hall, which opened into the several separate cloisters, but also into the staircase spiraling down to the entrance foyer, Rachel Vedette was greeting the ladies of the tour group, five of them. Her back was to Kavanagh, which relieved him, and he made for the stairwell, expecting not to encounter her again. He took the stairs at a clip.

By the time he reached the desk at the main entrance, he was aware that someone was coming after him, but he did not stop. He went past the prim attendant without looking at her. The cold air outside surprised him, as did the bright light.

"Father," she called.

But he kept going. He'd been dragged across a threshold into a forbidden room, and was now trying to crawl out of it again.

"Father!"

He stopped, and turned. She was there, behind him. Before, she had seemed collected, reserved—but no more. He recognized in her expression a version of the visceral impulsiveness that had seized him.

She gestured with her book, and said, "This is the story of Abelard, and the letters he exchanged with Héloïse. Today, earlier . . . already, before you came . . . they made me think of you."

"Abelard and Héloïse, the monk and nun?"

"Yes. Although 'monk and nun' hardly defines it. She was the greatest abbess of the age. He was the greatest scholar. I know their words by heart, yet I still long to understand. . . ." She could not finish.

"I hardly know them. Abelard was a hedonist, right? Not in the calendar of saints. Not in the canonical syllabus."

"To say that Abelard was a hedonist is . . . you say . . . *simpliste.*"

"Simplistic."

"He was the enemy of Bernard of Clairvaux, but . . ."

"Bernard we studied," he said. "*Saint* Bernard. Very canonical."

"But of course. Bernard was the victor. Victors define the syllabus. Those defeated are cast aside. But Abelard . . ." She hesitated again, clumsily, and he thought it was because their exchange had become so stilted, academic almost. *What is going on?*

But then, having centered herself, she continued, "There is religious grandeur in Abelard. Hedonism had nothing to do with it. That is the ancient slander. Bernard's slander."

Kavanagh said, "I thought Abelard and Héloïse stood convicted by their love affair."

"Which was the least of it. Well, perhaps not for Héloïse." She smiled slyly. "Héloïse is another matter." She pressed the book against herself, conveying its preciousness. "These letters show a great contest between two people, but also a contest *of* the two people against the whole rest of their age. They are humanists. The *first* humanists. But also mystics. The two things feed each other."

"I never heard that said."

"Héloïse has a deep attachment to the Holy"—the docent was speaking now in a rush of pent-up expression, as if a dam had burst inside her—"but also a savage indignation toward God. Abelard refuses to match her in that, but, because of her, he finds it possible to stand against the whole world—*for* the world. *For the human, and for the holy—both! How was that?* What sort of faith makes that possible? I have never discussed this with a priest."

"An ignorant priest."

"But a priest! It's why I have . . ." With a toss of her hands, she conveyed, *why I have so foolishly come after you.* She cared nothing, clearly, about the odd impression she was making. She was speaking like an unleashed person who had no choice but, yes, to speak. She said, "You live in their world of reference, no? The vocation? The call from God? Readiness to stake everything on the absolute. That is what compels me about them, but also mystifies me. I cannot let go of them, but neither can I . . . understand." Now her words, suddenly, began to come more slowly. "There is something essential that I miss . . . because . . . I . . . I do not believe in God." That she had made such an admission, Kavanagh saw, surprised her utterly. She underscored it with stern gravity, but also with palpable alarm.

Kavanagh thought back to his own moment on Madison Avenue. *"Non credo!"* What the hell was *that*? Then he thought of Bishop Donovan, and their sentimental exchange: " 'To daily go from men to God . . . to return from God to men, bringing pardon and hope . . .' " What was it the Bishop had said? "Not a bad vocation, that."

The woman pointed down the road, a serpentine curl through the overarching, bare November trees. She said, "There is a coffee shop halfway to the subway. I stop there sometimes, on my way home. Coffee keeps me alive."

"What time?"

"A bit after four o'clock."

Kavanagh could bring himself to do nothing more than nod.

Rachel Vedette turned and hurried back to the museum.

He watched her go, at first taking in the way her legs moved inside her long swirling skirt. Then he looked away, as a phrase popped into his aching head: "custody of the eyes."

THAT AFTERNOON, in his room at the rectory, Kavanagh had changed his mind twice before deciding, after all, to wear the Roman collar. He'd thought of going in his windbreaker, because that was how he'd first met her, but he knew now that the collar—his "world of reference"—defined her interest. He made the uniform complete by bringing his breviary, although, in leaving his room, he'd thought also to bring the Simone Weil book. But no. He left behind the French Jew's exchange of letters with a priest.

Though he had never been in the coffee shop, he'd been aware of it, a refurbished stone-and-timber Tudor cottage, the sort of little structure that a groundskeeper would have occupied in a more feudal age. Come to think of it, that's probably what it had been on the nineteenth-century robber-baron estate that Rockefeller would have requisitioned for his monastic museum folly. Inside, the place was linoleum tiles, Formica tables, glass-and-chrome sugar dispensers, tall-fold napkin holders, and round tin ashtrays. Kavanagh, the lone customer, took a table by the window, overlooking the road that cut through the hilly, wooded Fort Tryon Park. He lit a cigarette.

He saw her coming, but did not recognize her at first, so dramatically was her look altered by what she was wearing—a flowing black cape and a tight-fitting black turban. As she drew closer, he saw how the headdress pulled her brows down over the dark pool of her eyes, a slant that gave her face a hint of the East he had not seen before.

When she entered, he stood, cigarette in hand. She barely looked at him as she took a chair, on the opposite side of the small table. Before they spoke, a waitress appeared from behind the large refrigerated case that displayed pies and preset bowls of pudding. The waitress was a stout woman, wearing a pencil in the bun of her hair behind the pointed white headpiece. "Hiya, Father," she said happily, and even in that brisk greeting, the harp of her brogue played itself. "What'll it be? It's on the house." She said this without a glance at Rachel Vedette. Kavanagh exchanged rote pleasantries with the waitress, and he ordered two coffees.

While they waited, Kavanagh offered his cigarette pack. Miss Vedette took one and leaned forward for his light. They took refuge, each of them, in the business of smoking.

The waitress returned with the coffees, then disappeared again.

Miss Vedette said, "She serves me coffee most afternoons. She has never greeted me. I believe she has never seen me."

"Don't be offended. She didn't see me, either." Kavanagh lodged his cigarette between his lips and flicked his celluloid collar. He knew full well that this eccentric Frenchwoman, too, was seeing only that.

Rachel put her book on the table, next to his. Kavanagh extended his hand. "May I?"

She nodded.

He picked the volume up. The worn leather cover was smooth to the touch. The pages were edged with faded gold leaf. He opened the book to the title page: *Historia Calamitatum: Heloissae et Abaelardi Epistolae.* He turned the page. "It's in Latin," he said, showing surprise.

"Of course."

"But . . . Paris . . . I would have thought French."

"Early twelfth century, Father. French did not exist quite yet. The earliest *chanson de geste* came just a bit later. Educated people would have written to each other in Latin."

"And you know the language?"

"I attended the *lycée classique.* Latin was routine."

"And your English?"

"My English came later. It helped with my coming to America."

He offered the book back to her. "Would you read something?"

"But as a priest you know Latin."

"I know Church Latin. The Holy Office. The Mass. The Creed. Otherwise . . ." He shrugged, but, again, *"Non credo!"* popped into his mind.

"Thomas Aquinas?" she asked.

"Of course. Not so sure about Virgil."

She said, "This book is in the idiom of Aquinas, so you will know it." Still, she took the volume. She let her eyes settle on the first page, and, with a placid neutrality, began to translate. *"There was in Paris a young creature—ah! Philintus!—formed in a prodigality of Nature, to show mankind a finished composition. . . ."* She interrupted herself. "This is Abelard to Philintus, a friend."

"Dating from?"

"From 1132. He is describing Héloïse, as she was years earlier."

"Go on, please."

She found her place. *"Her wit and her beauty would have fired the dullest and most insensible heart; and her education was equally admirable."*

"Wow," Kavanagh said.

Rachel laughed abruptly. " 'Gee whiz!' " she said, and he realized that, once again, she was teasing him.

As if in apology, she said, "I told you before how sometimes you make me think of the men in movies, Jimmy Stewart."

Kavanagh rocked his chair back good-naturedly, cowboy-wise. But he jolted the table, the coffee. He said, "My goodness," but self-mockingly. Then he added, "Jimmy Stewart meets Simone Weil."

"Vey."

"What?"

"We did this yesterday. Not 'wile.' But 'vey.'"

"Okay." He grinned. "I stand corrected. But with your turban, if I may say, you don't resemble the famous"—he hesitated on the words "Jewish" and "French," and said neither—"martyr."

Rachel touched the black fabric at her ear. "There is a story about this head covering in France."

"What story?"

"It became the fashion after the war."

"That's it? The story?"

"Yes."

"You were in France?"

"But of course."

"A 'young creature in Paris,' like Héloïse?"

Rachel Vedette nodded. "My world and hers, so separated by time, coincided in space. Yes, Paris. They say she was about twenty when she and Abelard were together at Notre-Dame. When I was twenty, I used to walk past Notre-Dame every day, twice every day, back and forth, from Île Saint-Louis to the Musée de Cluny, on the Left Bank."

"You refer to Cluny in your docent speech."

"Yes. The great abbey was in Bourgogne, of course—nothing there but ruins today. But the Abbot had a palace in Paris, his, what do you say, town house. It is well preserved, now a museum of the Middle Ages."

"Like The Cloisters?"

She smiled. "Well, the *musée* is not a pastiche. But in feeling, yes—like The Cloisters, which, I admit, is what drew me here. I was hired first as a cleaner."

"Then they realized how much you know."

She smiled again, but vaguely. She rolled the tip of her cigarette in its ashes, and added, "Although in the Paris museum there is also the archive, and the scholarly center, the Institut Médiéval." She took a drag then, a hefty one. Smoke came out of her nostrils, as if she were a man. She said, "After the Revolution . . . 1789, no?"

"I've heard of it."

"I am sorry. The ladies in my tours think, *Revolution . . . 1776.* So, after the Revolution, the monasteries were destroyed—you know this, too. But the monastic *libraries* were also looted, the greatest medieval libraries in Europe—Cluny, but also Clairvaux, Clermont, Morimund, Bec. Terrible destruction, the coming of *laïcité*—you say 'secularism'? It was the hatred of everything Catholic, including books—including, also, the Roman writers and the Greeks. What was not destroyed was hidden. Thousands of codices, scrolls, and single leaves, many magnificently illuminated, were left on unmarked shelves across the country, slowly decomposing for a hundred years. Only in the twentieth century did scholars rescue the lost works that were suddenly deemed the patrimony of France. The Institut Médiéval became the main repository of the salvaged texts. One of those putting the fragments together was my father. I was his assistant."

"Really?"

"Yes."

"Working on what?"

"Abelard."

"But . . ."

"But what?"

"I thought you were Jewish."

She nodded. "My father began as a scholar of Talmud, Kabbalah, medieval Jewish texts. Tales of the Midrash: he retold them. The monasteries had collected all that, too. Professor Saul Vedette was famous as an expert on Moses Nachmanides."

"Maimonides?"

"Nachmanides. Someone else."

"Oh. I am sorry, I . . ."

"No matter. But then, of course, everything changed in France—little more than a decade ago. With the darkness, my father moved to the study of Abelard, who was his light. He was researching why such a figure was condemned by the Church."

"I don't know much, but I know Abelard was condemned because of Héloïse." Kavanagh gestured toward Rachel's book. "Maybe not hedonism, as you say, but as her lover, no? That was the offense."

"Oh, Father, forgive me, but that is a terrible distortion."

"Why, then?"

She laughed, "Well, for the much better reason that he was a heretic."

"A heretic? For what?"

"For what, among other things, he believed about Jews." Rachel Vedette pierced him with her dark eyes. Kavanagh recalled the image occurring to him earlier, that in this woman's presence he'd been dragged into another room, but now he thought, not a room, but a ledge—a ledge from which one could fall. It was a feeling he'd had before. When?

With Runner, that's when.

He saw it when she registered that he had no reply to make. She went on, "Saint Bernard saw to Abelard's being condemned, and he ordered his writings burned, which is why you have not studied them; why, apart from these letters"—she indicated the book—"you have not heard of Abelard's work."

"But Jews?" he asked, finally.

"Abelard was charged with multiple errors, one of which was his suggestion that Jews were not condemned by God for murdering Christ. Therefore—so my father argued—Jews remain beloved of God."

"I hold that. I'm not a heretic."

"You believe Jews are saved? Outside the Church?"

"If they act in good conscience, yes."

"Outside Jesus? Jews have no need of Jesus?"

"Well . . ." The words of Jesus from the Gospel of John popped open in Kavanagh's mind: "No man comes to the Father, but by me."

But he pushed those words away to say, "During the war, I closed the eyelids of dozens of boys. It never occurred to me that God's love for them depended on their being baptized."

"My father found that to be Abelard's position. Exactly. Abelard was condemned for it."

Kavanagh could not think what to say.

She said, "Abelard believed—and taught—that every person is saved by virtue of being created by the Creator. God is available in the human capacity for thought. That's all. No Church. No Jesus. Just Creation. Reason. For that, they burned his writings. My father was trying to retrieve them, from manuscripts that were hidden in medieval monasteries, then lost."

"But your father was a Talmud scholar?"

"Until 1940, yes."

"But . . . 1940?"

"You know of the Statut des Juifs? The Jewish Law. My father was creating an argument against those laws. Against Vichy. Not an argument, precisely. *Un récit*—a story. Its hero, Abelard, the great French Catholic, was to be my father's witness. A witness for the Jews. That was my father's great idea. But, naturally, the witness was never called." She lifted the book. "I nevertheless, ever since, have kept faith with Abelard. And with Héloïse."

"As witnesses? Or what?"

She shrugged. "I cannot let them go. What was your phrase yesterday? 'Death grip.'"

He shook his head. "I was thinking of the Irish—how we nurse the hurts of the past."

"Hurts need nursing, perhaps."

"Until the hurt is gone."

"And when is that, Father?" She fell silent.

Kavanagh sat in silence, too. Finally, he asked quietly, "What is the hurt?"

She lifted her shoulders. "That my father's great idea was foolish. He should not have been encouraged in it." Her shoulders fell.

"Who encouraged him?"

Rachel brought her eyes to the priest's. "I did."

"You say that as if you are admitting to something."

She shrugged again.

"Why foolish?" Kavanagh asked.

"Because it was dangerous."

"I don't understand."

"Dangerous," she said sharply, "for a Jew."

Kavanagh could not think what to say. The silence fell once more. At last, he asked, "You were twenty?"

"As the climax came, yes."

"That's young."

"And a long time ago."

"Walking past Notre-Dame every day," he said.

Rachel was relieved to laugh. "You pronounce it like the American football team."

Kavanagh blushed, the rube again. "Yeah, well . . ."

Veering away from both his embarrassment and the pit of her anguish, she said, "Coming from home on Île Saint-Louis, I approached the Cathedral from the rear, where there was an expanse of grass. I always stared up at the *arcs-boutants,* you say 'buttresses' . . ."

"Flying buttresses."

". . . yes, because I did not want to look at the men who were . . . at rest . . . lounging on the grass in that park beside the Cathedral. They were German soldiers. We Parisians called them *haricots verts,* because of their gray-green uniforms." Realizing that Kavanagh had missed the meaning, she said, "Green beans." Then she added, "But when I passed, they were half naked sunbathers, happy to be seen as decadent. They displayed themselves. I hated knowing that they were looking at me." She stubbed out her cigarette in the ashtray, forcefully. "But this is all too much about me."

"No, it's not."

"You began to explain. 'Thrown for a loop,' you said. A stranger at the Mass yesterday, the Bishop this morning."

"Not a stranger."

"Who, then?"

"This fellow from the seminary in Yonkers . . . when *I* was young. But it's embarrassing, really. Trivial. Compared to what you were dealing with at that age."

"Still, something is at stake, no?"

"His nickname was 'Runner,' because he was a track star. I was very close to him all those years ago. He disappeared. And then again yesterday, he disappeared. Suddenly, it mattered to me to find out why. I went downtown today and asked the Bishop. He knows, but he wouldn't tell me." Kavanagh shrugged. "That's all. It's nothing."

"But to you, the unknown answer carries weight, nonetheless."

"I guess so."

"So you should find it. You should go to this man 'Runner,' and ask him."

"But that's the point. I have no way to find him."

"That is not true. He came to you yesterday. He wants to be found. You can find him."

Kavanagh stared at her, marveling at the simplicity of her statement. He almost asked, *And how would I do that?*

As if in reply, she said, "The Bishop knows?"

"Yes. It surprised me, how unsettled I was when I realized he was keeping something from me, and had been all along. I am surprised at how shocked I was to recognize some kind of deception from the Bishop. He is a friend, but more than that. He is the Church itself to me, and he has deceived me. That is what I saw. 'A vocation that stakes everything on the absolute,' is that what you said before? Abelard and Héloïse, perhaps. But not me. In my case, I am realizing, the vocation is staked not on the absolute, but on something very shaky."

"All the more, then, Father. You must have your questions answered."

"You don't understand. There's this thing called 'the Seal.' Secrecy. The Bishop is bound by it."

"But you are not." She eyed him steadily. "There is a way to learn what you need to learn. You must find it." That she said this with such certainty made him realize that she had been through so much more than he had. She was a veteran of grim accomplishment.

Kavanagh found it possible to hold her gaze, but as he did, his mind went elsewhere. All at once, he was back in Bishop Donovan's outer office, with his eyes casting about the room. The receptionist, bent over her ledger, was resolutely ignoring him. What he saw now was the file cabinet behind her, the top drawer, a label that he had not consciously registered, but which he now saw as reading "Current Correspondence." He recalled Bishop Donovan's words, "a letter from him . . . Special Delivery, out of the blue."

"Yes," Kavanagh said. "I see what you mean." But he said it with finality, shutting the lid on the subject of his own uneasiness.

Rachel Vedette placed her hand on the leather-bound book of letters. She gave it the slightest nudge, bringing it together with his breviary, so that the two edges of leather touched. "Will you take this?" she asked. "My book? Read what's written here? To discuss it with me?"

"I've just told you. I know little or nothing of the absolute."

"This was my father's book. I have not parted with it since . . ."

In the silence, even Kavanagh knew better than to require her to finish the sentence. "Yes," he said. "I will be careful with it." He picked up her book, and also his own. Her request meant he would see her again.

CHAPTER ELEVEN

The deck cabin to which Héloïse had repaired, to be out of the sun, was one of two ad hoc structures standing at either end of the long, narrow river vessel. Since they were running with the current downstream, toward the river's mouth at the sea, only one sail had been deployed. For nearly four days, the wind had been fair, the boat's progress smooth. Now, as the sailing barge approached the voyage's end, Héloïse heard the pair of pole-men, who stood ready fore and aft, calling out numbers, alerting the barge master to the depth of the water. Soon enough, she felt the jolt when the boat ran aground. She lifted the tarp clear of her cabin opening, to look out. It was late afternoon, and though the sunlight had lost its edge, still, she found it necessary to shield her eyes, blinking in the brightness. The cutwater of the boat was at rest in the shallow elbow of shoreline between a watermill and a muddy beach from which the ground sloped gently up to a quayside thoroughfare. Along it, stone buildings and houses were organized around a stout Merovingian basilica.

So this was Nantes.

One crewman was dropping the sail, and another was looping the line around a stump on the shore. The party's second barge banged into them from behind, and the third approached. That last and largest barge was given over to the war dogs, who had offered protection from night bandits at their campsites, and the supplemental oarsmen and dray horses that would be needed when the barges made the return voyage, upstream. But the second boat, just kissing hers, was Peter's. She turned to see him.

From his place in the prow, Peter waved at her. Across the distance that separated them, his beaming smile spoke eloquently of their happiness. For Héloïse, the days since their departure from Paris had been dreamlike, especially once, away from the city, they could drop the pretense that they were not traveling in the same party. At a tributary of the Loire, below Chartres, they had bidden farewell to the wagons and armed escort her uncle had insisted on providing to that point, for what he took, with his leap from her half-truth, to be her journey to Bourgogne. From there, they had launched themselves on the soothing rhythms of flowing water. When their three-boat flotilla had come to the main river's northern bend, at Orléans, they had followed the flow to the west, instead of heading east, toward the ducal palace in Dijon. The barge master alone understood that their course was not what had been implied. Peter had smothered an outright deception with ambiguity, but he had also seen that the boatman's discretion was well rewarded.

Though Peter and Héloïse had not found it possible to be alone, in a trinity of small vessels carrying gossip-prone servants and crew, the simple fact of their escape from the confines of the Paris Cloister had been enough. As darkness fell at the end of each day, the barges had tied up on the shore, and in the servant bustle of encampment— the hour or so of boats being secured, dogs deployed, horses fed, fires stoked, shelters erected, and bedding laid—they had come together casually on the crossbeam of her vessel, pretending to share nothing more than a taste for the clean air and the golden flare of sunset. But for them, the air was freedom itself, and the fading light, glowing across open bogs or filtered through towering woodlands, offered a glimpse of heaven. For the first time in their lustful history, Héloïse sensed something wholly new in Peter—his capacity for calm affection. Until she felt herself the object of his quiet devotion, she had not known how, in addition to the ecstasies of Eros, she had been longing for this chaste counsel of contented intimacy, too.

Oddly, it was here, on the untamed river, that she felt her wild, uneven life coming finally into balance, and she wished that everything and everyone, except herself and Peter, as they were at these moments, would utterly disappear. Nothing on earth but the two of them: no past or future, only now. Surreptitiously at such instants, with one hand resting on her abdomen, where their child nested, she had reached with the other to take Peter's hand. When, in the magic of twilight, she felt his hand pressing hers in turn, a secret fever coursed through their fingers, heat beyond, if possible, what she'd felt in their frenzied, naked coupling in the dangerous shadows of Paris.

Now they were arrived, and Héloïse turned from looking at Peter to take in the sight of the prosperous river town, with its mill, grain house, animal pens, boatyard, stone dwellings, and substantial church. To her surprise, in this first glimpse of Nantes, the future seemed to show itself. She sensed that here events would form the hinge between the lost, if blustery, girl she'd been until now, and the unperturbed woman she would be once she had a healthy son and his faithful father settled, however their bond of love took shape in the world as it was.

Lucille was waiting for them on the rough ledge of the riverbank, where trodden grass held back the tidal mud. She was a pasty woman, looking, from the heft of her, to be well into her fourth decade. Her hair was hidden in the veil that creased her forehead. Her face, even shadowed, was bright with welcome. Hers was a familiar visage, since, as Héloïse saw at once, Lucille had Peter's sharp nose and his sweetly cleft chin. To her tawny skirts clung a diminutive, smock-clad child, while a pair of boys wrestled roughly at her feet. Beside her stood an even larger man, in whose arms squirmed an even younger child. Because the sun was low in the sky behind them, the man and woman, together with their children, were suspended in a radiant aura, making them seem a chosen family—or such was the fuzzy thought that came unbidden to Héloïse.

Enough of that! She focused. The man wore the sleeveless leather jerkin of an armorer, with a belt buckled at his ample belly by an oval of silver. A riot of long red hair and a rich red beard were organized around a broad smile, which made him seem the jolly fellow Peter had promised he would be: Marcus, then.

Héloïse was surprised to realize that she had, perhaps in a dream, anticipated such an arrival, imagining some while ago a world of contentment, even in exile. This unlikely expectation seemed fulfilled when Lucille, seeing them and scooping up her child, rushed forward happily. "Peter!" she cried. "Dear Peter! Praise God, you are here!"

As Peter scrambled across the mud to his sister, Héloïse took special notice of the deftness with which Lucille handled her child as she took her brother into her embrace. The woman's heart was large, and her manner competent.

Marcus, a skilled metal crafter and purveyor of breastplates and ring mail to the constables of the Duke of Bretagne, was a prosperous man. The house he provided for his family was large and well-built—a three-story stone-and-timber structure with decorated mullioned windows before which candles were set, and soon lit. Héloïse enjoyed watching the children rattle around the place. Given that guests were present, they seemed unusually free-spirited. After a raucous meal, and once the children were asleep, Lucille and Marcus sat formally with Héloïse and Abelard in the central ground-floor hall, before the warming hearth—the hosts in high-backed wooden chairs, the visitors on stools.

Peter made his explanations with a curl of feeling for which Héloïse loved him. When he'd finished, Lucille stood, crossed to Héloïse, took her hands into her own, and said, "Daughter, you are at home with us." And so she was.

Peter, comforted by the peace Héloïse had found in the embrace of his family, returned within weeks to Paris. But he was anxious, too, about what awaited him on the overheated island in the Seine. From his later recounting, Héloïse knew what he found at the Cloister of Notre-Dame. His wholly self-absorbed students had resented his unexplained absence from the dais, and more than three hundred rowdies had shown up for the first of his resumed lectures, which was teasingly announced on posters throughout the school with the one-word title *Ergo*. The implication of Master Peter's jibe was plain enough: "As you were about to conclude brilliantly before my absence so rudely interrupted you . . ."

When Peter mounted the platform, the students stomped, pounded, hectored, and whistled, demanding his apologetic explanation. Peter put them off with joviality that was as counterfeit as it was, in the end, rhetorically triumphant. With a single upraised arm, palm open, he waited for them to fall silent. Laying his trap, he asked meekly, "Does the truant Master owe his scholars an explanation?" They exploded again, with whistles and stomping, demanding it. Again, seeking silence, he waited them out. Then, suddenly stern, he demanded, "Did Socrates explain himself to Plato?" he asked. "Or Plato to Dion?" He struck a tone that, once recognized as a challenge, ignited a happy sequence of alternating—and competing—antiphons.

"Or Dion to Crean?" one called.

"Or Heraclitus to Cratylus?" cried another, setting them off.

"Or Aristotle to Timaeus?"

"Or Cicero to Atticus?" And so on, until, as such raucous exchanges always did, the thing came round to Master Peter Abelard again. The boys were not disappointed when he cauterized their passionate rudeness with "And did Zechariah owe an accounting to his ass?" The hoots at that could be heard across the river. The Master was back.

Over subsequent days, Peter Abelard learned that rumors had achieved the status of Holy Writ. His students had assured one another that his absence had been prompted by a summons from the Abbot Primate of Cluny, the monk-potentate seeking private forum counsel from the greatest teacher in Christendom. No, not Father Abbot, but the Cardinal of Sens. No, the school at Rheims had hired him as Rector. No, the Great Chapter at Chartres had finally issued its indictment, and Master Peter Abelard, in solemn disputation, had won the day at last against the White Monk, Bernard of Clairvaux, champion of a whole company of critics.

Among the Cathedral's other Masters of Philosophy, Abelard's intimate enemies, whisperers agreed that he was off with Jews; that his insults to the great Anselm and Roscellinus had reached the

King's ears; that he would therefore be expelled from the school; that, intimidated by the coming Great Chapter and the threat of Bernard, he had fled Paris to avoid the subpoena, which the Cardinal was certain to have authorized by now. The clucking of fishmongers was nothing to the noise his rivals made.

To Peter Abelard, however, there was only one figure whose current impression of him mattered, and that was Canon Fulbert. Peter was distressed to have learned that, as he feared, there had been one rumor that, although not rising to the credible level of others, had been discreetly passed among the inner circle of his admiring students, who, understanding its mortal danger, had apparently protected him by not spreading it more broadly: the tonsured Abelard was in violation of the vow of chastity with that fairest of girls oft seen in the Cloister. Had Canon Fulbert heard those whispers? What did he suspect? Indeed, what did he know?

On the Sunday after returning from Nantes, at solemn Vespers, Peter Abelard and Fulbert would be together in choir with their fellow Canons of Notre-Dame, and Peter resolved to approach him. There were two dozen Canons Regular, the senior clerics who served the Cathedral as sacramental ministers, officers of the diocese, chaplains to the Bishop, or, as in Abelard's case, Masters of the school. In the absence of the Bishop, Canon Fulbert presided at the festal ceremonies, and that was the case on this Sunday, as the evening celebration of the Divine Mystery unfolded. Into the dark reaches of the great vaulted nave soared the lilting chant of the Holy Office Psalter, together with pungent clouds of smoky incense. At the high altar, the Blessed Sacrament was lifted up in its crystal disc inside the hammered gold of the sunburst monstrance, which shimmered in the light of a score of candles and oil lamps. Once the adoration was accomplished, with the singing of "Panis Angelicus," the liturgical party—in addition to the Canons, there were deacon acolytes, thurifers, and untonsured members of the minor orders, all robed variously—formed a long procession that wound behind torch candlesticks from the sanctuary, down the center aisle, through the crossing, to the sacristy lodged in the north porch of the Cathedral.

Abelard was normally one to shed his *cappa nigra* promptly, hang the choir robe on its hook, and be off. But this evening, he lingered. A line of clerics waited for a word with Fulbert, their shaved heads shining in light reflected from the flaming wall sconces. Stout and perspiring, Fulbert openly delighted in this communal show of deference. He dispensed small servings of his attention like Communion wafers. At his elbow, waiting to receive his ceremonial *birettum* and cope, was his chaplain, but in the dark corner beyond the vestment case was the hunched form of Brother Thrall. Fulbert's waiflike *servus* was standing by with the Canon's cloak and staff, ready to be gestured forward.

Filius Nullius: son of no one. It shamed Peter suddenly to realize that he had hardly ever registered Canon Fulbert's omnipresent thrall, or the others like him scurrying about in the shadows of the Cathedral and its close, like the rats they were set to catch. How many of these church slaves were there, Peter wondered? And, apart from Fulbert's lackey, whom Peter vaguely recognized, how were they distinguished one from another? Dark phantoms crossed his mind, figures glimpsed throughout our Lady's precinct, but always on the edge of things, shoveling filth, hauling water, stacking firewood—or, if one of them was favored as the personal thrall of someone like Fulbert, holding ready the stave with which His Lordship might then stride off or, on a whim, turn and beat him. Peter felt a bolt of vomit rising in his throat—a rancid distillation of loathing at his own blind indifference to these sorry bastards until now, when it was possible that he himself had spawned a next one. He thought of his dear Héloïse, the certainty with which she dreaded the birth of a son, an incipient thrall, and for the first time, Peter Abelard felt the fear as she felt it— the sure knowledge that their child would be stolen from them, and stunted for life.

At last, Canon Fulbert turned to him. "Master Peter Abelard," he said, but icily. "How good of you to grace our Vespers with your presence."

Peter bowed, even while pushing down on the apprehension he felt at the Canon's undisguised pique. "Your Lordship. Peace be with you."

"And with you. What news from the infidel?"

"I beg your pardon?"

"The Bishop received an account of your absence from Paris. He is not pleased."

"I am surprised His Excellency takes note of my whereabouts. What account?" Peter's calm was counterfeit. This was not what he expected.

"Al-Andalus. You traveled across the southern mountains, and not as a pilgrim on the Way of Saint James."

Peter snorted. "A journey to and from Compostela, dear Canon, requires many weeks."

"The Jewish academy at Mainz, then. The Bishop knows you were away consulting Jews—again."

Peter Abelard shook his head. He reined in his disdain, but he was wary. "As you know, Canon, the Jewish academy at Mainz was destroyed by the rabble armies of Peter the Hermit, a destruction which the Pope himself condemned. Would that the Torah was still being studied along the Rhine. I was not there. The Bishop is misinformed."

"You are the one who brings the pagan texts to Paris. You receive them from the Jews."

"The pagan texts, Canon Fulbert? Cicero? Virgil? Plato, whom Justin Martyr called the 'unknowing Christian'? The loss of such texts to the Vandals was a catastrophe. Their recovery is a gift of Wisdom, which, of course, is a Name of God: 'Chokhmat Elohim.' "

Fulbert tossed his head, shaking off the better-knower's jab. "The Proverbs tell us, 'Wisdom's instruction is to fear the Lord.' "

"Indeed so," Abelard replied. "And also: 'The Lord giveth Wisdom. Out of His mouth cometh knowledge and understanding.' "

"But God's enemies trade in these pagan books—the Saracens and Jews."

Canon Fulbert was a formidable man, but he could also be dull-witted. Abelard knew that, if he was being patient, it was important not to be seen as being patient. He said, "You make a point, Canon. A serious one. Nevertheless, it remains that Saracens and Jews advance God's purposes in this one realm. The books they translate define the study of universals and particulars not only in our school, but in Orléans, Chartres, Rheims, Metz, and Cologne. Yet Paris is supreme. The library of philosophers over which you preside is unsurpassed in Christendom. Does the Bishop know of this preeminence? Surely, you have helped him to take pride in your school?"

Fulbert knew that the exchange had gone against him, but he had no idea what to do about it. Peter Abelard rescued him by saying simply, "As for my absence, I went away to visit my family in Bretagne."

Fulbert said nothing, standing immobile. His chaplain crooked a finger at Brother Thrall, who came forward with the cloak. The chaplain took it, and draped the Canon's shoulders. Then the staff was handed over. Fulbert closed his fat fingers around it.

Bowing, Peter Abelard said, "Canon Fulbert, I heartily wish to remain in your good graces. I am honored to be of your household."

Fulbert replied, "You have critics, Master Peter Abelard. The Bishop hears from them. I hear from the Bishop. No one hears from the legion of buffoonish boys who sit at your feet."

"Ah, but, Canon, that the boys are legion is the point. Their numbers define the triumph of our school. They are not buffoons. In their generation, the Gospel will be renewed throughout the world—by the Holy Spirit, making use of the learning they acquire *here*. The Holy Spirit is the wind that blows where it will, and our scholars have sailed upon it from all across Europe to the sacred college of thought you have created at Notre-Dame de Paris. My critics, as you know, are the disappointed Masters of the failing schools from which our lads have flown. Shall I meet with the Bishop to explain all this to him?"

"No." With a flip of his cloak, Fulbert made as if to go, but then stopped himself. "My household, you said. You are present to it for the sake of my niece, Héloïse."

"Indeed, so. A brilliant young woman."

"Does her brilliance shine better at night?" Fulbert's gaze hardened.

The question threw Peter. Without imagining ahead of time how it could go, he had hoped, in this encounter, to test Fulbert's readiness to hear him out. When in doubt, Peter had often advised others, proceed with the truth. It was advice he had given himself—against himself—for days now: somehow to lay the impossible truth of his love for Héloïse before Fulbert. But Fulbert was not to be predicted. Or, rather, Fulbert was to be predicted in nothing but in his being dangerous. Peter had come here like a blind man rubbing his hands across the rough surface of a wall, looking for an opening. But now the wall had closed around him, a jail cell.

What did Fulbert know of their secret life at night?

Peter recognized the Canon's question as a trap, but also as a signal that his suspicions, if he had them, were not confirmed. All Peter knew for certain was that he would not lie. He said, "We have it from the book of Job: some deep knowledge comes only in visions of the night. It is true, your niece and I have occasionally pursued . . . our work . . . beyond the coming of dusk. It is true, also, that I have never before . . . engaged with . . . such a one as this noble young woman. I look forward to informing you more fully, Reverend Canon, of our progress. I would like to say now that I . . ." Peter paused. The wall again, a blind search for an opening. ". . . have become mightily devoted to Héloïse."

Fulbert, having eyed Abelard carefully, looked sharply away, an evident act of deflection. "Yes. Well," he said. The Canon made a dismissive gesture with his free hand, and there was relief in it. "No matter now. Her lessons are suspended. Concluded, in fact. In your absence, my niece decamped for the court of the Duke of Bourgogne, who, you remember, is her dearly departed mother's cousin. It is not certain that Héloïse will return to Paris from Dijon. She is preparing there to become a Lady-in-Waiting to the mother of the Queen Consort. Héloïse is a credit to us. Who knows? Perhaps the Queen herself will tap her. Imagine, our Héloïse a member of the *Royal* Court. In that case"—with a wide grin, despite his resolve to be discreet, Fulbert betrayed his extreme delight—"she will return to Paris, but for the Royal *Palace.* I have advised the Bishop of this. He is awaiting an opportunity to recommend her to the Royal Court, and he will tell King Louis of our role in her preparation." Fulbert touched Peter's arm, almost fondly. "That would serve us both." He moved off before Peter could think what to say.

In Canon Fulbert's vacant after-space, Brother Thrall waited for Peter to look at him, and when he did, Peter flinched at the hatred he saw in the twisted creature's eyes. Once more, Peter thought of Héloïse, and their doomed son.

CHAPTER TWELVE

Immediately after the Six, Kavanagh took the parish car without asking. He drove downtown, arriving at the Villard Houses on Madison not long after seven-thirty, when the Chancery Offices, and hallways, would still be vacant.

Just visible, inside the elaborate double doors, the night watchman was still at his post in the great foyer, dwarfed by the gleaming chandelier that hung above him. He was a blue-suited, overweight retiree—an ex-cop, by Kavanagh's guess. With his shiny bald head forward, he was slumped in a purposely uncomfortable bentwood chair, next to a small square table holding his chrome Thermos and workman's lunch box. Kavanagh tapped softly on the door pane. The man snapped awake. He leapt to his feet. By crossing so quickly to the door, he displayed embarrassment at having been caught dozing, which Kavanagh knew could work for him.

The guard threw the lock and pulled the door open. "Sorry, Father," he said. Here, beyond all places, the Roman collar was a pass.

"No, Sarge. I'm the one who's sorry. It's too early by a mile. I hate to disturb you."

The guard pulled out a pocket watch, plainly relieved to read the time—more than twenty minutes to go before the building was to open.

"I left something upstairs yesterday," Kavanagh said. "I have to get it."

"Sure, Father. Sure."

It hit Kavanagh, how readily the lie had come. He said, "I don't need to bother you. Just let me borrow the master key, would you? I'll be just a minute."

The guard hesitated. A dozen or more priests manned offices here, and most of them, coming in late and leaving early, rarely crossed paths with a fellow on the night shift. But why wouldn't a Chancery official have his own key?

Kavanagh said, "I've just come from Mass. I have to get to the hospital." All true. "I'll just be a minute," he repeated.

The guard handed over the large ring with its set of four keys. "It's this one, Father. The big one."

"Thanks, Sarge."

The guard smiled. "I never made it off the beat, Father. You've promoted me."

"You deserve it, Sarge." Kavanagh saluted the man, then crossed into the regal main hall, his heels clicking on the high-polished marble. He made for the glittering grand staircase, the spine of the Renaissance palazzo. At its foot, he looked back and saw that the guard was unscrewing his Thermos—good. Kavanagh took the first several stairs with a hop, and successive treads two at a time. On the second floor, he was struck, again, by the life-sized portraits on the gilded wall to his left—saints and prelates, the gallery of God. Jogues, Rogues.

"Episcopal Vicar for Clergy," he read at Bishop Donovan's door. In short order, Kavanagh applied the key, threw the lock, and entered the outer office. The portrait of the Risen Christ now struck him as another watchman, and he avoided the Lord's gaze, to go directly to the file cabinet. The top drawer was marked, as he'd unconsciously noticed, "Current Correspondence," and he opened it. He found a rack of folders, the tabs of which were marked with numbers: dates, he realized. He quickly calculated—one folder for each week. He withdrew the first three and positioned them on the clear surface of the cabinet. He opened first one, then the second, and the third, arranging stacks. He fingered through odds and ends of letters and note cards, unsure what, exactly, he was looking for. John Malloy. Runner. No, John Malloy.

A school. New Jersey. "That kind of school," Agent had said. Therefore, quality paper, proper stationery.

Through each stack, Kavanagh found no Malloy. Complaints from pastors about curates, requests for transfer, condolence letters, recommendations—nothing from John Malloy. His pulse had quickened, and now he felt the muscles in his chest tighten, his heart rush. The crushing headache of the day before was gone, but he was alert for its return.

Once he'd visualized the file cabinet, and the drawer label; once he'd recalled Bishop Donovan's reference to the letter, "Special Delivery, out of the blue," he'd imagined a way forward. But this was a dead end.

"Out of the blue." The letter, he realized all at once, would have been addressed not to an official, the Vicar for Clergy, but to a long-lost friend. *Personal.* Therefore, not the bureaucracy file cabinet, but somewhere else: Donovan's desk.

Kavanagh gathered the letters and cards back into their folders, the folders back into their drawer. Now, though, there was a tremor in his hands. What was he doing? What was he thinking? A letter kept apart, out of the secretary's purview—what would that imply?

He went to the Bishop's door, ready to try the master key again, but the door was unlocked. He entered, crossed, and quickly found himself at the window alcove, inside the U-shaped desk. He was moving fast. If he stopped to think, he would simply stop. Instead, he efficiently set about opening drawers, first the center one, then the column of three on the right, in one of which, lying prone, was a pint of Jim Beam and a shot glass. Under the pint was a manila envelope with the letters "RIP" scrawled across it.

The left topmost drawer was cluttered with pencils, a pair of scissors, a box of clips, a blotter, a ball of rubber bands, erasers, a bottle of Carter's ink—all of which, as if set to do so, pressed down on a single business-sized envelope. He picked it up, like an item of contraband. Addressed in clear handwriting to "Bishop Sean Donovan, the

Chancery, Archdiocese of New York, Madison Avenue, New York," the envelope, aside from the Special Delivery stamp angled across the lower left corner, was otherwise blank—no return address.

The letter had been slit open, and Kavanagh withdrew its page—a formal, longhand note beginning, "Dear Bishop Donovan," and signed "Sincerely Yours, John Malloy." No address. The letter declared in three sentences Malloy's intention to come to Bishop Donovan's office for a brief visit at 4:00 p.m. on Monday, November 13—three days ago, the afternoon before Runner turned up at the Communion rail at Good Shepherd. The brevity of the note, its formality, the lack of any explanation or way to return contact, added up to the writer's wily caution. What was up with John Malloy? Not a hint. As had happened the other morning, such self-protection stymied Michael Kavanagh.

But he thought of Rachel Vedette: "There is a way to learn what you need to learn. You must find it." That was all.

He refolded the letter. As he returned it to its envelope, he looked at the written address again. Was it only the passage of time that made the penmanship unfamiliar? Yet the looped cursive, with a flourish of tag lines at the ends of words, conveyed a bright self-assurance that Kavanagh had associated with his old friend, and he felt the pang of having missed him all these years—and now, at this dead end, of missing him again.

But then he saw the postmark, with its flutter of lines canceling the stamp in the upper right-hand corner. The smudged black ink showed the date inside the circle of words: "Lake Durham, Sparta Township, N.J." He stared for a moment.

He put the envelope back in the drawer, replaced the desk paraphernalia as it had been, closed the drawer, and quickly left the Bishop's office. Clipping down the palazzo stairs, he glanced ahead and saw, just entering the grand hall, the schoolmarmish woman from the day before, Bishop Donovan's secretary. Caught!

Kavanagh slowed his pace so that their paths crossed at the foot of the stairs instead of closer to the night guard. He touched his forehead nonchalantly. "Morning, ma'am." She was startled, of course, and might have spoken—a query, at least; perhaps a challenge—but he kept going. At the door, still moving, he dropped the key ring on the square table, beside the lunch box. "Thanks, Sarge," he said, and tossed another salute. "Catch up on your sleep, now."

The parking garage at the Waldorf Astoria, two blocks away, welcomed the Cathedral clergy gratis, and that was where he had parked. He returned to the car, then had another thought. He grabbed his books and went into the hotel. From a phone booth in the lobby, he called Good Shepherd and asked Frank Russell to cover for him at the hospital. He thought of asking for the Monsignor, to request permission for use of the car, but instead told Frank to let the boss know he had it. What the hell.

He had to kill some time. He went to the corner coffee shop, took a table, and, leaving his breviary aside, opened the leather-bound book, picking a page at random. Translation, in truth, did not come easily to him: *The gossip at last reached Fulbert's ears. It was with great difficulty he gave credit to what he heard, for he loved his niece, and was prejudiced in my favor.* Kavanagh looked up, afraid all at once of appearing foolish. As had been true all those years before, in theology class, he marked the work of puzzling through Latin by moving his lips as he read, and he realized he'd been doing that now. He looked around. The shop was a-bustle with businessmen and tourists. No one cared a damn for a solitary priest with his little book of Latin. He focused on the page again, listening for Peter Abelard's voice, the story of his calamity. *But, upon closer examination, Fulbert began to be less incredulous. He surprised us in one of our quieter conversations. How fatal, sometimes, are the consequences of curiosity! The anger of Fulbert seemed to moderate on this occasion, and I feared in the end some more heavy revenge.*

Kavanagh looked up again, and this time he closed the book. "Readiness to stake everything on the absolute": Rachel Vedette's words weighed more in Kavanagh's mind than did the words of Abelard. A woman's words. For Abelard, hadn't the absolute come down to his feeling for a woman? Or was that Héloïse, in her feeling for a man? Kavanagh was struck by his own ignorance—how little he knew of these lovers, or any lovers. Across hundreds of hours, in the darkened booth on the priest's side of the Confessional, he had heard described every variation in the eternal saga of man and woman, but he knew as little of its deeper meaning as he did, well, of God's. The Absolute? He was struck, too, by his own distance from any sense of that word's meaning, whatsoever.

Had he presented himself falsely to the Frenchwoman at The Cloisters? The intensity of her declaration came back to him, the fierceness of her interest "Abelard finds it possible to stand against the whole world—for the world. For the human, and for the holy— both! How was that? What sort of faith makes that possible? I have never discussed this with a priest."

He was a "priest"—okay. But he was not remotely what she meant when she used that word. *Of course,* he'd presented himself falsely. To escape the shame of that recognition, Kavanagh lit a cigarette, distracting himself with the business of the match, the flame, the ashtray. But the train of thought ran on: *The human and the holy*—two realms in each of which he had, separately, constructed the fittings of a life, but the human and the holy *both*? What did he know of the realm in which they were *joined*? Nothing.

It was nine o'clock. He stubbed out his cigarette, paid his bill, and returned to the hotel lobby, for the phone booth. From Information, he got the number of the Sparta Township Chamber of Commerce. To the woman answering, he introduced himself as a prospective home- buyer interested in school options for his teenaged son. Private school, he said, close to Lake Durham, if possible. And that was how Kava- nagh learned of Saint Aiden's School, for boys in grades seven through twelve. "They take boarders," the Chamber woman said, "but with you living in the area, you won't want that. They have some day stu- dents. It's Protestant, if that matters to you. College prep. Ivy League. Like that." Kavanagh thanked her, and marveled, once again, at how easy it was to lie.

LAKE DURHAM, he read, was the largest private man-made body of water in New Jersey, with its westernmost shore just kissing the Pocono foothills that ran on into Pennsylvania. On that day, the lake was salted with whitecaps, running with the wind directly toward him. He stood near the town information board, on the edge of a tiered boardwalk. The planned community, a first of its kind, had been created by highflyers before the Crash, and, for the most part, it had maintained itself as an enclave of privilege ever since. Under bright sunshine, the lake rolled on for distant miles, in the bowl of hills that, with sharp peaks and jutting ledges, evoked an Alpine fantasy, although in miniature. Large houses—mansions—dotted the hills, dozens of them. The place looked to be a kind of inland Newport.

It had taken nearly two hours to drive here from New York. He was dressed now in the plaid shirt he'd worn under his rabat, and the windbreaker he'd tossed in the backseat of the car. The town center behind Kavanagh was defined, along the boardwalk, by a row of shops and offices in joined buildings that reiterated the Alpine motif, with steep roofs, timber-and-stucco siding, and fancifully cut gingerbread trim. At each end of the row stood a massive, multi-story chalet, each with exterior wooden stairs and craft-worked balconies. From the sharp peaks of both chalets wafted long red-and-blue pennants, showing the wind, despite the cloudless sky, for the near gale that it was.

Beyond the town center, the land sloped gradually away from the lake and its ring of hills, leveling out into pastures set off by pristine white fencing. Horses could be seen nibbling at the shorn November grass. Jump railings dotted the fields. Along the boardwalk, closer, town-and-country ladies in jodhpurs and hacking jackets crossed from the stores toward a parking lot and station wagons. The entire scene struck Kavanagh as a high-pedigree dream village. The only thing missing was a train set with railroad trestles and crossing posts ready to flash, ring, and bring down pole gates.

The hills, the bowl, the lake, the Alpine town, the fenced-off horse farms—all of it was, in addition to being so smugly itself, an exquisite setting for Saint Aiden's School, which stood at the far terminus of the boardwalk, on the other side of the hundred-foot-long river dam that held in place the water of Lake Durham. Through a sluice in that distant end of the dam crashed a waterfall over which, as it did everything in sight, presided the main school building. It was a Victorian version, in dark granite, of a sprawling Norman castle, with a pair of crenellated towers from each of which proudly flew—

there, too—a red-and-blue pennant. On the two visible sides of the building, expansive lawns sloped down to the lake, meeting it at a cuticle-shaped beach, where overturned sailboat hulls were arranged like piano ivories. A neo-Gothic chapel shared one remote stretch of grass with a U-shaped building—a dormitory?—which also featured blocked granite and arched leaded windows. In the distance, beyond the castle, rose a tall chimney, suggesting a stand-alone powerhouse. From back there, Kavanagh heard the faint pop of what sounded like a gunshot.

He followed the curving walkway up to the main building's large oaken door, which was so well balanced on its pins that it opened easily. Inside, in an office to the left, was the receptionist. She was a pleasant-looking young woman, standing at a bookshelf behind the desk, about to insert a volume into a set of matching books. When she saw Kavanagh in the threshold, she started to smile, but checked herself, assuming a willed solemnity. "Mr. Rohan?" she said.

"No, no. I'm not."

"Oh. I was expecting Mr. Rohan. A parent."

"I'm just passing by," Kavanagh said. "I thought I'd stop."

Now the woman smiled, patently pleased to be able to do so. "Oh, that's nice. Visitors are always welcome here."

"Thank you. Actually, I've dropped in, hoping to see an old friend. He's a teacher here. John Malloy."

"Oh." Once again her face darkened. "Yes, well . . ."

"I know it's a bad time. Classes are meeting, I assume."

"Yes. It's fourth period. Normally, Mr. Malloy would be in class, but . . ." She channeled her worried uncertainty into the act of pushing the volume into its place on the shelf.

Not knowing what else to do, Kavanagh waited her out. She said, "Mr. Malloy is out on the track, with Tommy Rohan. They are waiting for Tommy's father, who's coming to pick him up."

"Oh. Well, I don't want to interrupt. Is it okay if I just wander around the grounds a bit? It's beautiful here."

She did not answer. Kavanagh realized he had intruded on something, without any sense of what it was, but Mr. Malloy seemed to be involved. The young woman clearly had no authority, and he did not want her calling on someone who did. He backed out of the room. "I'll check in another time," he said. Leaving the building, he noticed in the foyer now what he had missed before—a midsized steamer trunk, a pair of suitcases, a braced tennis racket leaning on the trunk.

He wandered out into the grassy campus, and nonchalantly made his way across the lawns that led behind the castle. He saw the track, a great gray oval with a facing pair of goalposts as its elliptical focal points. The track and football field centered the even broader set of wide-open athletic fields that stretched off into the distance—including a pair of baseball diamonds, and a second football field. The expanse of green was broken only by a large boxlike building, up a slight incline from the track. That would be the field house. Looming over one side of the scene stood a monumental oak tree, with its gray cloud of bare branches. On the track beyond the tree, a lad in sweats could be seen crouched at starting blocks, the only runner in the middle of half a dozen lanes. Close by stood a lean man in a tweed suit and fedora, with his arm raised above his head. The only figures in the panorama, they seemed, at this distance, delicate, unreal. Kavanagh heard the pop again, a gunshot, and the boy took off, sprinting down the center lane. The man had fired a starter pistol.

After running perhaps fifty yards, the boy slowed, then stopped.

"Better," the man called to the boy, and the wind carried the word back to Kavanagh, who knew, despite the man's facing away, that it was Runner. He called, "Let's go again!"

The boy turned and jogged back to the blocks. Once more, he took his position, arched up, froze, waited. Runner raised the gun, and fired. Smoke puffed from his hand. The boy leapt forward into his sprint. After a dozen paces, as before, he pulled up. Malloy called something else again, words lost in the wind.

Kavanagh drew nearer, instinctively heading for the tree, which he kept between himself and his old friend. The boy glanced Kavanagh's way once, but took no notice.

Regretting the surreptitiousness of it, Kavanagh took up a place by the tree to watch. The drill continued: gunshot, jump, sprint, return; gunshot, jump, sprint, return. Shaving milliseconds off the completed dash was only one of the drill's purposes; winning the start was part one of winning the race.

Kavanagh was close enough to sense Runner's benign patience, and the sprint athlete's willing determination. But as he watched, Kavanagh saw that the boy, when he wasn't running, seemed high-strung, electric with nervousness, his arms jostling and tics jolting his head. Only once settled into his crouch, at the blocks, did he seem capable of focus. Into the instant before the start he poured concentration and discipline that seemed otherwise to elude him.

But if Runner was the coach, why was he in street clothes? Once more, Kavanagh was struck by his tailoring—the three-piece tweeds, the stylish hat, ankle boots. In the outdoor setting, from that distance, Runner came off as a gentleman farmer, but Kavanagh recalled from the other morning his ravaged face, his bloodshot eyes, misery etched into the way he carried himself. From where Kavanagh stood now, though, he could not see Runner's face.

Out of the wind, from behind Kavanagh, came the sharp cry, "Tommy!" It carried across the distance with urgency, and anger. The boy came up from his crouch at once, and he looked toward the voice with an expression both forlorn and frightened. Kavanagh turned, and saw crossing toward the track a pair of hatless men, one in a flapping tan topcoat, the other in a dark business suit. They took no more notice of Kavanagh, by the tree, than Malloy had. The man in the topcoat had rage in his face as he closed in on the boy.

I feared in the end—Abelard's words popped into Kavanagh's mind—*some more heavy revenge.*

Kavanagh guessed that this was Mr. Rohan, come to collect his son. The trunk and suitcases at the door suggested an expulsion, which would account for the father's anger. Yet, if the boy was leaving the school, why was Runner still coaching him?

The man charged toward the track, but before he reached the boy, Malloy stepped in his way. That Malloy was still holding the starter gun made the scene seem dangerous. Malloy spoke, but Kavanagh could not hear. The boy's father, if that's what he was, attempted to step past Malloy, but Malloy blocked him again. The boy shrank back.

The third man began to berate Malloy, then to plead with Mr. Rohan. Among the words that Kavanagh caught were ". . . disgruntled Latin teacher . . . track coach . . . don't listen to him . . ." The loud phrase that came most distinctly from John Malloy, addressed to the parent, was "Not true! Not true!" A moment later, Malloy turned to the other man and repeated it, more angrily.

Mr. Rohan seemed disgusted with both of the men. At last, he succeeded in grabbing his son's arm, but the boy shook free. Malloy dropped the pistol to reach for the boy, who eluded Malloy, too.

Mr. Rohan wheeled on the other man, whom Kavanagh had pegged by now as the school authority, the headmaster. The father spoke furiously, while the headmaster sought only to placate. At last, Mr. Rohan turned and brushed past Malloy and successfully seized his son's arm, pulled him roughly. Now the wind brought the words clear: "Come on! We're getting out of here!"

"No, Dad!" The boy jerked his arm free, a movement that ignited him. With clenched fists, he seemed ready to fight. Even across the distance, Kavanagh could see that his eyes were wide, maniacal. "Don't come near me," the boy cried.

"How dare you!" his father shouted. He reached for his son again, but the lad dropped to his knees, a move that seemed only like defeat, until he picked up the starter gun. He aimed it up at his father, and fired. The gunshot was hollow, but loud.

"Jesus!" Mr. Rohan cried, falling back.

The boy stood, his face twisted now. He closed on his father, and fired the gun again. Smoke burst from its barrel. The father shrank away, half running, and fell, as if he'd taken a bullet.

Malloy slapped the gun out of the boy's hand.

The boy turned to run, but Malloy stopped him, taking him by the shoulders. He pummeled Malloy, but Malloy overpowered him, taking him into his arms, a lock. At that point, the boy collapsed against Malloy, and began to sob. As Malloy held him, the muscular grip eased to become a most tender embrace. The boy wept and wept. Time stopped for a long moment. The boy's misery superseded everything.

Soon, a shaken Mr. Rohan came forward to stand with Malloy

and his son. Kavanagh saw that tears streaked the father's face, too. He tentatively touched the boy's hair, and spoke words that Kavanagh heard as, "Tommy, I'm sorry."

Malloy opened an arm, and gently nudged the weeping boy toward his father, who took him into his arms and patted him, as if saying, "There, there, Tommy." After some moments, the father and son, clinging to each other, turned and began to make their way up the sloping lawn, heading for the castle.

The third man, still in the grip of consternation, had not moved. Now, with the father and son at a distance, he craned toward Malloy and snarled a burst of hateful sentences, curses. Malloy ignored him. He stooped and picked the gun up, together with what Kavanagh saw as a box of cartridges. Malloy waved off the sputtering headmaster, who turned and stormed away, back toward the castle.

Runner stood there, looking after the man and, in the farther distance, the bereft father and son. Kavanagh had his best view yet of Runner's face, and saw that it was broken with grief. His eyes were pooled.

Kavanagh was not breathing. Half hidden by the tree, he thought of simply stepping fully behind it, never to be seen. But that would compound the violation of his intrusion with blatant dishonesty. He did not quite understand what he had witnessed, but his largest impression was of John Malloy's having cared for the boy, wanting to protect him.

As his old friend approached, Kavanagh moved away from the tree. "Hello, John," he called.

When Malloy saw Kavanagh, misery gave way to pure astonishment. "What?" That one word was all that he could manage: "What?"

Kavanagh walked toward him, aware of his own blushing. He was beyond embarrassed—hiding behind a tree, a sneak, a spy. Not knowing what he'd witnessed, he knew nevertheless what an interloper he was.

Malloy was aghast, barely able to believe his eyes. He said, "But what are you doing here?"

"Good question," Kavanagh answered. "It seems totally nuts right now, but I guess you could say . . . I tracked you down."

"Good Christ, Mike. Give me a minute." Malloy's eyes were rheumy, unfocused. He, too, was embarrassed.

"I followed you," Kavanagh said. "After you left Good Shepherd, I saw you go into the park, by The Cloisters." Kavanagh heard his own reference to the museum as meaningless here, but to him its relevance stood.

"Oh, man, Mike. Showing up at your church like that—I was drunk. I'm still drunk."

"You don't act drunk. I don't know what just happened, but I think I saw a good teacher trying to help his student."

"*Failing* to help his student. That boy is being kicked out for no good reason. Worse: he's being scapegoated."

"That gunshot—good Lord. I thought he'd actually—"

"Just blanks, a starter gun." Malloy gestured with the pistol, the cartridge box. "Tommy knew that."

"But—"

"The boy is troubled, that's for sure, but with every right. He's a misfit, but he's also an ace sprinter, best I've ever coached. The one uncomplicated thing about him. Away from the track, he's a mess. And now he's paying for it. A screwed-up athlete being screwed. Remind you of anyone?"

"You? Not as far as I knew."

"There's the point . . . how deeply buried it was." Malloy hesitated, then went on. "When Tommy told me I was the one teacher he could trust, I sensed what was coming." Again he paused, before continuing. "When he told me what was happening, I wanted nothing to do with him—just shut him off. This was last week. I ran from the kid instead of helping him. My own shit . . . out of nowhere . . . dumped all over me."

"What do you mean?"

"He came to me. I said I couldn't help him. I fled this place . . . went to New York, saw Father Donovan, got plastered. I was a pinball, slapped from pillar to post, until dawn . . . found myself at Good Shepherd, on my fucking knees, no idea how I got there. God, Mike, I apologize for that."

"What's going on, John?"

Malloy braced himself. He said, "Tommy was seduced by a teacher here. One of the gods. English teacher. An overnight field trip to Camden, visiting the grave of Walt Whitman, for Christ's sake. The asshole tapped Tommy as his hotel roommate. Back rubs. Massage. Singing the body electric. Fill in the blanks. The school is protecting the teacher. Ergo, they're screwing Tommy. They have to get rid of him. When they accused him of lying, the boy went berserk, which works for them, of course." Malloy stopped. A long silence. Then, "Obviously, I have my own issue here. What happened to Tommy— what they're doing to him now—it ambushed me."

To Kavanagh's surprise, tears began to wash down Malloy's cheeks. With the heel of one hand, he pushed into his eyes, trying to pull himself together. "Christ," he managed, "I'm astonished to see you."

Kavanagh replied, "That's how I felt Tuesday morning."

"You have no idea, Mike. No idea . . . This kid . . . He's what took me back, which obviously took me back to you. But then, when I actually laid eyes on you . . . at Mass . . . oh my God . . ."

"I don't get it, John." The word "ambushed" hung in Kavanagh's mind. He said, "I have my version of the same astonishment. Seeing you at the Communion rail—a ghost, then running away—threw me for a loop." His use of the cliché—again—made Kavanagh think of the Jewish woman. The Frenchwoman. That silenced him.

At last, Malloy found it possible to ask, "How'd you get here?"

"I have a car back in the village."

"There's a bar called the Swiss Alps. Give me an hour. I have to take another stab at getting to Tommy's father, before they leave. I have to get to him without having the headmaster block the way."

"Maybe I should just take off. This is—"

"No. No, Mike." Malloy stepped toward Kavanagh, with fresh urgency. "I need to talk to you. Kneeling before you at Good Shepherd, I saw something. An epiphany, sure as hell. Like waking up. It's why I took off like that. Foolish goddamn thing to do. But what I saw brought me rushing back here, to this Kingdom of the Blind Eye. No more blind eye for me. I had to help Tommy. Still do. Please, wait."

"Sure, Runner."

Malloy reacted as if slapped. "'Runner,'" he said. "Good God, nobody calls me that."

"It's how I think of you, still."

"Jesus, Mike . . ." Once again Malloy's eyes filled, but he fell silent.

To claw out of the swamp of feeling into which they'd sunk, Kavanagh asked, "You teach Latin?"

Malloy forced a grin. "What else could I do with my Dunwoodie education?"

"I ask because I'm reading a Latin book."

"What?"

"Historia Calamitatum."

"Really?"

"Yes," Kavanagh answered. "But you're surprised. Why?"

Malloy shrugged. "I had to leave the Church to read that," he said, palpably relieved to be discussing something else. "In our day, Abelard's misfortunes wouldn't have qualified as a priest's spiritual reading."

Kavanagh laughed, "Well, 'our day' is long over. And, oddly enough, I'm reading it because I followed you."

CHAPTER THIRTEEN

I endeavored to appease his anger by a sincere confession of all that was past, but he was only plotting a cruel revenge, as you will see by what follows. I took a journey into Bretagne, in order to bring back my dear Héloïse, whom I now considered as my wife. When I had acquainted her with what had passed between the Canon and me, I found she was of a contrary opinion to me.

"No, Peter," she said. "We will not. My uncle is a viper. Surely, you know that by now."

"He hisses, but has no fangs," Peter replied. "In any case, a viper can be handled."

"By a Saracen snake charmer. Fulbert cares nothing for your philosophy."

"He cares for himself. I can show him how he benefits from my release," Peter Abelard insisted. He was surprised that Héloïse, at this loaded moment, was mustering an argument against him. He went on: "Fulbert can intercede with the Bishop, who can sponsor the writ of my dispensation."

"Not dispensation. Banishment!" Her eyes flashed with feeling. She leaned toward him, saying, "You saw the Council decree: all marriages of clerics and monks invalid! A brutal reinforcement of Gregory's so-called reform! The power of Rome—and the protection of its treasure from the heirs of clergy—depend on this emasculation of men like you. As for the would-be wives of your kind, the Pope would have me sold into slavery. The Church, rejecting our marriage, would reject *me*. At best, I would be assigned a place at the Royal Court, not as a Lady, but as a courtesan—a universally available sex servant."

"Héloïse, you are—"

"And our son!" she cried. "Our son would certainly be seized by the Bishop. You know this! Our son a thrall! All this even before turning on you. Master Peter Abelard—deprived of his license! Muted forever! The power of the Church slammed down on you! You imagine pathetic Canon Fulbert as your sponsor now? That coward standing against an onslaught aimed at you? Never!"

Abelard shook his head. "Fulbert is tied to my case, whether he would be or not. His prestige is hostage to mine."

"*That* is what makes him dangerous," Héloïse insisted. "Even if he were inclined to untangle the knot for you, he would never do it for me. Not after his humiliation when my great coming out in the court at Bourgogne proved to be fiction."

"That humiliation is private. No one who matters knows of it. Only to the Bishop did he boast of your commendation, and the Bishop, in his wily prudence, forbade Fulbert to speak of your elevation at the Royal Court until the King was informed by the Duke, which never happened."

"Ah, but there it is," she said. "The Bishop was deceived, and Fulbert *lives* for his approval."

"If there was dishonor in the matter, reaching as high as the King, the Bishop of Paris will want it known no more than the Cathedral Canon. There *is* no scandal." Peter Abelard was carrying himself by now as if he were in disputation with his pupils.

"Nevertheless," she said, trying to rouse herself to the match, "the Bishop will want it adjudicated, the stain on his honor removed."

"Stains unseen, dear wife, are not stains."

"Do not 'wife' me, Peter. We are not married. We never will be."

Peter eyed her coldly. "You pretend to revere my intellect, but you hold my conscience in contempt. And conscience is the soul of intellect."

"I love your conscience, Peter. As I love you. Intellect. Soul. Body, too." She smiled, but wanly. Then she added, "I refuse to marry you, since marriage would destroy you." She was beginning to drift into another realm.

He missed that about her, and said blithely, "A lever and a place to stand! The prestige of the Cathedral school, which I enhance, is my ground. My lever is logic."

"Peter . . ."

"If need be, I will make our case to the Bishop. I will make it to the King."

"And the Pope?" she said, but wearily.

"Rome is full of concubines and whores. The Pope's apartments, too! This law of clerical chastity is empty."

"Ahhh . . ." The sound came from deep in her throat.

Still, he missed it. Peter rattled on, "Honesty, Héloïse. A simple statement of what is. Even those living in the lie must bend to the truth when faced with it. And I intend to face them."

"Concubines and whores . . ." Her voice faltered. "I never had such reason to think well of them"—she bent forward, then added, softly—"as now."

At last, Peter, the dunce, realized that the radiant cloud of heaven had come over her. She bucked and lurched, and clasped her heaving abdomen. "Oh, Peter, there! There it is . . . the gush of water! Fetch Lucille! Quickly!"

Peter rushed from her side. Héloïse was in her bed, in the small windowless room to which Lucille herself had repaired in the days before the births of two of her four children. Héloïse had been confined for seven days. For these last three, Peter, having come from Paris, had been with her. Her hair was unpinned, and she was wrapped in the pale blue coverlet—our Lady's color—that had seen Lucille through. A pair of candles stood on each of the bedside tables, throwing light to dance on the low, slanted ceiling.

Lucille, with her two serving girls, was soon ready with cloths and steaming water. They entered the room calmly. At the threshold, Lucille turned back to her brother, stopping him. "A while yet, Peter. I will let you know." She closed the door. Peter turned to Marcus, who said only, "*Terra incognita* to the likes of us."

When, some time later, Peter heard a torrent of screams, he could not help himself and crashed into the room. The three women were bending over Héloïse, at her knees. Peter went to her head. Her contorted face was a mess of hair and sweat. She was up on her elbows, off the bolster. From behind, he took the weight at her shoulders. At first, she continued screaming, apparently unaware of him. But the pain worsened to the point of silencing her. She turned a monstrously twisted face to him. He put his ear by her mouth. She managed to gasp, "Am I dying?"

"Yes, my darling," Peter whispered, "but not today. Today, you are life itself."

Timelessness, then. Not movement along the horizon of thought, one image parading past after another, but a penetration to the depth of awareness, one single feeling—pure absorbedness. Eternal consciousness. After what might have been moments, or hours, Lucille presented the swaddled child to Héloïse. The child was open-eyed and quiet.

Héloïse received the child, but tentatively. She looked up at Peter. "Was I wrong?"

Peter exchanged a look with Lucille, who said, "You have a fine son."

Héloïse said nothing, but her eyes overflowed, and Peter alone understood. Certain for many months of a coming male child, she had nonetheless prayed for a daughter instead—a child to whom the principalities and powers of the Church would be indifferent, and who could therefore live free. But now she shrugged that wish away, to draw their son into her absolute caress. She put her cheek against the infant's, washing him with her tears, loving him.

When, finally, she lifted her gaze from the baby's, she found Peter's eyes right beside her. Between sobs, she said, "He has your nose."

Peter nodded, and leaned yet closer. "You are magnificent," he said.

Across subsequent days, for the sake of their son, Héloïse told herself that perhaps her brilliant and courageous Peter was right in his blind certitude that some way forward could be found for them. She, far more than he, continued to be alive to the impossible reality of their condition, yet a startling new hope had become incarnate in the very person of their son. How vulnerable he was, how desperately in need of protection! The child was all in all to her, even while sealing the love she felt for Peter. Peter Abelard was her refuge, her protection, her everything.

Thus, it was the most natural thing in the world, when it came time to christen their baby, for Héloïse to want him named for his father. She ignored some deeply buried qualm to insist upon it.

The day came. Lucille, Marcus, and their children gathered with Peter, Héloïse, and the baby in the baptistry of the Nantes Cathedral. No one else was present; indeed, no one else knew of the occasion. The domed octagonal room replicated the form of the octagonal baptismal font around which the family drew itself. Each of the boys held one of the smaller sisters. Light poured in from the ring of clerestory windows above. The surrounding wall mosaic, made of gilded glass and marble chips of green and blue, glistened to show an aureoled Jesus before a skin-draped John. At the proper moment, Héloïse unswaddled the baby and handed him naked to Peter. As the liturgist, Peter was robed in white, an alb powdered with chalk, with the collar embroidered in blue and green. In preparation for the splash, his sleeves were rolled. The squirming child was poised to protest until Peter deftly soothed him by blowing softly in his ear, while swaying him slightly.

The baby remained calm while Peter enacted rubrics and said prayers, but then let out the inevitable shriek when Peter dipped him three times into the holy but frigid water. The child's cries bounced off the stone walls and echoed down from the womblike ceiling. Peter's voice, in pronouncing the sacramental formula, overrode the cries: *"Ego te baptizo in nomine Patris, et Filii, et Spiritus Sancti."* Hearing this, the child quieted, as his father went on to bestow his sacramental name by plucking a line from the Gospel of Matthew: *"Tu es Petrus"*—*Thou art Peter*—Peter Abelard declared, lifting the dripping child high above his head, "and the gates of hell shall not prevail against thee."

The child wailed once more, as if dangers implied by the prophecy registered, and Lucille stepped forward to take him. With the help of

Marcus, she efficiently wrapped him again in soft woolen apparels. Comforted, the baby fell silent. Attention centered on Peter Abelard, as all awaited the concluding prayer, but, still in his preacher's voice, he announced, "And now . . . *Kairos tou poiesai to Kyrio—the appointed time for the Lord to act—*one other sacrament, at this intersection with eternity." He turned to Héloïse.

"Meaning what?" she asked carefully.

Peter was shrugging off the white vestment, down to his black habit, but his eyes never left hers. "*Matrimonium sanctum.* We have our witnesses. We have the blessing of God, who made us as we are. We have each other."

Héloïse shook her head. "*Kairos* is the action of the Lord, not of men."

"The Lord acts *through* men, dear Héloïse. What else does our new theology mean?"

As he stepped to the altar and folded the vestment there, Héloïse exchanged a look with Lucille, who, with Marcus, was smiling benignly. Their children calmly looked on, enraptured by the glad solemnity they were witnessing.

Héloïse, understanding, faced Peter. "We have no celebrant but you," she said.

Peter laughed loudly, and so did his sister and her husband. "My being in Orders is irrelevant," he said. "The ministers of matrimony, as you well know, are the woman and the man themselves. The form and the matter belong to us. An illicit sacrament, perhaps, but nevertheless valid."

When he took her hand, she let him.

His eyes were intent upon hers. He said with grave deliberation, "Having long ago betrothed myself to you, I now offer this sign of my earnest pledge . . ." He turned briefly to Marcus, who placed something in his hand—a golden ring. Peter continued, ". . . if you freely receive me as your husband."

For a long moment, Héloïse said nothing. Peter's hand, with the ring, remained suspended between them, awaiting her finger. But Héloïse did not supply it. Instead, she turned to Lucille. "If you please, dear sister, your Agnus Dei." She gestured to the silver pendant at

Lucille's throat, a delicate piece of jewelry engraved with the Lamb, fashioned by Marcus. Without hesitating, Lucille whispered to Marcus, who stepped behind her and untied the waxed hemp cord from which the pendant hung—a short length, in fact, of bow string. Marcus removed his wife's medallion and handed the cord to Héloïse, who turned back to Peter. "I accept your pledge and this sign of it." She gave the cord to Peter and turned her back to him.

Peter saw. He threaded the cord through the ring and, lifting his arms over her head, tied it at the back of her neck.

When Héloïse turned to face him again, with the gold ring suspended on the top edge of her bodice, at the cleft of her breasts, she said, "I return your pledge with my own, dear husband." She took both of his hands in hers. "I will be a wife known but to you"—with that, she lifted one hand to make the ring disappear into the velvet at her bustline—"for as long as we live."

Peter drew her face to his. She parted her lips to receive his kiss.

He said, "What therefore God hath joined together, let not man put asunder."

They embraced. When Peter pulled back, he put his hand at her breast, to finger the ring beneath the fabric. He said in a less solemn but still earnest voice, "But, wife, when we return to Paris, we will find a way to make this marriage regular, settling this ring, thereby, on the hand where all can see it." He smiled suddenly. "And now that you are wife, you must obey."

Héloïse laughed, not perturbed in the least, but pushing back: "There is vanity in you, Master Peter Abelard, if you think, by mere words, you can shift the pillars of the age."

"The age is new, my lady. We are new. Substance matters more than form."

Héloïse put her hand at her breast. "This sign of our troth—form and substance both—will stay where it is."

"The treasure chest?" Peter said, happy enough to drop the subject.

Now when they kissed, Lucille, holding the infant, and Marcus, and all the children encircled them—a familial sacrament of joy.

As they moved to leave the baptistry, Lucille handed the baby back to Héloïse. Her heart swelled to receive the child. Yet, once again, she was overwhelmed with a sense of his vulnerability—and a sudden premonition of danger hit her. "Wait," she said.

All at once, she realized what that qualm had been, at the thought of his baptismal name. "We must not call him 'Peter.' He must not be known as the son of Peter Abelard, the son of a cleric. His true name, like our marriage, must be known but to us and God."

Peter put his arm around her. "I promise you, Héloïse, I will protect him, as I will protect you. I will make all things licit. I have power in Paris, beyond what you think."

"It may be as you say. But until then, our son will have another name."

"What name?"

Héloïse did not answer. The children, their patience exhausted, jostled against Marcus, who clapped one boy's ear, then the other's. He pushed them toward the door, and the boys rushed out into the afternoon. The girls followed.

Silence settled on the sacred space. At last, Héloïse said, "Astrolabe."

"What?" Peter asked.

"Astrolabe. You said we are 'new.' All right, then. Name our son for the precious instrument of star-science that comes to us from south of the Pyrenees. Measuring the heavens for guidance, he will know the way on earth. Our son, a secret Peter, will be known abroad as Astrolabe."

Peter Abelard was astonished—his face showed it—by the boldness of her unfettered declaration; by her, yes, newness. He leaned close and whispered, again, "You are magnificent."

He assumed he would be returning to Paris alone, but when it came time for him to depart Nantes—he was loading his bundle on the riverboat—she appeared. She carried a strapped bundle of her own. Lucille came up behind, holding the baby. Lucille's agitation—a red face, wet eyes wide—was apparent.

Héloïse, striding toward him, declared, "You will not be without me in that brood of vipers."

Peter, for all the confident assurance with which he'd been carrying himself, was not pleased, and took no pains to disguise what he felt. In the bosom of his family in Nantes, no harm would come to Héloïse. "You must remain here," he said.

"I will not."

Peter glanced back at Lucille, and at the baby. "But what of our son?"

"You and I have our defenses. Our son has none. He must remain here until our situation is resolved." Héloïse turned to Lucille. "The love of this family will be his fortress until the danger clears."

Lucille said, "Do not rebuke her, brother. Neither of you should return to Paris. Your wife would hear me on that no more than you. But if you must, your child is safe with us, until you return. That much I say without hesitation."

Peter faced Héloïse. "But the hill ahead," he said, "is for me to climb. We agreed on that."

"We agreed on nothing," Héloïse said. "You have not been listening to me, dear husband. You wanted marriage? All right. This is what it means. 'Whither thou goest, I will go.'"

"But that was Ruth, speaking as a daughter, not a wife."

Lucille, drawing close, put in, "I speak as a *sister*! You are both mad to return there."

"No," Héloïse said sharply, "Paris is the birthing room of the future. Peter must vindicate himself in Paris."

"Cockpit, more likely," Lucille spat.

"That, too," Héloïse answered. "Which is why I must go. Lucille, please. I beg you. Understand me. Your brother is at risk, and his denial makes the risk worse. I will be his shadow, the unknown figure in the back of the hall."

"Unknown, hah!" Lucile said. "You know the reports Marcus brings from the Duke's palace. You are both spoken of wherever snot-nosed scholars throw their knucklebones, wherever Court ladies sit at spindles. Not just bachelors of philosophy but itinerant jongleurs—singing the songs of lovers! Not just Paris, but even here—in Bretagne!"

Héloïse said, "Those songs tell of an unnamed Master and his comely pupil. No one thinks of us."

"Of course they do!" Lucille insisted. "Notre-Dame de Paris! Who else would it be? You, brother, count on your fame to part the sea ahead, but your fame is why you will drown in that sea."

Peter leapt onto the boat. "Our father taught us to swim, Lucille," he said jauntily. He looked back at Héloïse, and, after a long moment, he nodded. She handed her bundle over to the boatman. Peter took her by the hand and helped her across the side deck.

Marcus appeared, coming along the quay. He was accompanied by an even larger man, also dressed in leather—but even more so. He wore a spiked head covering, and his tunic had a metal breastplate. His leggings were proper to one of the Duke's marshals. A sword was sheathed at his hip, and a dagger was holstered at his calf. Marcus, who had outfitted the man-at-arms, called out, "One more for Paris!"

Peter exchanged an impatient glance with his sister, who shrugged, feigning ignorance.

Marcus and the marshal clambered onto the tiered dockside.

Peter Abelard said, "Marcus, I told you! No. No. My weapons are words. If I"—he glanced at Héloïse—"if *we* arrive at the Cloister with an armed escort, it will be taken as a sign that I doubt my ability to defend myself by explaining myself." Peter reached his open hand to the man-at-arms, who took it. They shook. Peter said, "Thank you, my friend, but no. This is the decision I made years ago, when I left the household of our father, who was one of the Duke's fine company, like yourself. I chose differently, and still do—the cowl, not the sword. Our protector is the Prince of Peace." Peter turned to Marcus and embraced him. "Thank you, brother," Peter said. "All will be well with us. And we shall return before long to collect our son."

Marcus nodded. "Young Astrolabe will be safe with us"—he grinned, draping an arm around Lucille—"until my children learn that the saint for whom he's named does not exist."

As the boat moved slowly away from the timber wharfing, Héloïse stared back at her son, asleep in their sister's arms. Héloïse clung to Peter, trusting him, but a tooth-edged blade was sawing through her heart.

.   .   .

AT NOTRE-DAME, the contest was soon joined. When Fulbert learned that Héloïse had reappeared and presented herself to the General Mistress of the Cloister, expecting to be shown to the rooms she'd occupied the year before, he did not wait, as protocol required, for his niece to be shown into his presence in the Great Hall. Instead, that very night, with his stick banging in stride, he went directly to her chamber and burst through the door. She was on her knees, before the image of our Lady, reciting Compline within the halo of the candle flame. She was clothed in her muslin sleeping gown. Even before she had come fully to her feet, he struck her with his stick. She fell. He was poised to hit her again, but the ferocity in her expression stopped him.

"You dare raise a staff against me?" she hissed. In the instant of his hesitation, she got to her feet and crossed to him, bringing her face close to his. "My mother should be alive to see this!"

"Your mother would be crushed with shame," Fulbert managed to say, but the energy of his long-nursed rage seemed drained.

Héloïse had not noticed, but in her fall the gold ring on its cord had come out from under the neck of her gown, and now hung quite openly at her breast.

"What is that?" Fulbert demanded.

Héloïse, realizing, put the ring back inside her garment.

Fulbert seized her now and clutched the cord at her throat, the unbreakable piece of hemp bow string. He twisted it, choking her. "What is it?" he cried. "What is it?" He jolted her up. "Are you married, or not? Is it true? Which? A monk's wife? Or a simple whore?" Again he jerked her. "Or both?"

She clawed at the cord, which, thinner than rope, cut into her flesh. She tried to scream, but gagged.

Fulbert might have choked her to death if Peter Abelard had not arrived at her chamber just then. He had stolen across the Cloister for one last loving word, but, seeing Fulbert bent over Héloïse, he threw himself on the Canon. He could not pull him back. Peter stooped for Fulbert's stick, and, swinging in a wide arc, brought its knob square against the Canon's head, knocking him back, dazed.

Héloïse gasped for breath. Peter untwisted the cord at her throat, then held her. In the moments it took for Héloïse to return to herself, Fulbert, too, recovered.

Peter rose to face him. "I will see you flayed for this crime. I will be at the Bishop's palace by Terce tomorrow."

"The Bishop, hah! He will have you seized."

"The *Royal* Palace, then. I will put the charge before the King. You dare to lay brutish hands on his kinswoman?"

"She has disgraced the King. You are the agent of her dishonor!"

Abelard took hold of Fulbert by the folds of his cloak. "I am the agent of her protection. The day you lay hands on her again will be your last. Do you hear me?"

Fulbert did not answer.

Peter twisted Fulbert's collar close around his throat, choking him as Fulbert had choked his niece. "Do you hear me?"

Gagging, Fulbert nodded.

"Answer! Speak! Your last day, do you hear me?"

"Yes," Fulbert managed, a whisper.

"Then go! Go!" Peter threw him to the floor. The Canon scrambled out of the room, half crawling. Out of nowhere, Fulbert's thrall appeared in the doorway, stooped and hesitant, with fear in his eyes. When Peter did not attack him, the thrall reached into the room to pick up Fulbert's stick. Then he, too, fled.

Peter closed the door. Héloïse had covered herself with the blanket, pulled to her throat, concealing whatever bruise had risen. Despite her unease, she found it possible to smile. "A man of the mind, are you? What was it you told Marcus: you use words?"

"But those *were* words, my dear one." He knelt at her bedside.

"Words full of threat. The threat seemed real."

"There's the trick," he said. "If the threat seems real, words suffice."

"The Philosopher Knight." She reached to his cheek, stroking. "Your father's son, after all."

He put his head by hers. She rested against him. After a time, recovering, she said quietly, "No wonder the hierarchs fear you. Now that you are returned to Paris, the Council will send its subpoena, the trap at last. William of Champeaux and his White Monk will have you where they want you. Threat of a different order."

"And I will meet it." Peter pulled the blanket down to look at the bruise on her throat. He touched it gently with the back of his forefinger. She did not wince. He let his finger fall to the lip of her gown, which fell in turn. When he cupped her bare breast, a customary initiation, she pressed her own hand onto his.

She shook her head. "We must not tempt the fates."

"The fates are with us." His hand went to the gold ring between her breasts.

"And they will be tomorrow. Be off." She moved his hand away. "Return to your quarters."

"I do not want you to be alone tonight. Not after—"

"After that, I am safe. Thanks to you. I am safe until the King's summons." She smiled, knowingly. "After you storm the palace tomorrow."

"Mere words, Héloïse."

"Simply putting the possibility of the King's involvement in play—"

"Fulbert crossed a line tonight, and knows it." Abelard touched the red band at her throat again, tenderly. "There's the proof."

"I will be wearing a high collar."

"We need not *actually* involve the King, and Fulbert would *dare* not. There is our protection. Fulbert falls if we fall."

"And *that,* as I said before, is what makes him dangerous. Not to me. To you. Therefore, caution, Peter. *Caution.* Beginning now. Be off."

"We must find another domicile for you, away from your uncle's household. What of your cousin?"

"That is for tomorrow. Now be off. I mean it."

He nodded, and said, "Meet me at the Cloister wall, after Lauds, before the light. We will take our steps in sequence, beginning with a safe place for you."

She felt the crest of his love breaking over her. She brought her hand gently to his throat, as if he were bruised. All at once, she felt the pulse of blood in her own fingertip, matching the pulse of the vein in his neck. That proximity was enough. She pulled his face down to hers, kissing him, shyly at first. When she lay back, she whispered, "Quickly!"

. . .

SLEEP, WHEN IT came to Peter, back in his rooms in the porch of the Cloister, was deep and dreamless. Lost in the labyrinth of his exhaustion, he did not hear the soft sound of his door being slowly pushed open. Indeed, he heard nothing until he heard the whoosh of his bed clothing being ripped away, followed by a loud bang, which, he realized vaguely, was the sound of his own head being slammed back against the bedstead. Dark forms of men showed in the doorway, against the gray of the fading night. Of the several figures closing on him, one carried himself in a familiar stoop—Fulbert's thrall. Peter Abelard's half-aware mind failed to register the intruders as his mortal enemies until too late, when they had pinned his arms and legs to the frame of the pallet.

He never saw the blade with which, in one cut, his penis and scrotum were severed from his body. The pain was as brief as it was intense, because he lost consciousness. With blood rushing out of the gash between his legs, he began to die.

HÉLOÏSE, FROM HER place in the women's balcony in the Cathedral, took the alarm from Peter's absence at Lauds. Straining to find his familiar profile among the Canons in the sanctuary stalls, she left her place, going to the railing, to concentrate on those figures whose cowls had been drawn forward. But he was not among them.

At the garden wall—his absence *there!*—she knew. She rushed to his rooms. She found him awash in blood, barely breathing. Oddly, a feeling of cold calm came over her—exactly what was required. Lifting and turning him, she quickly found the gaping wound between his legs. Wadded knots of the woolen blanket haphazardly bunched at his groin had enabled a partial clotting that had slowed the outflow, allowing him to live, but now the blood began to rush again. Clamping down on the bolt of her own nausea, she concentrated on stanching the bleeding with strips of cloth torn from her own underskirts. She dropped him half out of the bed, with his head and shoulders on the floor, to raise his waist above his heart. She steadied him there.

She rushed out into the Cloister arcade just as a trio of students were entering from the lane. One was Tomas Clare, a favorite of Peter's, and another was Theobald of Blois—a pair of Peter's protégés. Her sharp commands brought them to his room. Her example showed them how to ignore their own horror to tend to him, and her instruction told them how to prop him on the pallet, and turn its frame into a carry bench.

She led them from the porch, into the arcade, past the Chapter House, out of the Cloister, through the garden, into the streets, which were only then, as light crested the rooftops above, beginning to bustle with the morning market. She knew just where to go.

The young men took care to move Peter without jostling. He was their worshipped hero. Once Héloïse turned her back on them to lead the way, they began to exchange urgent oaths—swearing to see their Master avenged. As they crossed through the stinking fishmongers' quarter, with its crowd of busy stall-keepers, she whipped around to silence the boys, but was taken aback when Tomas Clare barked at her, "It was Canon Fulbert, was it not?" Instead of answering, she faced away again, to push through the growing crowd.

At the Jew's house, she banged on the door. "Please, Your Holiness! Please!"

CHAPTER FOURTEEN

Gongless cow bells, silenced cuckoo clocks, empty oxen yokes, and pewter-capped beer steins lining shelves too high to reach—the Swiss Alps was a profane sanctuary to kitsch. The waitress wore a smocked dirndl dress with puffed sleeves and an apron edged with tiny rosebuds. She was a pretty redhead, utterly at ease in her costume. The lunch crowd had drifted out into the early afternoon, leaving the booths and tables, mainly, to the shadows. Kavanagh nursed a beer, taking the place in, trying to remember when he'd last been in a dive in daylight. Not a dive, he corrected himself, but not so different from the Shamrock or Duffy's.

John Malloy's arrival, when it came, was an event. He swept into the place like an owner, with hi-signs in two directions, and a stop at the jukebox, after which wall speakers jumped to life with the first propulsive notes of Duke Ellington's "Take the A Train." Malloy half danced to the booth where Kavanagh waited, and he slid onto the bench with a small hitch in his shoulders that honored the music. It all seemed natural enough, but, given the contrast with his demeanor at Saint Aiden's, Kavanagh sensed that his old friend's snappy air was fake.

Kavanagh reached up a hand, and they shook. The aroma of Old Spice cologne hit him, the detail he'd first noticed at Good Shepherd.

"I'd say welcome, but who am I to welcome you here? Home court, obviously."

As if to underscore the point, the waitress promptly placed a V-shaped cocktail glass on the table. "Rob Roy, sweet, Mr. Malloy."

The glass was brimming. Rachel Vedette's *Historia* was on the table between them. Kavanagh moved it aside, to protect it from a splash. Malloy seemed not to notice.

"Thanks, Daisy." Malloy's smile was endearing, if still not quite authentic. Kavanagh was struck, in these shadows, by how laddered his friend's face had become—wrinkles, creases, and ridges climbing up the bones of his cheeks, past his eyes, to a heavily furrowed forehead. The skin was flushed, but his crows' feet featured tiny white claws, as if a permanent squint had kept an otherwise scorching sun at bay. He was a faded athlete whose world-weariness lent him, ironically, an eccentric glamour. In his brown tweeds, natty tan shirt, and perfectly knotted wool tie, he could, even with that face, have been a fashion model: Anglo-Decadence, Clothing and Apparel.

"Listen to those rails a-humming, Mike," he said, raising his glass to the swing. "In honor of Inwood."

Kavanagh lifted his beer, to clink. He said, "Good Shepherd would be marooned without the A Train."

"'A Train' equals Harlem," Malloy replied. "Who'd have thought the Darktown Express runs all the way to the Emerald Isle?"

"You would have—the other day. You took the A Train."

Kavanagh's comment stopped Malloy. He said, "What the hell, Mike?" Apparently, the "other day" was not on the table yet. That quickly, Malloy's jovial air was gone.

They watched their drinks. They listened to the Duke's music, the depth of longing, Sugar Hill, the excited rush of uptown dreams.

Kavanagh said at last, "Did you get to the boy's father?"

"Yes." Malloy grimaced. "Tommy hadn't told him about Camden. I was about to stumble into it. With a glance, the kid pleaded with me to hold my fire—not my place to lay the thing out. Tommy has to do that."

"Why does the father think his son is being expelled?"

"Booze. Cigarettes. Curfew. Grades. Call it—the usual. All true, as a matter of fact. The kid is a mid-century Bolshevik, or a slow-motion nervous breakdown. Take your pick. The only thing he's on top of is track."

"You."

Malloy shrugged and sipped. He said quietly, "Camden. Walt Whitman. Song of Himself, exactly—that teacher fuck. He has to be nailed. I am going to the trustees."

"The headmaster won't block you?"

"I'll nail him, too. He just threatened to fire me for being a drunk." Malloy grinned. "Which, of course, is true. But that won't stop me. I play tennis with the Board chair—Rodney Evans. A bigger lush than I am. Pulls on his flask between sets." Malloy took a hefty swallow, then said, "But I start with Mr. Rohan. I asked him back there if I could come visit. Morristown—not that far away. He said yes. I'll get to Tommy ahead of time, to help him. . . ." Malloy's voice faltered—no counterfeit breeziness on which to glide. "To be continued, as they say." He sipped his drink again.

In the silence now, Kavanagh picked up his smokes. He offered the pack to Malloy, who shook his head no. Kavanagh lit up, saying, "You saw yourself in Tommy?"

"Tried not to. After Tommy came to me last week, I told you: I put him off. His being gulled was the last thing I could deal with. But a blue rage hit me, and my mind leapt from Tommy right to Father Donovan, *Bishop* Donovan— Jesus Christ! *Bishop!* Holy shit, Mike, I went to his office—how stupid was that?" He shrugged. "What did I expect? Same old brick wall. Fucking stiff arm. From there, naturally, I hit a bar on Madison Avenue. *Sh-boom! Sh-boom!* The next thing I knew, Greenwich Village, here I come. One minute, I'm on my knees in an alley behind a Christopher Street bar, and then . . . I'm on my knees at the Communion rail in front of you." He stopped. "I'm sorry I said that, Mike." He shook his head, staring at his drink. "Oh, man." Silence, then. When he resumed talking, his voice had dropped. "I have no idea how I got up to Good Shepherd. The A Train, obviously. When I saw you in your vestments . . . just exuding goodness . . . as I said, fucking epiphany! The sky opened. I saw. *I saw,* Mike."

"Exuding goodness?" Kavanagh said quietly. The phrase stabbed him. He didn't know much, but he knew that, in his case, goodness was beside the point.

Malloy continued, "In you the other morning I glimpsed, intact, the innocence that was mine once. And, yes, I saw Tommy. I woke up. *What am I doing here?* I thought. *I have to get back to Saint Aiden's, to stand with that boy.* So I took off again. *Sh-boom!* It was crazy. I admit it."

Nor was innocence the point, Kavanagh thought. Something more like willful ignorance. What had Runner called it? Kingdom of the Blind Eye? Kavanagh asked quietly, "How were you and Tommy alike?"

Malloy stared at his drink. "He had his English teacher. I had Father Quinn."

"Father Quinn? At Dunwoodie? The Assistant Rector?"

"He was Assistant Rector in your day. Before that, he was a teacher at Saint Peter's—my day."

"The junior seminary?"

"You didn't go there."

"But I knew about it. Upstate someplace."

"Glens Falls. Near Albany. Boarding school, natch. I did all four years of high school there, before I knew you."

Kavanagh's breathing had slowed, a function of his wholly focused attention. "At Dunwoodie," he said, "we passed ourselves off as College Joes, but you Saint Peter's grads made the rest of us feel like rookies, like we'd missed something. Latin, for example. You guys actually understood it."

Malloy said, "You were—what?—eighteen when you entered? At Saint Peter's, that's what we called 'delayed vocation.' I went in at thirteen. Too young to know the difference between seminary and cemetery, which is what I kept calling it."

"Thirteen is very young."

"Fucking kidnapping."

"Except your mothers were thrilled."

"At Saint Peter's, Father Quinn was our Pat O'Brien, the fantasy priest, movie star. . . ." Malloy's voice had softened, taken on a disembodied tone. "He called us his Knights of the Round Table, and we loved it. Total magnetism. Masculinity. A jock."

Kavanagh could not picture it. He said, "The priests at Dunwoodie were removed—"

Malloy shook his head. "At Saint Peter's, he was King Arthur. . . . We were his good soldiers of Christ, the cross and the sword, him on a horse, leading the charge."

"And you—?"

"His chosen squire! In my mind, I held his fucking stirrup. I polished his armor. Beginning when I was fifteen . . . Tommy's age."

"Why don't I know about this?" Kavanagh stubbed out his cigarette, sharply.

Malloy shrugged. "'We few. We happy few.' You weren't one of us. 'We band of . . . little boys.' I served his Mass in the side chapel every morning during the school year. During the summer, I was head counselor at the choristers' camp he ran at Lake George. Do you remember that?"

"I heard of it."

"Then I graduated to Dunwoodie. Yonkers is a long way from Glens Falls, or so I thought. I expected to feel homesick for him, but in fact I felt free. I did not know until then how much I'd longed to get away. I didn't know shit from Shinola, but I knew that I'd been released. I *loved* Dunwoodie."

"That's how I remember you. Your loving the place helped me to love it."

"And then . . . when we were in First Theology—"

"What, two years later?" Kavanagh's memory quickened. He saw the place, the long, highly polished corridors, the gloomy chapel, Father Quinn striding into the refectory like a procession of one. "Quinn showed up at Dunwoodie as Assistant Rector."

"Three years later," Malloy corrected.

"I remember the impression he made," Kavanagh said. "You could focus a camera on the part in his slicked-back hair."

"Brylcreem." Malloy snorted.

"Man's man. Priest's priest." Kavanagh paused, then added, "Not to me, though. I didn't get the glow. He put me off; I didn't know why."

Malloy shrugged. "I remember that about you—your skepticism about Father Quinn. You kept your distance."

"Struck me as vain, his hair just so."

"Do you remember, one afternoon on the golf course, when I asked you to wait with me, while the other guys stowed their clubs?"

"No." Kavanagh leaned forward. What was this?

"I was desperate to talk to someone," Malloy said quietly. "I wanted to talk to you. . . ." His voice trailed off.

"Why didn't you?"

"You didn't wait," Malloy said, with a hint of accusation. But he shrugged. "The chapel bell had rung."

"Christ, John, we played golf dozens of times. You could have . . . Why didn't you stop me again?"

He shook his head. "At a certain point, talking about it was not an option. Not with you. Not with anyone."

"What was it, Runner? What did you want to tell me?"

"There it is again. 'Runner.'"

Kavanagh lit another cigarette, unsure what to say. What an unseeing youth he'd been.

After a time, Malloy said quietly, "At Dunwoodie, he left me alone at first. But just knowing he was back in my life undid me. He'd catch my eye at Meditation. He'd wink. Sure enough, one day he stopped me during the bustle after Sunday Mass. He put his finger to his lips, which I knew meant, *Wait for the others to leave the sacristy.*

"I recall thinking, *Pretend you don't understand and get out, too.* But I waited. And then we were alone. He drew close to me. I remembered from before the particular aroma that clung to his cassock: part tobacco, part Burma-Shave. His eyes were moist. He said in a whisper, 'Johnny, you've hurt my feelings.' My heart sank. Just fucking sank. I'd *hurt his feelings:* those three words defined my worst nightmare. What had I done to hurt his feelings? But I knew! I fucking knew! I had *hated* him—that's what. It was my deepest secret, but somehow he knew it. But *of course* he knew it, since he was the instrument of the Holy Ghost, who could read all minds. The Holy Ghost, the little turtledove, had told Father Quinn how I despised him. No—worse!—how I wanted him dead."

Malloy stopped, a faraway look in his eyes. His voice had become even quieter, and Kavanagh realized that he himself had leaned forward, to hear. His own face was only a few inches from Malloy's.

Malloy continued, "But, Mike . . . Mike . . . do you know what I said when he told me I'd hurt his feelings? I said, 'Oh, Father, I'm sorry. I'm sorry.'" Malloy now was almost whispering, his words weighted and slow. "Jesus Christ, Mike . . . *'I'm* sorry.' How fucked up is that?"

"It's fucked up, John."

Malloy nodded. "'I forgive you, Johnny,' Quinn said. Then he went on to explain that at Dunwoodie things would have to be different between us. As Assistant Rector, he couldn't be seen as having favorites, so we would have to be careful, since—'Of course,' he said, 'of course!'—I would *always* be his favorite."

Malloy stopped abruptly. Kavanagh had an impulse to tell him he needn't go on, but then recognized the impulse as itself the problem. He said nothing.

"At Dunwoodie . . ." Malloy was staring at his hands. He'd fallen into an inexpressive monotone. "I couldn't be his private altar boy anymore, but I *could* be one of his designated acolytes—the Holy Hours two or three evenings a month, sacred moments in the night, which were the Introibo to the liturgy that mattered, afterward, when all the others had drifted from the sacristy." Malloy stopped again. Kavanagh realized that the inexpressive monotone was itself the expression. He thought Malloy had finished.

But a moment later, Malloy continued, with the same dull cadence. "'We must put away childish things,' Father Quinn told me, which meant putting away the shy fondling that had defined our intimacy at Saint Peter's. Now we built the Temple of the Holy Ghost with the temples of our whole bodies." Malloy looked up sharply, meeting Kavanagh's eyes. "'*Hoc est enim Corpus Meum,*' he would whisper as he pushed into me. Not into *me,* but into the Body of Christ, which, he told me and told me and told me, is what I had become." Malloy stopped speaking, but he held Kavanagh's eyes.

Kavanagh longed to look away, but did not dare to. He leaned back, too stunned to speak.

Malloy said, "I'm sorry, Mike."

"Jesus, John! Don't say 'sorry' to me!"

"But it's true. I *am* sorry!" Tears had spilled onto Malloy's cheeks again. "I should have said no to him. At Dunwoodie, I *could* have said no." Malloy pressed the heels of his hands against his eyes, a cauterizing gesture he had used before. When he took his hands away, he was nearly in control.

Kavanagh said, "You were my best friend. I thought I knew everything that mattered about you. I knew nothing."

"I did not know it about myself, Mike. With Father Quinn, I was someone else. That's all. I was two different people. The one you knew—"

"Runner."

"All right, 'Runner.' There was Runner, and there was 'Johnny.'"

"I never heard you called 'Johnny.'"

"No one called me 'Johnny' except Father Quinn."

"But then what happened?"

"It took two years. Finding someone to tell."

"I'm sorry that wasn't me."

"You'd have been disgusted. As you are now."

"Not disgusted with you."

"So, obviously, since I was dutifully submitting to the Sacrament of Penance every Saturday—to Father Quinn, for Christ's sake— elaborately ticking off my litany of venial sins . . . well shit, what about my ongoing *mortal* sin? Debauchery committed by *concubinus clerici,* sacrilege raised to the power of infinity—and then *not referred* to in the Sacrament of Penance, because my Confessor himself was my *socius carnalis.* Do you see what good use I make of my Latin?" Malloy forced a grin that itself seemed degenerate, creepy. He quickly squelched the grin.

Kavanagh could not think what to say.

Malloy went on, "But that spring of Third Theology, our class was about to get ordained to the Deaconate. Remember that? Crossing the Rubicon. Holy Orders, at last. Our *own* perpetual vow of celibacy. My morals were in shreds, but still I couldn't do it. A solemn oath before God? I was to vow chastity for life? How about chastity for one night? I could not fucking take that oath. So I found another Confessor."

"Father Donovan?"

"On my knees on the floor in his room, I collapsed. I told him the whole thing. *Hoc est enim Corpus Meum*—and all. Donovan and the others took it from there. You know the rest."

"But *you* were kicked out."

"Encouraged to see that 'I did not have a vocation.' That seemed right to me. *I* was the occasion of sin. That's how fucked I was. The whole thing was *my* fault."

"You came to my room at dawn. You wanted to tell me."

"I couldn't."

"You told me to go ask Agent why you were leaving."

"'Agent'! Christ! What was it with the nicknames?"

"He told me you left because of me," Kavanagh said. "He didn't mention any of the other horror."

"Of course not. I was terrified—more than of anything, of *you* finding out what I was. I just wanted him to tell you that I cared about you. Nothing else."

"He said you had 'out of bounds' feelings for me. He said that was why you had to leave." Kavanagh paused. He was only now piecing the thing together. "Obviously, he needed to deflect attention away from the real problem. Quinn. Whether you meant him to or not, Donovan used me. Christ! 'Out of bounds.' His telling me that made *me* feel guilty. It panicked me, made me feel that I was . . ."

"Perverse," Malloy said with a snort. "There's the word."

"But our friendship was the furthest thing from perverse."

"Not to me, Mike. Here's the real secret . . . the real disgrace." Malloy suddenly drained his glass and held it up, casting his yellow eye about for Daisy. She swooped by and took the glass. He brought his gaze back to Kavanagh, now staring. He said, "When Father Quinn kissed me, it was your face I saw. Et cetera. I'd close my eyes, and it was always you. There's the grim fact of it, Mike. I dragged you 'out of bounds,' without your knowing it. I told Donovan as much, when everything poured out of me. So what Donovan told you was the truth. It *did* mean I had to leave. Even if Father Quinn had never come to Dunwoodie—I was already bent by then. I loved you, yes. Was *in love* with you. The purest affection . . . but still perverse. *Bent!* I couldn't be a priest."

"You'd have been a great priest. What I just saw with Tommy makes the point. I see again—so clearly—what was special about you." Kavanagh paused while the waitress placed Malloy's fresh drink in front of him. When she'd gone, Kavanagh leaned forward to say, with careful deliberation, "I would not have dared call what I felt for you 'love,' but that's what it was. After you left, I never felt that way again, about anyone. I clamped down."

"I clamped down as well, Mike. Ironically, the catastrophe made me chaste. A chaste prep-school teacher, anyway. I'm terrified of acting on my feelings for the boys, and so I never do. Never have. Not even close. We teachers are to protect these lads, not rape them. That's why what that fucker did to Tommy . . . what he obviously has done to others . . . so infuriates me."

"I see that," Kavanagh said. Then he added, "So you're alone?"

Instead of answering, Malloy sipped his drink, savoring it. Then he said, "I'm a Yankee Mr. Chips. I have the school. It's been enough. I said 'chaste teacher.' Emphasis on 'teacher,' not on 'chaste.' I slip away from Lake Durham now and then, in my cups. I head to Sheridan Square, certain bars where some guy will call me 'John' without knowing that's my name. Good enough. That's where I headed the other night, after leaving Donovan's office. *Sh-boom.*"

Kavanagh edged his cigarette in the ashtray with one hand, fiddled with his glass with the other. Seeing his friend so clearly was seeing, also, himself. He said quietly, "What I've realized over these last few days, John . . ." He paused, letting his friend's name resonate, briefly. ". . . is that what I felt back then for you was the best thing about me."

"But we are not talking about the same thing, Mike. I don't act on it except furtively and drunk, but I am defined by the erotic pull of men for men. You're not. You never were."

"How do you know?"

"Comes with the territory. We can tell. You were the straightest arrow in the quiver, pal. Still are, from what I can see."

"Maybe not," Kavanagh said. "I was a navy hospital chaplain. I loved the men I cared for, *loved* them. But I know what you mean, the difference." He paused. The straight-arrow image of Jimmy Stewart was what came to mind, the aw-shucks movie star meets Simone Weil, whose name he can't pronounce. "Still, I'm not as . . . unbent . . . as you think," he said.

"Try me."

The woman at The Cloisters, his tutor. To his "another time, another place," the day before, she'd said, in French, *"Impossible,"* as if he'd propositioned her. The memory mortified him. He could not speak of her. Instead, he said to Malloy, "I am most myself sitting at midnight in a canvas beach chair on the tar-paper roof of the rectory." He nodded at Malloy's glass. "Drink in hand."

"I don't see you as a drunk, either. I have antennae for that, too. I see you saying Mass, hearing Confessions, anointing the sick. Isn't that when you're most yourself?"

"I love all that. It's what has kept me at it. Not a day goes by that I don't help someone. At the hospital, I help a lot of people. It's just that . . ."

"What?"

He thought of Madison Avenue, the corner behind the Cathedral, how he'd almost fainted. He lifted up his glass, then put it down. "How do you say 'I do not believe' in Latin?"

"Non credo."

"Huh."

"Why?"

"That's what I blurted yesterday. I guess I knew what it meant. The opposite of *Credo.*"

"Si non credimus!" Malloy said. " '*We* don't believe.' I'm with you."

"No, I'm serious. I'd stumbled into a recognition."

"That's how recognition happens, Mike."

"Has to do with *you,* actually, your showing up the other day. The sight of you rang in me like a general-quarters alarm—*'Man your battle stations!'* Were you in the navy?"

"No. Infantry. Alabama. Never left the States."

"Me, either. But 'haze gray and underway' . . . ship alarms . . . We were trained to hear the whole panoply of signals in our sleep. Seeing you that morning was like surfacing when I didn't know I'd been submerged. I went to my beach chair on the roof that night—battle station on the deck—seeing something, but not knowing yet what. Then I went downtown to Bishop Donovan. I saw that he'd lied to me about you all those years ago. That lie was the rock on which my life was built. Not rock, therefore, but sand. I left his office, and outside, on the avenue, I was ambushed by those two words—*Non credo!* The loss of faith not in God, but in the Church."

"Don't kid yourself, Mike. If you lose faith in one, you lose faith in the other. There is no God without the Church."

"Then I *am* in trouble."

"All this because of a lie fourteen years ago?"

"Donovan is still lying to me."

"He did not want me talking to you."

"Obviously," Kavanagh said. Then he asked, "So what about Father Quinn?"

"I'd never imagined it, but turns out—what I did learn from Donovan—Father Quinn is long dead. Heart attack. A parish in New Rochelle. Seven years ago. You didn't know that?"

Kavanagh shook his head.

"The Bishop showed me the obituary. He'd kept it in a special drawer."

"In a manila envelope? 'RIP' scrawled across it?"

"Yes."

"I saw that envelope in the drawer, a pint of bourbon holding it in place. What other obits are in that envelope, do you suppose? I had no idea Quinn was dead. I'd had no reason to keep track of him."

"I felt nothing at the news. . . . Quinn dead? Turns out I did not give a shit. But I realized that, actually, my issue was as much with

Bishop Donovan as with him. Saint Aiden's School protecting a lecher by tossing Tommy Rohan overboard—that was my issue now. And, of course, that's what Father Donovan had done for Quinn, tossing me. A lie as the rock of your life? This was mine. It's what had blocked me from helping Tommy right away. Made me a coward. It was about time I dealt with it. At the Chancery, I confronted Donovan *about Donovan.* When I brought you up, he forbade me to get in touch with you. He said the Seal of the Confessional was still in force. What a crock."

"How odd, John. You start living in the truth, and it forces me to. I left Donovan's office yesterday, and nearly fainted on Madison Avenue with what I understood. Not just his lie, but my own. Going all the way back to my solemn vows. Even before I knew it, I knew it. Beginning with you. All along, at some level, I've known. The life is a lie. Hence my beach chair on the roof."

Malloy placed his hand on the leather volume. "Hence Abelard?"

"No. That would be something else."

"*Patron sanctorum* of lovesick priests and nuns." Malloy grinned. "You're not involved with some Mother Héloïse, are you, Mike? Some Sister Marie in the parish school?"

"How stupid do I look?"

"Not very. But I've heard the rumors—tunnels between convents and rectories."

"Also known as sewers. You spout the old slander like a teacher at a tony Protestant prep school." Kavanagh forced a smile, stubbing out his cigarette, aware that Malloy's reduction of Abelard and Héloïse, like his own a few days before, was a gross caricature. Malloy's grin made Kavanagh uneasy. He did not want to bring Rachel Vedette into this. This what? This thicket of malice and deceit.

But no. This was John Malloy. Runner. His best friend, once. And now? Then it hit him. Here was a good man to whom, already, he was explaining himself as he hadn't to anyone in years. And why should he not keep doing so? "I told you before," Kavanagh said, "that I'm reading the *Historia* because of you. When I followed you into the park the other day, I wound up at The Cloisters, where I met a Jewish woman. A museum docent. An expert on the Middle Ages."

He stopped. Why had he characterized her as Jewish, not French? He toyed with the dead butt of his cigarette in the ashtray. Explain himself? But how? Only two things occurred to him: Just as he'd begun to drown, Rachel Vedette had appeared out of nowhere, correcting his pronunciation and offering him rescue. And—her being a woman was incidental to why he'd reached toward her.

He said only, "This book is hers. I have to get it back."

CHAPTER FIFTEEN

"I cannot live like this," he whispered to her. She was bathing him, leaning close. The steaming cloths had been brought to the boil in the great kettle in the shed behind Prince Isaac's house. For almost three weeks, Peter had lain amid animal skins and coverlets on the sleeping bunk against the wall. Above him were the shelves holding jars and pots, from some of which had come the healing ointments, and the clotted spiderwebs used to purify the wound.

The room's table, with its lamp, inkhorn, parchments, and codices had been pushed against the far wall. The Jew, in caring for Peter, had surrendered the room to him, taking his own rest in some other corner of the house. Héloïse had come here from her cousin's place every day.

She replied to his whisper with one of her own: "Then do not."

"What?"

"Do not live like this."

"I am incontinent," he said, still a whisper, now an admission.

She smiled, indicating the cloth with which she was washing him, if now at his armpit. "I know." Her method was to respond to his bursts of despair with calm, mundane affirmation. She added, "And Prince Isaac assures you that control of your fluids will return. Why would you doubt him now?"

"I do not."

"Well, then."

"You should have let me die."

"Not true."

"They thought to kill me. . . ." Peter turned his face to the wall. "But, living, I am punished in the offending part. I am disqualified now from being yours, a fate that is meet and just."

"The only fate meet and just is what befell my villain uncle's henchmen."

"Ah, so now my own lads have joined in the evil. Eye for eye, blade for blade. Manhood for manhood. Where is justice there? One dishonor begets another, *ad infinitum*. As if the justice of God requires such mayhem. What God is that?"

She answered, "The God who welcomes Christ's death in atonement for Adam's sin."

"No," he said, "no. I will not hear of it."

"Then you are deaf, as well as wounded. That is the only God spoken of since Anselm."

"Anselm is poison to the faith. The honor of God has nothing to do with Christ's death, which was for love, not appeasement. As for honor, the only honor I care for is yours, and I bespoiled it."

She turned his upper body, to reach the warm moist cloth below his other armpit. "Are we in the hall of disputation here?" she asked. "Have you—yet again—reduced me to the role of victim in your tragic drama?"

"Do not make light of me, woman."

"You misunderstand if you sense lightness here. This is simply the refusal to die. My solemn request is that you join me in it, husband."

"Do not 'husband' me."

"I used to say as much to you—do not 'wife.' But that was before your own pronouncement: 'What therefore God hath joined, let not man tear asunder.' "

"But, Héloïse"—he faced her—"this *was* God. God's just punishment. *I* was torn asunder so that our marriage would be torn. Our marriage was false. It was a sin."

"Never, never will I join you in that belief. If it can be called 'belief.' I call it infidelity."

"Another sin. Which makes my point."

"Can you roll over?" She dipped the cloth in the steaming vat, and wrung it. "I would rub your back. That, at least, is innocent."

Behind Héloïse, Prince Isaac had taken a place in the threshold. Peter's eyes rose to him, and Héloïse turned. The Jew's white beard struck her, as always, like the white of milk, or of clouds, or of the skin inside her own thighs—which was an admittedly odd association, since the thought was that the whiteness of his beard was a signal of his goodness, his purity. Her thighs, so Peter would tell her now, were impure.

The features of the Jew's craggy face fell naturally into a consolingly benign expression. Where once she had seen him as Simeon, lately he had been striking her as the Prodigal's father, a man who could stand looking out at the lost horizon with longing for his lost son, with nothing but love in his eyes. More than ever, given Peter's mood, Héloïse welcomed the sight of the kind physician.

She said, "You have come to cleanse the dressing."

"Yes," Prince Isaac said. "That, too."

"What else?"

"To make my report to Master Peter. And you should hear it also."

"No," Peter said. "Not Héloïse."

Héloïse said nothing to this. She adjusted herself back from Peter's bed, to settle on the stool. She let the cloth fall into the steaming vat. She waited.

Prince Isaac, with his three-pointed hat, had to stoop slightly to cross into the room. He remained standing. He addressed himself to Peter. "What I have proposed for you, I know now, seems possible. Lady Héloïse is affected. It is right that she be included in our deliberation."

Peter touched the sleeve of Héloïse's gown. "Prince Isaac is leaving Paris. He was meant to depart weeks ago. He put the time off for my sake."

"Until I was certain that you would sustain yourself," the Jew said. "Now I believe you will."

Peter said to Héloïse, "Once I knew what was possible, I was going to tell you."

Héloïse had clamped down on herself. She turned calmly to the Jew. "Depart, Your Holiness?"

"Yes," he said. "To Ashkenaz. For the restoration of the Talmudic school."

Peter said, "The kingdom on the Rhine, Mainz."

Héloïse well knew of the place—how the cross-marked berserkers had descended on it, murdering Jews, torching their academies.

Peter pulled at Héloïse's sleeve, but she remained focused on the Jew. Peter said, "The Rishonim have summoned Prince Isaac. The Rabbis. They are rebuilding the yeshiva on the Rhine."

Héloïse choked off the alarm she felt, to remain focused on what was in front of her. She said to Prince Isaac, "But Peter is far from well. How can you leave him? He needs your ministrations still. Needs them badly."

"I am seeing to his future needs," the Jew said. "The Abbot granted my request for an audience. I have just come from meeting him."

"What Abbot?" she asked sharply.

"Saint-Denis."

"Abbot Adam?" Héloïse turned to Peter. "He was one of those preparing the subpoena against you! Forcing your disputation with Bernard!"

Peter said, wearily, "There will be no subpoena now, woman. No disputation."

Prince Isaac said to Peter, "Father Abbot was surprised that you are alive. The talk of Paris had come to him that you had taken refuge in the Vicus Judaeorum, but he did not believe it. When I explained, he counted your presence here, among the *deicidii,* as yet another offense."

"I warned you, Your Holiness," Peter said.

"But he seemed genuinely relieved to learn of your coming back to health. I believe that he bears you no ill will. Quite the contrary. He told me the best young monks of the entire Benedictine federation count themselves your disciples. The order needs their commitment. Your presence would reinforce it, even if unlicensed. On the terms you propose, he is prepared to welcome you."

"What terms?" Héloïse asked, with forced calm.

Neither Peter nor Prince Isaac answered.

"What terms?" she repeated.

Finally, Peter said, "I would be received into the community as a penitential monk."

"Penitential monk! What? A life of imposed silence? Of manual labor?" Héloïse was aghast. "What of your philosophy? What of the school?"

"The school is over for me, Héloïse. Surely, you see that. At Notre-Dame I am anathema."

"But there is Rheims. There is Rouen. Young scholars all over Europe would follow you anywhere. The rivals to Notre-Dame would vie for you."

Peter and Prince Isaac exchanged a look—more than a hint of patronizing skepticism, which made her anger flare. "Your Holiness! You, of all people, must see this. The wisdom of the Moors, who, with the Hebrew readers in Toledo, are bringing the ancient wisdom back to life—the rebirth of thinking! What you will be to Ashkenaz, Peter Abelard already is to Christendom. You *know* this. The Church needs him. And not only the Church. *You* need him."

"Lady Héloïse," the Jew said quietly, "Master Peter's physical rehabilitation is far from complete, as you yourself say. The fever always threatens. A great danger remains of poisons and humors, biles in the wound. Saint-Denis has the best infirmary in Paris."

Peter put in, "Because Prince Isaac instructed them."

Héloïse stood and rounded on Peter. "But what of us?" She drew the gold ring up and out from her bodice, bringing it as far forward as the cord allowed. "In a school—Rouen, Metz, even Canterbury—you have the freedom we need to be together in our way, with discretion, and with our son."

Prince Isaac interjected, "Your son is at issue."

"What?" Héloïse said.

"The Abbot expressed an interest. If the rumors about Peter Abelard and the Jews are true, he said, perhaps the rumor about a child is true as well."

Héloïse exchanged a look with Peter, then turned back to the Jew. "What did you answer?"

"That rumors are the night pollutions of Beelzebub. The Abbot seemed disinclined to pursue it, although he added that the Bishop is known to be asking if there is a child. He is asking if the child is male."

Peter said, "All the more reason for my permanent disappearance. As my name fades, the Bishop's interest will wane."

Prince Isaac leaned forward to venture, "It is unseemly for a Jew to express an opinion about interactions of Christian prelates, but the Abbot of Saint-Denis can be counted on to oppose the impulses of his rival, the Bishop of Paris."

Héloïse cared nothing for such intrigue. She said, "But, Peter, our dear infant! How can we—?"

Peter lifted up on the furs to say with feeling, "Violence! This violence!" He tapped his leg, indicating his wound. "The violence is unleashed because of me! I was blind to this threat, but no more! The threat continues! Our dear infant—yes! His hope lives with Lucille and Marcus, where he must remain, far away from this brutishness. You sensed as much when you turned from my name to the name Astrolabe." Clearly, Peter had considered this. He lay back, calmed himself. He added, more quietly, "In Nantes, our Astrolabe is safe. Anywhere else, he will be subject to sanctimonious conscription and enslavement."

Tears overflowed the eyes of Héloïse, yet she saw the thing clear—how she, too, in all her notoriety, was a danger to their child. Reflexively, she fingered the gold ring. After a heavy-laden silence, she found it possible to ask, "And what, then, of us?"

"Us? Us? Héloïse . . ." Peter was speaking out of an abyss of despair. "Have you troubled to take notice of my condition? I am a eunuch now."

"Not to me! Never to me!"

"Woman, how explicitly must I lay bare the depth of my shame?"

"You need not be ashamed with me."

"You are the *only* object of my shame. I have, in every way, dishonored you."

"I deny that. I forbid that. I love you. And you love me." She silenced herself, abruptly. When her silence fell upon the room now, it was a demand.

When Peter did not speak, she commanded, but quietly, "Say it." Nothing.

"Say it!"

In response, finally, he said, "You should have let me die." Again, he turned his face to the wall.

The Philosopher Knight, she thought—but not bitterly. She backed away from him. He was willing his own death, but she would not permit it. "Peter Abelard," she said, "I will never accept this from you. Are you hearing me?"

Far from unmoved, he yet remained at the wall, unmoving.

Wiping away her tears, Héloïse said with fresh firmness, "If you entomb yourself in strict monasticism because of what my wicked uncle did in the name of my honor, then I, too, will so entomb myself. In that way, I will be dead to everything in the world, and everyone— excepting only you."

Gently, she buried the gold ring back inside her clothes.

CHAPTER SIXTEEN

Once Rachel succeeded in getting Saul Vedette's blood-sugar levels stabilized, he returned to himself—not fully, by any means, but enough so that the prospect of his survival began to lengthen out from minutes and hours to days and weeks, if never months. Rachel began actually to imagine that the future tense, even foreshortened, might once more have meaning. As it happened, her father had regained the necessary strength just in time.

By the time the main Drancy population was set—something over six thousand in housing blocks built for seven hundred—the Gabardines had forced their French minions to impose a new, lasting discipline. Posters with commands and mottoes were hung on walls. One read *"Jedem das Seine,"* which Rachel's dull neighbors translated as "To each his own," but which she recognized as the threat it was: "To each one what he deserves." The imposed regimen divided prisoners by category—Jews, criminals, and politicals; yellow star, green star, red star. All prisoners were mustered for regular lice examinations, and they were checked for swollen bellies, jaundiced skin, and rashes. Large digits were painted on stairwells, rooms, and beds, and prisoners were supplied with cards that identified them by those numbers. That Rachel's father found it possible to leave his bunk for the roll call twice a day—once at eight in the morning, and once at six in

the evening—meant that he was not hauled off to the Drancy railhead, from which the sick-trains departed three times a week. Those
livestock cars carried whoever had become obviously infirm, as well
as troublemakers—and newly arrived small children. That the gendarmes herded all children onto the trains, ironically, convinced most
of the interned that the transported were not necessarily doomed.
Since the little ones would surely be left unharmed, perhaps the others would be, too.

Rachel and Saul alike mastered the habit of behaving as if they
always knew what to do, and as if they always understood what they
were told. With her bunk above his, they both slept with their most
precious possessions wrapped in bundles, ad hoc pillows. In Saul's
case, that meant the three small books his daughter had managed to
bring with them: the school edition of the Torah, footnoted with his
own commentary; the dog-eared copy of the treatise Nachmanides
wrote at the end of his life, *Torat Ha-Adam*, "The Law of Mankind,"
which was a meditation on the problem of evil; and the worn leather
volume of *Historia Calamitatum.* In Rachel's pillow was the insulin
kit, together with whatever stash she had of nuts, fruit, sugar cubes,
and, rarely, cigarettes for herself, which she always cut in half.

The insulin was ample, and readily obtained. For the nuts, fruit,
and sugar, she bartered with bread, but also with francs and ration
coupons, which to gullible inmates she insisted would have doubled in
worth by the time of their release, which she heard was coming soon.
For the insulin—and the unsought occasional bonus of tobacco—she
bartered, without her father's knowledge, with her body.

In the third week of their time at Drancy, the medical officer had
come upon her and the dispensary clerk having sex in the file room.
Instead of disciplining the clerk and sending Rachel to the railhead
for immediate transport to the East, the officer had arranged to have
her assigned as the dispensary night cleaner. From then on, the officer,
the clerk, and two other doctors—all considerate Frenchmen—had
their way with her in periodic rotation. This structured, almost polite
arrangement of nighttime liaison was insisted upon by the medical
officer, a man of authority. Rachel realized soon enough that her open
legs and willing lips were the solution to his staff morale problem.

She was the doctors' reward for putting up with Drancy, and the grim duty of selecting inmates for dispatch to the East. Rachel almost never had to be with more than one of them a night, and almost never for much more than an hour. Yet the ground of her new condition was clear: survival—her own, and her father's—depended on these men's enjoying her.

At a certain point, after the stroke of midnight, she regularly put aside her bucket and mop, loosened her hair, removed her shoes, and took her place on the largest cot in the intake room, which was down a long corridor from the overnight ward. A dozen beds stood in that ward, but because prisoners regarded it as the antechamber to the cattle car, they did everything to avoid being admitted there. What patients it held were too sick to notice the trysting down the hall. In truth, as she experienced the ordeal, the doctors and the clerk required practically nothing of her. The barest pretense of engagement—a receptive mouth, a rhythmic movement of her hips at the proper moments, a timely moan, a little smile at the end—was enough. She herself, meanwhile, developed the skill of *mental* transport, so that, as one grunter or another pawed her breasts, her mind took flight, carrying her elsewhere, like a great bird of rescue. Thus, she could find herself strolling, behind her firmly shut eyes, on the pebbly quay among the bridges of Paris on a summer afternoon, idling at the book stalls along the Seine. Or she could be bent over the filigreed leather desktop, focused on text work—Abelard's letter to Philintus, say— under the cone-shaped hanging lamps of the high-vaulted reading room of the Musée de Cluny. Oddly, perhaps—in this sustained trick of the mind—it was the figure of Héloïse who often came to her uninvited in the grotesque hours of sex. Considering that later, she guessed it was because Héloïse, too, had found it necessary to live in sin, refusing both to deny that's what it was, and to sink into regret. The bond between Héloïse and Rachel was forged, however dissimilar their experience, in the throes of what was most forbidden. For wholly different reasons, they were blasphemers both. Héloïse, alone of the women of whom Rachel knew, would have understood, and would have refused to condemn her.

Because Rachel's work assignment, as a night cleaner, occupied her through the hours of darkness, she was allowed to sleep during the day, which meant that she could be with her father, tending to him and protecting him. Rachel Vedette was surrounded by people who had lost all sense of purpose, but she had never felt hers more intensely.

At the Sorbonne through the 1930s, and until the Statut des Juifs banished him, Professor Vedette had famously transformed the ancient Talmudic tradition of *havruta* into an Age of Reason mode of communal textual analysis. His seminars in the literature of early-medieval France—the *chansons de geste,* for example, and the coming of the Crusader ethos—featured vigorous exchanges between teacher and students, which were themselves an instance of democratic liberalism. A stark exception to the *lecture formelle,* Vedette's method conveyed Vedette's message: that truth proceeds not from the conforming of one mind to another, but from multiple minds' taking off together from the given text—always attending to the *con*text of its provenance—to formulate thoughts that had never been ventured before. Saul Vedette, with his yarmulke, heavily framed spectacles, and rabbinic demeanor, had begun at the university as a narrowly perceived scholar of Hebrew studies, but, attracting students from an ever-broader set of concentrations, he had opened wide a gate into a new realm of the critical imagination.

Strangely enough, such an esoteric academic approach—interrogation over declamation—perfectly suited the profoundly unacademic condition of those interned at Drancy, where questions were all. With the building of a trustworthy structure of insulin supply, and the near normalizing of his blood sugar levels, Vedette regained enough of his former strength to make Rachel lift her gaze above the horizon of mere survival. She saw that his survival required more than medicine and proper nourishment.

In the Gabardine-imposed tightening of Drancy discipline, her father should have been reassigned to an all-male housing block, but, without officially citing the diabetes that would have had him promptly transported, the medical officer discreetly intervened to keep him where he was. The officer, an army captain, was a silent, middle-aged man whose delicate mouth and slender limbs hinted at the emotional fragility Rachel had come to sense in him. Because she seemed unjudging, he found himself confiding in her. His name was Jacques Rivière. He was from Toulouse. In civilian life, he had been a pediatrician. When war broke out, he'd been conscripted. He had then been forced into service at Drancy, where, to his unspoken horror, his main duty was not curing, but selecting. As the prison complex expanded with the arrival of more and more internees—Jews from all over France—Captain Rivière was charged with establishing satellite dispensaries throughout Drancy, which meant the transfer of members of his medical staff. This gave him the opportunity to dispatch the men with whom he could no longer bear to share the nighttime assignations with the *femme de ménage*. The sad *toubib* was infatuated with her. After a period of months, that is, this conflicted French physician had become the only man to whom Rachel had to make herself available on the intake cot, a relative intimacy that licensed him, apparently, to imagine that they were lovers. To protect that illusion, the doctor was prepared to protect Saul Vedette.

Thus, in the sprawling high-ceilinged dormitory room that was given over, mainly, to several dozens of elderly women, Saul Vedette continued to occupy the bunk below his daughter. That meant, once the population of Drancy internees had swelled, that he was the rare male in the entire complex with a bed to himself. Among the prisoners, such privilege loomed as blatant unfairness, and Rachel was aware of the resentful glances thrown her way by the fatherless and husbandless women around her. One in particular, Madame Picard, a former baker whose husband had disappeared in the first days of their time at Drancy, took to hissing *"Putain!"*—whore!—whenever Rachel passed by. Rachel, pretending to ignore such insults, understood them.

Saul Vedette did not register the umbrage of the women, and the men whom he brushed up against, if they knew of his privilege, preferred his company to complaining about him. Always hungry for bread, the inmates were hungry for talk as well. Males encountered one another in various settings: before and after roll call, in the dusty central square; in lines outside the latrines; on the stairwell landings where bread and gruel were distributed twice a day. In these circumstances, men—the still-stooped and the formerly upright alike—maneuvered in the queues to exchange a word with Monsieur le Professeur. Vedette seemed a rod around whom snatches of real conversation gyred, a longed-for antidote to the cryptic rumors, flash-point quarrels, or muttered inanities that flooded in on continuous waves of French, Hebrew, or, among the refugees from Germany or Poland, Yiddish. Such untethered fragments of expression made even the mute and the inhibited want more.

So it was that, with his daughter's help—she obtained the key to the cramped utility closet on the third floor of their housing block, a remote corner that the day guards ignored—Saul Vedette found himself at the center of an unnoticed weekly gathering of eight or nine men, including a Paris architect, a clerk from Marseille, a garment merchant, a lawyer from Hungary, a schoolteacher, a former member of the National Assembly, and a Pole whose teeth had been knocked out in an incident he refused to discuss. They met on Sunday mornings, because the ranks of the Gendarmerie were thinnest then. Despite the day's meaning for Catholics, these Jews, making the most of what they could get, regarded the Sunday-morning hours as an annex-in-time to Shabbat, and they thought of their cramped closet as a true Beit Midrash, a house of study. Having begun hoping only for conversation, they made a bold leap into nothing less than the study of Torah.

The architect, sitting proudly on a crate, was silver-haired and straight-featured, oddly Aryan-looking, the only sign of his Jewish-ness being the palm-sized, well-cut yellow star worn precisely at his lapel. The clerk, sitting on an upended bucket, was decked out in baggy overalls and a much-patched worker's smock, yet he still managed to sport a fastidious, pencil-thin mustache. The Hungarian was lithe, and claimed a ledge in the corner. The Pole with no teeth was content to hunch on the floor, beside and below the rancid mop sink. The only true chair, an armless straight-back, had a thronclike aspect in that space, and all took for granted that Vedette should avail himself of it. His daughter, on whose elbow the professor moved, was the only woman in regular attendance. She sat on the floor beside her father. She never spoke, and the men took no apparent notice of her.

She did not know if that was the unfeigned indifference of the Orthodox Jewish male, or the calculated snub of high-minded disapprovers who knew what she did at night. She did not care.

One day, the gathering came to a climax that she would not forget. Having settled on their crates, buckets, ledge, chair, and haunches, they let the silence fall, as usual—the silence that changed the foul little room into their yeshiva. They pulled from inside their shirts, coats, or trousers bits of cloth—soiled handkerchief, napkin, fragment of a sleeve—and covered their heads. Only Vedette and the architect had true yarmulkes.

"The Ramban says," the architect began, " *'Ein yisurim be-lo avon.'* Let that be our text. 'There is no suffering without sin.' " He spoke with the assurance of one picking up the thread of a fierce exchange, as if an intervening week had not interrupted their ongoing debate about theodicy.

Rachel expected her father to speak, and probably so did others, since "Ramban" referred to Moses Nachmanides, the thirteenth-century sage who was the subject of Saul Vedette's most widely cited book. But her father said nothing.

The mustachioed clerk put in cautiously, "That is what the friends of Job say, attributing sin to him to explain his woes, but they are wrong. Job was exceedingly righteous. The text is clear."

"Job was a Gentile," said the politician, happy as always to raise a flag of skepticism.

Rachel assumed that the man's point was that Job's experience counted for less if he was not a Jew. Yet Bible readers, she thought, were surely intended to sympathize with Job, whether he was a Jew or not. Well, the question was moot. The politician was not skeptical enough, since, as Rachel knew from her father, Job was a figment of Moses's imagination. Job did not exist. His story was a parable. For that matter, maybe Moses was not its author. Who actually wrote the books of the Pentateuch? Speaking of skepticism.

The architect had brought up the text to make a point, and now he pushed it. "God chastises a man so that he should return to the study of Torah," he said. " 'For whom the Lord loveth, He correcteth.' "

"Are we being corrected here?" the clerk asked bitterly. "How is this correction?"

"How is this love?" the politician asked.

"You say 'the Lord,'" the clerk declared with heat. "The Lord is gone!" The clerk turned fiercely on Saul Vedette. "You, Rabbi, tell us! Where is the Lord in this?"

Vedette smiled thinly. "Do not honor me with 'Rabbi,' friend. I am a simple citizen of God's holy nation."

"But you know the Ramban. He said that what we suffer here is somehow *our* fault! So we are punished. The Lord punishes us with His absence."

"The Lord's silence is not His absence," Rachel's father said, with a tranquillity that, for the hundredth time, astounded her.

"But suffering! The Lord visits suffering upon us because of sin. What sin for *this* suffering?"

Vedette was quiet. He let the silence settle once again. Finally, he said, "These are the great questions. We were put here to ask them—not to answer them."

"But there must be an answer."

Vedette nodded. "The answer to a text may be another text. Do you think that might be so?" Nothing in Vedette's tone was tentative, yet neither was there certitude. He seemed at home with query.

"What other text?" the architect asked.

"Perhaps someone has a suggestion," Vedette said. He looked from one man to another, exuding respect.

"You, Professor," the clerk said. "The text is yours to propose."

Vedette nodded: all right. "When the Lord looks at His people," he said calmly, "it is not sin that He sees. What he sees *is* suffering. He does not *inflict* suffering. He wants to end it."

"Where in the Rabbis do you find that?"

"I find it in Moses. There's the second text for today—an answer to the Ramban. 'And the Lord said, "I have surely seen the affliction of my people which are in Egypt, and have heard their cry by reason of their taskmasters; for I know their sorrows. And I am come down to deliver them out of the hand of the Egyptians, . . . unto a land flowing with milk and honey." ' Where in that, my friends, find you God concerned with *sin*?"

"But where in Drancy find you milk and honey?" the clerk asked.

"I find it in your fortitude, brother," Vedette said.

Rachel imagined her father adding, "I find it in the exquisite care you take with that perfect mustache of yours. Your mustache is a refusal to be reduced to the state of mere victim—a refusal that passes here for milk and honey."

"But the Ramban—"

"The Ramban was not in Pharaoh's Egypt," Vedette replied. "Nor is he in Hitler's Drancy. Not all suffering is the result of sin. On the Lord's scale, Moses tells us, suffering weighs more than sin. The Lord knows the sorrows of His people. And what happens then?"

"When?"

"After Egypt."

"Forty years of exile."

"And where was the Lord?"

The clerk did not reply, but the garment merchant spoke up. "The Lord went with them."

"And where was the Lord when Babylon destroyed the Temple and carried the people off to captivity?"

"With them," the merchant said.

"And after Rome destroyed the Temple and drove our fathers off?"

"With them."

Vedette waited. Rachel sensed that the men had joined him in the secret place of his magnanimity. Finally, he said, "And this presence of His, with the people in exile and in captivity—did the people see it? Or hear it? What do you think?"

"They saw the pillar of fire."

"A sign. But was that the Lord?"

"We do not see the Lord."

"Ah," Vedette said, "but we know nonetheless that the Lord is with us. No? With the Temple destroyed, where do we find the Temple?"

"In Shabbat, the Temple in time."

Vedette opened his hands. Here. He said, "If the Lord is struck dumb by what befalls us early and late, that is not absence. That is evidence of His presence. He is struck dumb, as we are."

"So the Lord's silence proves that He is with us?" The architect was clearly unconvinced.

Vedette shrugged. "What we have in Exodus is the start of our whole story. There it is, my good brother: 'For I know their sorrows.' Of whom is the Lord speaking when He says such a thing?"

"'For I know their *sins*.'" The architect put in. "That is the Ramban!"

"Would Rabbi ben Nachmanides choose his own disposition over what is given in Torah? By what authority say you so?"

"'*Ein yisurim be-lo avon*.'"

"I repeat myself, brother. The Ramban is not at Drancy. *Your* sin, perhaps, has put you here. Assuredly, mine has put me here." Vedette let his hand fall quietly on his daughter's head. "But that is not the Lord's concern. I repeat: sin is not the point. And not even suffering is the whole story. This place is alive with righteousness, the virtue of those who, in fortitude, hold fast. To the right of us, and to the left of us—there are those who hold fast, even as they see the little ones loaded onto cattle cars. Innocents. Pure innocents."

"And where is the Lord for them? The little ones?" The question came plaintively, from below. It was the toothless man, on the floor. This was his first intervention.

"The Lord knows their sorrows, too, brother," Vedette said with fresh gentleness. "That is the only word that Torah gives us to say. For the rest, we must be silent. As the Lord is silent. Silence now is the only way of speaking."

"No! No!" The man clambered to his feet. He shook his fist at Vedette, and fairly shouted, "We must speak by saying 'No!'"

"Ben Joseph, sit," the clerk said. "Sit! They will hear—"

"Let them hear! My children are gone! Carried to their deaths!"

"We do not know that—"

"Of course we know it! Do not speak to me of holding fast! You are fools, all of you! With your talk of Ramban and Rashi and Moses and the Lord! Who cares? Who cares?"

Vedette stood and, balancing himself unsteadily, drew close to the toothless man. He opened his arms, an implicit asking of permission. When the man did not back away, Vedette wrapped him with a stout embrace. The man fell against him, and his shoulders began to move. "We care," Vedette said. He repeated softly, "We care."

Rachel had an impulse to stand and join in her father's embrace, but she did not move. She sensed that the others, too, might have had such an impulse. Though no one moved, Rachel imagined them standing, one by one, to join in locking the heartbroken Pole in a mute circle of concern. That Vedette and the Pole remained, in fact, standing alone took nothing away from the air of potent solidarity that had all at once transformed the room. Silence was not absence.

Finally, her father said quietly, " '*Yitgadal v'yitkadash sh'mei raba.*' 'Exalted and hallowed be God's great name in the world which God created.' "

Rachel looked up at her father. Later, she would realize that she had not found it possible, while listening, to give real assent to anything he had said: to her, God's silence and God's absence were very much the same thing, and, from those days on, always would be. *Who am I now?* she would ask, wondering what it was to be an unbelieving Jew. But if she could not move her conscience to affirm the faith of her father, she could move her legs and her arms; she could come to her feet and stand, which, at that moment, had to be enough. And it was.

Soon all of the men had come to their feet. Each was careful to keep his distance, yet they joined, some more fluidly than others, in the solemn recitation of the prayer Saul Vedette had begun. It was the Mourners' Kaddish, and they knew it too well. As they prayed, the toothless man went on sobbing.

At that point, because of her father, the human capacity for fellow feeling still weighed more—on Rachel Vedette's scale, forgetting the Lord's—than the things that make for hate.

CHAPTER SEVENTEEN

A clap on the head, coming again and again, with the effect not of clouding her perception, but of sharpening it; accompanied by a nauseating sense of vertigo, as if she would never walk steadily again, or be at ease as herself in any circumstance—such was the experience Rachel had when she realized, after days of the priest's not returning to The Cloisters, that she had yet again betrayed her father—this time by carelessly giving his precious book away.

For more than five years, she had never been without that particular copy of *Historia Calamitatum: Heloissae et Abaelardi Epistolae.* A dozen times—with her father, and after him—she had hurriedly bundled a few possessions while moving, or being pushed along, or escaping, or following in a line of supplicants, or queuing before an intake officer's desk, or simply running. And each time, she'd found a way to bring his book. Alone of all she possessed, she had clung to it. It was not an amulet: what protection from harm had it offered? Nor was it a talisman: what luck had it ever brought? Not a relic, either: her father was no cult object, even to her. The book was simply the last point on a thread of connective tissue, palpably linking her to a past—and a deeper past—from which she'd sprung, and from which, in any case, she could not break free, even if she'd wanted to. But, above all, the book was her father's, not hers. Given all that was consumed in the fires of Europe, the book, despite its Christian content, enshrined that profoundly Jewish man's essential legacy, a hint of what he'd hoped for at the end. And now she'd lost it.

The strange priest cared nothing for what she'd entrusted to him. But why should he? What, to him, was one book among so many? Especially a book that, in the indomitable Héloïse, railed against all that any priest could be expected to revere? Rachel rebuked herself each time she thought of it.

Not in years had she so acted on impulse, and this was why. She should have known from that cursed late day in Drancy: impulse, for her, meant the doom of all she valued.

Again and again, she had circled back through the museum's varied arcades, gardens, galleries, and chapels to pass by the Chapter House in the central Cloister, the one from La Chapelle-sur-Loire, where they'd first met. Each time, she allowed herself to picture him, sitting there, his back straight against the cold stone wall, her father's book on the bench beside him. Sometimes she imagined him in the black suit and Roman collar, sometimes in his plaid shirt and windbreaker. But he never appeared. For the first time in the year and a half that she had been employed at The Cloisters, she'd begun to understand—no, she'd begun to *stand-under*—the museum's meaning as a monument to what was not there.

When she came outside at the end of her workday, the pale sun was already hovering just above the treeline of the forested Palisades across the river. She pulled the fabric of her cloak closer around her shoulders, and set out along the path that would take her to the subway stop. When, coming around a curve and up a slight hill, she approached the onetime gatehouse, now the coffee shop, she slowed her pace. She had done so each afternoon that week, picturing him there, too. She had imagined his profile in the window, the one beside the table where they had sat together. Twice, at the end of work, she had gone into the shop and taken that table, as if then he would come. The waitress had served her with the usual cold neutrality, having no idea with what frenzied agitation Rachel's mind was spinning. She rehearsed the conversation that she and the priest would have been having at that table: humanism and mysticism, yes; but also the theological roots of violence; the terrors of sexual restlessness; the real defeat of Abelard; the holy indignation of Héloïse; the Church's epochal amnesia; the twelfth century's curse on the twentieth. None of this was abstract to Rachel, but each time Father Kavanagh had failed to show, the recognition had come to her—how little any of what the medieval lovers had written to each other would have meant to a sane person living now; how little, apparently, it meant to him.

As for herself—well, why should shards of decisive days and nights at Drancy not have flashed across the field of her distraction all week, given what that priest had set loose in her?

She drew nearer to the coffee shop, and stopped.

There he was!

Now, when she saw his sharp profile in that window, she thought at first that she was once again imagining him. But he turned, and looked directly at her.

Him.

She resumed walking. By the time she climbed the few flagstone stairs to the entranceway, he was there, having moved to the door, waiting for her.

"Hello, miss," he said. His jovial air clashed with her mood. She would have liked to greet him with friendly goodwill, but managed only the barest nod. He was dressed in his black suit and collar. He gestured the way back to the table, where his cigarette smoldered on the lip of an ashtray, beside a half-empty coffee cup. Adjacent to the cup were two books—his breviary, and her *Historia*.

"I am happy to see my book," she blurted. "It was impulsive of me to give it to you." She added, "And it was rude." She picked the book up, to be sure.

"Rude? Why rude?"

"An imposition."

"No. No. Not at all. I found it fascinating," he said. "Even if I had to turn to Cassell's now and again. Héloïse uses words that old Aquinas didn't know." He laughed, still not picking up on Rachel's gravity.

Now that she had the book, her impulse was to turn and leave; she might in fact have done this, but she recognized the visceral urge as yet another instance of what had caused this trouble to begin with.

She said, despite herself, "I should have told you to return it to me sooner."

"Ah . . ." The priest showed with a passing grimace that he now sensed her anxiety. "I'm sorry," he said. "The truth is, I wanted to get here right away, after . . ." He stopped. She could not read him, but remembered his agitation from before. He continued, "I already told you some of it."

"An old friend, you said." She hesitated, then added, "An unanswered question."

"Yes. You told me I could find it . . . find him. And I did."

"And you spoke of your Bishop."

"I haven't been back to him yet. Time collapsed on me." He indicated her book. "You gave it to me on Wednesday. Thursday, I found my friend, far out in New Jersey. Friday is all day at the hospital, I can't miss it. Then the weekend . . ." A simple shrug conveyed a tangle of helplessness. "Hearing Confessions, writing a sermon, which, in my case, is a killer in the best of times . . . which, actually, this has not been." Now, when he grinned, she saw how forced the expression was, an attempt at self-deprecation. He said, "It is only now, on Sunday afternoon, through tomorrow, that I am free."

Rachel was startled to realize that the weekend had, indeed, come. She saw his point, how, whatever its challenges, he had simply been living his life, with no disrespect to her. She felt foolish for seeming to have rebuked him. "I did not think of that," she said. "Sunday at The Cloisters is just another day, but with more visitors. I cannot say, in reality, that I notice the days in this way."

"Not even Sunday?"

"No." It only now hit her that tomorrow was her day off, too. She hated her day off.

Kavanagh laughed again. "In the old days at The Cloisters, Sunday would have been the whole point. It's the whole point at Good Shepherd."

"Does that return us to your theme, then?" She forced a modicum of lightness into her voice. "How Mr. Rockefeller's sacred space is, in actuality, profane?"

"My theme? Profane? Did I say that?"

"Empty, then."

"Well, no sanctuary lamp. That's true. No Real Presence."

The absence of which Rachel had been aware that week was this priest's. She recalled her own words: "readiness to stake everything on the absolute." But he had demurred at that: not the absolute, in his case, he had said. Instead, "something very shaky." So that's what she had sensed in him, enough knowledge of the absolute to feel cut off from it. If she had reached out to him—that was why.

He pulled the chair out. "Shall we sit?"

Or, he seemed about to ask, *are you going to turn now and flee?*

She clutched the book, glad to have it back. And, yes, she was glad to see this man again. Not man. Priest.

He clearly read her hesitation, even if he could never have understood it. "Please," he said.

It was not his shakiness that struck her, but his kindness. Yes, she could see him in a hospital, dispensing care.

She sat. He helped her adjust her chair, and when she untied the neck strings of her cloak, he helped her arrange its folds on the back of the chair. She placed her book back on the table, beside his breviary.

Then he sat, too.

She said, "I might have tried to contact you."

"You know I am at Good Shepherd."

Once she had begun to fear that, through her own carelessness, her father's book was in danger of being lost, she had fallen back on an old stratagem: instructing herself not to trust or hope, but to detach and wait. She said, "An *infidèle,* calling at the rectory? No."

"It's allowed," he said. "Especially to discuss theology."

That he laughed seemed off to her.

"Anyway," he said, "here we are." He offered her a cigarette. She took it, and leaned to the flame. As she exhaled, she tugged absently at the edge of her turban. Her sleeve, having come loose from the elastic band that held it, began to fall from her upraised arm, baring her wrist. She lowered her hand promptly. It fell to her book. "So?" she asked, implying the text.

"Astounding," Kavanagh said.

"You did not know of them?"

"I knew their names, of course. But I told you, we studied Saint Bernard, not Abelard. And Héloïse, to us, was a temptress."

"And now?"

"As I say, astounding. Humanism and mysticism, you said. And I see what you mean. The human and the holy. Very human. Very holy. All the letters. But what strikes me most is his initiating letter—his misery. He calls it *the story of my misfortunes.*"

"Calamity. The word is stronger than 'misfortune.' Catastrophe."

"Okay. But what a contrast to her devotion. She is unrelenting. She refuses to see their story the way he does. She regrets nothing—except their separation. She loved him, totally. There's the astonishment: Héloïse."

Rachel was aware of his intensity of feeling, and saw that a blush had come into his face. She herself felt strangely awkward. But they were discussing lovers whose depth of passion had made them immortal. Why should such discussion not be awkward? Yet she found it possible to reply, in her usual docent-tone, "He learns from her—constantly—but, as she insists, it all starts with him. His *Historia* demands that we measure what we believe against what we *actually* experience." Rachel used a teacher's gesture, overturning her hand. "Experience over doctrine. Like Galileo, but five hundred years earlier. Abelard is the first 'modern.' In fact, he may have invented the word, taking off from *modo,* the Latin for 'now.'"

"Ah. There's the rub." The priest nodded, and with his hand—as if replying to hers—he waved dismissively. "'Modern' is a word the Church distrusts to this day. We have a heresy called 'Modernism.' I had to take an oath against it."

She laughed. "*Mon Dieu.* An oath against Abelard." The thought threw Rachel off. She took the reactionary character of Catholicism for granted, but in America she had not brushed up against it quite this closely. It was hard to square the priest's evident goodwill with his apparent readiness to surrender good thinking. But, then, which was more important? In a voice free of judgment, she said, "His thought would still be contentious, then." She added, "And Héloïse would still be prompting him to act. His love for her took the form of great courage, a magnificent struggle against his critics in the Church."

"Saint Bernard."

"Precisely. Known as the White Monk."

"Heresy, you said the other day. About the Jews."

"Yes."

"But he does not mention Jews in this book."

"True." She idled her cigarette. How to put this? "But the *Historia Calamitatum* shows the basis of his rare empathy," she explained—docent still. "Reflecting on his own suffering, he comes to see suffering itself as a sign of God's grace—not punishment. When he argues that God is close to the brokenhearted, and then when he looks about at the most brokenhearted of all God's creatures . . ." Despite herself, an unwanted emotion edged into her voice. Part anger, yes; but also part hurting wonder. *How could these things have happened? How can I be speaking of them?* "The first pogroms in Europe had occurred just then. Crusaders, rushing through the Rhineland en route to the Holy Land, attacking, first, the 'infidel near at hand.' Thousands upon thousands of Jews murdered in the name of Christ. Just then."

"By Crusaders? Why don't I know about this?"

"That is a good question, Father," she said with unwilled bitterness. She let the silence fall. One beat. Two beats. Three. Then she said, "Some local prelates denounced those attacks. Others encouraged them. But Abelard did something else entirely. He said that God is *with* the murdered Jews. *With the Jews,* Father! Do you hear me?"

"Yes. Yes."

"*Not* with their attackers. That changes everything."

"I see that. I do."

She checked herself. This man was not an attacker. She need not be a defender, therefore. Instructing again, she said, "Abelard takes the implications up in another work that might have been written later."

"What work?"

"*Collationes,* or Dialogue Between a Jew, a Philosopher, and a Christian, which is unique for engaging the conflict not between Church and synagogue, which had defined the entire genre for a thousand years. The antagonists here are the Jew and *the philosopher*; their argument is over the relation between reason and morality; and the Jew is given to articulate Abelard's *own* ethical position—the primacy of conscience. Do you see this? The Jew speaks for Abelard!"

"I see. Yes."

"Abelard gives us a Jew to be respected, a peer figure, not one to be baptized, and not one fated for an eternity of hellfire. In this book, written nearly a thousand years ago, *the Jew is a kind of hero.* And why should Abelard not have been condemned?"

"You've thought about this." Kavanagh's smile had nothing of the grin about it. He was only appreciative, only impressed.

When she nodded now, she meant it as a kind of thanks. He had been patient with her. He had, perhaps, learned from her. She said, "I can get a copy of the *Collationes* for you, which is itself a miracle. Unlike the highly romantic *Historia et Epistolae,* which the poets loved and, you could say, mass-produced, almost no manuscripts of the *Collationes* survived the twelfth century. After Abelard's condemnation, it was dangerous not to burn this text. Some heretically inclined monks saved it for us, in secret. By now, of course, I can get a copy for you . . . in English, if you prefer." She smiled, briefly.

Kavanagh laughed. "Is my mulishness with Latin that obvious?"

But she was still intent on what she was saying. "The mental spaciousness went beyond his kind portrayal of a Jewish character. Abelard attacked the ideology that made attacks on Jews inevitable. Not ideology. 'The ology.' He invented that word, too. Did you know that?"

"No. How do you know it?"

"I told you: my father. . . ." The thought of him made her stop. As she put the cigarette to her lips, she saw that her fingers were trembling slightly. In this priest's presence, she was strangely buffeted by an unprecedented impulse to reveal herself, which, at this moment, meant revealing her father and her father's hero. "I told you," she repeated. "I was my father's helper. At Cluny, he tracked down other writings by Abelard, records of disputations and councils; anonymous treatises; and notations of his students. Abelard inevitably criticized Jews for rejecting Christ, and my father's Catholic critics emphasized that. But my father saw that Abelard's innovation went further—to the very idea of God. His concern was with *God,* which is why he coined that word. *Theology.* For Abelard, everything follows from the first principle: The Creator loves what the Creator creates. Creation itself is God's act of love."

"You said something like that the other day," Kavanagh recalled, "that we're 'saved by virtue of being created.' No Church is needed. No Jesus. Just Creation."

"Including Jews."

The priest said nothing to that, and for a moment Rachel feared that he'd taken offense—or, worse, that he was appalled.

But then he spoke, and she saw that she was wrong. He said quite simply, "The idea stuck with me. I tried to work that . . . expansiveness . . . into my sermon this morning. Not successfully." Now his smile did have the aspect of a grin, and she was relieved to sense his self-deprecation. "At Good Shepherd," he continued, "the pews were full of blank stares."

"It is not such a hard idea," Rachel said softly.

"Actually, for us . . . it is. Jesus matters. Obviously. I mean, matters to us."

"Of course. But your theology, *avec tout mon respect, mon père,* follows from a fork in the road; a fork lit up by burning texts. There was another way to go at that fork, one the Church chose not to take." She extinguished what little remained of her cigarette. "That, at least, is what my father saw. He wanted the Catholics of France, of his own time, to claim this great Catholic champion from another time."

"Because of what was happening to Jews in your father's time."

"*Obviously,*" Rachel said, picking up his word. "Which was my time, too." She regretted the edge in her voice as soon as she heard it. But she had stopped herself from saying "when more than texts were burned." She disliked herself. She was lecturing this man—had been lecturing him all along.

After a long silence, Kavanagh asked, "What was your father's name?"

"Saul Vedette. A professor at the Sorbonne."

"Jacques Maritain was at the Sorbonne. The Catholic philosopher. He was a big deal in our seminary studies."

"My father knew him. Perhaps they were friends—I do not know. Once the Germans came, Professor Maritain fled to New York. Had he stayed in Paris, he might have helped my father—unlike those who remained. I do not know. Back then, getting out, Professor Maritain saw what I failed to see. My father and I stayed in Paris because we thought we needed medicine from the nearby chemist, but of course there are many ways to get medicine—as I learned." She paused, blanking from her mind that particular memory. Then she said, "We could have left. There came a moment when, had I insisted"—she blanked, as well, the hate-filled face of the bald inquisitor, in the threshold of their apartment—"my father would have agreed to leave. I misread the moment, and encouraged him to stay—to continue with his great work. I failed to imagine what was coming, at the start . . ." She looked away, then added, more quietly, ". . . and at the finish."

A silence fell between them then.

For a moment, she feared that she was sounding like a Catholic penitent, in one of their darkened booths. It panicked her to think the priest would now be pressing a Confessor's questions—questions about her. But to her surprise, he asked simply, "Medicine?"

"My father was diabetic."

"What happened to him?"

Rachel clasped her hands, a decisive gesture of self-protection. She knew it was impossible for her to answer. She knew, also, that, with unwilled coyness, she had made that unspeakable question inevitable. Not dislike, but loathe. She loathed herself.

KAVANAGH SENSED THAT his question about her father had shut her down. Yet his inquiry had seemed natural, the result of an instinctive pastoral feel for what she herself had wanted to discuss—a direct line from Abelard and his fate to Saul Vedette and his. But not so.

He let his eyes drift around the tidy coffee shop. The other tables, as usual, were empty. The waitress was hovering behind the counter, intermittently eyeing the clock and idling through a magazine. He brought his gaze back to Rachel Vedette, who was focused on smoke rising from his cigarette in the ashtray. He said, "Professor Vedette sounds like a very special man."

She did not react.

He said, "May I tell you about my father?"

Rachel looked up, surprise having brightened her face. "No one in America has ever said that to me."

"Pop was not special, except to us. His kids. Big Irish family. He was a lumper." Registering her quizzical look, he added, "A stevedore. We lived on Thirty-Eighth Street, Hell's Kitchen, near the West Side docks. That's been prettified by now, with a stretch of midtown piers for the big liners, mostly. Swell people wanting to arrive back from the Grand Tour within a short cab ride of the Plaza. Before the war, the dock trade was farther south, in Chelsea. Pop would show up at the wharves in the morning without a job, hoping to be tapped. Three days out of five, he would be. Unloading everything from steamer trunks to furniture to automobiles to bricks of salted meat and smoked fish. I can still smell the stench off my father's overalls— everything from motor oil to mackerel. But if he were here, he would sum up a lifetime of lashing barrels and hooking crates by telling you he helped unload the ship that had plucked survivors out of the sea after the *Titanic*."

"The *Titanic*?" Her surprise was complete.

"Yes. He never stopped talking about that day. Forty thousand New Yorkers showed up to stand on the docks when that accidental rescue ship pulled in, all completely silent. My father was given mooring lines to man. The ship came into its slip with no whistles, no horns, no sounds. They dropped the gangway, he said, without the usual noise. The first ones to disembark were the *Titanic* people. Pop said it was like watching a line of the walking dead come down the planks. Hundreds of them, many still wearing blankets, like cloaks. Dead people, he said, brought back to life—but barely. Their eyes, he said, were incapable of blinking. Mostly, it was women and children. He never got over it." Kavanagh stopped. After a moment, he said, "Goodness, how did I veer into that?"

Rachel said, unsteadily, "Yes, I ask myself that. How did you?"

She stared at him, deciphering. Then she said, "The image is strik-ing, *le débarquement* of the dead." She pulled her own pack of ciga-rettes from her pocket, and, with an agitation that made him think of her rush from the museum the other day, she had to strike her match repeatedly to get the flame. He recalled the womanly ease with which she'd leaned to his flame earlier, but he now understood that he should hold back from offering a match again. He knew not to intrude on whatever it was that had come over her.

Finally, she regained her composure, and said, "You report that so powerfully. But you were . . ."

"I was an infant, but that day was famous in our family. The older Pop got, the more he talked about it. He'd mock himself, and say that the shipwreck survivors cured him of the wish to go to sea. But we knew from Mom what a turning point it was. He quit drinking that day. She told us proudly that he never hit her again. He went to Mass every morning after that. Still, he never went up to Communion, because, as he would say, he felt unworthy. Somehow, in his mind, the gangplank-walking dead and his unworthiness were linked. But, in fact, he was a good man, and we all saw it. Odd, but our admiration for him, not to say affection, was tied to the *Titanic*." Again, Kava-nagh stopped. He was astounded at himself. He had not spoken in this way, of such things, in years—to anyone. But he knew that his thought was unfinished. He said, "We were humble people, but it lent us a kind of grandeur—the *Titanic*—that such a historic event should have touched us so personally. As I grew up, I would dream about those people, on the gangplank, with their eyes unblinking, as if I'd been there. I had that dream not long ago."

Rachel said quietly, "A parable of empathy, how a mere glimpse of such suffering changed your father." She spoke smoothly, having stifled her first reaction. She added, "Perhaps it explains something about yourself?"

Kavanagh laughed, claiming nothing. As if to scale back on the tragic grandiosity of what he'd reported, he resumed speaking, but more mundanely. "I have three sisters, and two brothers. One nun, Sister Teresa; one tugboat captain, Jerry; one office girl, Marie; one Brooklyn housewife, Sheila . . . Let's see, how many is that?"

"Four. You have neglected one."

"My brother Joe." Kavanagh nodded gravely. "I still count him. He died on Okinawa."

After a long pause, Rachel asked, "And your parents?"

"Both deceased. My mother died of pneumonia ten years ago, although my sisters swear she died of slow-motion grief. Pop had been taken off by a stroke years before that, but he was always part of us." Kavanagh fell silent. Then he added, "I am very lucky in my family."

"I can see that. And your friendships? The man you were seeking? Runner?"

Kavanagh laughed. "He hardly remembered that nickname. It's so vivid to me, like yesterday. He's a good man, too. A teacher. He showed up at Good Shepherd last week in the middle of some personal distress—"

"'Thrown for a loop.'"

"Yes, him too." Kavanagh laughed. "But he's handling it. For me, seeing him was a big relief. A recovery of something I'd thought I'd lost. Though it gives me some big business to tend to. Whether I can handle it is to be determined." He raised his brows. "It's more than you want to know. But, actually, you helped me the other day. I was stuck. And you told me to just get moving, and so then I did." He moved his hand to her book, covering it. "I brought this with me to New Jersey. You gave it to me, you said, so that we could discuss it. But your book . . . accompanied me."

She nodded. "It accompanies me. That is precisely what it does."

He sensed the block between them—what she would not or could not discuss. But he sensed also that that discussion had, perhaps, begun.

He said, "On Mondays, the biggest ocean liners set sail from the West Side Terminal. Did you know that?"

"No."

"Have you ever seen an ocean liner set sail? It's a festival. When I was a kid, it's what we did instead of the circus. It's still one of the best things in New York." He grinned. "And it's free."

She did not reply.

"The Cloisters museum is closed tomorrow?" he asked.

"Yes."

"I told you," he said. "Tomorrow is my day off, too. Would you let me show you? Three long, deafening blasts on the horn. Then the ship inches away from the pier, while all the dockside well-wishers are waving goodbye. The bands are playing. The whistles blow. People laugh and sing, the ship eases out, and when at last it's gone, everybody cries. It's grand. Only in New York! Plus, I could take you around my old neighborhood."

She smiled. Then, after a long time, and more quietly still, she said, "How could I resist, Father?"

CHAPTER EIGHTEEN

To his most beloved Lady, the memory of whom no forgetting can steal away, her most faithful one. May the first time I forget your name be when I no longer remember my own.

Héloïse looked up from the page. Its edges were yellow. Creases broke the page into quarters. It was one of his letters, written more than a decade before, when letters had flown between them. While waiting for the Abbot, she had, as she often did, drawn the folded parchment from inside her habit, less to read than simply to hold—her true periapt. Indeed, her eyes floated up from the letter to drift through the Cloister arcade to the rustic panorama beyond the cellarium, granary, and barns, where neatly ordered vineyards sloped down to the river basin. Its silvery water justified the name of the place—Argenteuil, her home. Within four years of her profession as a Benedictine nun here, she had been elected Prioress. Everything Mother Héloïse could see, including plowland stretching along the north bank of the Seine to the forested far hills, was hers.

Young Sister Célestine appeared in the arched entranceway, breathless. Twenty paces separated her from Héloïse, who was seated near the central fountain of the Cloister garden. The afternoon sun was gauzy with clouds, but the air was warm. Carefully trimmed hedges, bunched herbs, trellised roses, and potted jasmine stood between the women. "Father Abbot has arrived, Mother."

The portress, at twenty, was two-thirds the age of Héloïse, yet rank juvenescence showed in her agitation. She well knew who Abbot Suger was—Primate of Saint-Denis, the Bishop's rival, competing for preeminence as prelate of Paris. Héloïse, by contrast to the young nun, was serene, though she knew that the Abbot's sudden demand for an audience, received by messenger only that morning, could bode nothing but ill. Among the sisters of Argenteuil, the habitual calm of their Prioress seemed preternatural, a sign of sanctifying grace. To Héloïse, though, unruffled self-possession was less a virtue than a tactic. Rather than respond to the young nun, Héloïse dropped her eyes to the letter once more. *Farewell, my beauty, you who are incomparably sweeter than all sweet things. May you prolong your years as happily as I wish for you, for nothing better is needed.* Peter Abelard's words were all the blessing she would need. The parchment sheet fell easily into its creases as she folded it back into the sleeve hidden under her gray scapular, where, equally hidden, her golden ring rode on its cord. She pressed that lump against her breastbone, to remember that she existed. She stood.

Abbot Suger was a lean, tall man who, unusually for a monk, sported a thin mustache; it emphasized his tenebrous complexion, the stabbing darkness of his eyes, and the severe black of his religious garb. He habitually wore his cowl up, covering his head and, more to the point, keeping his face in shadow—*I see you; you cannot see me*—which was essential to his gift for intimidation. For a man of fifty, he was fit and agile, with something martial in his bearing. He swept into the Cloister garden with his robes swirling. Having removed his gloves, he paired them in his left hand and swatted his thigh as he strode. Because he wore heavy, ankle-high Norman shoes instead of sandals, his footfalls resounded. Approaching Héloïse, he bowed. "Good day, Reverend Mother."

Suger had been raised at Saint-Denis, and had served as clerk to Abbot Adam, whom he succeeded the year after Peter Abelard was forced to leave that monastery. Everyone knew that the wily Suger had been the instrument of Abelard's expulsion, and he had ridden that wave of triumph over the once-great Master into the Abbot's chair.

Saint-Denis was less than an hour's ride from Argenteuil, and, from the churning air with which the Abbot arrived, Héloïse understood that he had pushed his horse to get here quickly. When Sugar wanted something, he did not hold back.

Héloïse returned his bow with one of her own. He did not offer his ring hand, nor did she betoken readiness to kiss it. With an easy curl of her forearm, she indicated both the marble stool on which her visitor should sit, and the tray on which cups of barley tea and cider stood ready. "You are most welcome, Father," she said. Héloïse knew that reserving the cushioned armchair for herself would not be lost on Suger—a Prioress violating an Abbot's primacy. Indeed, she counted on his taking note.

"You honor us with your visitation." Héloïse sat, arranging the skirts of her habit as she did so. A simple toss of her head settled the drapes of her veil across her shoulders.

He sat. "You are gracious to receive me, Reverend Mother. I offer apologies for this intrusion." He dropped his gloves on the table, beside the cups.

Héloïse declined to offer him refreshment. Absently, she touched her starched white coif, but in a way that drew Suger's eyes directly into her own. "How can I help you, Father Abbot?"

"I fear I come with difficult words."

Héloïse only looked at him.

"Shall I simply speak my piece?"

She remained motionless.

Suger pulled a scroll from inside his habit, an unknowing match to the parchment sheet that was hidden on her. "This decree commands the removal of your convent from Argenteuil." He offered the page to Héloïse. She made no move to receive it.

He opened the scroll, and read. "The Holy Tribunal of the Metropolitan See of Sens, in the Kingdom of France in the twenty-second year of the reign of Louis VI, being of the intention to proceed against disorder, mischief, and scandal which increases to the prejudice of the Holy Faith, by command of the Most Eminent Lords Cardinal of this supreme and universal jurisdiction, and drawing on primacy recorded in the Donation of Clovis I, hereby removes and dissolves the Priory of Notre-Dame of Argenteuil. We pronounce, sentence, declare, and ordain the desacralization of the Benedictine Order of Argenteuil, pending the reconsecration of the monastic foundation by the Benedictine Order of the Abbey of Saint-Denis. By order of and signed, Henry, Archbishop of Sens; Samson, Archbishop of Reims; Stephen, Bishop of Paris."

Suger let the scroll curl back into its tube. When he looked up, he was jolted, if only slightly, to see that the piercing eyes of Héloïse had never left him. She was as still as a statue.

"Well?" Suger said, finally.

Héloïse said calmly, "This convent was founded by Princess Theodrade, the daughter of Charlemagne, more than three hundred years ago."

"Yes. And Saint-Denis was founded more than six hundred years before that by Dionysius the Areopagite, named in Acts as a convert of Saint Paul."

"I will leave that claim aside, Father. It is enough for me to observe that the monks of Saint-Denis, once each century, and always citing the spurious and long-discredited 'Donation of Clovis I,' make this bid for Notre-Dame, aiming to secure a port on the River Seine, not to mention the vineyards and contiguous demesne of Argenteuil. His Holiness the Pope always turns the essay back."

"In *this* century, Dear Mother, His Holiness the Pope is particularly concerned to suppress the source of scandal at Argenteuil. The Pope, furthermore, affirms the Donation. We have his writ. He is in France this very day."

"Which Pope?" she asked calmly. The question was a jibe because there were two papal claimants. She added, "Pope Innocent? Or Anacletus?"

"Innocent is Pope. Innocent II."

"But, Father Abbot, am I wrong to understand that the Petrine succession is in dispute, speaking of disorder? Simple nuns are less well informed than holy monks, but word has come here that the Cardinal Electors deem Innocent's election uncanonical. Pope Anacletus is recognized in Rome. Hence Innocent's flight northward across the Alps. So, of course, he is in France."

"Innocent is recognized by the Emperor, and, more to the point, by our own King Louis. And indeed, as you imply, a contested papal election is a matter beyond the competence of nuns in Lutetia."

"But Innocent, obviously, is beholden to you. Therefore, his writ lacks objectivity."

"Mother, this dissemblance—"

Héloïse cut him off with a raised hand. "Notre-Dame d'Argenteuil is under the patronage of Matilda, Countess of Champagne. Has Her Grace been informed of this interdict?"

"King Louis VI has been informed."

"Louis the Fat, your schoolmate at Saint-Denis. You were boys of the bench together."

"Mother, your disrespect makes my case. Need I remind you that your solemn vow of obedience, and that of every woman in this convent, is invoked?"

" 'Disorder, mischief, and scandal'—how dare you use such words of Argenteuil! What mischief? What scandal? I demand to know."

Abbot Suger craned forward, and with a lowered voice, he hissed, "The scandal here is well known."

"Canonical observance at Argenteuil is scrupulous in every regard. Consult your priests, who serve as chaplains here. There is no disorder. I demand that you specify your indictment."

Suger leaned back. "Look at you. Your very habit is a violation."

"The gray of our habit, the natural color of undyed wool, is an emblem of the simplicity for which we strive. Boiled wool and hemp cloth suffice."

"Peasant clothing."

"The repeal of luxury, Father Abbot, defines our reform."

"Reform! Hah! Vainglory, rather. To puff yourself up, you refuse the daughters of the well-born—"

"Not true. I refuse daughters who are sent here against their will."

"Instead, you receive women without dowry, which signifies their standing as harlots."

"Former harlots, yes. Some. Like the Gospel's own Mary of Magdala, perhaps. Repentant. Converted. Several of our most devout sisters."

"Admitted to the choir."

"We have abolished the distinction between choir nuns and lay sisters. Our women are equal before God. As your monks should be. Your lay brothers are no better than thralls."

"By what Rule do you live? Your nuns work on manuscripts, not embroidery. You presume to run a school for female children. You admit externs to the Cloister—"

"Never. We heal the sick who are brought to our gate. We feed the hungry. And, yes, we teach girls—as I myself was taught here, in the time of Mother Agnes. But our Cloister is inviolable, an enclosure absolutely restricted to those who are professed."

But Suger's litany rolled on, as he ticked offenses off with his fingers. "You instruct your sisters in writings of the pagans. You trade in Saracen texts. You forbid self-discipline—"

She interrupted with a sharply pointed finger. "Self-flagellation. Self-*mutilation*. Yes! The whip and thorn. Yes, I forbid that. Loving acceptance of the suffering attached to human life is all the corporal discipline we require. I forbid my sisters to torture themselves."

Suger made a sharp gesture of his own, the cracking of a whip. "Our Lord underwent flagellation, freely. He accepted thorns. Are we not called to imitation? Benedictines share in the Passion of Christ that they might share in His Kingdom. But you ignore Benedict's Rule. You presume to substitute—what?—the Rule of Héloïse?"

"Our house is reformed according to strict observance, Father. *Magnum silentium.* Fast and abstinence. The counsels of perfection. The furthest thing from 'mischief.' Again, I demand that you specify the indictment."

"Reverend Mother, I propose to spare you and your sisters the notoriety. But if you compel me, I will be merciless. I *have* consulted your chaplains. I am prepared to bring sworn testimony of holy men with certain knowledge of illicit, promiscuous, and decadent behavior by your women, one with another, and with themselves."

"Holy men, Abbot? Confessors? You would violate the sacred intimacy of the Sacrament?"

"No more than the *examen* of the Chapter House does."

Héloïse stared at him. After all these years—an epiphany. Early in her time at Argenteuil, she had sensed that the tonsured men on the other side of the Confessional screen, when presented with the once-notorious Héloïse, conjured lewd images and hoped to hear, in her *Me accusant,* details of her wicked carnal history. If she had never—never!—openly regretted her behavior with Peter, it was for the simple reason that she had never repented of it. As for the opinions of the priests, once she was elected Prioress, she had simply stopped presenting herself for Confession. Now, with this threat from Abbot Suger to exploit the sacred forum, she understood why. Her instincts had been correct.

She said calmly, if somewhat disingenuously, "My sisters regard the Sacrament of Penance as an encounter with Christ Himself. Would He so betray them?"

"'Whose soever sins ye remit, they are remitted unto them; and whose soever sins ye retain, they are retained.'" Suger smiled the smile of self-satisfaction. He continued, "Our Lord has given His ministers all authority to hold fast and to lay bare."

"Then use it." Héloïse stood, rattling the table holding the cups of cider. "Lay bare these charges. I demand a *public* accounting. You say the King knows of this interdict and its justification. I demand a hearing in the Royal presence. If Pope Innocent is involved, I demand a reckoning before His Holiness. My sisters are absolutely innocent. You say they are whores! I challenge you! I have no fear. Your holy men will be shown up as blatant liars, and then Saint-Denis will be the source of 'disorder, mischief, and scandal.' Not Notre-Dame d'Argenteuil."

"Mother, you are blind to what is most obvious." Now it was Suger who was calm. He looked up at her from his stool. "You are blind to your own standing in this matter. You *yourself* are the avatar of scandal never renounced. Your sisters' primordial offense subsists in their disregard of your *publica fama.* The disgrace of Argenteuil began with your election as Prioress, when you ceased being a penitential nun and became a false prophetess of virtue."

"I was never a penitential." Héloïse felt heat come into her face. She had long secretly suspected that her fellow nuns had elected her not despite her lewd history but because of it.

"Your so-called husband was a penitential—with us, if only for a time."

"And what good came of that for him?"

Suger shrugged. "We showed mercy to a man whose dismemberment was as much moral as physical."

"Your predecessor admitted Peter Abelard because a Jew whose knowledge of herbal medicine the Infirmarian coveted requested it."

"Peter Abelard was a Jew's friend, yes. Eventually, that corruption, too, showed itself."

"What showed itself was Peter Abelard's application of critical reason to the fairy tales of the Abbey of Saint-Denis. You claim to have been founded by Dionysius the Areopagite, Saint Paul's own convert. Peter Abelard, through careful study of history and Scripture, showed that to be impossible. He reduced your creed to the absurd. For which you banished him."

"Peter Abelard is degenerate, Mother—in thought as much as in deed. You are the living proof. The difference between you is that he has properly embraced his obscurity. Now it is time for you to embrace yours."

Héloïse, aware of the Abbot's advantage in his equanimity, was desperate to check the surge of anger coursing through her. As the organizer of Peter Abelard's shaming eviction eight years before, this man had been the object of her purest hatred even before this new outrage. Yet those early years came back to her now, and, for the needed brief interval, she took refuge in memory. Though her enclosure at Argenteuil, and Peter's at Saint-Denis, had been separated by only an hour's journey, she had never seen him. Yet she had been infinitely consoled to know that the same noonday sun made like shadows of their figures; the same rain fell on their upturned faces; and the same dark of night vaulted the ceilings above their narrow monastic pallets.

With a fresh pang, she recalled Peter's torment: first the long-in-healing catastrophe at the hands of Fulbert's henchmen; then betrayal by the monastery to which he'd entrusted himself; then, in the precincts of ecclesiastical power, almost universal disparagement, mockery, contempt. Once ostracized from Saint-Denis, and craving only solitude, he had built a hermitage a day's journey to the south-east, consecrating the place as the Paraclete to rebut adversaries who accused him of denigrating, in his theology, the Holy Spirit. Worship-ful would-be scholars—bless the young men!—pursued him there, and the place grew, willy-nilly, into a true religious foundation. But enemies followed, also, and the ever-famous Abelard was hounded away once again. The Paraclete fell derelict. Now he was ensconced on the far Atlantic coast, as the Abbot of a rough monastery of no importance on the wrong side of Christendom's most desolate frontier. Obscurity indeed. The great Peter Abelard, lost to the actual world forever: a chain of consequence that began with Abbot Suger, this man, here, in front of her. This villain.

To calm herself, she put her hand to her breast, to touch through the fabric the folded letter. *Farewell, my beauty . . . sweeter than all sweet things.*

The letter, yes. Her own Abelard.

Without ever imagining how such a thing might come to pass, Héloïse had long assumed that the day would arrive when they would once again turn toward each other. How could Abbot Suger's wrath-ful intervention become an occasion of grace if not by prompting that very pivot? Héloïse knew that Suger's bottomless ambition—not for Saint-Denis, or for King Louis, or for France, but for himself—required the takeover of Argenteuil. Lading traffic on the Seine had exploded in recent decades, carrying goods from Paris to Rouen and beyond, as well as pilgrims by the legion to and from Chartres. Héloïse had been expecting some move from the abbey to exploit the river's double-bend at Argenteuil—a landing site, a barrier-chain for tolls—and here it was. Suger would fortify the riverbanks and impose tariffs on every passing barge and cog. An endless supply of revenue was the issue, not the scandal given by promiscuous nuns. On mammon's account, there would be no deflecting the Abbot from his course. Even so, Héloïse would have fought him to the death if she alone were vulnerable to him.

He read her mind, for he said quietly, "I will summon each of your sisters to appear before the metropolitan tribunal. Your portress, for example—the girl who brought me in. Her name is . . . ?"

Héloïse did not answer.

". . . Célestine," Suger said, with a lewd sneer. He could not disguise the pleasure he took in this toying. "She will be required under oath to account for her night pollutions; what passions have her moaning to the point of communal disturbance?"

"Sister Célestine sleeps soundly."

"Perhaps so, Mother. But who of us knows what we do in the devil's company at night? All children have scruples. The *accusatio* can awaken them. Your sisters will be humiliated, one by one. Will you permit that?"

"No, Father. I will not." Héloïse stepped back, drawing close to the fountain that stood behind her in the center of the Cloister garden. "You have the power to desecrate the souls of the good women here, and I see that you will use it, even taking pleasure in the deed. I will not permit that. I see that it is pointless to resist you. Therefore, we will transfer this foundation, as you require, surrendering our ancient freehold in Argenteuil. But I will not dissolve this community. I am bound by my oath to the preservation of Notre-Dame. I am bound by love to each of its members. Love in your view, perhaps, is salacious. For us, it is sacred. We love the Lord by loving one another. Not Eros but Agape. Upholding that virtue requires me, as Mother Superior, to make a demand of you: before obeying your malign command, I must have time to arrange for an alternative conventual domicile."

"You will find no such alternative."

"In which case, your burden will be light. But if I do, Saint-Denis will cover the cost of our reestablishment. Not only accommodation for my sisters, but for those of our pledged feudatories who choose to accompany us."

"Serfs do not choose."

"Notre-Dame's sworn homage to its servants and laborers stands. I will leave it to them to determine the standing of their sworn fealty. This mutual allegiance carries an obligation that I will fulfill. You will support me in that. Am I clear?"

Héloïse waited. The power she had over this man resided only in her will. But it was power.

Finally, Suger said, "Yes."

"So—my first requirement is time. My second is provision. My third is discretion. I will not reveal to my sisters what you compel until I know what awaits us. Is *that* clear?"

"Yes."

"I will inform you when these preparations are accomplished. Now, Father Abbot, if you please . . ." Héloïse gestured, again, with a sweep of her forearm: *This conference is over.*

When Abbot Suger had departed, Héloïse summoned her chief horseman and instructed him to prepare himself for a long journey. She then went directly to her cell. The complications of what she felt made her light-headed, and she had to resist the urge to lie down on her cot. The impending loss of Argenteuil staggered her. Anguish attached to her own flawed character's having enabled that loss—her cursed reputation!—was beyond reckoning. Suger's cruelest thrust was true: the sisters *had* made themselves vulnerable by electing her as Prioress.

But desolation was only half of what she felt, for in the thick of contention a long-shut door had sprung open in her mind at the thought of the Paraclete—*his* Paraclete. She had just decided to put Peter Abelard's name on the page again—at last. Her heart had leapt at that, a kind of levitation. Her flawed character be damned.

She prepared her materials quickly, then wrote, "*Magistro suo nobilissimo atque doctissimo . . .*" She stopped. She knew at once that her choice of grammatical person was wrong: she should not be writing in the third person, but in the first. In her haste, she did not restart the letter, but continued. Peter Abelard would note the change, and would understand it, since—as she now realized for the first time—he had made the same adjustment in the letter she carried at her breast. She wrote, "*Fidem meam, et cum omni devocione meipsam quamdiu vivam.*"

"To her most noble and most learned teacher: my faith and my very self with all my devotion, as long as I live."

THE WAY IN WHICH the Paraclete had come to Peter Abelard was peculiar, intimately involving, as it did, the catastrophe of his mutilation, as well as, in a wholly other context, a mother's declaration that her oldest son was an imbecile. Theobald, the *second* son of Stephen II, the Count of Meaux and Blois, had, as befit his station in the age of primogeniture, taken the tonsure at a young age—anticipating life as a cleric. He was a bright lad, and at Paris he had embraced the ambition of becoming a Master at a school. He had been one of Peter Abelard's most devoted students, and happened to be passing by that dawn when the frantic Héloïse summoned him and two others to carry the bloodied Master to the physician's house in the Jewish quarter—a trauma Theobald had never wholly shaken. That Peter Abelard had then disappeared from his life had remained a source of grief.

Some years later, Theobald's father died of injuries suffered in a joust, and his mother, Adela, boldly declared Theobald's hare-brained older brother incapacitated. She appointed Theobald as heir, which is how an Abelard disciple became head of the House of Blois, one of the great dynasties of France. As it happened, that was the year of Abelard's expulsion from Saint-Denis, and Theobald, hearing of that further humiliation of his mentor, had responded with an irrevocable grant of an extensive demesne in the county over which he ruled— plowland, fishing reserves, and leasehold forest sufficient to support a pious enterprise worthy of the great teacher. The Catholic hierarchy in the region was long subservient to the House of Blois, so the local Bishop of Troyes had no choice but to sanction the benefice. Hence the founding of an oratory as a place of prayer, reservation of the Blessed Sacrament, and celebration of Mass—under the aegis of the infamous Peter Abelard.

Master Peter welcomed the gift of independence and protection, but, shaken by the forced exile from Saint-Denis, he began at the Paraclete as a reclusive anchorite, renouncing all worldly ambition. He wanted only to be alone. Yet this embrace of ascetic discipline enhanced his reputation with the young scholars who had not forgotten him, and they, together with juniors for whom he was legend, flocked to the Paraclete. The oratory was soon the center of an ad hoc village, part Cloister, part academy, part rough encampment— all sunk in a valley that had been cut over eons by a river that was, by now, a meandering, middling stream. For a time, because of the self-invited scholars, Count Theobald imagined himself as the patron of the first important school not sponsored by a cathedral or centered in a city. That was not to be, for the ever more eccentric Abelard discouraged the lads, and, after only two years, he abandoned the oratory and disappeared. Eventually, word came that he had accepted the commendation, elected as Abbot, of an obscure monastery in the uncharted west. Still the faithful Theobald refused to withdraw support from his mentor. The young Count insisted that the grant held: the Paraclete, and its lands, would perpetually belong to Abelard, or to whomever he conveyed it.

Now, once again, upon the arrival of the women from Argenteuil, the Paraclete was a hive of activity, with workers busily repairing old structures—the public chapel, hospice, schoolrooms, kitchen, stables—and building new ones, centered on a true monastic Cloister: Chapter House to the east, choir at the crossing, *scriptorium,* library, refectory, bathing room, and, on a second story, encircling the enclosure, a row of cells for professed sisters. The gray-robed women, with preternatural detachment, observed the hours of the Divine Office, maintained the Great Silence, and visibly upheld the contemplative ideal, as if the spinning world of which they were the mystical center were absolutely still. Indeed, the focal point of that whirl, being built, would be a looming bell tower that would transform the hours into knelling praise.

This reconsecration of the Paraclete involved dozens of workingmen, who, in a swarm of activity, tended fires at forges and brickworks, hauled carts, turned a water mill. Masons and thatchers scampered on scaffolding. Carpenters and joiners hoisted timbers. Artisans of various guilds supervised the firing of bricks, the smithing of iron, the cutting of stone, the erection of frames, and the application of lime mortar over wattling. These masters, in turn, were managed by the job steward, who met twice daily with Reverend Mother Héloïse in the windowless room adjacent to the Cloister that she referred to as her chancery. Bent over its tables, the nun, above a spread of drawings and ledgers, gave instruction to men who had never before taken it from a woman. Because she was as competent and sure of what she required as she was respectful, the steward and his craftsmen honored her by obeying. The monastic commune was accomplishing an astounding reinvention.

One day, as the steward left her alone in her chancery, Héloïse hesitated. Normally, she would have joined her sisters in the choir for the chanting of the midafternoon office, but she stalled, not knowing why. Spread before her was a finely drafted rendering of the timber inner structure of the new barn, and her eyes were fixed on the angled tracing. Yet she was aware of a numinous presence before any actual sensation signaled it.

At a soft rap on the door, she said simply, "Come."

When she looked up to find Peter Abelard in the threshold, her thought was: *At last.*

Neither spoke. They looked at each other unblinkingly. Héloïse was aware of the heat in her cheeks, and she was sure that his brightened face, too, was a function more of feeling than of sun. He was taller than she remembered. The door frame made him stoop. She had always imagined seeing him at this moment as if he were young, his expression glad with the fervor of their just-finished play. But his mouth was unhappily clenched, his skin was blotched, and the dust of an unforgiving conscience, like an unkind wind upon the sea, shuddered across the pool of his eyes. When, finally, he said, "Reverend Mother," a tremor in his voice made it wholly unfamiliar.

She surprised them both by laughing. "You call me Mother?"

He was taken aback. "What then? Sister?"

Without thinking, she answered, "Call me wife, dear Peter. In my sleep, I call you husband."

Now his eyes fell, conveying that this was what he'd dreaded. How quickly she had pierced to their conundrum. "We are full-awake here," he said. "Wakefulness requires prudence." This sternness, she realized, was mainly with himself. His brow was lined, and the dark stain of weariness made hollows of his eye sockets. Time had touched him roughly. He said, "Although seeing what you have done with the Paraclete is like a dream. I come here from meeting with Count Theobald. It is no wonder that he is pleased."

"Count Theobald is gracious, but you, Peter Abelard, are my true benefactor. I am glad to thank you. It was impudent of me to write to you of my distress. I was desperate. You rescued us."

At her gesture, he stepped into her room, so that he could stand straight, but he remained by the door. She remained seated, at her table. He said, "I was appalled to learn of what Suger did to you at Argenteuil. If you had not made your direct request, I would not have dared propose this solution. I am glad of your request."

"You proposed your solution through Theobald. It was rude of you not to answer my letter direct *to me*. All these years . . . not a word of consolation from you. Nothing. How is that? Once, letters flew between us."

"Yes."

"I have saved your every one. Have you?"

"Saved your letters?" he asked.

"Yes. Have you?"

He blushed. "It is a womanly thing to do. I am not a woman."

"You have not answered my question."

"We have not written to one another since . . ."

"Your wound," she said. His womanly wound.

"I left your letters behind, in Paris," he said. "With everything of that life. I am fully a monk now. An Abbot. A priest."

She smiled. "And I am a fully vowed woman. Doubly vowed. Once to Christ. And ever to you. That has not changed."

That he said nothing to this hurt her, but she would not let him see it. She smiled. "You did not write. You did not come. You worry about appearances. The storied Abelard and Héloïse together again, spawning gossip. That is what has kept you away."

"I am here now."

"Because Count Theobald summoned you. He told me. That is why I am not surprised to see you. His Lordship, in consultation with the Abbot Primate of Cluny, has seen to the elevation of the Paraclete from oratory to conventual priory. But the granting of the monastic charter for women requires the naming of an ecclesiastical patron, whose seal must be applied to the charter, and His Lordship has seen to your appointment as our patron."

"Because you insisted upon it," he said. "Despite the Bishop's objection."

"The Bishop is a fool. The Count is right to ignore him. You have agreed to the appointment?"

"Yes," Peter said, and she was relieved. But then he added, "Although I had a condition."

"What?"

"The elevation from oratory to priory. I rejected that."

"I required it," she said coldly. What was this? Peter Abelard undercutting her?

But she was wrong. "At my insistence," he said, "the elevation is to a status above priory, to abbey." He smiled, expecting her to be pleased. "The Paraclete is to be an abbey with canonical exemption. You are to be an Abbess." He paused, letting the full weight of the good news land. Then he added, "You will have the right to the crozier and the ring." Abelard's smile broadened. "You and Suger will be peers."

"I care nothing for Suger," she said, not expecting to be believed. Suger was her nemesis, and this turn would punish him. Her smile matched Peter's, and conveyed her delighted surprise. "You are the peer I want," she said. And then, boldly, she asked, "Will you stay with us?"

"That is impossible, sister."

"Appearances?"

"I am the Abbot of Saint-Gildas-de-Rhuys."

"*Hic sunt leones,*" she said. "Your monastery is in the faraway land of dragons and lions, where the language of the Celts is spoken."

"Yes. Far away, dear sister."

"In the west, well north of Nantes." She paused, allowing the laden place name to fall between them with all its weight. Then she asked quietly, "What word have you . . . ?" She could not bring herself to mention him, their son.

But Peter understood. "Lucille has sent word on occasion. He fares well. He folds in fully with the growing children of Marcus. He is beloved and safe. We were right in what we did."

"I have him in my nocturnal litany," she said. "Habitually, I hand him over to the care of our heavenly Father."

"As do I." He smiled. "But by what name? As Peter? Or Astrolabe?"

"As both." Héloïse laughed, and then he did. Their bond of love, still vital despite everything, was a triple weave, including their child—evermore.

Relief had come into her heart, and it prompted her to push him, as she had of old. She said, "I ask for your presence at the Paraclete, and you decline. So be it. But you should be where the influence of Master Peter Abelard can be felt. As it is, in your remote outpost, you are almost ignored. I know that you fear gossip, but you are in danger of being remembered more for the scandal we caused long ago than for your current application of reason to belief. Is this obscurity what you truly want?"

"My influence is a matter of my writing now," he said steadily. "I am at my table all through daylight, and even with candles at night. I have scribes at my elbow, taking dictation."

"So your monks know Latin?"

Abelard shrugged, conveying disdain for his own situation. "Some do."

"Enough, apparently." She nodded. "The writing of Peter Abelard travels. Your books are copied, and passed from one *scriptorium* to another—including mine. I have them. Your *Treatise on Ezekiel*. Your *Theologia*. Your *Sic et Non*. I read you." The warmth of her regard made her voice full-throated now. "But apart from your most devoted followers, and from disapproving critics, your readers are far fewer than is right. The Master Teacher's lectern, raised upon a podium, is where you belong, not the *scriptorium*. You belong in the city, not the edge of wilderness; a school, not a monastery. Your work as a writer will find its future only in your work as a Master. Even more than here at the Paraclete, you belong back in Paris, Peter Abelard."

"I am content to make my case on the page."

"Your case is too important to remain there. Limbo, for example."

"Limbo? What of it?"

"You openly question Saint Augustine's doctrine that unbaptized infants are doomed. And what is your argument? That such cruelty to the little ones renders meaningless the love of God. There's the key: you use love as the measure of truth—not Church discipline. Not tradition. Not the Sacraments. Love. You must expand upon that."

"How?"

"Moving from infants to infidels. God loves them, too. Make *that* case."

"Infants, by definition, are innocent."

"Was the thief on the cross beside our Lord innocent? Was he baptized, for that matter? Yet he was promised paradise."

"You have honed your disputation skills, sister."

She nodded. She was surprisingly at ease. Her hands were at rest upon the architect's drawings, a vivid symbol of her authority. Authority braced her tone. "Your own *Theologia Christiana* points to how infidels, too, can be innocent," she declared. "Pagan philosophers. Hebrews of old. Jews of today. All of us sinners. The loving Father takes into account what his children intend. *All* his children. Including your humble servant." Here she half bowed, with more than a hint of self-mockery. "I learned this lesson well from you, how to trust my own desire. Yes, husband, *desire!* This is why I refuse to regret who we were to one another. Who, in my case, I still am. Your God, when I knew you, was not a God of law, but of love. I am your living reminder of that."

Abelard faced away. Framed by the doorway behind him, he stood tall. He, too, was strong. She was relieved to sense that he was, still, a match to her. He said, "The law is what love looks like, sister, when it comes to us in time and finitude." He paused. Strong, yes. But not stone. His voice shook slightly when he added, "As for *our* love, I would that you transfer what you felt for me to the love of Christ."

"Not 'felt.'"

"Still, it is Christ—"

She cut him off. "My Christ," she said, "is the Christ I have from you." Héloïse refused to lower her eyes. She waited for him to turn back to her. When he did not, she said, "Not the God who wills sacrificial suffering, but the Lord who rushes out to greet the wayward child."

"Sacrificial suffering, sister, looks different to me now. When we were young, life was grand. That changed, for me at least. Now it is in sorrows that I meet the Holy One."

"Forgive me if I presume to say . . . one can be too fond of tribulation."

At last, he turned back to her. "In my case," he said, "the sorrows are deserved."

"Because of me?"

"I was properly punished," he said firmly. "I do not judge what you were. What you *are*—that is admirable."

"People who admire me now as chaste do not know what a hypocrite I am. God knows, however. I have not changed since lust defined me. Lust for you."

His faced burned at her words, at least that. If there had been another chair by her table, she'd have invited him to sit. That he remained standing was making their encounter all too formal. That formality was the hedge behind which he could hide. But what did she expect, using the word "lust"? Even in their heyday, he colored at that.

She went on, "God knows this of me—my unrepentant longing—and still declines to judge. God is no heavenly magistrate, balancing scales, offense against punishment. I learned this from you as well, Peter Abelard. There is no appeasing God, because God does not need appeasement. God is love, pure and simple. That was your lyric."

"I no longer write songs."

"Good. You write theology now. Do that, Peter Abelard. Make your case with power. Speak it aloud. Follow your logic wherever it leads. That is what you used to demand of me."

"And now, demanding it of me, you would see my books burned."

"No!" She slapped her hand down on the table. "I would see them *read*! Once read, your words will fly. Your scholars, and then your readers, will see to your vindication, how the logic of Peter Abelard leads inexorably to the One True Faith."

"Ah, but there you miss the delicate point, sister. What makes me contentious is that I give primacy to logic, *not* faith. I think! That begins everything. I think! We cannot believe what we do not understand. I am accused of preferring thought to faith—and of that I am guilty. I presume to contradict the great Anselm, who has become holy writ. But I must do it from afar. To hold what I hold is dangerous. That is why I retired from the schools."

Héloïse heard these words with a heavy heart. The great man of her youth—still emasculated? But sensing his bleak condition opened her, all at once, to her own responsibility. Her role now was to help Master Peter Abelard to be Master Peter Abelard.

She said quietly, "Far off, in the Celtic hinterland, you are living in the past. The future needs you in the present. The Church needs you in the fray. And so do I."

"Leave the Church aside, sister. What do you need of me?"

"Apart from another form of address than 'sister'?"

"There can be no other."

"Then be a Father to the Paraclete. Be our counselor and guide, even if from a distance, and only by your writing."

"How so?"

"The Rule, for example. Abbot Suger made it clear that our Rule is inadequate."

"The Rule of Benedict—"

"—is for men. I need a Rule for women, legislating matters from the ridiculous to the sublime."

"What is ridiculous?"

"Benedict's Rule forbids underwear. I care not to speak for monks, but nuns need underwear—for one week a month, at least." She paused, then added with a soft smile, "Once, I could have said such a thing without causing you to blush."

But she'd misunderstood his embarrassment, as she saw when he said, "I wear underwear, needing it more than once a month." This reference to a condition caused by his castration silenced her, but only for a moment. She said quietly, "That has never mattered to me."

"Still, it matters." He forced a smile. "So much for ridiculous. What is your *sublime* reason for needing a Rule?"

She wanted simply to stand, and go to him. She wanted to take him in her arms. But she was confused now. Was this feeling the old longing for her lover? Or was it pity? She reined in the emotion to say, with what detachment she could muster, "The Rule for the Abbey of the Paraclete should measure duties and responsibilities of nuns against the duties and responsibilities of the women whom our Lord called as Apostles."

"Disciples, not Apostles."

"But you yourself say otherwise, calling Mary of Magdala 'Apostle to the Apostles.' Her anointing of Jesus is what made Him Christ, the Anointed One—so *you* say. Mary is the exemplar of love. Love must be the soul of the Rule. Teach us that! In your writing you deny that women were taken from Adam's rib! Women, too—directly from the hand of God! Declare that aloud! Construct a Rule on it! Give us the true mysteries of faith! Write to us! I will turn the refectory into the repository of your instruction. At each meal, my postulants will read aloud everything you send. May I depend on it?"

"Yes, sister. You may."

"Thank you, Peter Abelard."

She had succeeded in restoring the necessary equilibrium, and so had he. It wasn't what she wanted, but it was what their condition required if they were to have a future. A future! Enough!

She stood. She came out from behind her table. When he made no move toward her, she simply pointed the way with her hand, and, obedient, he turned. Héloïse walked with him then, but only as far as the pile of stones that would become the garden wall. They parted without touching. As she watched him go, she touched her breast, for the substance of his hidden letter, and for the compact mass of the ring she had from him. She thought, *He imagines me as a bride of Christ, but I am a Stoic of Rome.*

CHAPTER NINETEEN

Rachel Vedette routinely rode the bus from Hoboken into the city, but today, instead of filing with the morning commuters into the tunnel complex of the subway, she found herself strolling in the early afternoon from the bus terminal at Forty-First Street to the western extremity of Fiftieth Street, where, if he was right, she would find Pier 88.

A dusting of snow was swirling about, but the November sky was brightly organized around the yellow haze of an insistent sun, a benign promise that seemed wrong, given the dark weather of her own feelings. What did she want? Why had she agreed to this? She was a fool.

First to appear as she approached the river was neither a moored ship nor the massive terminal he had described but, rather, the hulking elevated highway that cut the city off from its Hudson waterfront. In the shadows of the steel-and-concrete structure, the cobblestone street bustled with trucks and taxis, vying for curb space or pushing into the cavernous cargo halls of the pier storehouses. Men in overalls and caps tugged at dollies or shouldered wheeled carts loaded down with steamer trunks and luggage. At corners, policemen waved and whistled as streams of well-dressed New Yorkers moved at a happy clip through the chilled underworld below the highway. Rachel fell in with them, to all appearances just another gawker come to see a ship set sail. But to her, the scene, extending for blocks, was chaotic, not festive. The frenzy only heightened her sense of dislocation. She had been at these piers once before, but not like this.

Rounding a corner at the last of the looming storehouses, and suddenly emerging from beneath the highway, she found herself in the open, confronted with a long view of a mammoth ocean liner moored to a pier across a broad stretch of harbor backwater. The ship was the size of a Manhattan skyscraper, as if toppled on its side and reaching far out into the river. The hull was black, the decks rising up were white, and from a pair of slanted-back oval-shaped funnels flew lines aflutter with hundreds of triangle pennants—red, white, and blue. Strains of some snappy show tune could be heard drifting from the ship across the distance, and reflections off an orchestra's brass and silver instruments could be seen to shimmer on the deck just below the captain's bridge. Tiny figures lined the railings. Emblazoned across the hull, in gleaming white letters amidships, was the word "America." Now the lightly falling flakes, salting the scene like the flitter of a child's crystal snow-globe, seemed a function of magic. For a moment, Rachel let go of her habitual wariness, releasing herself to the spectacle.

"Amazing, eh?"

She knew his voice at once—Father Michael Kavanagh, speaking from only steps behind her.

She turned. His face was vivid with delight. He seemed slightly winded, having apparently just crossed out from under the girders. He was bareheaded, wearing an open-collared blue shirt, but also, against the chill, a long black topcoat—the outer garb of a priest. At the sight of him, her heart, from its place of uplift, sank.

She was alone on Mondays because solitude was her natural state. His evident accessibility, by contrast, underscored the depth of her reticence, which, in turn, made this defiance of it feel dangerous. Why had she come here? But instead of turning to walk away, she found it possible to say, "Hello, Father."

Her diffidence was nothing to him, nor, she realized then, had his elation to do with her. His eyes were on the ship. He seemed younger than before. "She casts off in less than an hour," he said. "We should make our way over there, to the port-side dock, where the send-off gang gathers. That's us." Now he looked at her, grinning. She sensed that he was going to take her by the elbow, but instead he pointed, "Here come the tugboats."

He led the way through the crowd, moving gracefully, a man accustomed to deference but not forcing it. He was easy to follow. They lost sight of the ship as they drew even with a three-story red-brick building with a flamboyantly carved pediment reaching skyward above a columned portico—the marine terminal, standing between the endpoint of the pier and the street. They joined a line patiently filing through the terminal gate and out onto the dock. When Kavanagh and Rachel cleared the entrance, the first thing that registered, immediately to the left, was the looming bow of the ship. Seen up close and from below, it seemed more like a mammoth black wall than the graceful cutwater Rachel had seen from the distance. But then, coming fully onto the pier, as its planks broadened and ran out into the water for nearly the entire length of the SS *America,* Rachel saw the most startling vista of all: down from the soaring decks of the ship were drifting dozens—hundreds; no, thousands—of delicate ribbons, thin streamers in every color of the rainbow. Most were already fixed, wafting in the breeze, and impossibly tangled, a gossamer web, but other streamers were still falling, unfurling, like lines connecting the dots of the tiny bits of snow. Indeed, the snow itself was compounded now by, in addition to streamers, thrown confetti. The very air had color. The sight made Rachel gasp—a visceral elation with which she was entirely unacquainted. She almost reached ahead to Michael Kavanagh, but he pressed on through the crowd. Still, as if he'd sensed her uncharacteristic impulse, he did then let his arm drift back toward her, apparently aiming to pull her along. Though she did not take his hand, she quickened her pace, to stay up.

The streamers fluttered. She saw what was happening: from the decks, the ships' passengers were throwing colored discs into the air, while holding fast to one end. The ribbons spooled out as they fell. Only when Kavanagh, half leaping, caught the loose end of a ribbon did she realize that such snagging, on the pier, was the point.

All around them, the festive well-wishers were seizing streamers that linked them randomly to the travelers high above. With shouts and waves, though, some landlubbers were ecstatic to find themselves joined to particular people who, equally thrilled, could be seen craning down over the ship's railing. Kavanagh clutched a second streamer, and turned and handed her the end. Red.

"Look up," he said happily. "Figure out who this ribbon pairs you with. That's who you've come to send off."

Through the tangle of elongated tapes, confetti, and the swirling snow, Rachel traced the color red of her particular thread, up and up. Well free of a snarl above the midpoint of the hull, the red streamer, proudly distinct, looped up to the rail of the main deck. There, holding the other end, was an adolescent girl in a bright green beret and a matching green coat. She was wearing white gloves, which made the wild waving of her free hand all the more jubilant. With her other hand, she held the red ribbon up in the triumph of having identified Rachel, her partner! The girl called down to her, words that Rachel could not make out in the cacophony, which included, as she heard it now, the orchestra's rendition of "Happy Days Are Here Again."

"Wave to her," Kavanagh said gently. Only then did Rachel realize that she'd been standing like a statue, conveying nothing of her buoyant absorbedness. She did wave, but cautiously.

Kavanagh's streamer was purple. He leaned to Rachel and said, "The red ones are the best. Red means you, too, will take a trip."

"Why should red mean that?"

He shrugged. "Red for the navigational slogan 'red right return.' You'll be sailing home."

His words meant nothing to her. She wrapped the end of her ribbon twice around her hand, while still waving shyly. Above, the girl in green tugged at the man beside her, a father perhaps, and now he, too, waved down. Rachel was aware of the snow upon her own upturned face, but otherwise the field of her concentration had been taken over entirely by the girl.

The sounds of music, laughter, joyous shouting were all surpassed suddenly by the soaring blast of the ship's horn. Like the hands of many others, Rachel's went involuntarily to her ears, although she, like the others, continued to clutch the ribbon. The horn fell silent as abruptly as it had sounded. All other noise had quieted.

Kavanagh leaned to her again. "Brace yourself. Two more blasts. The signal that she's moving astern."

The second sharp horn sound was, if anything, louder.

The girl on the deck above was clutching her ears, too, but her gaze was fixed upon Rachel, and then she was waving again.

No sooner had the third blast sounded than the ship began to ease away. Now a cry went up, in unison, from the dockside crowd, and their waving took on a frantic edge. The onboard band broke into "Auld Lang Syne." As the ship moved, the streamers, held fast in a thousand fists, began to go taut. Curls and loops disappeared as, one by one, the ribbons stretched. On board the ship, the passengers waved and waved. Hands went to mouths for the blowing of kisses.

The draping red ribbon that joined Rachel to the girl in green went straight, and other ribbons now began to snap as the ship pulled away. The rainbow tracery was breaking apart.

No, Rachel thought. It suddenly mattered that her one precious streamer not break. Eyeing the girl, Rachel pushed past Kavanagh to go with the ship, to keep the tape intact. It grew tighter and tighter, but held. The ribbon held! How could such a thing have significance? Yet it did. Rachel began to throw kisses to the girl, who threw them back, and once again began calling to her. Now, though, Rachel heard the words: "I love you!" the girl cried. "I love you!"

At that, Rachel's streamer went slack, and the broken end fell from high up—curling down, down, into the channel of seething water that separated the dock from the hull. Rachel continued to hold on to the remnant tape, unconsciously winding it around her hand. The ship made way, ever more swiftly. The bow, passing by, loomed with a menace that drew Rachel's gaze high up to the word "America," emblazoned above the anchor flukes. She cast her eyes forward once more to find the girl in green, but the child was lost in the suddenly undifferentiated mass of passengers at the rail. Gone.

Rachel realized that Kavanagh, standing nearby, was staring at her. She saw that his cheeks were awash with tears, which startled her, but also underscored how unmoored she herself had become. She was given neither to tears nor to ready sentiment of any kind—yet she had just been unaccountably moved by a stilted commercial ritual, a debarkation she knew was staged. Still, the stirred feelings were real. She felt drawn to the priest simply because he was a fellow human being who had, for his own reasons—a long-lost father? a mystery friend returned?—been ambushed by a grief of farewell to which he was, unlike her, capable of giving expression. His show of feeling forced her to acknowledge, if only to herself, that she, too, had been waylaid.

Then, abruptly, she realized her enormous mistake. His face was wet not with tears but with melted snow. Her own cheeks, she realized, were wet for the same reason. She turned away from him. Mere foolishness could not define her. It was not that she had mis-read the man. It was that she had *wanted* him to be weeping, so that the difference between them could be clear. She had forgotten for a moment what she was—an orphaned animal, alone, hungry, and perhaps dangerous.

That an abyss had opened between her and everything else was the indelible fact of her condition. Who was she to imagine that a line could be thrown to her, or that she would, in any case, know how to reach for it? To have been dropped, with the snapping of that ridicu-lous streamer, back into the bottomless pit of desolation made her joltingly short of breath. She brought a hand to her chest, to press her lungs, the hand around which, by now, was wrapped the red ribbon.

With the ship under way, the send-off gang slouched back toward the city, lazily funneling through the gates at the marine terminal. As abruptly as the flurries of snow had come, now they disappeared, as if its own romantic weather accompanied the departing ship. Without waiting for instruction from the priest, Rachel turned and went the other way—toward the river, not the streets. He followed her, but she did not care.

They advanced against the crowd, pushing farther out toward the pier head, as if hawsered to the ship, which was sliding into the open river with remarkable speed. Having begun to move her legs and arms, blood pumping, Rachel found that the unexpected flood of emotion started to ebb, which enabled her to resume breathing almost normally. Yet she was still in the grip of the oceanic free-fall through the cavern of her chest. To come out of herself, she focused on the surrounding scene, and was immediately struck by the dapper look of the ladies and gentlemen shouldering past: the coiffed hair, bright scarves, suede gloves, fedoras, coat collars upturned just so—an inventory of style. Most seemed paired off as couples, with arms linked. They carried on an easy interchange of laughing chatter.

The laughter was like an unknown foreign language, sparking an alienation that drew her back into preoccupation with herself. She was dressed in black, as always, yet today, away from her workplace, she was wearing loose-fitting black trousers instead of a long skirt. That, together with her cloak and turban, set her apart—a woman of sorrows compared with these partygoers, assuming they even saw her. But with her cape flying as she pushed through, of course they saw her.

Rachel chastised herself for being a willful misfit—a *gitane,* the Gypsy card-reader for whom the rough French cigarette was named. But she rebuked herself for foolishness again. What is a Gypsy here? Who reads cards? And what, for that matter, in this city of Technicolor dreams, is a woman in black if not one hoping to be gawked at? She was pathetic.

Soon she was free of the crowd, and Kavanagh was right behind her. She slowed her pace. He caught up, and they walked shoulder to shoulder, rattling the planking as they went. Again she took in the scene, to escape herself. Across the water, tugboats nudged the magnificent SS *America,* turning it slowly, so that, soon enough, it once again showed itself broadside.

She turned to him, pointing at the ship. "Your brother, perhaps? You said he's a tugboat captain?"

Kavanagh laughed. "No. Jerry's is a push boat—barges and scows, not ocean liners. Nothing glamorous, like this. Staten Island with the working stiffs, not Manhattan with the swells."

Rachel watched the ship for a moment longer, then resumed

walking. At the end of the long wharf, beside a flagstaff flying the eagle-adorned ensign of the United States Lines, was a slatted wooden bench. The sun had broken fully through, a completed shift in weather that invited them to sit.

In silence, they watched the ocean liner gliding downriver, toward the Statue of Liberty. Tugboats drifted away from her—first one, then a second, then a third—leaving the ship to her transcendent solitude. Rachel, for her part, was glad for company now: a rescue from bleak inwardness. She wanted to ask the priest a question, but it refused to take shape in her mind. Obviously, because of the ever-shrinking ship, the question had to do with departure. She toyed with the red streamer on her hand, rewinding it around the spool of her fist.

"During the war," Kavanagh said quietly, "she carried troops. Her hull was painted a swirling gray and white and silver—camouflage. She's so fast she would outrun her destroyer escorts, so she would cross the Atlantic alone. She outran the U-boats, too. I used to watch her come and go from Brooklyn."

"But were there streamers?" she asked.

"No." Kavanagh laughed. "Although the navy band was there, playing 'Anchors Aweigh' instead of 'Auld Lang Syne.'"

Rachel surprised herself by saying, "I looked at you back there and thought that I saw tears on your face, but it was melting snow."

"It might have been tears," he answered kindly. "Who's to say?"

But when he smiled, she thought perhaps he was teasing her. Then she saw he was teasing himself. He said, "I saw the snow on your face, too."

She said, "Yes, snow. Only snow. Still, I was not prepared for such feeling. It was, we say, *heureuse et triste.* Happy-sad. That young girl at the rail above. Did you see her?"

"In green. *Your* girl. You had her streamer. Holding the other end, she was calling to you."

"Yes." Rachel could not bring herself to say, *I think she was calling, "I love you."* Instead, Rachel gestured with the ribbon on her hand, and said, "The surprise was in what this . . . *a établi*—you say 'established'?—established between us. Then, when it broke . . ."

"You found that sad?" Kavanagh asked.

"I was invaded by feelings. *Envahie.*"

"There was a man with the girl," Kavanagh said. "Perhaps you noticed. I suppose it was her father."

"Yes. I saw."

"And perhaps that made you think of your father, if you don't mind my mentioning him. A father and daughter."

Already in this conversation Rachel felt not only that she was impersonating someone—*la gitane?*—but that, by contrast, he was being entirely himself. How had he come so quickly back to Papa? He knew to do that because, yesterday, when he broached the subject, she had cut him off, which only flagged her father as unfinished business.

Now Kavanagh was gently returning to it, having prepared the way by speaking of the ship and its service in the war; by taking seriously the implications of her red ribbon; by having noted what passed between her and the girl. But, then, was this not what a good priest did? Observe. Listen. By observing and listening, understand? Then she wondered, how had she come to the knowledge of his goodness? Yesterday, she had pictured him with patients at the hospital, but that had been abstract. Was this what priests did when hearing Confessions?

She turned her face to him, the day's first direct meeting of their eyes. Yes, he listened. He understood. And he offered an opening—one through which she was not yet prepared to go. She veered, saying, "I thought, in bringing me to the West Side docks, you were inviting me to know *your* father, the longshoreman. Was that not the point? What this place means to *you?*"

He answered, "This pier wasn't here in Pop's day. There was a shorter one, all slanted pilings and creosote and splinters galore, but out here, jutting into the Hudson, it feels the same. This was my special place. My brothers and I were river rats, taking every chance we got to clamber aboard a boat, usually a work skiff or a dinghy. It's how Jerry wound up in tugboats, and I would have, too, but . . ." He hesitated, and had to make a fresh decision, whether to go on. He said,

"Actually, I was a solitary boy, most myself out here alone, looking across the river to the other shore. In those days, you saw no buildings over there, just woods. I used to feel that I was looking not so much at Jersey, but at the whole rest of the country. Go west, young man, go west! After Pop died, this was where I did my thinking about him, the feel of my hand in his, which was callused but always gentle. The aroma of his skin, the rough stubble on his cheek when he kissed me good night. He was everything I loved about where I was from. But where was I going? Out here, the past bled into the future. So what I saw, stretching out past Jersey, was the whole span of time, too. I loved the feeling, here, that I was looking at my life to come."

"Your life in the Church?"

"From a certain point on, sure. From harbor boats to the Barque of Saint Peter." He laughed, and he looked away. His discomfort showed, and she sensed how rare this was, his explaining himself. With his gaze soft upon the far riverbank, he went on: "The parish priest was the neighborhood hero, and it seemed normal—inevitable—to want to be like him. It doesn't take a psychiatrist to get the connection between the father I'd lost and the father I soon found. Becoming a priest, obviously, was the answer to a question I'd begun to ask when Pop died. But it took me a while to get there. Looking back, I see that that's what I was doing, with my solitary brooding out here on the pier."

"Brooding?"

He shrugged. "I would learn to call it 'contemplation.' But before I settled on the seminary, I wasn't attuned so much to 'a' future, with a whole lot of specifics defining it, but to 'the' future, if you catch the distinction. Open-ended, the way that landscape across the river struck me, rolling on from sea to shining sea. Looking west is an American habit, they say, because it's as wide open as tomorrow. Geography and time—reflecting one another. Is that the difference between Europe and the States? One looks back, the other looks ahead? The past is what makes you French. The future is what makes you American."

"Me?"

"Yes."

"Am I American?"

"If you want to be." He faced her again, to say emphatically, "You get to decide."

"One does not get to decide about the givens of the past."

"That's true. But you decide what they *mean* to you. Isn't that what your father's project was, regarding Abelard? Trying to change what Abelard's *meaning* was?" He waited for her to affirm what he'd said. When she remained silent, he went on, "From what you said, your father didn't regard the givens of Abelard's past—or past understandings about him—as closing off a different future. Or is that presumptuous of me?"

"No. It suggests that you have been listening." She did not know when she had looked so steadily into the eyes of a man.

He did not look away. He said, "You told me you wanted to talk about it."

"Yes. About Abelard and Héloïse."

"Which means your father."

"Yes. Although I did not realize that . . . until . . . you . . ." At last, she dropped her gaze; her eyes settled on her hands, which were clasped in her lap. She'd forgotten the red ribbon. Feelings stirred up in the wake of the ship's departure still washed through her, a complicating countercurrent to far older feelings from which she was normally walled off. Though it seemed obvious, now that she saw it, Rachel was startled to recognize that her impulsively giving the *Historia* to the priest was as much about her father as about the text. With this stranger, she was at last forcing herself to reckon with her own, yes, grotesquely unfinished business.

She said, "I have not talked about my father, or 'his project,' as you call it, because he failed." Rachel stopped. What she had just said was false. The truth was, she did not talk about her father because of *her* failure, not his.

She allowed the silence to settle, and soon the silence became its own palpable presence, like a third party between them. Once again, her mute immobility was a cul-de-sac from which there would be no exit. But no: this time she was not alone, and her partner in the silence could break it.

Understanding, apparently, the need for a pivot, Kavanagh said with a self-mocking laugh, "That was some U.S. civics lesson of mine, eh? The great American narrative: looking west; the mythic power of the future; time and space joined on the wild frontier—which is what we New Yorkers call New Jersey!"

His inflection signaled the punch line of a joke, but she did not get it.

He continued, "That unfenced future is why, though I could never become French, you could certainly become American. Open-endedness makes for the famous American innocence."

"Innocence?"

"Innocents abroad. How we Americans are always starting over. Moving on. Who knows what's out there? Believe it or not, I've been feeling that way myself, for the first time in years . . . this week, since I met you. 'Experience over doctrine,' you said yesterday. You were talking about Abelard and you mentioned Galileo, but you could have been talking about me."

"Your business with the Bishop?"

"A long time ago, he lied to me. That lie—experience—is like a flawed brick down low in a wall—doctrine. If you cut into the wall to replace the brick, pretty soon you're having to move every other brick in the entire structure."

"Does the wall fall?"

"That is the question, Miss Vedette. That sure is the question. I have to take it up with His Excellency. I'll begin by explaining about ethics over creed." Kavanagh grinned. "Maybe I'll quote Abelard."

"Quote Héloïse. She's the true genius."

He laughed, and nodded—a wholehearted gesture of agreement. Then he veered: "Maybe I'll just tell the Bishop about the coming and going of ships—what started us on this."

"Us?" she asked. What had she to do with his Bishop?

He shrugged. "Yesterday I suggested we come down here to the docks just for the fun of it, but 'fun' hardly applies to this chat of ours. Wouldn't you say?"

"You have a history here, and it carries weight."

"Because of Pop, that's true. But also because of the war." He was suddenly solemn. "Did I say I was in the navy?"

"You said Brooklyn, just now."

"The Brooklyn Navy Hospital. Chaplain."

"And you still serve a hospital."

"Yes. It's the heart of what I do. A priest at the side of the patient's bed. That experience, actually, is what passes for my doctrine. The bedside of those in pain is where I most belong. But during the war I was down on the docks all the time, too, sending my lads off on troop ships. And then . . . receiving them when they came home. Speaking of sad."

"And, in your case, haunting everything—the *Titanic*."

"So we have a theme going here. What was it you said, '*heureuse* . . . or *triste*'?" Kavanagh pulled a pack of cigarettes from his pocket. A bit presumptuously, he put two in his mouth and lit them, then handed one to Rachel. She took it, gratefully. He said, "But you must have arrived in New York by ship, no?"

"Yes. Down there." She tossed her head toward the Statue of Liberty.

"Ellis Island," he supplied.

"And the very long lines."

"When was that?"

"More than a year ago. Nearly two years."

"You mean 1948?"

"Yes. Why?"

"The year Truman let the DPs in. Was that you?"

She considered what to say, then spoke slowly. "It was carefully explained to me that I was not 'displaced.' I was not 'stateless.' I was French. Nevertheless, I was expelled from Europe. We were *all* called 'DPs,' because Truman could not bring himself to call us Jews. But that is what we were. Israélites. In France, I stopped being French."

"You were in a camp?"

Rachel, instead of replying, focused on the study of her cigarette. That this man—a stranger, really—had pushed through to that question might have surprised her, but she coldly acknowledged its inevitability. She herself had made it inevitable. Now that the word had been spoken, and spoken by him, there was no question of not answering. "More than one," she said. "A camp for Jews, run by Germans. And then, after the liberation, a second camp, for, shall we say, *les délinquantes*. Liberation, for some of us, was delayed."

"I don't understand," he said.

She looked at him sharply. "Collaborators. Traitors. *C'est moi*. Surely you heard how we French turned on one another at the war's end." She shrugged—a willed gesture of indifference. Of course he would not understand. She went on: "And then, third, a 'relocation camp,' which was organized by the Americans. From that camp, I came here, to the United States. By then I was, yes, 'displaced,' no matter what they called me." She took a hefty drag on her cigarette. In exhaling, it was as if she had just taken her first breath in years. Also as if she would not be allowed another. "It is a long story," she said, by which she meant there was nothing more to say. She would go back to holding her breath.

She looked downriver. The ship was small, beyond the statue, approaching the mouth of the harbor. Its one streamer now was a thin line of smoke, trailing from one of the two funnels. She thought of the ship, suddenly, as an emblem of herself. She was gone like that, sailed away. She said, "It is cold. Are you not cold?"

"Yes, but . . ."

She looked at him and, despite herself, asked, "What?"

"I am trying to understand what has brought us to this moment. I came upon you at The Cloisters, a place, to my surprise, full of implication for both of us. I did not intend to impose on you, but, because of events unleashed in my own life just now, I seem to have done just that. You have been helpful to me—as I navigate some unexpected swells. Also, I get the feeling that I can, perhaps, be helpful to you. That is all I mean."

"Thank you, Father. You do help me. I am glad to have come here to be with you. But there is a limit. We have reached it."

"Sometimes it is at the limit that breakthroughs occur."

"Breakthrough? From what to what?" It was true: she *had* stopped breathing.

"Well," he said, "in your language . . . perhaps . . . from *triste* to *heureuse*? Isn't talking about it what we've been given to do? I do not mean to be presumptuous, but you can talk to me."

"What do you imagine I could possibly talk about with you?"

"Besides Abelard and Héloïse, you mean?"

The delicacy in his statement made her realize how she had used the medieval couple as an invitation to this unfamiliar intimacy. He was careful. He was respectful. For these reasons, suddenly, he seemed dangerous to her. When, nevertheless, she then said "Yes," she knew she was in some way giving him permission.

He nodded and said, "Well, then . . . I have noticed your sleeve. How you protect your forearm. Your left sleeve is always tightly buttoned, unlike your right. You wear that elastic band."

Rachel was taken aback. "That is not your concern, Father," she said sharply. Her use of his title, at this point, was a withdrawal of whatever permission he thought he had.

"I know that, miss," he said. "And I know it is rude of me. But my concern by now is with you. I am concerned to know you, and you have seemed concerned to let me know you. Am I wrong?"

Rachel began to say, *Yes, you are wrong,* but, unaccountably, she did not.

Therefore, he continued, "Your forearm tells the story, no?"

She stared at him, astounded. He held her eyes. She snapped her cigarette away.

She lifted her left arm, free of her black cloak. She unbuttoned the cuff of her sleeve, pulled away the elastic band, and pushed the cloth roughly back. *"Voilà!"* she said.

Kavanagh lurched back with surprise.

She said calmly, "For sure, you imagined numbers, a tattooed line of numbers."

What she showed was a savage, knotty scar at her wrist. *Not* numbers, but the gnarly evidence of self-mutilation, a failed attempt at suicide. Searing her open hand, tangled with the shirt elastic, was the tightly wound farewell streamer, as red as blood.

"'American innocence,' you said before, Father. But you should have said 'American *ignorance.*'" She was speaking calmly. This was *her* civics lesson. "Americans hear lurid stories about tattoos, how the German guards put numbers on the arms of prisoners. That was at one camp in Poland. *One* camp! There were dozens of camps, hundreds of camps. Everywhere in Europe. *Camps everywhere!* In Paris, too—the City of Light. Imagine! And not just German guards. During the war, and for a year after the war, my guards were French. Fascists first, and then heroes of the Resistance. Good Catholics all, Father, by the way. Then my guards, for another year, were American, and they were not innocent, either. Believe me. Tattoos were the least of the impositions."

She closed the sleeve around her wrist, fastened the button, and pulled up the elastic. "So. I repeat myself. It is cold."

FOR WEEKS, RUMORS had told of the coming Americans, and now Roosevelt's army was said to be closing in on Paris. Rachel Vedette had learned to discount rumors unless they foretold a deepening misery, yet the frenzy of Drancy guards, including many newly arrived Germans, suggested this one might be true. New barriers of barbed wire were strung on the perimeter of the compound and at the railhead, and gun mounts were hastily constructed at the gates. The senior-most officers, with their lightning-bolt black collar badges, disappeared, but further rumors had it that they were being replaced by hardened leaders of the Death's Head Unit, come to incinerate the camp rather than see it taken.

In fact, only half-panicked *Unterführer*s were in evidence now, ranting at ever more harried inmates, who were mustered repeatedly, counted off, made to stand for hours, and then dismissed. No explanation was given for these unprecedented exercises, and most prisoners assumed that mere harassment was the motive, although Rachel realized that note-taking guards, moving through the ranks, were recording housing-block numbers. The mass assemblies in the vast courtyard were made more difficult when bonfires were lit at both ends, fouling the air with smoke, but at least the purpose of the conflagrations was clear. Through darkness and daylight, camp functionaries emptied hundreds of file drawers into sacks and hauled the documents to the fires—meticulously kept records, presumably, of the many thousands who had been processed for transport to the East.

And then—an ominous signal—a train with a larger-than-usual number of freight cars and stock wagons had appeared at the railhead. The glad rumor of a coming liberation was trumped now by the recognition that yet another selection was imminent. But even that suggested the end was near, and French prisoners assured one another in whispers that this time Ukrainians and Poles would be the ones taken.

Rachel Vedette and her father were among the decided minority of those first arrested who, all these many months later, still remained in Drancy. And why should she not have allowed herself, as the horror showed real signs of climax, to believe that their luck would hold? Their survival, of course, had not been a matter of luck. Rachel's dependable access to the pharmacy at the main infirmary had protected the supply of insulin, which, together with steadily purloined honey, apples, and oranges, allowed them to navigate the highs and lows of her father's blood-sugar levels. Weakness, blurred vision, confusion, the drift toward coma, occasional convulsions—the old man had mostly managed to hold the worst effects of the disease at bay, and, most crucially, to keep from drawing untoward attention to himself.

The professor's informal *havruta* group had long before stopped gathering: when one member or another had disappeared, those remaining feared that their discreet Shabbat fellowship was itself the reason. Eventually, everyone who ever joined the group vanished. Saul Vedette alone remained. As Drancy became less a true internment camp than, for more and more of the prisoners, a mere transit point, internees wrapped themselves anew in a cocoon of indifference toward everything that was not food or sleep or distance from the Gabardines and jackboots. In contrast to the early days, that indifference extended to how the once-noted professor was regarded. No one cared who Saul Vedette had been. He was left to pore over his Hebrew texts alone. His daughter, in this void, took to pretending that she had recovered her long-lost interest in Torah study, and joined him in it. To her surprise, if not his, they found a new kind of intimacy, side by side, in keeping their eyes cast down upon the same page. But, in fact, cast down was how they kept their eyes when they were apart, too. They had embraced the survivor's superstition that if they did not see they would not be seen.

As the hazy light of dawn was brightening the stairwell windows one morning in that time of heightened rumors, she was, as usual, coming down from the infirmary at the end of her cleaning shift—which included, as it did once or twice a week, the numb assignation with Dr. Rivière—when she first sensed that something was wrong below. The infirmary was on the back side of the mammoth building, facing away from the U-shaped courtyard around which life in the camp revolved. Through the night, she had heard no noises from that enclosure, but now the crowd murmurs, coughing motors, and occasional shouts that defined daytime activity sounded from the large quadrangle. Commotion so early was unprecedented. She picked up her pace as she descended the last of the stairs that brought her to the third floor. The landing was vacant, but the door into the cavernous bunk room was ajar. A clamp closed on her chest.

The double- and triple-tiered bunks were still arranged more or less in their orderly aisles, but there were no sleepers. The beds were empty. Here and there, tattered nightshirts and undergarments pooled on the floor, suggesting how hastily the roughly eighty inmates, mainly old women and a few old men, had been made to dress. They were gone.

Pale sunlight filtered in through the many large windows, and fleets of dust motes swirled in the shafts of haze. Rachel heard an air of urgency in the distant courtyard sounds, but she focused on the scene before her. Mattresses and blankets were strewn about, and the boxes and trunks that held the prisoners' meager belongings were opened, with contents spilled. She might have shrieked "Papa!" and run through the maze to the farthest corner, but a ruthless discipline steadied her. She crossed the dormitory, apparently calm. The niche she shared with her father was defined by their two-tiered bunk and two square meters of surrounding space, hedged in by the suitcase, a chair, and two footlockers, a cagelike area that had come to seem a sanctuary. Now it was a heap. Bedding had spilled from the bunks, and the lower mattress was upended—her father's. The suitcase and lockers were askew and open. Clothing was piled on the floor, torn pages scattered across it. Rachel knelt and found the leather valise in which she kept her father's insulin kit. It was, amazingly, intact; its straps were still buckled. When she lifted a shirt, she found under it her father's spectacles, crushed.

The dozens of pages scattered about bore the sharply angled block script of Hebrew. The pages had been ripped from her father's Torah, but also from *Torat Ha-Adam,* the Nachmanides volume. Both had been utterly destroyed. Intact on the floor, unmolested, she found *Historia Calamitatum,* the only book not in the divine language from which the entire cosmos was created.

Holding the *Historia* and the valise, she began to leave the room, but her composure failed and she broke into a run, tore down the two remaining flights of stairs and out into the U-shaped courtyard. What she saw stopped her. The nearest part of the quadrangle was vacant, but at its far end a throng of inmates was clustered inside the recently erected funnel of barbed wire. The limit of the courtyard was defined by the platform at the terminal point of the railway track. Rachel ran toward the crowd of prisoners, but as she approached, she saw smaller knots of soldiers, and stopped. To one side, they wore the brown uniforms of the Gendarmerie, and to the other, the gray-green of German infantry, soldiers who carried rifles. Closer to the inmates stood other Germans, whose status as officers was indicated by braided shoulder boards and holstered pistols instead of rifles. Intent upon the crowd at the railhead, none of these uniformed figures seemed to notice her. She moved slowly forward. In the process of observing and assessing, the necessary calm came over her.

The penned prisoners numbered in the hundreds. Those closest to her wore the rough shawls, wooden shoes, and babushkas of Ukrainians and Poles, a sight that gave her hope. She kept moving forward, more quickly. The Slavs were mute, and Rachel saw now that they were being channeled through the wire and along the row of freight cars. In line ahead of them, alas, were prisoners dressed in the tattered remnants of more familiar clothing—French. Rachel drew closer. Those inmates were at the train already; numbers of them had been herded into boxcars, the sliding doors of which were slamming shut.

Soldiers covered the nearer cars of the train, rifles ready, while their comrades, farther down the queue, were forcing more inmates into the rail wagons. Meanwhile, dozens of other prisoners had drifted into the courtyard from dormitories that had not been targeted. This was a bold move, even if now they timidly kept their distance, observing from the safe side of the barbed wire, an ad hoc formation all along the track; they were not spectators, but witnesses. They clung to one another, yet also gestured and waved toward those who were being taken. Rachel drew closer still. The guards seemed to require of these watching prisoners only that they keep their distance back from the barbed wire. Their exemption suggested with what rigid methods the selection was being carried out. Certain groups, like the Slavs, had been chosen, along with particular dormitory blocks, including her own—all singled out, perhaps, at random. Other groups had not been chosen. That was all. The distinction was as absolute as the order it implied.

The chosen people, she thought bitterly.

Her attention turned to an officer standing beside the rail platform, only a few feet from the line of selected prisoners. His highly polished knee-boots and riding breeches set him apart from other Germans, marking him, perhaps, as one of the newly arrived hard men of whom the rumors had spoken. For sure, the band beneath the splayed eagle on his hat flaunted a skull—the Death's Head. A skull adorned the right patch at his collar. Next to him was a young girl, as still as a statue. She was barefoot; her dress was torn. The officer was holding his drawn pistol to her head, and the message to the internees was clear: at the first commotion, much less resistance, the girl would be shot.

Rachel, moving outside the wire, eyed the French prisoners as they shuffled along. She recognized an old woman. Rachel quickened her pace. She recognized another, and another—and then she recognized the whole clutch of bent people she knew from her dormitory.

She searched for her father's stooped figure, but before she found him, one of the women pointed at her, and screeched, *"Putain! Putain!"* Whore! Whore!

It was Madame Picard, shriveled with age. Her bed had been opposite the Vedettes' corner. Rachel had long ignored her reproving eye. The woman's voice pierced the air, sucking all attention to itself. Heads turned. Madame's voice shot up in pitch, painfully shrill: "She is one of us! She is one of us! Take her, too!"

Rachel drew back, but the hag's gnarled finger followed her. Into rage at the whore's escape from this final tribulation, Madame Picard poured all of her desperation, dread, and revenge. She screamed again, "Take her! She is one of our group! *Putain!*"

The officer with the skull on his hatband came toward Rachel, hauling the young girl with him.

Madame Picard cried now, "The whore is his daughter!" and she pointed to the bent man just ahead of her—Saul Vedette. "*His* daughter!"

Saul was moving slowly forward, ignoring everything around him, staring at the ground as he tottered along.

The SS officer, inside the barbed wire, had come between Madame Picard and Rachel. A rifle-bearing soldier, outside the wire with Rachel, closed on her. The SS officer brandished his pistol at her. "Is that true?" he demanded, in clipped French.

"She is his daughter!" Madame Picard screamed again.

Rachel stared at her father, who was resolutely ignoring her. She'd have given anything for him to turn, for the chance to meet his eyes.

"Is that true!" the officer demanded once more. "You are his daughter?"

Here it was: the perverse fulfillment of her refrain, *Who am I now?* Against the current of everything she felt and had ever done, and with absolutely no knowledge of what she was saying or why, Rachel Vedette answered, "No."

At that, the officer released the girl, wheeled, aimed his pistol at Madame Picard, and fired. She fell. Saul Vedette, having refused to look at his daughter, knelt to the old woman, as if to help her.

The barefoot girl collapsed in front of the officer. He ignored that.

Instead, he turned back to Rachel. When he saw the horror on her face—admission enough—he whipped around toward the prisoners again, raised his gun, and fired. Battlesight zero: the old man's skull. Saul Vedette fell over, dead.

Now, when the German turned back to the lying whore, a smile had crossed his face. It said, *I will let you live with what you just did.*

Instead of shooting Rachel, he shot the girl at his feet, and went back to his place at the railhead.

CHAPTER TWENTY

Patricia Murphy's, near the corner of Madison and East Sixtieth Street, was to high-end restaurants what "Danny Boy" was to the hit parade. With Irish table linen, Waterford chandeliers and glassware, Wedgwood china, candles on every table, every table with its bud vase, and murals showing scenes from the Gap of Dunloe and the Ring of Kerry, the place always had a line at the door—a line to the head of which every arriving Catholic priest was always ushered. "This way, Father," the tuxedoed maître d' would say, gesturing the waiting diners to step aside—which they did willingly. But tonight was different, for Patricia Murphy's was entirely given over to the men in Roman collars—the Cardinal's Thanksgiving Eve gala dinner for the priests of New York.

More than two hundred clergymen had shown, and by the time Father Michael Kavanagh arrived, the jovial air was well fueled. Black suits, a few cassocks, white neck-tabs, red faces, flashing cuff links, and hearty laughter. *Gaudeamus igitur:* let us rejoice, indeed. The men were standing in knots among the tables, glasses in hand. The large U-shaped room, occupying the joined first floors of what had been two buildings, bracketed a glassed-in courtyard onto which, in good weather, expansive French doors opened. The courtyard now was an off-season sunroom, with spotlighted shrubs and potted plants hardy enough to survive without heat. Waitresses in puffy-sleeved peasant dresses were placing baskets of the famous popovers on each table. Kavanagh, in his black suit, rabat, and collar, eased into the crowd, making for the bar. He would not have come, but Bishop Donovan, whose secretary blamed the Bishop's impossible schedule on an upcoming trip to Rome, had refused to see him. This was Kavanagh's one shot. Kavanagh's fellow priests registered his arrival with nods, but they also recognized a man in need of a drink and made way, leaving the hearty hello for when he would return, fully armed.

At the bar, Kavanagh found himself next to Joe Gallen. "Hello, Suede," he said with a friendly grin.

Gallen arched an eyebrow, the necessary, if minimal, show of displeasure at the moniker. "Hi, Mike," he answered. "Where've you been? Haven't seen you all week."

"Busy days, Joe. Busy days."

Gallen turned to the priest beside him and said, "Mike is lost in Simone Weil. Imagine that."

Kavanagh said, "It's 'Vey,' Joe."

"What?"

"Not 'Wile.' 'Vey.' Her name." Kavanagh turned to the bartender. "Jack Daniel's, please. On ice. Short glass. Thanks."

The other priest extended his hand to Kavanagh. "Seamus Riordan. I'm at Saint Paul the Apostle, on the West Side."

"A hint of the harp, Seamus?" Kavanagh said warmly, as they shook.

"Righto. Tipperary."

The priest looked to be about thirty.

Gallen continued, "Mike thinks Simone *Vey* was an anti-Semite because she was offended by the Old Testament God."

"The God who killed children, according to Joe," Kavanagh said. He raised his glass to clink with the others. "Which puts me in mind of the hospital, my rounds today. Just finished." Kavanagh hesitated. This was not the scene for an earnest report, but what the hell. He would give expression for once to what mattered. He continued: "I was with a family whose week-old infant is in an incubator. I was standing with the father, looking through the window of the preemie nursery. There were maybe half a dozen incubators, all these infants in trouble, struggling to live. And the dad says to me, 'Pray for our little Eileen, Father. Bring God down to save her, would you?' And I thought, What kind of God is that? Was God waiting for me to pray for the rescue of Eileen? Was I to ask the Lord to save Eileen, and not the others? And then what? The others die? Because they have no priest saying the hocus-pocus? What do you think, fellows? Old Testament God? Or Catholic God? What do you think?"

Gallen and Riordan exchanged a look. Gallen said, "Hocus-pocus, Father?"

"*Hoc est enim Corpus Meum,* Joe. It's where the magic formula comes from. You didn't know that? It's what the people expect from us. Magic." Kavanagh sipped his drink, surprised at himself. Despite his trenchant words, there was nothing sarcastic in his manner. John Malloy had referred horribly to the words of consecration—Quinn's *des*ecration—but Kavanagh pushed that aside, to focus on the memory of the hospital. "I did as the poor man asked, of course. I got out the oils, put on the gown and mask, went into the isolation unit, and anointed the little girl. I said the sacramental prayers for Eileen, and not for the others. But that's when it really hit me. God made *all* those babies, right? God loves them. When we administer the Extreme Unction, are we asking Him to come down and choose one, while ignoring the others? What do you think?"

Riordan said, "Father, I think you need your drink."

Kavanagh continued, "Afterward, I held the child's weeping father in my arms, and I went in and blessed her mother. I didn't tell them what I was thinking. This was two hours ago. So I am telling you."

Gallen said quietly, "It's a mystery, Mike."

"Mystery, Joe? That's the word we throw over what makes no sense. When we do our job and the great thing happens—a miracle! But what is it? One child saved, the others dead? If that's not a killer-God, what is? Who, actually, are we praying to? And for what?" Kavanagh sipped his drink as a way of veiling the cloud in his face. He forced a smile. "Just wondering."

A waitress came through, saying with an Irish lilt, "Please be seated, Fathers. Dinner is served. Thank you, Fathers."

Gallen moved swiftly away from Kavanagh, who did not blame him. Kavanagh had not realized how unsettled he'd been by the baby in the incubator, and he felt guilty for having wielded that memory as a blade. But he could not pretend that the hospital scene was all that had cut him adrift. For a week now, he'd been unmoored.

His colleagues began to circle the tables and seat themselves, and as he watched them, Kavanagh was buoyed by the recognition of their virtue. A happy throng right now, but they were a collection of men in whom the habit of empathy was ingrained. There were Frank Russell and Billy Mitchell, jostling each other like the chums they were. There was Kavanagh's own boss, Monsignor Stevens, with his red collar notch and ample waistline. They were generous, kind, and surprisingly unselfish for a group of sanctified bachelors. Then, too, the priests of New York also included savvy operators who knew how to budge City Hall in the interests of parishioners; who did not hesitate to weigh in with employers, landlords, neighborhood thugs, and cops; who played, depending on circumstances, mean games of stickball, gin rummy, candlepins, and—skirts high—hopscotch. He knew of the inbred loneliness of their kind, born of the necessary limit of every encounter, but he also knew of their rare capacity for fraternal good feeling—and that was powerfully on display right here.

Kavanagh's affection for the group blanked the fact that no particular man in the room qualified as what he would call an actual friend, what Runner would surely have been had he survived. As the crossed wires of his conversation with Gallen and Riordan just emphasized, there was no one to whom he could possibly explain what he was experiencing. No one but Bishop Donovan, although that explanation, which was what had brought him here, would not be offered in friendship.

There was a bustle at the entrance, and the clergy, having mostly taken their seats, immediately stood again to offer chipper applause as Cardinal Spellman glided into the sprawling restaurant. Short and rotund, he smiled broadly and waved at his priests, crossing into the room. His crimson cassock hid his legs, of course, and his movement was more like floating than walking. Not for the first time, His Eminence made Kavanagh think of the Little King, the cartoon character who never spoke, and whose shenanigans made the very idea of divine-right rule ridiculous.

Behind Spellman, in a procession of flashing purple and red, came the Auxiliary Bishops, Seminary Rectors, and Vicars, led by His Excellency Sean Donovan, the Vicar for Priests. He was the only prelate wearing a street suit. Spellman and his apparatchiks took their places at the round table under the largest chandelier. The idea for this banquet had been Donovan's, which is why Spellman deferred to him when it came to Grace.

"*Oculi omnium in te sperant, Domine,*" Donovan intoned. And the responsive antiphon came in one full-throated voice that boomed through the room, "*Et tu das escam illorum in tempore opportuno.*" The eyes of all look to Thee, O Lord . . . and Thou givest them food in due season. "*In nomine Patris, et Filii, et Spiritu Sancti . . .*" And the pack they'd become as they signed themselves with the cross answered, "*Amen!*"

It was like Donovan—to the point, a little loose with tradition, jovial—to offer an abbreviated Grace. Also like him that it would be the Latin verses the men had recited three times a day through their seminary years. The room now became noisy with scraping chairs—the renewed bustle of conviviality. Kavanagh remained where he was for a moment, ready for Donovan to look his way. But the Bishop did not. So Kavanagh headed into the heart of the room and took a seat between priests who were glad to see him.

As the main-course plates were being cleared, Bishop Donovan rose and made for the restroom, down one of the wings that bracketed the courtyard. Kavanagh bunched his napkin, dropped it, rose, and followed. He waited opposite the restroom, at the pair of French doors that opened into the winter garden.

Donovan appeared, and Kavanagh stepped into his path.

"Michael," the Bishop said, surprised.

"Hello, Bishop."

"My goodness, you startled me. And as I recall, you told me you wouldn't get here this evening."

"Change of plans. I need a minute with you." Kavanagh opened the French door, and gestured into the courtyard.

"Oh my, I should get back."

"Just a word or two."

"Call my secretary, Mike. Come and see me—anytime."

"I've called her three times this week," Kavanagh said easily. He felt surprisingly sure of himself. "She said she told you as much. You won't see me until the week before Christmas. A month from now."

"Well, I'll be in Rome—"

Kavanagh took the Bishop's arm. "So give me a minute. Now."

The Bishop shook his head no.

Kavanagh said, "Paul Quinn."

Donovan stared at him. The mask of geniality fell away, replaced by a stone-cold stare.

Kavanagh said, "I saw John Malloy. I know what you did." Kavanagh released Donovan's arm, and led the way into the chilly atrium. Once the Bishop had joined him, he closed the door behind them. It was eerie. They were all at once alone, yet surrounded, through the muting glass, by hundreds of black clad partygoers.

Kavanagh and Donovan faced off. Kavanagh said, "Deceit and self-deceit, Sean. I finally see why I've never trusted my vocation. Except for snatches of time during the war, I've been going through the motions—a pretend priest. I thought it was me, something wrong with me. Like a virus. But it's a virus I got from you."

"What are you talking about?" The Bishop's hand went to the gold pectoral cross at his breast. He clutched it.

"My priesthood rests on a lie. Your lie. You betrayed Runner. You betrayed me. You did both to cover for Paul Quinn. Last week, you did it again."

"I did not betray John Malloy. I protected him."

"By making him a scapegoat? He was Quinn's victim. From childhood on. For years. He turned to you for help. He told you everything. He told you how Quinn would recite *Hoc est enim Corpus Meum* as he pushed into him. Didn't he tell you that?"

Donovan flinched, but managed to say, "And I'm telling you, I protected that boy."

"You threw him overboard. You protected Quinn."

"I protected John from scandal. The scandal would have ruined his life." Donovan's eyes were wide. His head was back. He seemed ready to run. He added, "I got Father Quinn removed from Dunwoodie."

"To a parish! Jesus, Sean." Without consciously deciding to, Kavanagh poked the Bishop, the tip of his forefinger just below the pectoral cross. "You made him a pastor."

"Not me."

"Spellman, then. Is that because you failed to tell the Cardinal what Quinn was? Or because the Cardinal didn't care?"

"Of course he cared. We all cared. From then on, Father Quinn behaved."

"Those bastards behave when they're dead. Is that why you have him in the secret RIP file you have in your drawer? Keeping track of the priest-perverts? Obituaries to show their victims when they finally come to you from the wreckage of their lives?"

"You were in my desk? How dare you!"

"Is that the offense here, Sean?" Kavanagh's face by now was only inches from Donovan's. "My little burglary?"

"This is all confidential. You don't know what you're talking about." By now, the Bishop's hand was a clenched fist around his cross—a shield from Kavanagh's poking.

"How many 'private altar boys' did Quinn go on to have?" Kavanagh demanded. "That's what Runner was. His 'private altar boy.'"

"You have no evidence—"

"So you're denying it?"

"No. Not denying—"

"You let Quinn keep running that summer camp for boys."

"A choristers' camp. Father Quinn was the archdiocesan music director. He behaved, I tell you."

"Then why was the boys' choir eventually disbanded? I wondered that at the time."

"That had nothing to do with Father Quinn."

"Sean, you're lying to me still. Right now. You know it. I know it."

"These are things I cannot discuss with you."

"The Seal? The private forum of the Sacrament of Penance? You used that with me before. You told me that *I* was Runner's problem. He and I were 'out of bounds,' you said. You didn't seem to remember that phrase the other day. I never forgot it. Do you know what that did to me? All these years? And I could never discuss it with anybody, because it was God's secret. What you did was a sacrilege. But even that wasn't the crime, Sean. It was the evidence! Something far deeper has been wrong with us all this time." Kavanagh threw an arm toward the restaurant. "Look at them. Good men all. But there's a lie at the bottom of everything they do. Everything they believe."

"That's foolishness. What lie?"

"The Jews."

"What?"

Kavanagh was as startled by his blurted statement as Donovan was. The Jews? He had drawn no conscious line of connection between Donovan's lie about Runner and the—what?—lie of the ancient slander against the Christ killers? But there it was. Malloy had said recognitions come in bursts of the unexpected, and if ever a recognition was unexpected, this was.

Yet, even as he'd spoken the words, Kavanagh knew they were true. A silence opened between him and Donovan, a yawning abyss across which their locked eyes fell like an iron plank. But there was also a kind of abyss separating Kavanagh from the man he'd been an hour before. "The Jews," he repeated at last, but with an assurance that surprised even him. "What just happened in Europe: where did that come from?"

"You are talking nonsense now, Father."

The Bishop turned to go, but Kavanagh seized his arm. "Where?" Kavanagh's voice had dropped into an unyielding whisper.

"The Germans. The Nazis. That's where." The Bishop's hand fluttered up from his cross, as if to ward off blows.

Kavanagh said, "The Jews are God's mortal enemies, Sean. Because they crucified Christ. That's *Church* teaching. The Jews are damned to hellfire in the afterlife. Why not hellfire in *this* life? That comes from *us*."

Donovan pulled his arm, but Kavanagh only tightened his grip. "You were our professor of Church history, for Christ's sake. You never mentioned what the Church did to the Jews. Why did we never hear about Abelard?"

"Abelard! Good God, what are you talking about now? Are you drunk?"

Kavanagh said, "Abelard said the Jews were *not* damned, and the Church condemned him for it."

"Where are you getting this?"

"Denzinger, the *Enchiridion.* Decrees of the Solemn Magisterium. 'Abelard's Errors: That they have *not* sinned who have crucified Christ.' The Jews were not guilty! So said Abelard." Donovan winced at how fiercely Kavanagh was squeezing his arm. Kavanagh's mouth was by Donovan's ear, but his fury was so efficiently channeled now that his voice came in the steady cadence of an indictment reciter. "And the Church Council declared *'Damnamus'!* When you wouldn't see me yesterday, I used the time to go to the theology library up at Dunwoodie. The Church said *'Damnamus'* to Abelard because he refused to say it to Jews. They put his books on the Index."

"Well, maybe that's why I didn't teach him." Donovan jerked his arm, attempting to free it, but Kavanagh held him. Despite the chill in the courtyard, a broad film of perspiration had broken out on the Bishop's ample forehead.

Kavanagh said, "Abelard wrote a dozen major treatises—on ethics, the Trinity, Scripture. Dunwoodie has none of them. At the New York Public Library, Sean, I found a copy of his *Collationes,* in which Jewish suffering is described *from the point of view of Jews*! The Public Library! At Dunwoodie, the librarian has never heard of it. Abelard was one of the greatest Catholic thinkers who ever lived, and the only text that Dunwoodie has is the famous love letters exchanged with Héloïse. Why is that?"

"You just said it. Heresy, that's why."

"So God *did* damn the Jews? Is that what you believe? Do we learn *nothing* from what just happened in Germany? And not just Germany. Catholic France. Catholic Italy. Catholic Poland, too. Something evil *in us* was just laid bare. An epiphany! The Jews are central to the revelation, but the lecherous Quinn is part of it, too."

"They have nothing in common."

"They have a damning God in common. A killer-God, who's just panting to send His enemies to hell. Including those of us who are declared 'out of bounds.' Out of bounds, there is no salvation! *There's the heresy.*" Finally, Kavanagh let Donovan's arm go, and Donovan immediately made for the door. Kavanagh said, "You should ask the Cardinal about this killer-God. When you're in Rome, you should ask the Pope. *Damnamus!* There's a lie at the heart of the faith, Sean. I'm telling you—a lie!"

Donovan went through the door, back into the restaurant.

Kavanagh stood there like a man in a glass chamber, wholly disoriented at one level, but entirely clear at another. Clear for the first time in his life. Kavanagh only now understood what John Malloy had told him: *No more blind eye for me.*

On the other side of the windows, the priests were still happily at one another, laughing, gossiping, clapping shoulders, breaking out cigars, passing along bottles of brandy and port. To that company, Kavanagh simply did not exist—much less belong. Good men all, he thought again. Which made the hidden truth all the sadder—their sanctifying power, and their precious clerical status, depending utterly on a lie.

To collect himself, he lit a cigarette. Now, when he looked around the courtyard, with its paving stones, illuminated boxwood hedges, and potted plants, he saw it as the winter garden of a medieval Cloister.

WHOEVER THINKS THAT *we shall receive no reward for continuing to bear so much suffering through our loyalty to God must imagine that God is extremely cruel. Indeed, there is no people which has ever been known or even believed to have suffered so much for God.* The voice was that of a Jew, explaining himself to a philosopher and a Christian. The author of the voice was Peter Abelard. How was this possible? Michael Kavanagh, as it were, took a mental step back from the book he was holding. If turning it this way and that could have made it seem less exotic, he'd have set the book rotating. The Jew's narration felt like something bootlegged, properly delivered in a brown paper wrapper. He continued to read. *Dispersed among all the nations, without a king or earthly*

*ruler, are we not alone encumbered with such demands that almost every day
we pay an intolerable ransom for our wretched lives. Indeed, we are thought by
everyone to be worthy of such hatred and contempt, that whoever does us injury
believes it to be the height of justice and a deed pleasing to God.*

Kavanagh brought his eyes up from the book. He was sitting, as
at the beginning, on the cold stone wall-bench of the Chapter House
in La Chapelle-sur-Loire, which, a thousand years after its original
construction, now sat on its bluff overlooking the long-tamed Hudson.

It was late morning, Friday—his hospital day. This time, Billy
Mitchell was covering for him. The Inwood hospital was a mile and
a world away. It surprised Kavanagh how its wards, many of whose
patients he knew by name, might as well have been in Brooklyn—the
navy yard, so central to his identity before, now so forcefully a matter
of the left-behind. Once, he'd have asked Billy to take his rounds only
for an acute emergency. But what, in fact, was this? This . . . this . . .

This *museum*, a hospital in which to put the past itself on life
support. A few yards away, a steady stream of visitors was funneling
through the monastic arcade, an attendance uptick on this day after
Thanksgiving. From her place at the head of a tour group, nearly half
an hour ago, Rachel Vedette had registered his presence with a quick
double-take, nothing more.

He was dressed in his navy-issue turtleneck, fetched that morning from the high shelf in his closet. His pea coat was on the bench
beside him. The day outside was cold but sunny, and light washed in
through the glazed canopy of the Cloister garden.

He returned to the book. *Even when we sleep, we may think of nothing
but the danger of being murdered, the threat looming over our throats.*

Throats being slit—that stopped him. Kavanagh recalled
Rachel Vedette's words from the week before: "The first pogroms in
Europe . . . Crusaders, rushing through the Rhineland . . . Thousands
upon thousands of Jews murdered in the name of Christ." That he
had been ignorant of all this shamed him now, but one thing he had
always known: the Crusader's cry was "God wills it!"

*We are allowed to possess neither fields, nor vineyards, nor any sort of
landed property because there is no one who could protect them for us from open*

or covert despoilment. And so the main way which remains for us to earn an income to support our wretched lives is by lending out money at interest, and this just brings the hatred of Christians who think they are being oppressed by it.

The Jew's voice was direct, unflinching, coldly factual—the furthest thing from pleading. Most astounding, the Jew's lament was offered as a Jew would make it, not a Christian. Yet a Christian was its author, writing while other Christians committed sanctioned murder.

This was Kavanagh's third or fourth plunge into the text, and it confirmed what set Abelard apart—an intimate grasp of a despised people's tragic experience, at a time when the tragedy was taken to be the Gospel's triumph. Who *was* this man? Where did such empathy come from? The so-called *Dialogue Among a Philosopher, a Jew, and a Christian* purported to be a dream, with the three figures carrying out a debate of which Abelard himself was to be the judge. But after hearing the Jew's testimony, he declined to judge. *Abelard declined to judge.* He preferred, instead, to go on listening: *A wise man by listening,* he declared, *will be wiser.*

It was nearly one o'clock when she appeared. He was engrossed in the page, and looked up to find her already standing mutely before him. She was not wearing her cardigan sweater. He was struck at once by her pressed white shirt, the cuffs tightly closed. Without the turban that she wore outdoors, her very short black hair was striking, and it registered freshly how it emphasized her long, gaunt neck, the thinness of her face. She said, "I imagined I would not see you."

"I felt bad that our outing ended so abruptly . . . because of me."

She said nothing to that.

He lifted the book. "After we parted on Monday, I went to the library. First Dunwoodie, then Forty-Second Street. I found it."

"The *Collationes?*"

"I see what you mean. I've been reading the Jew's discourse. Your father was on to something. Something important."

She wrapped herself in her long arms. "He made an important discovery about *The Dialogue.*" Kavanagh recognized the abrupt shift in her tone of voice, and was surprised that he knew her well enough to be familiar with the way she took refuge in exposition. Docent. She went on, "Before the Statut expelled him from the Medieval Institute, my father had come upon another medieval text, contemporaneous to Abelard, similarly arranged, a trialogue of the same kind: a Jew, a Christian, a Muslim, engaging each other in debate before a judge. It was also in the form of a dream. The dreamer, in this text, was the King of the Khazars—"

"Of what?"

"Khazars. A nomad people, in Turkey. The King was also the judge, just as the dreamer Abelard, in *his* text, was judge. The King—after hearing statements in his dream from the Christian, the Muslim, and the Rabbi—the King converted, to become a Jew. The story explains how the Khazars became Hebrews—that is its purpose. My father had discovered the text that Abelard used as his model. For certain. A tremendous discovery, because the author of the text was Judah Halevi, a great Spanish sage. No Christian took instruction from a Jew in the twelfth century. For Abelard, just to read Halevi would have been an offense, not to mention being generous toward Halevi's point of view."

"Did your father publish—?"

Rachel shook her head so dismissively that Kavanagh stopped, seeing at once the stupidity of his question. Speaking of offense.

She said: "If he had published, he would have been roundly criticized for a partial reading of Abelard—as indeed he was in private by Catholic colleagues who read his manuscript. After the Statut, I told you, I did his research at the institute. From a certain point on, I became more than his assistant—I became his chief encourager, especially once those colleagues dismissed him. Even when it made no sense to go on, even when it became dangerous, I encouraged him." She paused, falling silent for a moment. Then she continued, "I told you before that I encouraged him for the sake of his great work. But that is not true. I was protecting the dream I had of my strong, heroic father. I could not allow him to fail because I could not allow him to be just another man. Staying, continuing . . . was my need, not his. I was locked in myself, and therefore he died." Her voice drifted off.

Kavanagh said quietly, "That seems unnecessarily—"

"Harsh?" she said sharply. "Judgmental? Self-hating? What?"

He knew better than to speak. To Kavanagh at that moment, she was impenetrable. Having just imagined that he knew her, he saw that he did not. She was indignant, yes—but with herself. He thought of her wrist, its message of the suicidal ledge from which she'd almost leapt. He wanted to pull her back. Indicating the book, he tacked, to say, "Still, the attitudes here are striking. Abelard says that Jewish Law is sufficient for salvation."

"Yes. That contradicts what he wrote earlier, which my father's critic insisted on. The *Collationes* may come very late—not long before Abelard died, perhaps. You notice that the text is incomplete."

"No. I hadn't noticed that."

"You will. Either he did not live to finish it, or scandalized monks destroyed what he wrote."

"Heresy."

She answered, "Jews are the first heretics."

"But not the last," he replied. The recognition was about himself—heretic. For him, that word had always been tied to a fuse. No more. "I see that now."

"Now?"

In using that word, he hadn't been aware of its weight. "Now" was a pivot, and she'd invited him to turn upon it. "Since meeting you," he said, hardly breathing. "I came here today hoping we could . . ." What? He did not know what to say.

Then he did. It was obvious. "I am sorry that I intruded on you Monday, when we were on the pier. I was out of bounds." When those toxic words—the goddamn "bounds" again—snapped from his mouth, he realized how off balance he was. He glanced around. "In the Chapter House, we tell the truth. Isn't that it?"

"They say."

He nodded. "I came here at lunchtime on purpose, thinking you might take your break with me. I wondered if you, too, felt like we'd begun a conversation we haven't finished."

Instead of answering, she just stood there, holding herself, hiding behind her dark eyes. Kavanagh felt remarkably calm. No matter what happened, he would have all that had passed between them up until now—and he would have it forever. He would have the recognitions and the resolutions and the truth that had changed his life. He would have the recovery he'd begun to make, and he would go ahead with it. He would have all of that, no matter what she said or what she thought. But he wanted her to understand that he had it because of her.

He said, "I know you prefer not to eat at lunchtime, but the park outside is sunny. The paths are sheltered from the wind. It's not so cold. We could take a walk." He lifted the book. *"A wise man by listening,"* he said, *"will be wiser."* He grinned. "Imagine, then, how much wiser a dolt will be."

He waited for her at the museum entrance, feeling self-conscious in his navy coat, the rakish collar of which he had not turned up. When she appeared a few moments later, she was in her cloak and turban, a getup that took him back to the gleeful scene among all the fancy people at the SS *America,* where, at first, she'd seemed a different person—almost glamorous. Diana Vreeland.

But no. Rachel Vedette was authentic to the bone. Kavanagh, on the other hand, sensed something of the impostor in himself, and hated it.

The silence, as they walked along the serpentine path, was easy. Neither seemed in a hurry to break it.

Kavanagh had slipped the *Collationes* into the ample pocket of his pea coat. He closed his fingers around the book, and it gave him, finally, something to say. "What made the difference between the early Abelard and the later?" he asked. "You told me the other day that the key was his suffering. The 'calamity.' Is that it?"

"In part. Sure," Rachel answered. "But, of course, something else. Something far more important."

"What?"

"Héloïse," she said so simply.

A man under the influence of a woman. There was the simplicity. "I think I get that." He laughed. "I think."

"Except for him, she was *détachée,*" Rachel said. Then added, "Unbound."

That word again. It hit Kavanagh—that if any two people were

ever "out of bounds," Héloïse and Abelard were. But "unbound," as
Rachel's use of French suggested, meant detachment, too. Detachment from everything but each other made the lovers masters of
everything else—even faith. "Out of bounds" was the point.

As for Kavanagh himself? The strangest thing about his unsettled condition was the way in which he had begun to face it expressly
in relation to this woman, yet that she was a woman was *not* the point.
He, too, was a man under the influence of a woman, but differently.
She was the entirely unexpected occasion of this reckoning, but was
nothing like its cause. How was that?

Night after night, shivering in his beach chair on the tar-paper
deck of the rectory roof, he had examined this. He was at the mercy of
his habitual scrupulosity, yes, but this examination of conscience had
been for the sake of a purification—for her. What were his motives?
He had taken the celibate life and its disciplines for granted, which,
he could admit, had more to do with inhibition than with virtue. He
knew what it was to be snagged by the glimpse of a well-turned ankle,
the sway of pleated dresses, moist pooling in wide female eyes, but he
knew nothing of unleashed erotic impulses. The ready flow of feeling
for his patients at the hospital, for the kids he sprang from jail, for
rosary sayers at the wake, or for the heavyhearted mothers who knelt
before him at the Communion rail rarely equated to feelings about
or for himself. Sublimation, in his case, meant redirection—that's
all. That he was almost unacquainted with sexual longing must, of
course, have had to do with the vise he'd closed on desire of every sort
after Runner Malloy. There it was, indeed: vise, not virtue. He knew
nothing real of intimacy, or its pursuit. His navy years had scraped
him free of naïveté, but had, ironically, reinforced his repression. He
was not a man on the make. That was why, he saw just then, this otherwise inscrutable woman was walking with him along this winding
path. Her evident history of troubles had not stopped her from trusting him at least this much. He was relieved to believe that she could.

Out of the silence, she said, with the directness he'd learned to
expect when the subject was not herself, "How has it been with you,
going around your 'loop'?"

He laughed. But also he realized that she was inviting him to declare himself. If not with her, with whom? He said, "I have come to a big decision. I made a mistake when I was young . . . when I became a priest. I have decided to undo it."

"What does that mean?"

"I am going to leave Good Shepherd. Not immediately. But soon." In these straightforward words, he was laying before her the jumble of his whole life. He had never imagined speaking the words with such equanimity. "I am going to leave the priesthood."

She stopped and faced him, her face alive with surprise. "You are such a good priest."

He laughed. "How would you know that?"

"I know it because already that is what you have been to me."

She turned away from him, which at first he misunderstood. But she crossed to a bench before a great overgrown juniper shrub that gave the seat a thronelike aspect. She sat and looked back at him, regally. *We must discuss this,* her manner declared.

He joined her. Now he did lift the collar of his navy jacket, for warmth.

She pulled her cloak closed in front of her, hiding her hands, which she clasped on her lap. She faced him. " 'A big decision,' you said. Are you all right?"

"Yes. I am fine. I'm not quite at peace with myself, but I'm getting there." He might have added, *That's what brought me here today.*

"I have never known a priest. Never heard of a priest stopping."

"It's like leaving a marriage, I imagine. But no one's heartbroken."

"Perhaps the Church, in some way."

"The Church gets pissed off, then pretends you never existed."

"But your people . . . ?"

"The parish? Sad, yes. Some of them, when they hear. Disappointed. But not for long. And it will only be discussed in whispers. Because of the violation, the shame. I will be a shamed person. But I am not ashamed."

He was aware of her taking this in, and he expected her comment. But she said nothing. She looked down at her hands, hidden in the folds of her cloak, as if she could see them. Eventually, she said quietly, "A good priest helps sinners acknowledge their sin. Just now, what I told you about my father's project—how I encouraged him past the point of prudence; how I failed to trust him, that he could be a simple man, without heroic work; that I willfully refused to face the truth of our situation—all that was a grievous failure. I have never before spoken of it. I spoke to you."

"I understood what you were telling me, how it pains you."

She nodded. "You took the trouble to learn what my father saw. You told me he was 'on to something . . . something important.' You told me that, wanting to relieve my remorse. A good priest does that, too. It does not relieve what I feel, but it reverses a prior verdict." She shrugged. "Anyway, one must reserve despair for what is unforgivable."

"I hope you won't think me presumptuous if I say nothing is unforgivable."

She smiled thinly. He knew to take her silence as rebuttal.

He said, "My friend who reappeared at Good Shepherd last week, and whom you encouraged me to find, is homosexual. I had been blind to that, and to much else. When we were young, I loved him, but naïvely. The Church made him its whipping boy. I cooperated in that. I've lived a lie for more than a dozen years. This week, with your help, I began to face that, and many other things have become clear. The Church has other whipping boys. Which means I do, too."

"Jews," she said calmly.

"Exactly. I know how outrageous it is—to compare anything to what . . . just happened in Europe . . . what just happened . . . to you. . . ." He paused, waiting for her to stop him, lecture him, rebuke him. She sat unmoving, but listening. He continued, "The Bishop told me the two things have nothing in common, but they do. The whipping. They have the whipping in common."

"I do not presume to speak of your friend. I have had my say, with you, speaking as a Jew. But, in other realms, some whipping is deserved."

"Realms? Like what? Realms of yours? You can tell me more, Rachel, if you like. You can tell me the story."

"No. I cannot," she said, so simply.

Kavanagh realized only now that he had called her by name. She seemed not to notice. He said, "You told me the other day that we are at the mercy of 'the givens of the past.' That's been my question this week. Do you believe that I can change my life?"

"If you tell me you can, I believe it."

"The priesthood, the ultimate given, is supposed to be for keeps. I will be a pariah to my kind. If my parents were alive, this would kill them. My sisters won't disown me, but they'll never forgive me."

"Your brother?"

"Jerry's the only one I've told. I'll start my new life at his tugboat company—business manager, deckhand, something. He's divorced, so he welcomes me to the Pale." He paused, then added, "Do you know what 'the Pale' is?"

"No."

"It's the part of Ireland that the Protestants control."

"You'll be a Protestant?"

"No. I'll always be a Catholic. Which means I'll always be responsible for what we did." He let the two words hang there—"we" and "did"—obvious.

After a long time, Kavanagh became convinced that their conversation was over. He saw that she was exhausted, emptied. Because of his forcing, she had forced herself to come with him, out of mere politeness. Or was it pity? To have imagined in her any semblance of the wish that had returned him to The Cloisters, to her, was not only foolish but selfish, and insulting. Yet he could not bring himself to end their time together. The stillness between them was the furthest thing from tranquillity. But it went on.

At last, she said, "I was in Drancy, what you would call 'the camp,' for a full year *after* the liberation. I referred to this, but incompletely. You should understand that I was *une femme tondue*, a shorn woman."

"What's that?"

"It's why we took to wearing this." Without raising her eyes, she touched her turban. "The postwar head covering *de rigueur*. So the baldness would not show. We were the *collaboratrices horizontales*. Many, many of us. Our Nazi jailers were replaced by Heroes of the French Resistance. They took turns with us. As our defilers, the Frenchmen were worse. Punishment, they called it. Although . . . in my case, it was justified."

"I doubt that."

She lifted her eyes and looked at him so sharply that he said, "I'm sorry."

Only then did he realize what a further defilement cheap courtesy could be. He knew from secrets entrusted to him by bedridden lads at the navy hospital that a chasm had separated him from the real ravages of the war. That chasm was open here, between him and this woman.

She had, however, begun to speak to him from her side of that pit, and, with her voice not much above a whisper, she continued. "I was released from Drancy by the Resistance fighters only when I became pregnant by one of them, a troubled pregnancy. I was sent to the Bon Secours Sisters. I lost the child, of course."

When she fell silent, Kavanagh had to rein in the impulse to reach a hand across to her.

As if she'd read that in him, she looked away.

With her eyes averted now, she resumed, "From the hospital, free, I went at once to Île Saint-Louis, the neighborhood in Paris where we lived. I went to our apartment. I was like a madwoman. The concierge was still there from before the war, Madame Boudreau. I terrified her. Why not? Once, I smashed her statue of the Virgin to the floor—a grotesque act, which, to this day, I do not regret. Naturally, so afraid, she admitted me. Our apartment had been stolen, but the thieving occupant was not there. Madame Boudreau gave me the key and let me go up. The last thing I had done on the day my father was arrested was hide his manuscript—*Abélard et Israël*—under the floorboards of the closet. I went directly there and threw myself on my knees. Some stranger's clothing and shoes—I pushed it all aside. Already I could hear scurrying noises from below. I knew where to press. The boards came loose, and my father's pages were there, still in their satchel, undisturbed by all except the rats whose nest I had disturbed. But then I saw: the leather of the satchel had been chewed away, into gray tissue. Reaching for the pages, I found that the rats had shredded the paper—all of it—into millions of fine pieces. And, with urine, into paste."

"Dear God, Rachel," Kavanagh whispered. "Dear God."

She said, "I had imagined that, with my father's treatise on Abelard, I could keep my father alive. That purpose had kept *me* alive. I was living to retrieve that text into which he had poured himself at the end. I aimed to finish it by correcting any errors his critics had identified. With that work, *I was going to repair my terrible mistake.* When I saw what the rats had done . . . an utter obliteration . . . that was the end. *C'est tout.* My father dead. His Abelard dead. Because of me. That is when . . ." She uncuffed her sleeve, to display her wrist. She ran her forefinger across the scar, gently—but still retracing the slice of the blade. What had been Kavanagh's imposition on Monday was now her act of trust. She said, "Madame Boudreau found me after I cut myself. She did me one great service. Through everything until then, for three years, I had clutched my father's small copy of the *Historia.* That book was all I had of him. It was on the floor beside me. She put it on the stretcher when the police took me away."

"Do you have it with you now?"

"No. Which surprises me. Since I shared it with you, I have not felt the same compulsion to carry it everywhere. . . ." She shrugged. "I never imagined telling any of this to anyone."

" 'Givens of the past.' They never go away, but you change what they mean by putting them into words. All of them."

"There are no words for all of them. The worst remains unsaid. And always will."

"What could be worse?" he asked quietly.

Once again, a sharp, cutting look. "Is that a Confessor's question?"

"No," he answered firmly. "Nor is this Confession." Yet her rebuke jolted Kavanagh, and he was shocked by what came to mind then. She had trusted him *because* he was a priest, and yet, to himself already, he was a priest no more. Just your average knucklehead—who had glided past what she had told him. The words that Abelard gave the Jew to say returned to him: *Indeed, there is no people which has ever been known or even believed to have suffered so much. . . .*

But were Jews nothing more than that? A people whose eternal fate is to endure? Was that her point? The source of her resentment?

Morally, yes: there *was* something worse than victimhood. Worse than being slain, surely, was to be a slayer. But that moral horror, he was certain, could not have belonged to her. Kavanagh was not sitting beside a victim or a slayer; beside a "people" or even "a Jew." He was sitting beside a rare and precious person. A woman.

He realized only now that he had used her name again—*Rachel*—as he had shortly before. By what right had he done that?

She misread the cloud that had come over him. She met his eyes with her own, to say, with a note of apology, "Not Confession. No, of course not. Not at all. And I was wrong in what I said before. It is not your being a good priest that drew me to you. What drew me, despite myself, to say this much . . . to say . . . too much . . . is your simple human kindness. But there is not enough kindness in the world for what remains unsaid." He heard her as if she were speaking, say, to a fellow traveler on a train, someone in whom to confide precisely because he would never be seen again. She fastened the button at her wrist. "I should get back. *Adieu.*"

A week ago, he had imagined them at a threshold together. But they were on its opposite sides. She had not said *au revoir.* He heard her firm statement as what it was—the closing of the door.

CHAPTER TWENTY-ONE

Héloïse went round and round, up the spiraling stone shaft to the small chamber beneath the belfry proper, a space to which sentries were dispatched at word of marauders in the region. But to her, the perch high above the Cloister served far more often as her personal anchorite cell, a locating refuge to which she had regularly repaired across eight years of life at the Paraclete. What drew her was not the view of the monastery's surrounding dominion, distant forests and nearby fields bisected by the meandering stream, so much as the mesmerizing point above the treeline, in an undefined middle distance, the realm of contemplation. Levitating here, in detached solitude, she could be who she truly was.

But today detachment was unthinkable. She'd come here simply to be alone, again, with the text that had been brought to her three days before, surreptitiously delivered by a seneschal from the Royal Palace in Paris. She'd carried the scroll under her arm as she mounted the stairs. Now she sat on the plain wooden stool, looking out. The stout bell above her was silent. At the mercy of an inchoate dread, she hesitated to unfurl the message once more and reread the foul words. Instead, she took in the view, a closer survey of the Paraclete's demesne. The stream, swollen by spring rains, was high. In the fields it watered, the monastery's men were harrowing the rough-plowed soil and sowing the April barley seed. The sun was bright and the air was mild. The soothing mantle of Eastertide had settled on the world, but not on her.

She focused on the drovers' road that ran along the ridgeline from which the fields fell away on two sides. On that road, abbey livestock were regularly driven from one pasture to another, and, periodically, harvest crops were carted off to market in Nogent-sur-Seine. Pilgrims appeared on the road occasionally, come to venerate the relics of Saint Angilbert, which Charlemagne's daughter Theodrade had entrusted to Argenteuil, and which were now housed in the golden reliquary beside the tabernacle in the chapel below. All persons coming to the Paraclete had to pass on that road, and on that road, two days before, she'd sent her messenger riding off to the river, for the barge to Paris, carrying the urgent summons to Peter Abelard. Now she expected him to appear at any moment, riding in the horse cart she had posted for him at the river landing stage.

She unfurled the scroll and read, *He has defiled the Church; he has infected with his own blight the minds of simple people.* She had to stop. Whose mind was simpler, Héloïse wondered, than the young fool to whom this brutal indictment of Peter Abelard was addressed—King Louis VII? Eighteen years old, he was on the throne less than two years, and was already wholly at the mercy of the wily White Monk, the letter's author. The young King's authority was being tested by burghers in Toulouse, Poitiers, and Bourges. Dukes and Counts were poised to take advantage of a weakened sovereign, with the strongest challenge coming already from Theobald, Count of Blois. Bernard of Clairvaux had convinced King Louis that religious dissent fed the roots of political discord, and the taproot of such dissent was Peter Abelard, who was known, after all, to be a favorite of Theobald's. Bernard's solution to the King's great problem was to scour his realm clean of heresy, and the insecure monarch embraced it. Bernard of Clairvaux was Louis's ferret and his war dog.

If Mother Héloïse had been secretly provided a copy of the White Monk's screed, it was only because the King's even younger wife—Eleanor, daughter of the Duke of Aquitaine, aged seventeen—was herself in thrall to the mawkish love-fables of the much-storied

316 JAMES CARROLL

Abbess herself. The Queen cared nothing for the intricacies of Abelard's theology, only for the legend of his early life as a thwarted lover.
Héloïse disdained Eleanor's girlish fancy, but thought it harmless, and
was prepared to turn it to her own ends. The Honorable Lady had vis-
ited the Paraclete. Upon meeting the Mother Abbess, Queen Eleanor
had been struck by her unfaded beauty, which was, if anything, made
more alluring by being clothed in chastity. The Queen had happily
accepted the invitation of Mother Héloïse to become the abbey's prin-
cipal patroness.

The nun steeled herself to read on. *He tries to explore with his reason
what the devout mind grasps at once with vigorous faith. Faith believes, it does
not dispute. But this man, apparently holding God suspect, will not believe
anything until he has first examined it with his reason.*

Héloïse had to smile. At least that accusation was true. But
Bernard's purpose was deadly. His letter to the King proposed the
launching of a campaign, a rank attempt to undermine the resounding prestige Peter Abelard had reclaimed for himself in Paris. Peter's
new school at Mont-Sainte-Geneviève, on the hilly left bank of the
Seine, loomed fittingly above Notre-Dame, from which he was still
banished. If Bernard could, simply by this philippic, discredit Abelard, then the young scholars who were flocking to him again would
not acquire the Church-sanctioned bachelor's license recently made
necessary to become a Master. Bernard's mischief threatened, at the
very least, the survival of Abelard's school.

But Héloïse sensed that more than mere rivalry fueled the White
Monk's assault. The interdiction was *ad hominem* in the extreme.
*His venomous books do not lie peacefully on bookshelves. No, they are read
at crossroads. His books have wings. He fills cities and castles with darkness instead of light, with poison instead of honey, or rather, with poison
in honey.* And how? By undermining the very principle of religious
and therefore social order, extending beyond the Kingdom of France.
More than King Louis VII's standing was at stake. Bernard was warning of a threat to the universal cohesion that the Church herself had
only recently reclaimed after the disastrous papal schism, when a
pair of manic Popes had excommunicated each other. Innocent II's
hold on power after his triumph over Anacletus II was still fragile,

which meant all of Christendom was fragile. *A new gospel is being forged for peoples and for nations, a new faith is being propounded, and a new foundation is being laid. Peter Abelard is a man who does not know his limitations, making void the virtue of the Cross by the cleverness of his words.*

The cross. There it was. Yes, Abelard was making void all that was claimed for the cross as the emblem of what a violent Father required of His only beloved Son. If one Person of the Trinity could so ordain the torture of another, imagine what the Divine Threesome could do to the exiled brood of Adam and Eve. Peter's argument was simplicity itself. Reason tells us that a loving God cannot be cruel; therefore, cruelty in the name of God, whether in this life or in the life to come, cannot be holy. The cross, cruelty itself, cannot have been willed by God as the mode of God's redemption. Any theology that says so is wrong. "The virtue of the Cross" is not only void, but a lie.

What a spacious faith he had. How she loved him. The passion of her youth had never cooled, really, but it had, in these recent years, mellowed into an abiding and affectionate respect. Since he had returned, six years ago, from his hinterland self-exile at Saint-Gildas-de-Rhuys to re-engage the great disputes of the Paris-centered scholars, he had carried himself with an equanimity of which he had known nothing in his youth. He had learned to do without antagonism. That was so even as, in the sacred arena of contention, he continued to dispel the obfuscations known as holy mystery with simple common sense. The God of Love loves—that is all. Abelard's poise in the face of disputation now was a matter of self-acceptance. *Loves him!*

Even more than before, Abelard said what he thought because he thought it. He no longer courted magnification of himself in the gaze of his young charges, nor sought he the approval of his rivals. He had *her* approval, and he knew it. Apparently, for him, that was enough. Hers, she dared believe, was the sacrament of love that graced him. As the ecclesiastical patron of the Paraclete, Peter made two apostolic visitations to her convent a year, and, formal though those canonical encounters were, to her they were enough. He was her sacrament, too.

The sun had dropped in the sky, and just as she began to think the day would end with his not having come, a horse and cart rounded the farthest turn of the road; one of the two riders wore the black habit of a Benedictine monk. The horse was running at a three-beat gait, less than the gallop of Héloïse's heart. She let the parchment snap back into its cylinder and, gathering the skirts of her habit, threw herself into the narrow shaft and down the winding stairs.

By the time she reached the monastery gate, the cart was there. The groom leapt down from its bench and took in hand the bridle of the horse, but Peter Abelard was slow to dismount, which was the first suggestion of the difference in him. The second was the slight tremble in his hand as he lifted his personal satchel, the leather pouch that would have carried his books, candles, tablet, and hard biscuits. He used his second hand to steady the first as he handed the bag to the groom. When he turned to Héloïse, she noticed at once that he was slightly, but uncharacteristically, stooped. Though his habit cloaked his frame, she saw in his face that, since he'd last been here months before, he had shed weight. Time had been striking him hard for three score years, and he looked it. When their eyes met, though, his expression of plain relief at the sight of her could not have been more familiar. He bowed to her, and said, "Holy Mother."

She laughed. "Holy" had become his way of teasing her, for, in her letters, she always insisted on—nay, reveled in—her unworthiness. And he knew how she detested the title "Mother" when it came from him. She bent her knees slightly, one invisible foot in front of the other, and said, "Salutations, Peter Abelard. Welcome home, dear man." To herself, she added "husband." Unknown to him, beneath her scapular, her hand went to her breast, for the feel of his gold ring, hidden there. She pressed it against her flesh, for the sweet pain. They remained still, smiling at each other, a pose that stood in for the embrace that was forbidden. The bell for Vespers rang just then, which Héloïse welcomed, though she meant to ignore the summons. If she left the rote chanting of the Holy Office to her sisters, she and Abelard would have the Cloister garden to themselves. She led the way there. The setting sun left the quad in shadow, but the air was warm still, and the day's fading was a poignant caress.

She had not imagined that anything would come before questions of Bernard's indicting letter, yet she had noticed, in addition to his tremulous hand and slouching posture, a slight shuffle in his step. She gestured with the scroll, pointing at the hand with which he adjusted his habit as he sat on the bench beside her. "Is that a tremble I see in your hand?" she asked.

He looked at his hand. "It is nothing. A small pain in the nerves. I have unguent for it. Why have you summoned me? Your message said 'dire.' What trouble?"

She unscrolled the parchment and read, "'Concerning Certain Heresies of Peter Abelard.' This is correspondence from Bernard of Clairvaux to King Louis. The White Monk dangerously slanders you."

Abelard nodded, then recited from memory, "'He has infected with his own blight the minds of simple people. . . .'" Abelard shook his head, but calmly. "I have read what Bernard wrote. He sent the same allegations to the Pope, and to the Archbishops of Sens, Rheims, and Paris as well. So much chaff to the wind."

"The infecting blight, it says, is Abelard himself." She slapped the parchment. "This marks Bernard's long-plotted offensive against you."

"But is it slander? Most of what he writes is true."

"He calls it heresy. Coming from him, the King's confidant, that is dangerous, if it goes unanswered."

"How do you have it?"

"The Queen has confidantes, too. I am one. She is enchanted with the rose-water legend of our youth." Heloïse smiled. "Naturally, she assumes my interest in what concerns you. Her nervous husband showed her the letter. She had it copied. She sent it to me."

"I mistook your summons. I came so promptly because I thought you had other news. More pressing news by far than intrigues of the craven Cistercian."

"What could be more pressing?"

"Something that threatens not the reputation of one poor monk, but the moral spine of all Christendom. Have you heard the news from Mainz?"

"No."

"On Holy Friday last, after the Solemnities of the Lord's Passion in the Cathedral, there was a massacre in the Talmudic academy, situated not far away. Having venerated the cross, devout Catholic worshippers stormed out of the Cathedral to avenge the murder of the Lord Christ. Hundreds of the so-called Christ killers were slain. It is said that many others threw themselves into the Rhine, together with their children. Jews. All Jews."

"Hundreds?" Héloïse asked, not breathing.

"Isaac ben Joseph Benveniste."

"Prince Isaac?"

"Yes. It is said that he stood at the gate of the Vicus Judaeorum, barring the way. He was the first to fall before the mob."

"Oh, Peter . . ." Words failed her. When she saw that he had nothing to add, she said quietly, "Such a thing happened in Mainz before."

"Yes. Pope Urban's war. Then, too—preaching on the day of the Lord's Passion lit the flame. Now a new War of the Cross is being summoned, and preachers are calling again for the killing of Jews. *Christ's cross must be avenged! God wills it!*" Peter was speaking more mournfully than bitterly. After a pause, he added, "It was not only that the Rabbi saved my life. He was my great teacher. He was my friend."

"I never saw you hand yourself over to anyone as you did to him. Not even to me, your wife."

Abelard nodded. To her surprise, he reached his hand to hers, and rested two fingers on her one. His hand weighed nothing. He said softly, "After Canon Fulbert's men finished with me, I had no choice but to give myself to Prince Isaac. With you, it had been a choice in every way. But, like you, the Rabbi received me. I deeply grieve his death. As a man of the Church, I share the culpability, which compounds the grief. Dear Héloïse, I had to come to you with this anguish. I cannot bear it alone. *This* is why I am here."

She put the scroll aside to cover his hand with hers. They sat like that, hands joined in her lap, in silence.

It was Héloïse who spoke first. She took up the scroll again. "Bernard is the great war-preacher now. Queen Eleanor wrote to me describing his sermons: 'O mighty soldiers, O men of war, you have a cause in which to conquer is glorious and for which to die is gain.'"

"He puffs himself up with such blood hosannas," Abelard replied. "To knights and rabble both, he promises the papal plenary indulgence, a sure road to heaven. The cross once again is on battle flags in churches. No doubt, it was in the Mainz Cathedral."

Héloïse said: "I have a letter from the Queen in which she says her husband has had his armor tunic marked with the cross. She mocks him for strutting about the palace wearing it, but then she tells of her own intention to accompany him to Jerusalem. For this holy pilgrimage, she requests our monastic prayers." The nun forced a derisive burst of breath through her nose. "That the Royals love his great new escapade enhances Bernard's standing everywhere. I did not see this before, but that is why he is moving *now* against you." She gestured sharply with the scroll. "And *of course* his charge indicts you for 'making void the virtue of the cross.' Bernard's cross is a weapon. The God you are preaching, Peter, is not a God who wills such a war."

His appreciative smile pleased her, but when he nodded, it was with a jerking motion. He said, "You are indomitable."

"But what will you do?"

"Do? The man spews his filth. My enemies will suck on it. My friends will know what it is."

"No. He twists the mind of the King against you. The prelates are one thing, but the King can hurt you," she said.

Indeed, the King was already moving against Abelard's patron, Count Theobald, and he was tilting toward Bernard's Cistercian monks against the black robes of Cluny. Because of Italian intrigues, the Pope stood sorely in need of the French King, and so Louis could hurt Abelard in Rome, too.

Héloïse added, "And Bernard's preaching rises to a pitch before the rabble. The executioner of heretics is the mob, Peter. The man is a danger, I say. You must challenge Bernard."

"In my youth, I challenged the fox that dared to cross my path in the forest. I challenged the sun not to rise. I challenged the bells of Notre-Dame to be silent."

"When you challenged philosophers, you won," she insisted. "It made your reputation. More to the point, it vindicated your thinking."

"My reputation stands, Héloïse. I think what I think. I say so, and I let my words defend themselves. So far, they have."

"*Are* you a heretic?"

Her question surprised both of them.

"No. Absolutely not," he said forcefully. "The measure of my thought is nothing but the Gospel, elevated by reason, which is the true mind of the Church."

"Then show it. Bernard must be stopped. His manipulation of the boy King must be stopped. His assault on Cluny must be stopped. His War of the Cross must be stopped. You can stop him. He has made himself vulnerable to you."

Abelard laughed. "How so, Mother?"

"Do not 'Mother' me, Peter Abelard."

"How so, then?"

"He has defamed you with the charge of heresy. Make him prove it. Demand a hearing. It is your right. He has involved the King and the Pope. Therefore, demand a Church Council, the bishops gathered with universal authority. The King presiding, with papal license. Dispute the White Monk in that setting and, when you demolish his charges, the anathema will come down on him—not you. The serpent will be defanged."

"I went through a heresy trial once before."

"That was a long time ago, and it was because of me. You were being tried, no matter the pretext, because they hated your proven capacity for love. Now I am an aged Abbess, forever cloaked in gray, the color of death. The comely Héloïse lives on only in the songs of troubadours, which no one takes seriously. At issue against Bernard will be nothing but ideas and doctrines, finally. The disputation will shape the future of the faith. It will avenge Prince Isaac."

"I seek vengeance no more," Abelard said, his voice muted. "As for the slaughter of Prince Isaac, I doubt that Bernard, for all his venom, is one of those preaching death to Jews."

"Perhaps not. But his theology makes such preaching inevitable."

"Is this why you summoned me? To stiffen my spine for the mêlée? To make me young again—but without the comely Héloïse?"

"Ah, sir . . . but you do have her." She covered his hand once more. "Our secret." She still knew how to read him, and knew that he had accepted what she'd proposed. He welcomed it. He would be her champion, and she would be his unknown lady. He would vanquish his enemy and live! That, in combination with their physical touch, however bare, should have made her pleasure exquisite. But in his hand, she felt his tremor.

CHAPTER TWENTY-TWO

Good Shepherd Church at Midnight Mass on Christmas Eve was crowded. Along the side aisles, car-sized radiators hissed plumes of steam, and up the length of the center aisle a river of undulating linoleum floor tile shone with festal polish. The stained-glass windows, usually so vivid in the daylight, were opaque now; the darkness outside blanked out the colorful saints and martyrs, whose peaked hands, tilted heads, and halos were evident only in outlines of lead. The organ was playing a singsong "Silent Night," and the congregation was quietly trilling along, even as latecomers shook out their heavy coats and timidly sought places in the packed pews, or in the rearmost corners, to stand. The large church seemed small with this turnout. Though the willful gestures of its architecture—embedded half-pillars instead of true columns; groined arches made of plaster; chandeliers blazing with flame-pointed lightbulbs—fell short of the great Gothic spaces of the Catholic past, the sweeping power of the place came from the overflowing devotion of the Mass-goers. They were here because, on this night above all others, more than *longing* for Good News, they *had* it.

Michael Kavanagh faced the congregation from the altar, and his heart brimmed with love for each of them, and for all of them together. If human life is made for more than itself, that *more* was present—not in the sacrament, or in the Church, but in the good people themselves.

And what else, he wondered as he stood with hands steepled at his chin, does Christmas celebrate than that? *Hic Incarnatus Est.* God is here. Now. Not in a newborn babe, but in us.

He was wearing the jubilant gold vestments that the sacristan broke out only once a year—tonight. Behind him stood altar boys, candle bearers, acolytes, a crucifer, and a thurifer, whose brass incense pot spewed forth a billowing cloud that had everyone in the sanctuary squinting. Beside him were Frank Russell and Billy Mitchell, decked out in the vestments of Deacon and Subdeacon. Kavanagh was glad they were with him. Old fuddy-duddies both, yet he was in touch with how fond he'd become of them, especially Billy, whose glass eye always seemed to be weeping but never was. Billy and Frank had no idea that this was to be his last Mass as a priest. Without knowing it, they were stand-ins for the entire fraternity from which he would walk away tonight. When they exchanged the ritual kiss of peace, he would bid adieu, through them, to all the brothers of the common life. In this one instance, perhaps, he would let the war-wounded Billy's tears be a sign of actual feeling.

What most surprised Kavanagh was the equanimity with which he'd come to this moment. Over the last month, two or three nights a week, he'd taken to shivering in his beach chair on the rectory roof, smoking and nursing the one bourbon he allowed himself. But mostly he had spent his time on a last turn through the parish rounds, earnestly connecting with all those who'd depended on him—the nuns in the school, the hospital staff, certain long-term patients, lads on the basketball court, the penitents who'd so trusted him. Without their knowing, he was saying goodbye. It was out of the question that he reveal his plan simply to disappear from Inwood on the day after Christmas. "Thou art a priest forever" was the rubric, and, to the "good people of Good Shepherd," the violation of his ordination vow would be a sacrilege, a scandal. Even those who loved him would feel betrayed. That was why he'd chosen not to burden the parish Christmas by leaving weeks ago. Not even the Monsignor knew.

Apart from his sisters and brother, the only person he'd sought to tell was Runner. At that Swiss-themed bar in New Jersey, Kavanagh had described to him the Madison Avenue moment of *Non credo!* and so John Malloy would not be surprised. Malloy had said that a shattered faith in the Church equated to the loss of God, but that had not been Kavanagh's experience. On the contrary, God's love for him was simply no longer contingent on his being a priest—there was the liberation. Kavanagh had said as much in the letter he wrote to Malloy, but Malloy had not answered. That lack of response was the negative echo of what else was missing.

Only a week ago, he'd finally yielded to a feeling not so much of longing as of incompleteness, and he'd allowed himself to return to The Cloisters. He'd rehearsed what he would say to her—that he'd come to the museum only to close the "loop" for which he'd been thrown. But he learned from the desk lady at the museum entrance that Rachel Vedette had abruptly quit her job at the beginning of December. She'd left no forwarding contact information—which Kavanagh, in his narcissism, took as a message sent to him. Fair enough, he told himself, and put whatever else he might have felt second to his hope for that grave woman's happiness.

Her disappearance, together with his old friend's lack of response, had simply cauterized the precipice-anguish of an unknown future. In an odd way, this pointed solitude seemed fitting, which perhaps explained his unexpected moral poise. For the first time in his life, he was acting on an impulse that belonged to him alone. The surprise was in finding that, apparently, he was up to it.

After the sung Kyrie, and the Gloria in Excelsis Deo, Kavanagh sat, flanked by altar boys, to hear the Epistle read by Billy Mitchell, a passage from the Letter to the Hebrews. Because of his glass eye, Billy always read the text with his head at an angle. Kavanagh listened in particular for the Letter's definition of Christ: "He is the brightness of God's glory and the exact imprint of God's substance, and he upholds all things by the word of his power." After the Epistle, and the rustle of the congregation's rising to its feet, came the Gospel. Frank Russell swung the thurible with panache, then read the text from John, which famously concluded, as Kavanagh had been relieved to find when he worked on his sermon, "And the Word was made flesh and dwelt among us, and we saw his glory, the glory as it were of the only begotten of the Father, full of grace and truth."

The congregation, acting in sync, sat down again. When Father Michael Kavanagh mounted the pulpit, it was less for a finale than for an initiation; the time had come to declare himself. "My dear friends," he said softly. "Merry Christmas." There was a stir as the decorum-minded people, all but one child, stifled the urge to reply. Yet the child spoke for the church, calling out, "Merry Christmas, Father." Kavanagh smiled broadly, encouraging a buzz of laughter. He felt the wave of their affection cresting toward him, and his eyes burned suddenly. He said, " 'Full of grace and truth': that's not me, God knows. But I want to speak—if not gracefully—at least truthfully about why God comes to us in Jesus tonight. I hope you'll bear with me."

Kavanagh's earnest feeling drew them in. He was quiet for a moment, and the congregation, too, became unusually hushed. Already, they sensed something out of the ordinary.

"When I was growing up," he said, "they told me that I was in trouble from the minute I was born. Original Sin . . . you know. They told me that I was on the wrong side of a huge gulf between me on this side and God in heaven on the other. An abyss. I had no idea how I'd come to be on its wrong side, but there I was—with all of you, 'poor banished children of Eve.' And they told us—didn't they?—that by ourselves there was nothing we could do to get across that gulf. To God. We were damned if we did, and damned if we didn't. You know the feeling. Damned. Damned."

He paused, letting the nods of the people speak, not only to him, but to one another. "Here's how they explained it to us: Because Adam's sin offended God's honor, and threw the whole moral structure of Creation out of kilter, we humans became ugly, and Creation became 'fallen.' God had no choice but to turn against what He had made until, somehow, that Original Sin could be atoned for—counterbalanced with some infinite act of virtue. We humans could not do it, because the status of the One offended was divine, while our status was menial. God the Father, by Himself, could not repair the breach, because, far away in heaven, He was too remote—too unlike us. Only a Being who had something of both—human *and* divine—

could bridge the gap between man and God. And the only way such a human-divine Being could accomplish this atonement was by offering Himself as a sacrifice—offering infinite suffering to outweigh the infinite offense on the scales of cosmic justice. So, they explained, God sent His only beloved Son to be this God-Man, bridging the divine-human abyss by fulfilling the Father's will and dying on the cross, so that the Creator's mind could be changed back from damning His Creation to loving it. This is what, on Christmas, the Church calls the 'Good News.'

"Come again? My friends, what is 'good' in this news? Do we really believe that God, as a loving Father, could possibly require the brutal death of His beloved Son *for any reason*? On the night of his death, Jesus prayed, 'Not my will but Thine be done.' God's will was Calvary? For what? To restore offended honor? What kind of father does that? Would you do it to your child—require his brutal death to satisfy some need of yours? Who here would do such a thing?"

He waited. Not a muscle moved, anywhere.

"No one," Kavanagh said. "No parent here would do what we are sometimes told our heavenly Father did."

Again, he let the silence build.

When he resumed, his tone had changed. He was a neighbor now, a friend—parsing through a mystery. "We are sometimes told that, because Jesus has taken our place and died for our sins, restoring the balance that had been thrown out of whack by Adam's sin, anyone who is baptized in His name is 'saved.' That is, anyone who is baptized will be spared from being damned by God to an eternity in the lake of fire. Not just the wrong side of the abyss, but engulfed in flames! Forever! That is why we are so intent on baptizing our little babies, because if they die without the sacrament they die without being beloved of God. We can't bring ourselves to picture the little ones in hell, so we imagine a place called limbo, which may be free of fire but amounts, in fact, to an eternity of unhappy exile. Come again? Our innocent babies? Who have done nothing wrong? God does not love them? Because no priest happened to be there in time, to baptize them? Come again?

"My friends, what kind of God is this? Do we really believe it took the brutal crucifixion of Jesus to change God's mind from damnation to love? Do we believe the Creator of the vast cosmos turned against His own Creation because of one measly sin committed eons ago by one naked guy living in a garden? Do we believe, for that matter, that God only loves baptized Catholics? *No salvation outside the Church?* Yes, Popes and Church Councils seem to have taught that, but do we really believe it?

"Think of your Inwood neighbors, living on Seaman Avenue, or Park Terrace—neighbors named, let's say, Cohen and Ginsberg, good people to whom you would entrust your own children in an emergency, or with whose daughters and sons your own kids play, or to whom you might simply be devoted as a friendly neighbor. How many of you men here tonight shared foxholes or cockpits or tin cans with fellas named Cohen and Ginsberg? Did you damn them, or did you thank God for them? Do we believe that the Cohens and Ginsbergs are, by definition and through no fault of their own, condemned to an eternity in hell for being Jews? Come again? Do we believe in a God who is that unjust?

"My friends, I do not believe it. *Non credo!* And, to tell you the truth, I don't think you believe it, either. *Si non credimus!*" Father Kavanagh grinned suddenly. "If I put this in Latin, maybe it will seem less outlandish. What do you think?" He waited. Sensing the priest's permission, the people laughed. Perplexity was palpable in the air, but so was relief. They were leaning forward, listening hard.

He went on: "So, if it is literally unbelievable that Jesus Christ, the Son of God, came down on Christmas night to change the mind of our heavenly Father from damnation to salvation—if we can't believe that—what can we believe? Simply this: Jesus did not come—and He certainly did not die—*to change the mind of God.* The mind of God, Jesus told us and told us and told us again, does not need to be changed. God is love, Jesus said. Always was and always will be. Constant. Faithful. Universal. The Creator *never* turned against the Creation—no matter what Adam did. The Father *never* ordered the death of His Son—no matter what unfolded in Jerusalem all those years ago. And our God *never* wills the suffering—now, or in the life to come—of *any* of His children.

"No. What happened as a result of the sin of Adam was that we, the sons and daughters of Adam and Eve, *imagined* that we were damned. We 'poor banished children of Eve' banished *ourselves.* God did not do that. *God does not damn.* We invented that monster-God *ourselves,* because, for reasons we do not understand, we are born inclined to feel that we deserve a monstrous fate. But that is *our* mistake: our *original* mistake. Leave sin out of it.

"And, seeing our mistake, what God did in response was to send us word that we were wrong about Him. The Word that became flesh—tonight!—and lived among us. There *is* no gulf! There *is* no abyss! Now, *that* is Good News!"

Kavanagh fell silent for a moment, and he let his gaze move slowly and deliberately across the congregation, making eye contact with one parishioner after another.

Then, more quietly, he said: "Please remember what I am telling you tonight, and please remember it about me. I used to think that God loved me because I was good; because I was a priest. If I were otherwise, I would be damned. But I know now that that is not so. God loves me because God made me, and I exist. Period. And I invite you to take seriously your own experience of that same reality. You came into the world, in the words of the Epistle tonight, as 'the *exact* imprint of God's substance.' That's you! Therefore, trust yourselves. Trust your experience. Hey, if you think well of the Ginsbergs, God must think well of them. Anything that contradicts the knowledge that we have from our own lives cannot be true, and it cannot be the true faith of the Church.

"How do we know all this? Like the old spiritual says, *Jesus told us so.* That's how. Remember His story of the Prodigal Son? How the father never stopped loving the wayward lad who squandered his inheritance and broke his father's heart; and how the father, *even then,* when he glimpsed the runaway boy off in the distance, rushed out to greet him; and how the father had the huge banquet in his son's honor, with the fatted calf and all? Jesus said—*that* is what God is like. The prodigal *father*—prodigal in love. So stop thinking God is the monster up there who is out to get you. Out to punish you. Out to send you to hell if you so much as have a bad thought, or disobey a rule, or eat a hot dog on a Friday, or fail to believe every little thing some preacher tells you to believe—including this one.

"Jesus Christ, the Son of God, did not come down from heaven on Christmas night to save us. He came down to tell us that we are all *already* saved! The only doom is what we make for ourselves. It is not God's mind that needs to be changed, but *ours*. Saint Paul said it: nothing we *ever* do can separate us from the love of God. And if that is true of us Catholics, it is true of everybody! The Creator loves what He creates. *That* is the Good News. There is no salvation outside . . . Creation!"

To his surprise, Kavanagh realized that he had made a fist, and elevated it above his head, a gesture of unbridled feeling. Without his knowing it, his voice had risen with his declaration, his passionate announcement of the gladdest tidings he'd ever heard.

"Let me say the thing again"—both hands were now spread before him—"offering it as my Christmas present to you, my last and best gift ever: salvation is knowing that you are all *already* saved. In Jesus Christ, who came down from heaven not to die a miserable death, or to form an exclusive group called 'the Church,' but to live a selfless life that makes plain to *all* of God's children His universal and everlasting love."

Kavanagh fell silent. The counterpart silence of the church was absolute. It lasted for as long as Kavanagh remained unmoving in the pulpit. Finally, with a wide, shit-eating grin, he asked, "So why should we not greet one another in happiness tonight, saying, 'Merry, merry Christmas'?"

To which that same child called out, once more, "Merry Christmas, Father." And all the people laughed, hard.

A FEW MINUTES later, the Midnight Mass communicants were presenting themselves at the gleaming brass rail, rolling waves of kneeling men and women, boys and girls—all dressed up in their Christmas best. To Kavanagh, they were saints. As he placed the Host on each one's tongue, he had an impulse, also, to cover their heads with his hand, to press down with affection and farewell. To all appearances, he was a blithely efficient priest, passing out the Body of Christ, but inwardly, he was brimming with emotion—gratitude, and love.

And then, swinging to his right, he saw the sandy, well-coiffed head of a bowing gentleman in a tweed suit. Even before John Malloy brought his face up, Kavanagh recognized him. Their eyes met briefly, before Malloy's lids fluttered shut as he extended his tongue. Placing the Host, Kavanagh's hand trembled. Malloy kept his head bowed as he blessed himself. He stood and turned away without making further eye contact, leaving Kavanagh with the sense that, for Malloy, this moment was less about their friendship than about the Sacrament, Jesus Christ, God.

After the Mass, Michael Kavanagh, still in his vestments, stood in the chilly night, outside the church door, exchanging Christmas salutations with one and all. His breath came in puffs. His left hand was cold, but his right was warm, from all the heartfelt handshakes.

John Malloy waited, holding back, and appearing only when the other Mass-goers had drifted off. Then he and Kavanagh were alone on the top step of the broad staircase that ran down to Broadway.

"They love you, Mike," Malloy said.

"I love them." Kavanagh smiled broadly. "Not to mention you." They clasped hands. "Merry Christmas, Runner."

"Merry Christmas, Mike. But 'Runner'! Jesus! There it is again."

"Runner Malloy. Stayer Kavanagh. I didn't expect to see you."

"I only got your letter three days ago. The school secretary didn't forward it to me, because, she said, everybody hoped I'd be back."

"To Saint Aiden's? Back?"

"The prick headmaster tried to can me. I was put on leave . . . until the trustees' meeting last week. They heard me out. Tables turned. Mr. Rohan had written them a letter. As of the new term, by unanimous vote of the board, *I* am interim headmaster. Emphasis on 'interim.'"

"No shit! That is great!" Kavanagh only now released Malloy's hand, and slapped his shoulder. "What about Tommy?"

"Reinstated." Malloy smiled happily. "The lecherous English teacher is gone. You brought me luck that day."

Kavanagh matched his friend's smile. "Speaking of tables turned, you received Communion tonight."

"You noticed. After that sermon, how could I not?" Grinning, Malloy spread his hands. "Prodigal son."

Kavanagh laughed. "I got the best part from you. *Si non credimus!*" Then, more seriously, he added, "It was a privilege to say what I don't believe, and what I do believe."

"But, Mike, does the Church believe it?"

"Everything I said is in the tradition."

"If so, it's a minority report."

"So it needs to be brought forward," Kavanagh said. "You saw the people nodding. About unbaptized babies. About the Cohens and the Ginsbergs. About the monster-Father. Commonsense Gospel, John. The people, when they hear it, know it's true . . . even if the clergy don't."

"Do they know about you?"

"The folks here? No. Nobody knows. My brother and sisters, that's it."

"What did Bishop Donovan say?"

Kavanagh shook his head. "He doesn't know yet, either. If I'd told Donovan that I'd be leaving, he'd have gone to the Cardinal immediately, and they'd have made sure I didn't say this Mass tonight. I wasn't going to let them stop me from this farewell. I'll be leaving letters on my desk, one each to the Monsignor, Donovan, and Spellman, explaining my decision. The housekeeper will find the letters tomorrow, after I clear out. The letters are thank-you notes, really. At this point, my gratitude for what I could do as a priest, despite the bullshit that began when they dumped you, outweighs the regret."

"Your gratitude was on full display tonight. You seem okay about what you're doing."

"I am. Better than okay. 'Stayer' Kavanagh is not staying. No more nicknames. I'm at peace, John. First time in years."

Malloy grinned. "Because of some nun?"

Kavanagh shook his head. He said, without levity, "My only nun was Héloïse. What I preached tonight came from her."

CHAPTER TWENTY-THREE

To the Cathedral of Sens, for the great Council in May 1141 and its contest of giants, came all the notables of France—the King, the Queen, Dukes and Counts, dozens of courtiers, Archbishops and Bishops, Abbots and Priors, together with what yeomen, merchants, artisans, and minor clergy could crowd into the great Merovingian basilica. The thick walls and small windows meant the dark interior space was illuminated by dozens of torches and candles, placed high on ledges and low on side altars—everywhere. Shadows danced in sync with the flickering flames. Here and there could be seen black-robed Benedictines and white-robed Cistercians. With their cowls drawn over their heads, such rival monks were like pepper and salt, seasoning the throng.

Raised high on a chancel dais, King Louis VII and Queen Eleanor, looking too young, giddy, and thrilled, were enthroned side by side under the ceremonial canopy, the shimmering purple of which draped down behind them to form the cloth of honor. Her Majesty had reserved the loggia high above the Gospel side of the altar for her personal party, the Ladies-in-Waiting who accompanied her everywhere, a happy chorus of good fortune. They craned down like fairgoers, although one of the women in the Queen's party held back. In a corner of the gallery, behind the grille and the giddy attendants, was a figure heavily cloaked in mourning dress and veil, the Queen's cousin—recently widowed, from the look of her apparel. She was, in actuality and unknown to all but Eleanor, Mother Héloïse, Abbess of the Paraclete.

Under the domed apse, two dozen mitered prelates were positioned in rows of stout chairs fanning out on either side of the Royals. The gold and silver threads of their headgear and vestments glistened in the candlelight. Immediately in front of the bishops' crescent was the small rostrum with railings, the stage on which the antagonists would face each other.

The only figure of prominence to be absent was Peter of Montboissier, Abbot of Cluny. More was at stake in this disputation for him than for most others, and his truancy was taken to indicate his insecurity. An ornate chair on the upper level of the sanctuary, near the King, had been purposefully left vacant to show that the Abbot Primate had been summoned and had not appeared: Cluny was in decline.

From the sanctuary, Their Majesties, Their Eminences, Their Graces, and Their Excellencies faced the untitled throng that crowded into the transept, held back by men-at-arms—or, rather, by cross-marked knights of the Jerusalem-based monkish order, the so-called Poor Fellow-Soldiers of Christ, whose spiritual father was the illustrious Bernard. The crush of spectators filled the nave, a jocular multitude for whom the solemn proceedings held the promise of a joust. No one would acknowledge attending a knights' tournament in the hope of seeing combatants killed, but if they were not regularly killed, no one would attend. A heresy trial was like that, but different. The risk of death here was the immortal soul's, not the mere body's: the stacked wood and kindling in the Cathedral plaza outside would fuel the burning of the condemned codex manuscripts and scrolls, not the blasphemer himself. Although, in these latter days, upon the bishops' command, the lightning bolt from heaven could strike, igniting a spontaneous execution. A man, too, might be set aflame, the famous Abelard himself—which added to the excited suspense.

What few in the gathering knew, as they crowded into the Cathedral early that morning, was that, at the bishops-only banquet after the Vespers Mass the night before, the dramatic contest had already been decided—in the accused's absence. To a series of propositions said to be drawn from Peter Abelard's own work and read out by Bernard, the bishops had, to a man, cried *"Damnamus."* That the public formalities of the Council of Sens, now to begin, were all but meaningless would soon become clear.

As across waves of wheat bending in the wind, a buzzing rustle spread through the assembly when Master Peter Abelard appeared at the Cathedral entrance. A black-robed monk, framed by the rounded arch of the narthex against the bright light of the open door, he wore the aura of morning as if he'd been born to it. For the first time, silence fell upon the Cathedral. It had been rumored that Theobald, Count of Blois, was providing an armed escort for Abelard, but he was alone. His solitude was magnificent. He stood there in defiance. His air of vulnerability made courage his armor. Even his antagonists were stirred. Those who were not standing, including all in the chancel, save the King and Queen, came to their feet.

Only now did Héloïse push forward to the edge of the balcony, and what she saw made her heart sink. As Peter moved slowly into the Cathedral proper, down the aisle that opened for him as the crowd drew back, his gait was uneven. Normally a man of erect posture, he tilted forward. He carried his right arm in his left hand. His head was to the side. Even across the distance, she saw, as he shuffled more than walked, how much more pronounced the tremors had become since she had seen him. She realized what she had fended off before, that Peter Abelard had the palsy. It had him.

Waiting for Abelard at the forward edge of the top step of the sanctuary, standing above the rostrum, with the array of dignitaries behind him, was Bernard of Clairvaux. The White Monk was a large, bald man. His striking pristine habit caught the flickers of torchlight, which lent him, altogether, an otherworldly luminescence. He held a parchment scroll in both hands, horizontally before his chest. His dark eyes were fiercely concentrated on the approaching black figure. When, at last, Abelard mounted the one step to the rostrum and, with evident relief, balanced himself with a hand on its railing, Bernard made a slight lowering motion with the scroll, and those in the Cathedral with stools or room to crouch sat down. That simply,

Bernard claimed the presider's authority. Against expectations, he was going to be less a participant in a disputation than the man in control of proceedings.

With a flourish, he opened the scroll and began to read. His voice was steady, confident, loud. "Having assembled under the authority of the Sacred Canons, as the Pontifical Delegates of the Bishop of Rome, Vicar of Jesus Christ, Successor of the Prince of the Apostles, Supreme Pontiff of the Universal Church, Innocent II; and with the intention to proceed against disorder and the increase of prejudice to the Holy Faith; this Holy Tribunal does issue, promulgate, and declare these condemnations of the heresies of Peter Abelard, Master of the School at Mont-Sainte-Geneviève in Paris, aged sixty-one. . . ."

Bernard turned slightly and, with a thrown glance, cued the bishops, who, with rough scraping of chairs, coughing, and adjustments of miters, came once more to their feet. Most of them had their eyes cast down, and they gave off an air of unease.

From her place, an alarmed Héloïse craned forward to search Peter Abelard's face for some sign that he was less startled by this turn than she: a promulgation already? His expression was impassive, impossible to read.

"Erratum!" Bernard said in a now declaiming voice: "That the Father has full power, the Son a certain power, the Holy Spirit no power."

He looked briefly back, and the bishops, more or less in unison, declared the one word, *"Damnamus!"*

Bernard addressed Peter Abelard, "Do you abjure this teaching?"

Peter Abelard, looking directly back at Bernard, said nothing.

After a moment's uncertainty, Bernard returned to his text. *"Erratum!* That the Holy Spirit is not of the substance of the Father or of the Son."

The bishops said, more forcefully, *"Damnamus!"*

Bernard again asked, "Do you abjure this teaching?"

Again, Abelard said nothing. Héloïse saw the thing clear. This was no disputation. This was a sentencing. Abelard had already been convicted—and of what? Of the sacrilege of *thinking* about the mystery of the Most Holy Trinity. He was standing not on a debaters' rostrum, but in a criminal's dock. The coward Bernard had sprung a trap.

"*Erratum!* That Christ did not assume flesh to free us from the yoke of the devil."

"*Damnamus!*"

"Do you abjure this teaching?"

Silence. Indeed, Abelard's silence was amplified by the absolute silence that had fallen over the Cathedral. Hardly a breath was being drawn by that multitude.

"*Erratum!* That we have not contracted sin from Adam, but only punishment."

"*Damnamus!*"

Bernard continued the recitation of errors, and the putting of the questions to Abelard, but the pattern was unvaried, climaxing again and again with Abelard's refusal to speak.

"*Erratum!* That the power of binding and loosing was given to the Apostles only, not to their successors."

"*Damnamus!*"

"*Erratum!* That they have not sinned who being ignorant have crucified Christ."

There they were: the Christ crucifiers! That a shift in the standing of Jews in the Christian mind would necessarily follow from Abelard's schema made the transgression mortal, malefaction beyond all the rest. The Jew's place in the tapestry of redemption—no place—depended absolutely on the Jew's guilt. Untie that knot, and the entire tapestry would unravel. *Jews have not sinned!*

"*Damnamus!*"

Throughout, Héloïse heard hints of Abelard's positions in the indictments, together with implications of what would offend a false prophet like Bernard, and she readily conjured the rebuttals Peter would have thrown back, forcing Bernard's pomposity to swallow itself. That the accusations were not, in fact, precisely accurate representations of Abelard's teaching did not take away from the fact that running below all the imputations were, yes, the assumptions of a critical mind at work on reimagining the faith; submitting faith to a test of reason, and to a test of love that was true to Jesus but that, in this age of odium, had been forgotten. These bishops had already pronounced the verdict: *any reimagining of the faith was the offense.*

Indeed, Héloïse saw it all. She understood that these anathemas marked a decisive break with the authentic tradition—anathemas she had herself entirely failed to anticipate. The future of belief was being set here, but so was Peter Abelard's future. The most grievous recognition came all at once: Yes, Peter had been trapped, but by Héloïse herself. By challenging him to be here, *she* had set the snare.

After the last *"Damnamus!"* Bernard drew himself up to demand, "Do you abjure these teachings or not!" The White Monk was beside himself with rage, clearly taking the heretic's repeated refusal to respond as contemptuous, even as it was blazingly apparent that, to the transfixed Cathedral throng, Abelard's bold spurning had become magnificent.

To Héloïse, his standing there, supporting himself with a trembling hand on the rostrum railing, had the transcendent dignity of the mute Jesus Christ before Pontius Pilate, refusing to answer the fabricated Roman charges. Yet, if Abelard was Christ, who was she but one of those who, having failed to see the stakes—or dangers—of what he confronted, had utterly failed him? She was Judas.

Bernard looked quickly back toward the King, who was leaning forward, with his chin upon his fist. The bishops were exchanging nervous glances. Bernard returned to his proclamation, the peroration, but he read nervously now: "Whereas you, Peter Abelard, cling to these grave and pernicious errors, and that they may not go altogether unpunished, and that you may be an example to others who would undermine the order of the One, Holy, Catholic, and Apostolic Church . . ." The monk's voice was drained of its former authority, which made the stark declaration odd. Still, its words were shocking to all who heard. ". . . this Plenary Tribunal ordains that the books of your hand be prohibited by public edict. Furthermore, we prescribe and enjoin that you, Peter Abelard, are everywhere to be denounced publicly as excommunicated . . ." Bernard looked up nervously from the parchment, but when his eyes met the unflinching Abelard's, he dropped them again, and read on. ". . . accursed . . . condemned . . . and interdicted. We condemn you to perpetual silence and enforced monastic confinement for the duration of our pleasure."

Again, Bernard looked up from the page. Abelard was, if anything, more stoic than before. He, too, had drawn himself up. He was standing with his hand free of the railing now, and the tremor of his head, by an evident act of will, was stilled. Indeed, his head was thrown back—a stance of pure defiance.

Bernard took refuge once again in the sheet of parchment, but his voice faltered even more. The arrogant firmness with which he'd begun had become uncertain, almost apologetic. He recited, "So we say, pronounce, sentence, declare, and ordain." He looked up, and added, evidently of his own accord, in search of vigor, "God wills it! *Deus vult!*"

No sooner had Bernard brought the page down than Peter Abelard, raising a steady hand as if to swear an oath, finally broke his silence by declaring, in an unwavering voice that carried all across the Cathedral—the voice, it almost seemed, of God—"I appeal this unholy verdict to the Primacy of the Roman Pontiff!"

With a mass intake of breath, the Cathedral silence became an astonished hush. Bernard did not react at first, then swung around to look at the King, who had turned to look at the Queen. The dilemma was immediate and clear. After Pope Innocent II had finally calmed the storm stirred by the antipope Anacletus II at the Second Lateran Council two years before, the now fortified Pontiff had issued a solemn Great Bull, reserving to himself all authority to resolve every and any dispute involving papal jurisdiction. Had Peter Abelard just invoked that privilege, superseding the present jurisdiction? When the King finally met Bernard's eyes, the current of anxiety ran in both directions. The imperious Pope in Rome could not be crossed.

Bernard turned back to Abelard, and, with the air of a man scrambling, said, "The Apostolic See authorized this Tribunal, in concert with His Majesty, the Sovereign King of France. The Canonical Adjudication of this Council will be forwarded to Rome. Apostolic approbation will be forthcoming." Bernard, at the edge of catastrophe, had recovered himself. He poured all authority—all memory of authority—into his spontaneous decree. With upraised hand, he said, "While formalities of the magisterial appeal are observed, the order for the silencing and confinement of Master Peter Abelard stands." With a flick of his fingers, Bernard gestured to the nearby Fellow-Soldiers of Christ, the Knights Templar. "Take him," he ordered.

Héloïse nearly cried out, but if one thing would make Peter Abelard's condition even worse, it would be the scandalous discovery *here* of his onetime lover. She looked to the Queen, hoping to find a way to spark her intervention, but the Honorable Lady, like the balcony girls with whom Héloïse was standing, was happily transported by what she was seeing. To the young women of the Royal household, including Her Majesty, this tragic turn in Peter Abelard's saga was the fitting dénouement to the lyric romance begun with his lusty transgression more than twenty years before. Héloïse saw suddenly how the tittering Eleanor of Aquitaine and her commissioned minstrels, now that they had an end to the story, would banalize the interrupted ardor—the impossible love—of Héloïse and Abelard. She despised that prospect, and despised herself for having so unworthily enabled it.

"No!" A stirring voice resounded from the center of the Cathedral nave, well back in the gathering of commoners. Heads turned. Bernard of Clairvaux, blindsided again, craned forward to see. The Knights Templar remained back, leaving Abelard alone at the railing.

A black-robed Benedictine moved forward and stepped into the open space at the front edge of the transept crossing. He dropped his cowl, showing his face, which all in the Cathedral chancel recognized. Nevertheless, he announced himself: "I am Peter of Montboissier, Abbot Primate of Cluny." He stepped forward, to face the white-robed Bernard, his great rival. Peter Abelard, standing between them, was all at once the prize.

In a voice that carried throughout the cavernous space, the Abbot Primate declared, "This man is a professed monk of the Benedictine Order, of which I am Abbot Primate in the Kingdom of France, and in the One, Holy, Catholic, and Apostolic Church. This man is the ecclesiastical patron of a monastery in confederation with the Abbey of Cluny, which has universal preeminence. Therefore, his any and all canonical sanctions fall under my authority. Supreme papal jurisdiction has been invoked. While the matter of this Tribunal is resolved by the Holy Father, Pope Innocent II, Master Peter Abelard is remanded to the custody of Cluny." With that, the Abbot crossed to the rostrum and raised his hand to Abelard, who reached for it. Abelard had to steady himself on the Abbot's shoulder as he took the step down. The Abbot and Abelard stood shoulder to shoulder, ignoring Bernard but facing the King, waiting for a sign of the sovereign's dismissal. King Louis, with relief in his expression, nodded.

Abelard's eye was snagged by Queen Eleanor, whose back was half turned on the King. She was looking up at the loggia, and Abelard, following her gaze, saw then what the Queen was seeing. Abelard saw Héloïse.

She was looking only at him. They held each other's eyes for the briefest of moments, but it was enough. They saw their entire life together, and its unbroken, unconditioned mutual regard.

Leaning on the stalwart Abbot of Cluny, Peter Abelard then turned and shuffled out of the stunned Cathedral. Héloïse was aware of the break in history she had just witnessed, but also of her own enabling hubris. Had she not forecast Peter's fate by her garb? Had she not foreordained it? How dare she come here clothed in the black drapery of a widow?

CHAPTER TWENTY-FOUR

You are towing a large barge on a hawser, Michael Kavanagh read. *Your main engine suddenly fails. What is the greatest danger?*

He was at his desk in the small, cluttered company office, in one of several ramshackle single-story, multi-tenant buildings nestled together at the head of a narrow Staten Island finger pier, just east of the looming ferry terminal. The golden light of a bright May morning poured in through the wall of paned windows. It was a Sunday, so Betty-May, the bookkeeper, wasn't there, and the three Kavanagh tugs were in their berths outside, snug in the crotch of the pier. The surrounding yard was quiet.

Kavanagh was reviewing questions for his upcoming Mate's License exam. It was a laughable project to him, since he was barely qualified as a deckhand, and had, in fact, spent most of his five months at Kavanagh Tug Company organizing his brother's office. Since mustering out of the Merchant Marine, Jerry Kavanagh had scored bank loans that enabled him to buy first one army-surplus tugboat, then a second, and a third, and to take on crews for each. He'd steered his fleet of three into the narrow but booming "car barge" niche of the New York Harbor tugboat trade; he'd nailed down contracts with the railroads, come to terms with the union, and accepted a pay-to-play arrangement with the waterfront boss. But except for the latter, that all involved paperwork that the grease-monkey Master Mariner had left in various stages of undone. Jerry was right to regard his well-organized older brother's arrival—no offense—as a Godsend.

But if Kavanagh Tug was to become, as Jerry insisted it would, Kavanagh *Brothers* Tug, he was right to insist that Michael get licensed.

Back to the greatest danger—choose one: "The tug and the tow will go aground." "The tow will endanger other traffic." "The tow will overrun tug." "The tow will block the channel."

Obviously, "The tow will overrun tug." Ten thousand gross tons of barge weight crushing the engineless tugboat—there's the danger. Fuck the channel. Michael slapped the pocket of his denim shirt, for his cigarettes.

A runaway tow wasn't a hazard he was likely to face. Jerry's boats specialized in bringing loaded freight-car barges from Jersey City to Brooklyn, and empty ones back; but that involved the tug's tying alongside the barge instead of pulling it with hawsers. There was no "tow." Given that dozens of rail floats made the transit every day, the confluence of the Hudson and the East Rivers, at Upper Bay, was too congested for hawser towing. That Kavanagh tugs were married to their barges meant Michael hadn't learned much about towline maneuvers. But he knew that, if his main engine failed while he was tied gunnel to gunnel to a scow weighed down by a dozen fully loaded boxcars, the East River tides would carry them crashing out into Lower Bay, wreaking havoc with the tankers and freighters swinging at anchor. Nobody would give a crap whether the asshole helmsman had successfully passed his Coastal Tug Mate exam.

Next question: "The compass heading of a vessel differs from the true heading by—"

Kavanagh had no idea. He looked out the window, like a kid longing for recess. The harbor vista always drew him. He had discovered a whole new way to cherish New York. What he'd really loved in these months were the hours on the open water: the inland bay, with glimpses of the far Atlantic; the rivers; the cable-grid bridges overhead; forests of cranes and derricks sprouting from the piers and wharves; the sleek liners with their ship-assist tugs. He would leave the wheelhouse to have the wind in his face, welcoming even the rain when it came. He would spread his feet for the rhythmic swell of the cross-flooding wakes, feeling the music of motion in his chest—more alive to the present moment than ever. No satisfaction could compare to throwing the wheel and kicking the engine into reverse at exactly the right instant, so that the tire-fendered gunnel kissed the dock with no need for the braided line.

As a chaplain, he'd loved the navy for its camaraderie, the lads, and the cause, but the Navy Yard Hospital was not a ship, and he'd rarely been at sea. He'd never imagined himself as a bluejacket. But now all the river-rat fantasies of a longshoreman's child were coming true. Aboard one of his brother's muscular workboats, with its engine's smooth vibrations, the purr in his fingers on the wheel, the steady cruise out into the magnificent open harbor, he'd come to feel entirely at home—as, so many years before, he'd imagined he would. No matter the weather, his eyes took a warm bath in the sight of the city skyline, which, he knew only now, was meant to be seen from the water. What cathedral towers and buttresses had been to him, the skyscrapers were now. He'd come into a familiar dream without remembering it was his until long after waking.

But the Mariner's exam: he looked back to it. If the questions were not multiple-choice, he'd be screwed. "The Compass heading . . . the true heading" . . . what? "Compass error"? "Variation"? "Magnetic dip"? "Deviation"? He liked the sound of "magnetic dip," and, indeed, vaguely remembered Jerry's having said something about magnetic lines of force not actually being parallel to the earth's surface, making the compass needle jostle up slightly in the Northern Hemisphere, and jostle down in the Southern. Maybe the jostle is the dip. *Magnetic dip,* therefore. Good enough.

He was just lighting his cigarette when he saw a shadow fall across the glass panes of the door, and he looked up. He glimpsed a figure in tan moving away from the door. The docks here were given over to the day boats and rarely saw activity on Sundays, so he was curious. He placed his cigarette in the ashtray, rose, crossed to the door, and opened it. There, to his right, staring at him, was a woman in round, rimless sunglasses, wearing a loosely belted tan trench coat and a blue beret from which black hair curled down over her ears. She looked so unlike the turbaned, black-cloaked, short-haired woman of The Cloisters that it took Kavanagh a moment to recognize Rachel Vedette. A leather bag was slung over her shoulder. She was holding in her two hands, as if to fend him off, a white envelope.

"My goodness," Kavanagh said. "Miss Vedette." He heard the leap in his voice, and only then felt the full surge of his surprise. She had never struck him as stylish, yet, in this ragtag working boatyard, she seemed a figure, nearly, of glamour.

"I am sorry," she said. "I did not expect—"

"It's all right. It's quite all right," Kavanagh said. "I am glad to see you. I almost didn't recognize you."

She removed her sunglasses and held out the envelope. "I meant only to leave this for you."

He did not take the envelope. He said, "For me?"

"A letter."

"How did you find me?"

She glanced at the sign above the door, "Kavanagh Tug." "A tug-boat captain. You told me your brother was a tugboat captain, in Staten Island. You told me you would go to work with him."

Kavanagh grinned. "I did?" But then he remembered. "God, that's right. You were the first person to whom I . . . spoke." Spoke of what he was doing. After a moment, he added, "That's so long ago. But even before I left Inwood, you left the museum."

"Yes. I am a teacher now. I teach French to girls."

"Ah. Good," Kavanagh said, nodding. Then he said, "I went to The Cloisters once, asking for you. I owed you a lot. I thought of try-ing to track you down, but then realized you probably didn't want that."

"That was true." She hesitated, and he sensed her need to make a decision, whether to explain. To his relief, she then added, "But the months passed. I realized that I, too, owed a debt. To you." Now she pushed the envelope toward him again.

He took the letter, but made no move to open it.

"I thought on a Sunday," she said, "the office here would be closed. I did not expect to see you."

"How did you get here?"

She pointed up the waterfront. "The famous Staten Island Ferry," she said, welcoming the neutral subject. "For five cents, an ocean voyage. I often come and go, just for the salt air. It surprised me, when I finally looked for you, that you were nearby the . . . *crosser* . . . *le traversier* . . . which I regard as my luxury liner." She almost smiled, saying, "Of course, whenever I see the great ships being turned by the tugboats, I think of you."

Kavanagh laughed. "No. No. We push scows around the harbor, barges. Workboats. Not the SS *America*. Too fancy for the likes of the Kavanaghs."

She nodded. "I remember." She stepped back. "I meant only to put my letter here, where you would find it. I will go now."

He gestured with the letter. "What's it say?"

She shook her head.

"May I read it? Then, we could talk. Look, come on inside. It's a mess, but I have coffee on the hot plate. Will you have some?"

She shook her head no. But she did not move.

Kavanagh stood aside, opening the way for her. "Please," he said. After a moment's further hesitation, she went into the office. He pulled the door shut, moved a stack of tech manuals from Betty-May's chair, and pulled it free of the table. "Shall I take your coat?"

"No. I will be only a moment here." Rachel sat.

Kavanagh poured a fresh cup of coffee, and topped off his own. "This is rotten," he said, "but it's hot." He handed the cup to her, and, pulling his own chair out from behind the desk, closer, he sat. He reached for the ashtray to stub out his still smoldering cigarette. Indicating her envelope, he checked again: "Should I?"

She shrugged. "Why not? It will embarrass me. But why not?" Her tone of voice was matter-of-fact, sure. "While you read . . ." She reached into her coat pocket for her own cigarettes, and went about the business of lighting up.

Kavanagh opened the envelope and removed the letter—a page of neat handwriting.

Dear friend, he read silently. *I was* une femme incomplète *when we met, an incomplete woman. I remain so. But one does not begin to amend oneself until one understands. One does not understand until one speaks. I spoke to you. As you know, it was a matter of importance. You listened to me. It was enough. In these months, I have come to see as a gift what to you must have been a mere passing encounter. I am obliged to offer this word of thanks.*

I am in a new place. So, I see, are you. Good luck to us both.—Rachel Vedette. Below her signature was an address. Hoboken.

Kavanagh looked up. "It wasn't a 'mere passing encounter' to me. You could have no idea. . . ." Kavanagh was suddenly choked with feeling. "I had been waiting a long time to change my life. Then I walked into The Cloisters that day, after years of ignoring the place. It was like coming out of dark woods into a sunlit meadow. Not The Cloisters itself, but . . . where I got to."

Rachel stared at the tip of her cigarette.

He said: "If you are in a new place, it must be a good place. You seem . . . better." He took in her appearance more closely. Her legs were crossed. She was wearing a brown skirt that came to her calves, and black fabric shoes with rope soles. Her ankles struck him. Though she was lean, as before, the hint of emaciation was gone. There was a shadow of gauntness in her cheeks, still—but only a shadow. Under the sleeve of her belted coat he saw the edge of a shirt cuff, and thought of her wrist. He gestured with the letter. "The 'matter of importance,'" he said. "I am glad you told me."

She raised her eyes to his. "I wrote my address on the letter, just there. . . ."

"Yes. I see. Hoboken. We pick up Lackawanna barges there, twice a week."

"I was meaning to leave it for you to decide whether to reply. I was thinking that, if you did reply, perhaps we could meet briefly. Then I was going to give you something . . ."

"So here we are, meeting."

". . . something I would not just leave. . . ." She glanced about the office. "That is, I had to be certain you would receive it."

Kavanagh smiled. "Well, here I am."

After a moment, Rachel stubbed out her cigarette in the ashtray and reached into her bag. She brought out a book, and Kavanagh recognized it at once—the leather-bound antique, *Historia Calamitatum: Heloissae et Abaelardi Epistolae*. She offered it to him.

"Your father's book," he said.

"Yes. The time is here for me to leave it behind. I would leave it with you."

Instead of answering, or reaching to take the book, Kavanagh turned toward his desk and pulled open a drawer from which he withdrew a book of his own—the same book, also antique, also in Latin, also bound in leather, but without gold leafing. He held it out, side by side with Rachel's volume. "I found it in a used-book store off Washington Square. You taught me to treasure their letters. As you did."

"I still treasure it," she said haltingly. Rachel's breath caught, and she clutched her book back to her breast, nearly overcome. Tears flooded her eyes, but did not overflow. She had a rigid grip on herself. "It fills me . . . that you found your own copy . . ." She stopped, nearly overcome. Then she went on, "After I spoke with you, I realized how this book had become the . . . *signifiant* . . . the signifier of my *father's* Abelard, as if I could still complete his work. But with you I saw that my father himself was what mattered. This book, I mean, embodied my distraction—a mistake I could not correct. It was too late."

"It is never too late," Kavanagh said, but immediately he understood the callowness of his remark. He placed his book on the edge of the desk, taking her misery fully in. But he was also aware that her blurted explanation was triggered by his having produced his own copy of the Abelard and Héloïse, which hit her like an "Open Sesame!" The book itself was the key to the deep mystery—the Ali Baba's cave—of both their lives. He dared not say more.

But what he'd said was enough to display his shallowness. *"Never too late"—Christ!*

It was as if she felt obliged, but without malice, to rebut his glib statement. Still hovering on the edge of tears, she said with forced calm, "I spoke to you, when we sat on that bench near The Cloisters, words that began my . . . what to call it? . . . reckoning. I have continued it in these months . . . a drastic reckoning. But in speaking to you that day, I did not say the worst thing. I had not said it yet to myself."

In the face of her silence, and only because he sensed her need, he found it possible to ask, "Will you say it now?"

"I denied my father. That is it. I denied my father."

He was motionless.

"At the end, in Drancy . . ." she continued. She held her book to her chest as if it were a life buoy. ". . . they were taking him away. They would have taken me. I said I was not his daughter." Her sobs came, finally, but she spoke through them. "I do not know why I said that. Not for life, because I was only living for him. Not for fear. I was afraid only for him. It was just . . . the German asked me, was I his daughter? I said no. No. I do not know why I said this. I do not understand. It was a lie with no purpose. I had always been asking, 'Who am I now?' And at last that was the answer. A daughter without loyalty. The German did not even believe me." She was speaking in a rush. She rushed on. "He shot my father dead because of me, but already I myself had done the worst. The German knew that. It was his triumph. We were alike. He was happy at my betrayal, and let me live. He was right. Living was worse, after that, far worse. . . ." She stopped.

Kavanagh knew better than to think that this fresh, visceral flood of admission had anything to do with him. She had come to the point of having to put this horror into words—that was all. That he, Michael Kavanagh, was the recipient of her expression was incidental.

She collected herself enough to go on. "I carried this book with me everywhere, as evidence of my *first* betrayal, how I had failed to see what threatened, encouraging him in what kept us in jeopardy. Abelard was a friend to Jews, perhaps, although to us, at the end, he was just another dangerous Catholic. But then came this, my second betrayal, and it was mortal. Literally, since, in the next moment, Papa was killed. So I carried the book as if Abelard and Héloïse would absolve me, if only I clung to them. In the camps; in Paris, where I could not possibly live again; in coming to America; in living inside the fantasy world of that museum in your parish—I could not face the truth. That there is no absolution. I said in my letter to you 'incomplete woman.' I almost wrote 'unforgiven woman.' *Non pardonnée.*"

"But, Miss Vedette, if I may . . . ?" He was asking permission to say what was in his mind. She did not offer a signal, and so he did not speak.

She repeated the phrase, *"Non pardonnée,"* and then continued, "But here is the surprise, that I have found it possible to live, precisely, as that. Unforgiven. In these months since I met you, I have begun to accept that there is no forgetting. I am who I am. I did what I did. There is no undoing. This book had become to me what it became to my father, but for a different reason—a book of wishes I need no longer entertain. Therefore, I will leave it behind."

Kavanagh took a breath, and realized it was his first in some moments. Rachel Vedette seemed to have finished her explanation, but he wasn't sure he understood. He felt the burden of his own recognition, but was afraid of expressing it. Rather than speak, he took a pair of cigarettes and lit them, offering one to her. It was a gesture he had made on that park bench, when it had seemed inappropriately intimate. Now it seemed right, and she took the cigarette.

After exhaling, she said, more calmly, "Yet, because it *was* my father's, the *Historia et Epistolae* remains a treasure. When I first took the Staten Island Ferry, I thought I would drop it into the sea, and have done with it that way. But I could not. After all, I first came to Staten Island because you mentioned it once. Having thought of you, I saw what to do. I would give my father's book to its new friend. But, then, seeing just now that you have your own copy of the *Historia* completely surprises me. Undoes me. What a companion you are to Abelard and Héloïse. . . . It made me think, for a moment, just now, that we must be alike."

"Was your father there, nearby?"

"Yes. In the line of prisoners. But he would not look at me."

"Did he hear you? When you said 'No'?" Kavanagh was speaking carefully.

"Yes," she answered.

"And still he did not look at you?"

"No. It is how I know he was hurt. Betrayed."

"Is it possible his refusal to look was his protection of you? If he looked, they would know for sure you were his daughter? If they did *not* know, they would not take you? Was that his purpose?"

Rachel considered this. "Yes," she said. "Perhaps."

Kavanagh said quietly, cautiously, "If your father did not want them to know you were his daughter, how was it betrayal when you denied it? You were doing as he wanted. He wanted you to live."

"Even so." She shook her head brusquely, dismissively. "What I said was unforgivable. It does not matter what my father thought. *Unforgivable!* I knew that as soon as I said 'No.' So did the German. The German condemned me to live with that knowledge. He was right."

Kavanagh had spent more than a decade as a facile dispenser of forgiveness, and he realized that that was what he had just attempted to do now. Better, he realized, to utter the separate truth he'd come to, even at the risk of being misunderstood. "But . . ." About to say "miss" again, he stopped. Instead, he said, "Rachel." He waited. She did not indicate that his use of her name was wrong. He continued, "There is something else besides your experience of that situation, perhaps something larger."

"What?"

"The situation itself—who created that? Not you. Not your father. The German certainly did, but not even he was acting out of a vacuum. You said before that Abelard, even despite himself, was a 'dangerous Catholic'—just another one. There's the point. None of what you went through, including the loss of your father, would have happened but for Catholic teaching about Jews. Twenty centuries of it. I myself, in that sense, am a 'dangerous Catholic.' The crime you described, what requires pardoning, was not yours. In a way, it was mine."

She stared at him. An amazed expression had come over her face.

"Don't misunderstand," he added quickly. "I know the crime was Hitler's, and the crime was that German officer's, with his gun. He—

they—were the murderers. But someone handed them the loaded gun. What I've understood is . . . we did that. We followers of Jesus . . . we have been, what to call it? The gun loaders. The arms suppliers, maybe. The Germans could not have done what they did without what went before. You referred to this with me—the French Catholic support for Vichy. Where did that come from? And among the things I learned from you, and I guess that means from your father, is that, with Abelard, the story could have gone another way. You told me this, and now I get it. Abelard marked a fork in the road—the Church's wrong turn. Wasn't that what your father saw? The dangers in our theology?"

"Yes."

Kavanagh picked up his copy of the *Historia*. "Peter Abelard gave the great warning, and thank God for him. But, as I read them, it was Héloïse who made the difference to me," he said. "Not just because she pushed him to become the hero he was, but because she herself so heroically refused to live with illusions. All her railing against convention, and against the Church even—I see it now as being about the underlying truth she saw. I have come to my small version of that. Until I met you, I was terrified of facing up to the unreality of my situation, because, as a Catholic, I knew that ordination to the priesthood is forever, an 'indelible mark on the soul.' My solemn vow—broken. Quitting the priesthood is an unforgivable sin . . . for us . . . truly unforgivable." He paused, aware of having not said this to anyone before, acknowledging the breadth and depth of his offense. But then it hit him—how trivial his problem was, how pathetic.

He said again, "Don't misunderstand. I am not comparing my situation to yours. I know they are incomparable. I am only trying to explain why I came to treasure this book you brought me to, why—once, finally, I *did* leave the priesthood—I then haunted used-book stores looking for my own copy. These people"—he held the volume up, eyeing it with more feeling than he knew he had—"*that woman,* actually. Her. She exposed the lie that I'd built my life on. Yet Héloïse could denounce it—not against the Church, but within and for the Church."

He stopped. He said quietly, "Because I believe in God, the God

I have from the Catholic tradition, I am still a part of it. But perhaps I am a Catholic now in the way Héloïse was. I haven't left the Church. I have only moved to the edge, as she did. She is the gift you gave me."

He waited for Rachel Vedette to speak. She said nothing, but her gaze, fast on his eyes, did not shift. She knew, before he did, that his thought was not complete. Her silence was an invitation to go on, even if his thought would now extend to her. He said, "And one more thing, speaking of *non pardonné . . .* I am only now seeing this, but . . . wasn't Héloïse *defined* by her status as unforgiven? And how she accepted it? Her unforgivable offense, of course—*as she saw it*—was not against the Church or God, but against the one she loved, for whose, yes, *calamitous* fate she accepted responsibility. Is it that you, in the acceptance you describe, have become like Héloïse—not as a Catholic, of course, but exactly in being the Jewish daughter of your Jewish father?" Seeing the gleam of recognition in her pooling eyes, a further permission, he continued: "Being like Héloïse, ironically, requires you to let go of what she wrote. Is that it? You are still instructing me, Rachel. You want to give me your father's book not to be rid of it, but because you are finished with the task it came to represent. Forgive me if I presume, but . . . hurts need nursing, you said. Until they are gone."

"No," she said, "Not 'gone.' Until they are different." She brought the back of one wrist to her face, to wipe it dry of tears. Her sleeve was no longer bound with an elastic band. He saw her scar.

She said softly, "Your Héloïse, perhaps, is like my father's Abelard—a screen on which to flash images of the world as we would have it."

Kavanagh laughed. "Whoa! Speaking of the rejection of illusions."

Rachel smiled faintly. "So you are like my father. And because you are . . . *le voilà*!" She reached her book out to Kavanagh, who took it and paired it with his own.

He said, "I will accept your book, but only as its safekeeper. One day, it will no longer be what you called it, a 'signifier.' It will be only what it is. And then, perhaps, if you will have it back, I will return it to you."

She gave no indication that she heard in what he said the implication of a future. She stood, and fastened the belt of her trench coat. "So now I will go. You have been kind—" She cut herself off, and he realized that she'd almost called him "Father." She said, "From the start, you have been kind. I am grateful."

He stood. "Hoboken, you said."

"Yes."

"I told you, we go there twice a week. Let me take you."

She did not understand.

"If you go by ferry, then the subway, then the bus," he said, "what's that, two hours? On a Sunday, three? I can have you at the Hoboken dock in half an hour." He reached for his jacket.

"By boat?" she asked.

"The *Catherine Marie.* Named for my mother. It's right outside. I can use the log time." He gestured at his Mariner's exam prep. "I still need another thirty hours at the helm for my Mate's License. You'd be helping me. We'd document the trip as vessel inspection." He laughed, and led the way.

At the midpoint between Staten Island and Hoboken was Liberty Island, and as they drew abreast of it, Kavanagh pulled the throttle back. The engine noise eased off. Rachel was sitting on the jump seat beside him. "There she is"—he pointed through the glass of the wheelhouse—"in all her glory." Seen up close, the enormity of the green statue was what registered.

"The day of my arrival," Rachel said, "she was lost in fog. But when we finally saw her from the rail, people around me wept."

"Not you?"

"No. I never weep." When she looked at Kavanagh, she was blushing: her face still showed the slight smear of tears. She smiled. She teased herself by adding, "Never."

"Me, neither," he said, laughing. But he thought of that day they'd seen the SS *America* off, when a departing girl had cried down to Rachel, "I love you!" And he'd mistaken snowflakes on her face for tears.

He gestured at the water around them. "This marks the actual mouth of the Hudson. Some days, when I'm logging time, I go upriver a ways, past the bridge. Have you ever seen The Cloisters from the water?"

"No."

"Would you like to?"

She did not reply at first. Then she said, "No. I've left that behind, too. No, thank you . . . Michael." She fell silent.

EPILOGUE

If there is any thing which may properly be called happiness here below, I am persuaded it is in the union of two persons who love each other with perfect liberty, who are united by a secret inclination, and satisfied with each other's merit; their hearts are full and leave no vacancy for any other passion; they enjoy perpetual tranquillity.

Mother Héloïse looked up from the page—script in her own hand. These were words she'd written to him three decades ago, but what struck her now was the one word—"happiness." Peter was long dead, and, as she well knew, she was soon to follow, at last.

She was propped up on the pallet she'd had brought into the Chapter House two days before. The stolid room was serving as her vestibule of darkness. Because it opened on her beloved Cloister garden, she would spend her last hours within sight of the earth's most precious corner. Amid the paving stones just inside the arched ambulatory was the marble disc carved with the letter "A," the marker of his grave. Twenty years before, she had chosen that spot on the path from garden to sanctuary so that the nuns, with heads bowed on the way to choir, would see his place and then carry him with chanted Psalms to God. While her good sisters had prayed "for" Peter Abelard all these years, she had been praying "to."

Mother Héloïse realized that someone was standing in the Gothic archway, waiting. The cranelike form was familiar: Sister Célestine, the Novice Mistress. She had been acting as provisional Superior since Mother herself was stricken. It was certain, such was the esteem in which the sisters held her, that Célestine would be the successor Abbess. Célestine was Héloïse's intimate friend.

"Dear sister," Héloïse said, and she let the vellum page fall into its folds. The Novice Mistress came forward. At the edge of the pallet, she bowed. "Bless me, Mother."

"You are blessed beyond any blessing I could bestow."

The nun was carrying a flagon and a cup. "This is lemon water, Mother. You should drink." She helped Héloïse to sit forward, and put the cup to her lips. Sister Célestine then placed the flagon and cup on the nearby table, beside a bowl that was alive with steam. She adjusted the white draperies of the bed, even as Mother Héloïse tugged her veil back into place, saying, "There is vanity, still, in a wizened old nun."

"Your vanity, Mother, is justified. You are ever beautiful."

"Still vain." She held the page up to Célestine. "Put this back with the compendium, sister. You have tended to the compilation, as I asked? The codices, scrolls, manuscript leaves, all of it?"

"Yes, Mother. When I have replaced this missive, the lot will be sealed in the iron-bound chest and secured in the groin of the tower vaulting."

"And registered in the *scriptorium*?"

"Yes, Mother."

"And the *Dialogue with the Jew,* in particular, noted in the 'Index Reserved'?"

"Yes, Mother."

"I depend on you, sister. And I will depend on your successor, when the time comes. See to the fast-keeping of Master Peter's writing, one Abbess instructing the next, *in perpetuum.* I depend on you," she repeated, but now breathlessly. She had kept his writings intact across the most dangerous decades, through the frenzied destructions that followed King Louis's mad Crusade, the requisitions imposed upon Cluny after the ascent of Bernard, the savage assaults against

Jews wherever they clustered, and the heresy hunts launched through-out France by the ever-threatened Italian Popes. Again and again, the white-robed zealot monks had stormed the gate of the Paraclete, but Héloïse had kept it barred. If Peter Abelard's writings could be held safe through these bloody years, why not forever?

Sister Célestine pressed her beloved mentor's arm. She turned to the table, and from the steaming bowl took a cloth and squeezed it free of warm water. She applied the cloth to the brow of the Abbess, who lay back, eyes closed—soothed. Yes, her promise to the Abbot Primate, long ago, was kept. Her promise to Peter. His thought preserved until new thinkers could join him in it.

More absently now, as if entranced, Mother Héloïse said, "I just read of 'happiness,' a word that once came glibly from my pen. Happiness for me now consists of two gifts, both coming from you. The first is that protection of his work of which I just spoke. The victory of the wicked will be reversed when men sing of Peter Abelard, who, in the Church of darkness, pointed to the way of light. Men will curse our age for the devils it set loose—a stampede of devils against which Peter Abelard stood alone."

"Not alone, Mother," Sister Célestine ventured, but quietly.

"Protect his writings, sister, so that the future can redeem this past."

"Yes, Mother. You have my vow. I understand."

"Peter Abelard . . ." The voice of Héloïse faltered. ". . . will yet help . . . Mother Church . . . to recover herself."

"But you said *two* gifts for happiness, Mother. What is the second?"

"Master Peter's marker."

"Mother?"

"The marble disc in the pavement."

"Yes, Mother."

"Side by side with the letter 'A,' have the mason carve the let-ter 'H.' "

Sister Célestine said nothing to this.

Héloïse continued with mustered strength, "Open Peter's grave. Have it ready. When my Requiem concludes, have each sister approach the bier and bless me with a kiss. Then carry me to Peter." Héloïse stopped. She clutched the edge of her bed gown and pulled it aside, baring her breast. Her fingers went to the gold ring, nestled in the hollow of her throat. "Take this ring from its cord. Place it on my finger. Remove my habit. Unclothe me fully. Place me naked in the grave with him, to his left side. You will find that he is laid out with his feet to the east. Align my feet likewise, so that when the Lord Christ comes on the Last Day, Peter and I will be together for the universal Resurrection, our mortal bodies made immortal, lifted up as one body—in the Lord."

Sister Célestine's ear by now was near the mouth of Mother Abbess—so softly had she been speaking. The silence that came over Héloïse then was absolute.

Acknowledgments

Among the many authors on whose work I drew for this book, the following deserve special acknowledgment: Kevin Madigan, *Medieval Christianity: A New History;* Diarmaid MacCulloch, *A History of Christianity;* Jaroslav Pelikan, *Jesus Through the Centuries;* Étienne Gilson, *Heloise and Abelard;* James Ramsay McCallum, *Abelard's Christian Theology;* M. T. Clanchy, *Abelard: A Medieval Life;* Constant J. Mews, *Abelard and Heloise* and *The Lost Love Letters of Heloise and Abelard;* Jeffrey E. Brower and Kevin Guilfoy (eds.), *The Cambridge Companion to Abelard;* Eileen C. Sweeney, "Abelard and the Jews," in Babette S. Hellemans (ed.), *Rethinking Abelard;* Jeremy Cohen, *Living Letters of the Law: Ideas of the Jew in Medieval Christianity;* Norman F. Cantor, *Inventing the Middle Ages;* Philippe Wolff, *The Awakening of Europe;* Robert Chazan, *In the Year 1096: The First Crusade and the Jews* and *From Anti-Judaism to Anti-Semitism;* Margaret Collins Weitz, *Sisters in the Resistance;* Ronald C. Rosbottom, *When Paris Went Dark;* Michael R. Marrus and Robert O. Paxton, *Vichy France and the Jews.* The conclusions I draw from these authors, including any erroneous ones, belong to me alone.

My first readers were Alexandra Marshall and William D. Phillips, whose early insights were a crucial help in my finding the way. Others who generously read the work in progress and made important suggestions were Bernard Avishai, Rachel Jacoff, Kevin Madigan, and Milton Gatch. I gratefully acknowledge the help of Barbara Drake Boehm, senior curator for The

Met Cloisters, and all of the Cloisters staff. I did research for this book as an Associate of the Mahindra Humanities Center at Harvard University. Special thanks to the Center's director, Homi K. Bhabha, and its administrator, Mary Halpenny-Killip.

I have been more than fortunate to have as my editor Nan A. Talese, to whom I am profoundly grateful. Thanks also to the editors and staff of Nan A. Talese / Doubleday who helped this book at every turn. Tina Bennett, my agent, was the first to encourage this project, and her support never flagged. My gratitude to her is larger than I can say.

I am sustained by my family. Thanks to our son, Patrick; our daughter, Lizzy; her husband, James; and their children, Annie and Julia. This book, like every book I have published across more than forty years, owes its existence to the support I receive every day from my wife, the writer Alexandra Marshall. Thank you, Lexa.